Praise for Marcia Clark's
GUILT BY DEGREES

"It's no big surprise that Marcia Clark knows her way around a courtroom, and a murder mystery—but she's also a terrific writer and storyteller." —James Patterson

"This sequel to her remarkably accomplished debut...proves that former prosecutor Clark is no one-book wonder....Clark has a winning cast of characters, a strong plot, and plenty of smart and sassy dialogue (particularly when Knight and her BFFs gather for after-work martinis), and she heightens interest in Knight's next appearance by establishing the psychopathic Bayer as her nemesis. A superlative series bringing together elements of both legal thrillers and police procedurals." —Michele Leber, *Booklist*

"Clark humanizes her tough lead, and gets the mixture of action and investigative legwork just right, more than making the case for a long life for this West Coast analogue to Linda Fairstein's Alex Cooper."
—*Publishers Weekly* (starred review)

"Well-developed characters and a story arc that leaves the reader hanging are a surefire way to bring fans back for the next installment, and Clark has wisely left that door wide open. This should appeal to fans of Lisa Scottoline and David Baldacci." —Stacy Alesi, *Library Journal*

"With *Guilt by Degrees,* Clark has managed to do the arduous and make it look easy: she has taken the strongest elements from an already assured debut and melded them into near perfection. The dialogue is razor sharp, the humor laugh-out-loud funny, and the pacing relentless. Further, Clark infuses the narrative with a wealth of expertly informed details shaped by the years that she spent living and breathing her protagonist's life. Bullets may fly on the page, but it's readers that will ultimately be blown away."

—John Valeri, *Hartford Books Examiner*

"Marcia Clark knows her villains, and *Guilt by Degrees* gives us one you won't forget. She also gives us one of the toughest and most appealing heroes to come along in a very long time. Prosecutor Rachel Knight is smart, funny, and just about fearless in her pursuit of justice and a good martini. *Guilt by Degrees* kept me guessing to the last page—and then impatient to read more about Rachel Knight."

—Joseph Finder, *New York Times* bestselling author of *High Crimes* and *Vanished*

"Given her background, it's no surprise that Clark's writing crackles with authenticity. The courtroom exchanges in her latest novel are crisp and brimming with tension. The lawyers, cops, and bad guys feel real. The story is fast-paced and will keep readers interested to the end."

—Christian DuChateau, CNN.com

"The second *Guilt* book by author Marcia Clark reintroduces the tough DA Rachel Knight. And if readers liked her in the first, they will like her even better this time around....The book offers a more in-depth exploration of crime and punishment, which is—of course—what Marcia Clark is good at. The suspects are beyond interesting, and the plot is extremely dark, allowing the character of Rachel Knight to really shine through. A great thriller!"

—*Suspense Magazine*

GUILT BY
DEGREES

MARCIA CLARK

GUILT BY DEGREES

A NOVEL

MULHOLLAND BOOKS

LITTLE, BROWN AND COMPANY

NEW YORK   BOSTON   LONDON

Copyright © 2012 by Marcia Clark
Excerpt from *Killer Ambition* copyright © 2013 by Marcia Clark

Mulholland Books / Little, Brown and Company
Hachette Book Group
237 Park Avenue
New York, NY 10017
mulhollandbooks.com

The publisher is not responsible for websites (or their content) that are not owned by the publisher.

Printed in the United States of America

Originally published in hardcover by Mulholland Books / Little, Brown and Company, May 2012
First Mulholland Books mass market edition, April 2013

10 9 8 7 6 5 4 3 2 1

ATTENTION CORPORATIONS AND ORGANIZATIONS:

Most Hachette Book Group books are available at quantity discounts with bulk purchase for educational, business, or sales promotional use. For information, please call or write:

**Special Markets Department, Hachette Book Group
237 Park Avenue, New York, NY 10017
Telephone: 1-800-222-6747 Fax: 1-800-477-5925**

*This book is dedicated to the memory of
a true hero, Hugo Tale-Yax, whose selfless rescue of
another cost him his life.*

GUILT BY
DEGREES

PROLOGUE

He stood still, listening as the car pulled out of the driveway. When the sound of the engine faded into the distance, Zack looked at his watch: 9:36 a.m. Perfect. Three solid hours of "me" time. He eagerly trotted down the thinly carpeted stairs to the basement, the heavy bass thud of his work boots echoing through the empty house. Clutched in his hand was the magazine photograph of the canopy he intended to build. He figured it would've cost a small fortune at one of those fancy designer stores, but the copy he'd make would be just as good, if not better—and for less than a tenth of the price. A smile curled Zack's lips as he enjoyed the mental image of Lilah's naked body framed by gauzy curtains hanging from the canopy, wafting seductively around the bed. He inhaled, imagining her perfume as he savored the fantasy.

Zack jumped down the last step and moved to the corkboard hanging above his workbench. He tacked up the magazine photo, pulled out the armless secretary chair with the bouncy backrest, and sat down heavily. The squeak of the overburdened springs jangled in the stillness of the dank air. The room was little more than a cement-floored cell, but it was Zack's paradise, filled to bursting with the highest quality carpentry tools he could afford, acquired slowly and lovingly over the years. Since he was a kid, he'd found that making things with his hands had the power to both calm and inspire him. His brother, Simon, said it was his form of Zen. Zack shook his head. Simon would've made a great hippie if he hadn't been born about twenty years too late.

Hanging on the walls were framed photographs of Zack's completed projects: the seven-tiered bookcase, the cedar trunk with inset shelving, the wine cabinet. Each one had come out better than the last. His gaze lingered on the photograph of the wine cabinet as he remembered how he'd labored to carve the grape leaves on its doors. It had to be worth at least five hundred dollars.

Zack turned to the bench. He pulled a steno notepad off the shelf above it and snagged a pencil from the beer stein where he kept his drafting tools. The stein had been a Christmas gift from his rookie partner, who hadn't yet learned that, unlike the other cops in their division, he wasn't much of a drinker.

He rolled his chair back, put his feet up on the desk, and began to sketch. Minutes later, he'd finished the broad outline. He held the drawing at arm's length to get a better perspective when a sound—a soft rustling somewhere behind him—made Zack stop, pad still poised in midair. He dropped his feet to the floor and carefully began to scan the room.

He sensed rather than saw the sudden motion in his periphery. Before he could react, the weight of an anvil crashed into the side of his head. Blood-filled stars exploded behind his eyes as he flew off the chair and landed on his back on the hard cement.

Zack opened his eyes, dimly aware of a voice—his own?—crying out in pain. Someone was poised above him. Again he sensed movement, something cutting through the air. In a hideous moment of clarity, Zack saw what it was. An ax.

He watched in mute horror as the blade came whistling down. At the last second, he squeezed his eyes shut— hoping to make the nightmare go away. But the ax plunged deep and hard, the blade slicing cruelly through his neck, right down to the vertebrae. As the blade yanked out, his body arched up, then collapsed back to the ground, and blood spurted from his severed carotid. The ax rose again, then hurtled downward, blood flying off its edge and onto the walls. Again and again, the blade rose and fell in a steady, inexorable rhythm, severing arms and legs, splitting the abdomen, unleashing coiled intestines and a foul odor. When at last the bloody ax dropped to the floor, a fine red spray spattered the walls and the shiny trophy photographs of Zack's creations.

1

TWO YEARS LATER

He moved with purpose. That alone might have drawn attention to the man in the soiled wool overcoat, but the postlunch crowd was a briskly flowing river of bodies.

The homeless man picked up his pace, his eyes focused with a burning intensity on the woman ahead of him. Suddenly he thrust out his hand and gripped her forearm. Stunned, the woman turned to look at her attacker. Shock gave way to outrage, then fear, as she twisted violently in an effort to wrest her arm away. They struggled for a few seconds in their awkward pas de deux, but just as the woman raised a hand to shove him back, the man abruptly released his grip. The woman immediately fled into the crowd. The man doubled over and began to sink to the ground, his face contorted in a grimace of pain. But even as his body sagged, his eyes bored into the crowd, searching for her, as though by sheer dint of will they could pull her back.

Finally, though, unable to resist the undertow, he sank down onto the filthy sidewalk, turned on his side, and began to rock back and forth like a child. The river of pedestrians flowed on, pausing only long enough to wind around him and then merge again. After half an hour, the rocking stopped. A passerby in a janitor's uniform leaned down to look at the man for a brief moment, then continued on his way. A young girl pointed her cell phone at him and took a picture, then moved on as well.

It would be another hour before anyone noticed the spreading crimson stain under the homeless man's body. Another hour after that before anyone thought to call the police.

2

TWELVE DAYS LATER

I looked out the window of my office on the eighteenth
floor of the Criminal Courts Building, sipping my third
cup of coffee of the morning and savoring the view—one
of my favorite pastimes. It had poured last night; early
this morning, an unexpected wind kicked up. All vestiges
of smog were wiped out, bequeathing to the citizens of
L.A. an uncommonly sparkling day. I watched the sunlight dance over the leaves of tall trees whose branches
whipped to and fro, threatening to crack the heads of
those scurrying up the street toward the courthouse.

"Rachel, don't you have a preliminary hearing on that
arson murder in Judge Foster's court this morning?"
asked Eric Northrup, my boss and the head deputy of the
Special Trials Unit.

As with all cases in Special Trials, my arson murder
case was that ugly combination of complex and high-
profile. Proving arson is seldom as simple as it sounds.
You have to rule out all accidental and natural causes,
and frequently the necessary evidence burns up with the
victims—who in this case were the elderly parents of the

murderer. The press probably wouldn't hang around for the preliminary hearing, but they'd been making noises about wanting to cover the trial. And that meant I'd have them breathing down my neck while I slogged through the reams of testimony required to stitch together a million little pieces of evidence, praying that the jury didn't get lost along the way. Fun. But ever since I'd joined the district attorney's office eight years ago, I'd dreamed of being one of the few handpicked deputies in Special Trials. And this kind of gnarly beast of a case, which swallowed up any semblance of a personal life, was exactly what I'd signed up for.

"Yep," I replied. My motto: Keep it simple and never offer more than the question asks for. With a little luck, the questioner gives up and goes away. That motto is less effective when the questioner happens to be your boss and you're in your office when you're supposed to be in court doing a preliminary hearing on a murder case.

Eric put his hands on his hips and looked at me expectantly. "I know you hate waiting in court, but..."

I hate waiting in general, but I especially hate it in court, where you're not allowed to do anything except sit there and watch proceedings so boring they make you want to bang your head against a wall.

I held up a hand. "You don't have to tell me," I said. I'd heard that Judge Foster was on the rampage about having to wait for DAs to show up. "But he's got another murder on the calendar before mine, so I've got—" At just that moment, my phone rang.

I motioned for Eric to give me a second as I picked up. It was Manny, the clerk/watchdog in Judge Foster's court.

"Rachel!" Manny whispered. "Stop eyeballing the calendar and get down here. Are you out of your mind? You know what'll—"

I refused to give Eric the satisfaction of knowing I was already on the verge of being chewed out, so I did my best to put on a relaxed smile. "I'm so glad you called," I said cheerily, as though I'd just heard from a beloved sorority sister, which it might have been...if I'd ever joined a sorority. "I was hoping we'd get a chance to talk!"

Manny, momentarily nonplussed, sputtered, "What the...?"

I mouthed *sorry* at Eric and again smiled pleasantly. Eric raised a suspicious eyebrow but moved off down the hall.

I waited a couple of beats to make sure he was gone, then curtly answered, "I'll be down in fifteen seconds." I snatched my file and scrambled out the door, strategically heading for the hallway less traveled.

I'd made it down two corridors and was just about to dash out to the bank of elevators when a voice behind me said, "In a hurry, Knight?"

I abruptly downshifted and turned back to see Eric standing at the other end of the hall, his arms folded.

Exhaling through my nose in a futile effort to hide my recent sprint, I forced a calm tone. "No, but I figured I should go see what's happening, just to be on the safe side."

He shot me a knowing look, turned, and walked into his office.

I trotted out to the elevator, wondering why on earth I'd ever thought I could fool Eric. Four stops and twelve additional bodies later, the elevator bumped to a halt on the fifth floor. I pushed through the shoulder-to-shoulder crowd and made my way to court.

3

I moved swiftly into the courtroom, trying to keep a low profile so Judge Foster wouldn't notice me. The case before mine was still in play, and defense counsel was making an objection that, fortunately for me, kept the judge occupied. But it didn't shield me from the wrath of Manny. He gave me a stern look and shook his head. I pointed to the lawyers as if to say, *What? No one's waiting.* Manny just rolled his eyes. I took a seat at the back of the courtroom; that way, when they called my case, it would look to Judge Foster like I'd been there all along. It doesn't matter whether it's a murder trial or a blind date—it's always about strategy.

The judge overruled the defense objection, and the deputy district attorney resumed direct examination with the standard nonleading question: "Tell us what you saw."

The prosecutor looked vaguely familiar, though his name escaped me. He was in his early thirties, and his carefully coiffed brown hair, perfectly tailored navy-blue suit, red power tie, and French cuffs sporting pricey-looking cuff links said that he didn't have to rely on his civil servant's salary to pay the rent. Or that he was still getting a free ride with Mommy and Daddy.

The witness, a surfer dude with long, bleached-out hair, stroked his sparse soul patch and licked his lips nervously before answering. "Uh, he reached out toward that lady, and the next thing I knew, he was lying on the ground."

"And when you saw he was on the ground, what did you do?" the prosecutor asked. "Did you call the police?"

The witness bent his head and hunched over. He looked away from the prosecutor, and his eyes darted between the floor and the top of counsel table for a few long seconds. Finally he sighed and replied in a quiet voice, "No. I, like, I don't know. I guess I thought he was just drunk or high or something." The low hum of whispers and shuffled papers suddenly stopped, opening a vacuum of silence around the witness's last words. The surfer dude reddened, darted another look around the courtroom at all the eyes now fixed on him, and added defensively, "No one else thought it was a big deal either. I mean, no one called...at least, not for a while."

Every face in the courtroom—with the exception of the prosecutor, who'd been expecting that answer—reflected the ugliness of the mental image those words had painted: of people callously stepping over a man who lay dying on the sidewalk. For me, that image immediately sparked the thought of Cletus, my homeless buddy, who made his bed just south of the courthouse on most Wednesday nights. I'd been bringing him Chinese takeout from the Oolong Café nearly every week for the past couple of years. I imagined Cletus slowly bleeding out onto the cold concrete while people stepped around him as though he were an overturned garbage can. I didn't know who this victim was, but it didn't matter. No one should die like that.

"Objection, irrelevant," the defense attorney said in a bored voice. I recognized him as Walter Schoenfeld, a seasoned public defender. "And no question pending," he added.

"Sustained," the judge ruled, his voice equally flat.

It was just a preliminary hearing, so there was no jury and the prosecution only had to show probable cause, not proof beyond a reasonable doubt. That meant the objections, while legally proper, didn't matter much. The judge could winnow the wheat from the chaff.

"So you saw the man fall to the ground and stay there. What happened next?"

"I saw the cops come, and one of them came into the shop and asked if any of us had seen anything—"

"Objection to whatever the cops said," Walter interjected. "Hearsay."

"Overruled. 'Did you see anything?' It's a question. Questions aren't hearsay."

"Do I keep going?" the witness asked.

"Yes." The judge sighed. "*Overruled* means you're in the clear."

The witness went on. "And then Keshia, uh, the other counter person that day, told them she saw me out by the homeless guy before he, ahh..."

Gun-shy after the reaction to his last mention of the man he'd abandoned to die on the sidewalk, the witness trailed off.

"And then you told them what you've told us here today?"

The witness nodded.

"You have to answer out loud," the prosecutor instructed. His *duh* was implied.

"Yeah, yes."

"Do you see the man in court who stabbed the homeless guy?" asked the deputy district attorney.

"Wait, excuse me," the judge said, stopping the witness and turning to the prosecutor. "'The homeless guy'? He had a name, and I'm sure it wasn't 'homeless guy.' Have the People not come up with any identification for him yet?"

"No, Your Honor. The defense refused to waive time, and so far he hasn't turned up in any database."

So not only was he left to die on a city sidewalk but we couldn't even acknowledge his passing with a name. The sheer loneliness of it all was a lead weight in my chest.

The judge cast a disapproving look at the deputy. "Then, Mr. Prosecutor, the appropriate term would be either *victim* or *John Doe*—not *homeless guy*." He turned to the witness. "Is the person who stabbed the victim here in this courtroom?"

"Uh, well..." The surfer dude nervously looked around the room.

The prosecutor sighed impatiently. Now it was bugging me—I knew I'd seen him around before. What was his name? I mentally scanned the nameplates on the doors in the DA's office. It took a moment, but I finally had it: Brandon Averill. Though I didn't know him, I knew the type. He was one of those young Turks who are self-impressed, self-promoting, always on the hunt for fame and glory, and just handsome enough to entice press photographers. Everything about his attitude said this case wasn't worth his precious time.

After more silence from the witness stand, Averill became visibly irritated. "Try looking over there," he said, pointing to the defense table.

The defendant pulled his head down toward his shoulders, shrinking to make himself a smaller target.

Defense counsel jumped up. "Objection! Suggestive and improper! Motion to strike!"

Judge Foster raised an eyebrow. "Are you sure you want me to strike that, Counsel? You can't think of a way to use that brilliant move in front of a jury?" he said, the word *brilliant* soaked in sarcasm.

Walter smiled. "Withdrawn."

"Indeed," the judge said.

By forcing the witness to focus on the defendant, Brandon had basically tubed his own case. Now, even if the surfer dude did identify the defendant, Schoenfeld would be able to tell the jury that the witness had been strong-armed into it.

The judge's tone had been relatively mild, given his notorious distaste for all counsel. I figured he must have a soft spot for Walter. Judge Foster was a big man, six feet three barefoot and about 270 pounds. As smart as he was impatient, he didn't need a microphone to be heard in court. When an attorney got on his nerves—a more than daily occurrence—you could hear it in the cafeteria, five floors below. I'd always liked him because, although he was a tough old bird, he was equally nasty to everyone. In my book, the perfect judge.

The witness did as he was told and looked straight at the defendant, who was so nervous I could hear him sweating.

"Nuh...uh, no," the witness said in a thin, wobbly

voice. "I seen him there, on the street, but I din't see him stab nobody."

"But isn't it true that you told the police at the scene that *this* man," Averill said, pointing to the defendant, "was the man who'd done the stabbing?"

The defense attorney was on his feet again. "Objection! Improper impeachment!"

But the judge waved him off. "Have a seat, Counsel. Maybe it is, and maybe it isn't. But let's cut to the chase, shall we? It's just a preliminary hearing. No sense pussy-footing around." The judge turned to the witness. "Did you tell the police this was the man who did the stabbing? Yes or no?"

The witness rubbed his soul patch, clearly torn. "Well...uh. Not exactly... Your...uh... Your Worship."

"Just a simple *Your Honor* will do," Judge Foster said. "Then what *did* you tell the police?"

"I just said I seen the dude," he said, turning toward the defendant, a man named Yamaguchi. "He was, like, nearby, you know? But I din't ever say I saw him, like, stab nobody, you know?"

Brandon Averill was red-faced. "Wait a minute, you mean you're denying that you pointed out this defendant at the scene and told the cop that you saw him stab that guy?"

"Yuh...uh, yeah," the witness said, casting a furtive look at the defendant. "I'm denying it."

Brandon turned back to counsel table and shuffled through some papers as the courtroom again fell silent, waiting. Judge Foster had just opened his mouth to tell the prosecutor something he undoubtedly wouldn't be happy to hear when Averill produced a report with a flourish and marched up to the witness stand.

"Isn't that your name?" he asked, pointing to the top of the page. "Charlie Fern?"

The witness mouthed the words quietly. "Uh, yeah."

"Then read this statement aloud for us," the prosecutor demanded, pointing to a line on the page.

"Objection! Hearsay! What the cop wrote on that report is hearsay!" Schoenfeld shouted, again on his feet.

"It is," the judge agreed. "Sustained."

Brandon Averill's mouth opened and closed without sound like a netted fish's while he tried to grab hold of a thought. "It's not admitted for the truth of the matter. It's…uh, well, it's offered to prove the witness's state of mind."

"And this witness's state of mind is in issue because…?" Judge Foster asked, his tone sarcastic. "He's here to identify the defendant as the stabber, true or false?"

"True, Your Honor. But I—," Averill began.

The judge cut him off.

"There is no *but,* Counsel." The judge's merely annoyed tone of a few minutes ago had given way to truly pissed off. Of all the judges in the building, Brandon had picked the worst one to hear a case this weak, this poorly prepared. The only things Judge Foster hated more than unprepared lawyers were cases that were too thin to be in court. He'd called the district attorney's filing unit more than once to "order" them not to file cases that couldn't make it past a preliminary hearing. If a case wasn't even strong enough to show probable cause, which boiled down to the standard of "more likely than not," then it shouldn't be in court, wasting his time.

Now he turned to Brandon Averill, his bushy brows

pulled down, his voice ominously low. "Your eyewitness has denied making the statement attributed to him by the officer. If you want to get that statement into evidence, you'll have to call the officer. This gentleman"—the judge gestured to Charlie Fern, who'd probably never been called that before in his life—"does not seem inclined to go along with the program."

I could see the skin around Brandon Averill's collar turn red. "Can I have a moment to call the investigating officer, Your Honor?"

"You may have exactly one minute, Counsel," Judge Foster said, his voice beginning to rise. "In the meantime, I presume we're finished with this witness? That is, unless defense counsel would like to try and change his mind?"

"No, thank you," Walter Schoenfeld quickly replied. "No questions, Your Honor."

The judge turned to Charlie Fern. "You're excused, sir."

Sir. I had a feeling this was yet another first for the redoubtable Mr. Fern.

I saw the bailiff, clerk, and court reporter brace themselves, having recognized the signs of an imminent eruption. Ordinarily I would've felt codependently nervous for the prosecutor, but Brandon Averill's cavalier attitude had me actively rooting for an ass-kicking. I sat tall and suppressed a smile. How often in life do you get to see the right foot meet the right ass at kicking time?

Brandon walked quickly out of the courtroom, and when the door swung shut behind him, the entire place fell silent. Everyone looked away from the bench; eye contact might invite the judge to find a new focus for his palpably growing ire. Walter turned and whispered to his client, and the other waiting lawyers huddled and spoke softly among themselves. One minute ticked by, then two.

"Bailiff," the judge intoned loudly, "please go and fetch our prosecutor."

"Yes, Your Honor," the bailiff said.

"And if he hesitates," the judge added, "shoot to kill."

The bailiff was smiling as he walked down the aisle, his rubber soles squeaking on the linoleum. Seconds later, he returned with Brandon in tow. The prosecutor was not smiling.

"Your Honor," Brandon said, out of breath, "I need a recess to locate the officer."

"No, Counsel, you may *not* have a recess," the judge's voice boomed.

The looks on the faces of Clerk Manny and the court reporter told me the festivities had begun. Manny grabbed the water glass he kept on the shelf above his desk, and the court reporter's expression hardened as she prepared her fingers for flight.

"As you know very well, Counsel, the defense has a right to a continuous preliminary hearing. Do you see all these lawyers lined up here?" the judge shouted in his thunderous baritone.

Averill nodded. I noticed the tips of his ears redden, matching the skin above his shirt collar.

The judge continued, "I'll be damned if I make an entire calendar cool its heels while you figure out where your witnesses are!"

Brandon touched the knot of his tie like a condemned man fingering his noose. "Perhaps the defense will waive the right to a continuous preliminary hearing so the court can take up the next case while I locate my witness?"

"Oh, indeed?" the judge replied acidly. "Let's find out, shall we?" He turned to the defense. "Counsel, do you waive your right to a continuous preliminary hearing?"

"No, Your Honor," said the attorney. "The defense does not waive."

"Shocking," the judge said. "Any other bright ideas, Mr. Prosecutor? Or, better yet, any other witnesses? Some *incriminating* evidence for a change?"

"I don't have any other witnesses, Judge," Brandon said, trying to regain his cool with a nonchalant shrug.

"People rest?"

"I suppose so."

"I have a motion, Your Honor," Schoenfeld said, beginning to rise.

"Don't bother, Counsel," the judge said, signaling him to sit down.

The judge banged his gavel and barked, "Dismissed."

4

The spectators gave a collective gasp, then erupted in a buzz that built and rolled through the courtroom. The dismissal of a homicide wasn't a typical day for even the most seasoned courtroom veterans.

The defendant, a wiry, lean, young Asian male with black shoulder-length hair, sat quietly at first, absorbing the shock. Then, all of a sudden, it seemed to hit him like a thunderclap. He thumped his fist on the table, the clanking of his waist-to-handcuff chains underscoring the gesture, and turned to his lawyer. "I told you! I told you it wasn't me!"

Judge Foster gave another loud rap of his gavel, stopping the defendant in mid–fist pump. "This is a court of law, not a sports bar!" he thundered. "Get your client under control immediately, or I'll do it for you!"

Walter grabbed Yamaguchi by the arm and whispered through gritted teeth. I couldn't hear what he said, but it worked. The defendant folded his hands on the table and sat quietly.

Legally speaking, the dismissal was well justified. But

it rankled. Maybe this defendant really wasn't the guy. And maybe I would've let it go at that if it hadn't been for the "I could give a shit" look on Brandon's face. Because maybe it *was* him, and the murderer was about to walk out of that courtroom and away from this victim for no good reason—just like everyone else had walked away while he bled out on the sidewalk.

I couldn't just sit there and let it happen. For Cletus, and for all the others who wound up on the periphery of an overpopulated, uncaring world, I had to do something. I quickly moved up the aisle and walked over to Brandon.

"What the hell?" I whispered heatedly. "Where's your cop? Did you subpoena him?"

Brandon glared at me wordlessly for a moment. "Of course I subpoenaed his ass," he shot back.

"Then tell the court you're going to refile so they don't let this guy out," I said as I watched the bailiff take the defendant back into the holding tank.

By law, the prosecution can refile a case that gets dismissed at the preliminary hearing, and we usually do if it's been dismissed just because a witness didn't show up. But the sheriffs don't have bed space to waste. If Brandon didn't tell them he intended to refile, the defendant would be released.

"You're never going to find this defendant again," I said heatedly. "He'll be in the wind the minute they open the gate."

Averill threw the last report into his file. "Tell me, since when does a Special Trials hotshot give a shit about some homeless guy?"

"Tell me, since when did it matter whether a victim drove a Mercedes or a shopping cart?" I fired back.

"Maybe since the 'victim,'" he said, making air quotes—which I hate almost as much as I detest snotty prosecutors—"had just grabbed a lady and was probably going to rob her."

"Based on?"

"Based on the fact that he was found holding a box cutter, and surprisingly we didn't find any packing tape nearby."

"But surprisingly he's the only one who's dead, and if someone killed him in self-defense, then how come they're not around to say so?"

"You're so fired up about this dog, why don't *you* re-file?" he said with a smirk. "Be nice to see one of you Special Trials hotshots get down in the muck with the rest of us."

If he hadn't been such a huge jerk, I might've taken a moment to think about whether there was any hope for this case. But as it was, he'd pissed me off so royally on so many levels that I didn't pause for a second. I grabbed the file out of his hand and turned to the judge.

"Excuse me, Your Honor," I said, loud enough to break through the courtroom chatter. "I'd like to notify the court that the People will be refiling the case of"—I paused to look at the file—"People versus Ronald Yamaguchi."

Judge Foster raised an eyebrow. "I had no idea the Special Trials deputies were in the business of trolling for cases. Must be my lucky day," he said dryly. "Deputy Stevenson," he said, addressing the bailiff, "tell your folks not to rush. It appears Mr. Yamaguchi will be staying with us a little longer."

The bailiff nodded and picked up the phone on his desk.

"And I have the next case, Your Honor," I said, setting down the murder book—the binder cops put together that holds all the reports on a murder case—on counsel table with a heavy thump.

"You ready?" the judge asked.

"I am," I replied.

"But I'm not, Your Honor. Sam Zucker for the defendant." He was a really young, slick-haired type in a chocolate-brown pin-striped suit that said wowee-look-at-me-I'm-a-lawyer. "I'm standing in for Newt Hamilton, who's got the flu. We'll be asking for two weeks—or more if the People want."

Since Newt Hamilton had been privately retained, I had the feeling the onset of his "flu" might be related to the defendant's lack of cash. I knew the judge wouldn't force a stand-in to go forward on a murder case, so I didn't bother to object. We quickly picked a new date, and as the judge called the next case, I saw a detective come barreling in, his eyes on fire and his jaw working sideways. He headed straight for the clerk's desk.

"Detective Stoner, investigating officer on the Yamaguchi case." He pulled out his badge and handed Manny his card. "I just heard the case got dismissed," he said, his voice tight with barely restrained fury.

Manny, who'd had enough fury for one day, quickly pointed to me. "Yeah, but she's refiling."

Thanks, Manny. The detective turned to look at me, steam blowing out of his ears. I motioned for him to meet me out in the hallway and braced myself for the nuclear blast. He nodded curtly, turned on his heel, and headed for the door in rapid, angry strides. Although I was closer to the exit, he moved so fast he got there ten steps ahead of me.

I found the detective out in the hallway and walked over to introduce myself. "Hi, I'm Rachel Knight. Guess I'll be handling the case—," I began.

The detective turned toward me, but before he could respond, his attention was drawn to a point over my left shoulder. His eyes narrowed and his chest filled. "Excuse me," he said roughly, and marched past me.

I turned to see where he was headed, and there was Brandon, sauntering out of the snack bar, carrying—what else?—a cinnamon-covered latte.

Detective Stoner flew at him like a heat-seeking missile. "Why the hell didn't you give me a subpoena for the uniform?"

Brandon had enough sense to blanch, but not enough to back down. He took exactly one second to find his voice. "I did. I sent it over. You just never picked it up. You blew it, Stoner, so don't try to blame me for your fuckup."

"You never sent anything over, you dumb punk! And I can prove it! The subpoena records show nothing was ever issued for the uniform!"

"Yeah? And who controls those records?" Brandon said in a grating voice that'd probably set people's teeth grinding since he was in kindergarten. "Oh, that's right, *you guys.*"

Everyone has a breaking point. Brandon had just found Stoner's.

The detective pulled back his right fist with a vengeance that would've knocked Brandon into his next life if he hadn't flinched just in time. The potentially lethal blow glanced off Brandon's left shoulder. Even so, the force was enough to send him and his latte flying.

Stoner's momentum carried him forward, knocking them both to the floor. The detective seized the opportunity to land a solid punch to the kidney.

Brandon managed a strangled "Help!"

I wasn't strong enough to break up the fight if I'd wanted to—though I admit I didn't mind having an excuse to stand by and let Averill get what he so richly deserved. But there were about twenty cops standing around at the time who were more than capable of taking control. They gave Stoner at least a solid minute before stepping in. I made a mental note to get all of their names. I wanted to personally write them thank-you cards.

It took three of them to pull Stoner off, and when they yanked Brandon to his feet, still dripping with the remains of his latte, he couldn't straighten up. But did that stop him from yapping? Holding his side with one hand and the wall with another, he went off: "I want that asshole arrested! He attacked me! You all saw it!"

We glanced at one another blankly. Nobody moved. Stoner looked Brandon over with hooded eyes, then, cool as a cucumber, flipped open his cell phone and called for the paramedics.

After they'd carted Brandon off to get checked for any possible major damage, I turned to Stoner.

"Want to try again?" I said, extending my hand. "I'm Rachel Knight."

"Stoner," he said, taking it and giving it a firm shake.

"No first name?"

"None I want to share," he said flatly.

"Fair enough."

"You really going to refile?" he asked as he straightened his sports jacket and adjusted his tie.

I paused. Common sense was beginning to enter the picture. "You really think it's a righteous case?"

"We got blood on the defendant's sleeve," he replied. "No lab results yet, but it looks good so far."

Meaning: enough to keep the case alive and see what else pans out. But I had one big question before I took the plunge.

"What about that box cutter? You think our victim was about to mug someone?"

Stoner shrugged. "It's possible. You know, cut the purse straps and run."

I nodded.

My expression must've shown my reservations. Stoner went on, "I know what you're thinking. It looks like a possible self-defense case. Tell you the truth, I would've been willing to let this one go as a manslaughter, if the suspect had said the guy threatened him."

"The defendant didn't say he'd been attacked?" I asked.

"Nope. Claimed he wasn't there when the victim got stabbed."

It was classic. Suspects generally don't get nailed by confessing. They get nailed by saying something provably false. Like claiming they'd never been in a house after their fingerprints were found all over the place.

"But your eyewitness backed up on you big-time," I pointed out. Translation: maybe this defendant is telling the truth.

"Our eyewitness is a little sketchy," he admitted.

I nodded, but if the only eyewitness was sketchy—and from what I saw, that description seemed accurate—that didn't leave much to rely on. Again, Stoner read my expression.

"Look, I'm one hundred percent aware that we're going to need a lot more," he said. "Just give me the time to get it."

"And if you don't?"

"Then I'll be the first to say, let it go."

They always say that. Maybe no-first-name Stoner was one of the few who meant it.

But I knew that if I didn't refile the case now, it might never see the light of day. A victim with a box cutter looked bad, but neither the defendant nor anyone else had claimed that the victim tried to attack them, which told me this probably wasn't a self-defense killing. If so, our homeless man was a real murder victim. I didn't know much about the case, but I knew one thing for sure: he didn't deserve to die nameless and abandoned on a dirty stretch of concrete.

"I'll go put the paperwork through," I said.

"I'll make sure the defendant stays in pocket." Stoner turned to go, then stopped. "I may not be able to keep the case if that DA makes a stink about this. So...thanks," he said. "In case I don't get the chance to tell you later."

"Glad to help," I replied. "And thank you too. On behalf of those who didn't get to see you in action." I had a feeling there were many who would've danced in the streets if they'd witnessed Stoner bitch-slapping Brandon.

The detective nodded.

5

It took the better part of the morning for Sabrina to go from head-turningly gorgeous to invisible functionary, but the success of her efforts was undeniable. No one noticed the woman in the dull brown pantsuit with the flat-colored hair that lay in a low bun against her neck. She moved around the edges of the cocktail-wielding guests in tentative steps, blinking rapidly, nervously pushing her glasses up the bridge of her nose. A timid little mud bird, so inconsequential that even the security at the door hadn't given her credentials more than a fleeting glance.

Not that the others around her exactly glittered. It was a low-key-looking bunch: pearls and tastefully small diamonds, navy blue and black, pumps and wing tips. But a word from any one of the men and several of the women in that room could shake Wall Street and rattle the NASDAQ. And, in fact, they had.

Sabrina was unaccompanied, but she was not alone. Now and then, she'd duck her head and offer a twitch of a smile to a man or woman passing by. They weren't friends. Every single one of them worked for her. Sabrina moved from the fringes of one group to another, watching each individual with a fierce, penetrating intensity. That gaze would have been disturbing had it not been effectively masked by frequent sips from her drink—water disguised as vodka—and fidgeting with her glasses. Sabrina could "watch" like no other—it was one of the many unusual arrows in her quiver that made her the best at what she did. With the patience of a sniper, she surreptitiously tracked every nod, turn of the head, and gesture made by the key figures, but she made sure to take in the more peripheral figures as well: noting who spoke to whom, who leaned in closely to whisper, who left with whom. In that time, she'd seen what no one else would ever have noticed... and then some.

Finally, she signaled to a waiter (another of her employees), put her half-empty glass on his tray, and—shoulders hunched, head tilted obsequiously—approached the circle of suits surrounding the congressman, a tall, slender man whose blond head hovered above the crowd.

A lull in the conversation gave her an opening. "Congressman, it's an honor to meet you." She extended her hand. "Sabrina McCullough. I was wondering whether you intend to oppose the cap and trade bill?"

The congressman glanced at her, then turned a warm smile on the circle surrounding him. "That's a complex bill. I never like to form any final conclusions until I've had the chance to consider all of the possible ramifications. But I'd love to hear what you gentlemen think of it." Dismissing Sabrina completely, the congressman put his hand on the shoulder of a solid man with heavy jowls that swayed with every turn of his head. "Senator Beasley?"

Sabrina nodded, though she knew he wasn't looking and didn't care. Frankly, neither did she. She'd made the necessary contact with her target. Her employees, especially Chase, had pointed out the danger of these encounters, insisted they weren't worth the risk. But Sabrina said that the personal contact, however brief, gave her unique insight. The truth that she didn't admit, even to herself, was she craved the adrenaline rush of physical proximity to her targets—it was an addiction, not a choice.

Sabrina waited to find out if the congressman would say anything of interest. But after the senator "fumphed" his nonreply regarding the cap and trade bill, someone changed the subject to the congressman's upcoming vacation to Martha's Vineyard, which set him off on a journey of boring reminiscences about his boyhood summers on the Cape. Sabrina slowly melted out of the room. On her way down the stairs—she avoided elevators, which threatened tight proximity with too many eyes, not to mention the close-up security cameras—she took off her glasses and, masking her movements from any unseen surveillance, removed a small item from the frame. Just before stepping out into the lobby, she put on her sunglasses. One of the valets came to attention, and when she nodded, he ran to get her car. His tip came wrapped around Sabrina's microcamera—which he quickly pocketed. Sabrina never traveled with anything that could be traced back to her job. The valet would send his intel about all of the guests, along with the camera, by a well-established secure route.

The next morning dawned bright and warm. Sabrina

tossed her carry-on into the backseat and tilted her face up to the sun. Winter in Miami—there was nothing like it. Even California didn't have it this good. She started the engine, pushed the button to roll back the convertible roof, and sped off to the airport, her long black hair a darkly glowing streamer in the wind.

She pulled out her cell phone and hit the number 1.

" 'Lo?" Chase answered, his voice thick with sleep.

She'd forgotten she was three hours ahead, but she didn't care. An early start wouldn't kill him. "I'm done here."

"When do we have to deliver?"

"Yesterday."

Silence. Chase always got nervous with tight deadlines. But she knew he worked best under pressure.

"You find our friend yet?" she asked.

"No. But we know he's not in any of the hospitals."

"You saw him go down? You're sure?"

"There's no doubt," Chase replied.

Sabrina nodded to herself. So far, so good. As long as he stayed down.

6

Paperwork in hand, I headed to the clerk's office and got lucky to find Rosario, one of the more efficient filers, on duty. She let me in behind the counter, where I'd be able to avoid the usual obnoxiously long lines. Then I got even luckier and ran into Toni LaCollier—fellow denizen of the Special Trials Unit and one of my two "besties."

I gave her the lowdown on my eventful morning.

"Girl, trouble and you are like white girls and Justin Bieber—one always chasing the other," Toni said, shaking her head.

"Kind of like black girls and Usher?"

"We don't have to chase," Toni sniffed. "We just have to slow down." She looked around and lowered her voice. "But, seriously, you need to watch out for that little tool, Brandon."

"You know him?"

"I know of him." The clerk passed Toni the complaint for her case—the initial charging document—and she signed it.

"From?" I asked.

"J.D."

Judge J. D. Morgan was Toni's on-again, off-again boyfriend. Perfectly suited for each other, they had all the bad *and* the good things in common. Since both were commitment-phobic, this meant that one or the other would inevitably back away after they'd been together for any length of time. And once they'd been apart for a while, one would eventually sidle up to the other. They were currently in one of their "on" phases.

"He tried a case in front of J.D.," Toni said. "According to him, the guy was a showboat—without the boat."

"That fits," I replied. "And he's got a big hard-on for Special Trials."

"Want to know why?" she asked.

"No," I replied.

Toni ignored me. "Guess who's his boss and big angel in the office?"

"No clue," I said, shaking my head.

"Phil Hemet," Toni replied.

"You've got to be kidding," I said, stricken. "The idiot who lost the only case he ever tried?" I fished through my memory. "A caught-inside-the-car joyriding case."

"A genius he ain't," Toni agreed. "But he's a world-class brownnoser."

"Right. Got promoted to director of central operations at one point, didn't he?"

"Yeah," Toni snorted. "And on his way up, he headed Special Trials for about five minutes."

"Thank God we weren't around for that. But how did they let a fool like that run a unit like Special Trials?"

"How do they do anything around here?"

The clerk pushed the complaint for my case over to me, and I stopped to sign it.

"I will tell you this, though," Toni said. "I heard that the deputies in the unit gave him endless shit. Refused to talk to him about their cases, never listened to a word he said, and if he called a meeting, no one would show. They'd all say they had to be in court." Toni recounted the story with relish.

"Sounds like good, responsible lawyering on their part," I replied.

"Most definitely," Toni agreed. "But you know who demoted his ass?"

I shook my head.

"Your buddy, District Attorney Vanderhorn," she said.

"Nooo!" I replied, truly shocked.

Toni held up her hand. "If I'm lyin', I'm flyin'."

Vanderhorn and I were like oil and water. He thought I was insubordinate and unpredictable. I thought he was a boneheaded politico with no legal skills whatsoever. On any given day, we could both be right. But apparently he'd had a rare fit of good judgment where Hemet was concerned.

"Well, you know what they say . . ."

"Yeah, I do, so spare me," Toni said, knowing what was coming.

I continued, undaunted. "Even a clock that's broken is right twice a day."

Toni walked out ahead of me, muttering to herself—something about gagging.

7

I knew the defense would jam me into the earliest possible date for the preliminary hearing, which meant I wouldn't have much time to pull everything together. From what I'd heard in court, and the flimsiness of the file in my hand, there was still a lot of work to do, not the least of which was to figure out who my victim, currently listed as "John Doe," was. So I turned down Toni's offer to hit Little Tokyo for a sushi lunch and grabbed a no-guilt turkey-and-lettuce sandwich to eat at my desk while I worked.

By the time I settled in and spread out the file, the eighteenth floor was largely deserted. Quiet and empty, just the way I liked it. I shoved the murder book onto the table next to the window and tried not to look at the teetering pile of *other* murder books and case files that were starting to impinge on my treasured ninety-degree view. I opened the bottom drawer of my desk, dropped my purse on top of the bottle of Glenlivet, and propped my feet up on the edge of the drawer.

I flipped open the slender file. My John Doe had been

walking north on Hope—insert irony here—between Fourth and Fifth Street, when he lunged out and grabbed a woman's arm. They struggled for a moment, and that's where the narrative got murky. Either she broke free and then the victim fell to the ground, or he fell to the ground and then she got loose. The report quoted witness Charlie Fern as saying that the defendant, Ronald Yamaguchi, was standing right next to John Doe, so he had to have done the stabbing, though Fern hadn't exactly seen it.

It was an interesting twist on what Fern had said in court. Not so much a contradiction as a difference in emphasis. The gap was right there in plain sight: he "hadn't exactly seen" the stabbing. Why he'd shaved down his statement in court was anybody's guess. Taking the oath can make witnesses nervous, but it was equally possible that Fern had exaggerated what he'd seen when he'd spoken to the cops. Regardless, the statement itself gave fair warning of a possible problem, and a prosecutor who was paying attention would've noticed that and either taken some time to interview Fern before the prelim or at least anticipated a possible snag on the witness stand. In other words, if "I could give a shit" Brandon Averill had been doing his job instead of his hair, he would've made sure the cop who took that report had his butt firmly planted in the seat next to him before he even thought about announcing "ready" in court.

As a general rule, I don't like to second-guess fellow deputies. No one but the trial deputy really knows what's going on, and sometimes his smartest moves are the ones he *doesn't* make. But there was no benefit of the doubt to be given here. Not after what I'd seen in the report. I had no doubt that Stoner was telling the truth and Averill had forgotten to issue the subpoena.

So how had Fern fingered Yamaguchi for the police in the first place if, as Fern claimed, he didn't know Yamaguchi?

I quickly paged over to the arrest report. Apparently Yamaguchi had been in the crowd of gawkers who'd gathered when the police had finally been called to the scene. Charlie'd noticed him there and pointed him out. Odd. Why would Yamaguchi return to the scene when he'd gotten away free and clear? Then again, he wouldn't be the first defendant to get off on watching the police work the crime scene he'd created.

And who was our John Doe, who lay alone and ignored on a filthy sidewalk while his life seeped away? I imagined a mother looking down at her newborn's face, full of hopes and dreams.

I pushed aside the depressing thought and refocused on the report. John Doe'd had a box cutter in his pocket, and he'd grabbed that woman. It was possible the killer had stabbed John Doe in response to a threat. But if it wasn't a self-defense killing, then I owed it to John Doe to make his murderer pay, or at least to give it a fair try.

The crime scene was just a short hike from the office and only a few blocks away from my home—a suite at the Biltmore Hotel, a grand historical landmark in the heart of downtown L.A. I'd been lucky enough to score a sweet deal as a long-term resident after getting a sentence of life without parole for the murderer of the CEO's wife. Recently, the CEO had upgraded me to a suite with two bedrooms, claiming it wasn't getting much use anyway. I'd been a little reluctant to be on the receiving end of even more of his generosity. But when he continued to insist, I caved in. It did make sense that my old room, being smaller and more affordable, was easier to book.

I picked up the phone and punched in Bailey's number. Being at a crime scene always gives me a firsthand feeling for how everything went down—gives me ideas about where to look and what to look for. And it always helps to have the benefit of Bailey's discerning eye.

"Detective Keller, please," I said.

I gazed out at my view of downtown Los Angeles. Having a window office had thrilled me from the moment I'd landed here, in my dream job as a prosecutor in the Special Trials Unit. I made it a point to enjoy the spectacular view every day, no matter what else was going on. The wind was still wreaking havoc with skirts, hats, and hair. A young couple in jackets that were way too thin for the wintry cold shivered and clung to each other as they waited to cross Spring Street. An older woman—who'd unfortunately chosen to wear a wide skirt—awkwardly walked with one hand pressed to her thigh as she hugged the shoulder strap of her purse with the other hand. Behind her a teenage boy mugged for his friends, pretending to be Marilyn Monroe in the famous skirt-blowing scene. He pressed his hands to the legs of his jeans and puckered his mouth as the others snickered. *Yeah*, I thought, *you try walking downhill in a skirt and heels in this wind, smart-ass.*

My call was put through.

"Keller."

"Knight here. Want to walk a crime scene?"

"John Doe stabbing?"

How the hell...?

"It's all over the station, Knight. But how'd *you* wind up with this case? It's not exactly Special Trials material."

"The guy who had the case was a useless sack—"

"Who was gonna dump it, so you got pissed off and grabbed it. And, now that you're in this thing up to your ears, it turns out the case is a dog." Bailey sighed. "You know, I get your whole 'justice for all' thing. What I don't get is why it means *I* have to be roped in."

As if Bailey—or Toni, for that matter—was all that different from me. This wasn't just a nine-to-five job for any of us. But given Bailey's current attitude, not to mention the fact that she was right about the case being a dog, I decided now was not the best time to point that out. "Because you'll get to give me hell about my lack of impulse control?"

"I can do that anyway, and besides, I'm in the middle of a report..."

I saw that I'd have to up the ante. "I'll give you the blow-by-blow on what happened in—and *out of*—court."

Bailey exhaled. "Where's the scene?"

The lure of gossip. It seldom fails. I told her.

"Meet you in ten," she said, and hung up.

It gets tiresome the way Bailey goes on and on.

8

I called Melia, the unit secretary, and told her I'd be going out to a crime scene. Then I pulled on my coat, reached into the pocket for my .22 Beretta, flipped off the safety, and headed out.

I found Bailey standing at the corner of Hope and Fourth Street, her short sandy-blond hair barely ruffled by the heavy wind. Only the tall and lean Bailey could pull off a midcalf-length camel-hair coat. The day was cold enough to make even the weatherproof detective wrap a scarf around her neck, and its jewel-toned colors brought out the green in her eyes. If she weren't one of my besties, I'd hate her guts.

"According to the report," I said by way of greeting, "our John Doe was slightly more than halfway between Fourth and Fifth when they found him."

We headed toward the spot.

"I didn't leave my cozy cubby just to walk a scene with you. What the hell happened in court?"

I filled her in.

"Jeez," she said with a sigh when I'd finished. "Poor Stoner. He's had it rough lately."

"So you know him?"

"We worked together in Hollywood Division a while back. Really good guy, and a great cop."

"So I should believe him when he says he won't give me grief if the case goes south?" I asked.

Bailey hesitated. This did not reassure me.

"What?" I asked impatiently.

"Yeah, he'll probably be okay," she said, then stopped and looked off down the street. "It's just that he's going through a real bitch of a divorce. It's got him a little...un-hinged. Otherwise he never would've gone off on some dumb-punk DA, no matter what he said." Bailey put her hands into her pockets and looked at the ground for a moment. "But you did him a solid—pulled his case out of the Dumpster. I'd think you'd be bulletproof where he's concerned."

I didn't care for the choice of words, reminding me as it did that if Stoner lost it, I might literally need to be bul-letproof.

A group of men in business suits who were trying to navigate the sidewalk and talk at the same time created a moving roadblock, so I stepped to the curb to avoid a col-lision. They never even broke stride or seemed to notice that they'd commandeered the sidewalk. They'd probably walked around my John Doe with equal oblivion.

"Anyway, it may all be moot," Bailey continued. "If that DDA beefs Stoner, they'll make him ride a desk until it all gets sorted out."

"So who'll I get?"

"Depends on who's up." Bailey shrugged, then gave

me a little smile. "But I'd take the hit and work with you for Stoner's sake."

Bailey and I had met and bonded over a serial-killer case we'd worked together six years ago. We'd wound up becoming best friends and had finagled our way into working more than our fair share of cases together. But then Bailey got transferred into the elite Robbery-Homicide Division, and we didn't need to finagle anymore. It was common practice for Robbery-Homicide to funnel nearly all of their cases to the Special Trials Unit.

Bailey thought a moment. "I could probably get clearance to babysit the case until Stoner's beef is settled. That should be long enough to at least get it through the preliminary hearing."

"Yeah, and I'll bet no one's going to fight to get their hands on this one."

"True story." Bailey sighed and shot me a sour look. "Seriously, Knight, would it kill you to get me in on an easy one for a change?"

"Apparently," I said with a shrug. I did seem to have a habit of sticking us with some of the nastier messes. "You want to call Stoner and let him know we're out here?"

"Probably be the smart thing to do."

Bailey opened her cell, and I looked around at the businesses on this stretch of Hope Street: a travel agency advertising low-fare tickets to Costa Rica, a dry cleaner whose window afforded a view of racks filled with men's dress shirts, a bank, a liquor store, and a Subway sandwich shop. I watched a man in a flannel lumberjack coat bite into a thick, juicy meatball-and-cheese submarine and remembered that I'd been too angry to finish my wafer-thin turkey-and-lettuce sandwich. I felt my stomach rumble as I watched the tomato sauce drip onto the paper wrapper he'd spread on the table. I was just about to throw caution to the wind and go order one for myself when Bailey snapped her phone shut. Her expression was grim.

"What? Is he pissed?" I asked. Maybe we should've gotten his okay before invading his turf.

"Apparently that asshole, Averill, already beefed him. Stoner's gonna be stuck at his desk for a while." Bailey shook her head. "The good news is, he's glad to have me help out. For now anyway."

This had clearly put Bailey in one funky mood, but since there was no chance she'd get a whole lot happier in the next hour or so, I decided the only thing to do was to roll on with the business at hand.

"Most of these places have surveillance cameras, don't they?" I asked.

"They should." Bailey looked up and down the street for a moment, then stopped and gazed at a storefront near the northwest corner of Hope and Fifth. "Especially that one."

I followed her gaze and saw that there was a check-cashing store across the street. I hadn't noticed it before, because the sign was so small. I figured that was a testament to the business's popularity. I peered at the building and thought I could see a camera mounted above the storefront window.

It was the start of rush hour, and traffic was beginning to get serious, so we walked up to the corner and waited for the light. Between the commuters in a hurry to beat the bottlenecks and the homicidal taxi drivers, jaywalking was tantamount to a death wish.

"Wouldn't you think Stoner would've done this already?" I asked.

"Maybe he did and just didn't have the video in time for court."

"Or maybe he got it and it didn't help," I said.

Bailey nodded. Neither of us voiced the third possibility: that Stoner had dropped the ball because his life was falling apart. That was definitely not Bailey's style. Or mine. We were great at what shrinks call *compartmentalizing.* Frankly, I think being able to keep your worlds separate is a great thing. Keeps me sane. Or close to it.

9

As check-cashing places go, it was relatively discreet. Just a cursive neon sign in the window to let people know they could get fleeced in exchange for a fast return. We entered the small store and walked up to the counter, where an older Asian man with wire-rimmed glasses and a few strands of comb-over hair sat on a high stool behind a cash register.

Bailey flashed her badge. "LAPD, homicide investigation. I'd like to speak to the manager."

He calmly inspected the badge and glanced at Bailey to match the photograph, then sat back. "First time I see detective as good-looking as you," he said, his speech accented but very intelligible. He seemed appreciative in a completely nonlascivious way. "What can I do for you, ma'am?"

"Does your surveillance camera pick up a view of the street?" Bailey asked.

"Of course," the man replied. "You talking about the day that homeless guy died?"

We both nodded.

"I hear he lay there long time before someone call," the man said, shaking his head. "Sad business, very sad."

I was glad to find someone who seemed to get that.

"You have exact date when it happened?" he asked. "Camera record on a loop. After so long, record over itself."

"It was twelve days ago," I said. *Please don't let it be a ten-day loop.*

He smiled. "You in luck. It's fourteen-day loop."

He called out, and an older woman in thick-soled rubber shoes and polyester pants and blouse shuffled out from the back of the store.

"Show them tape for twelve days ago," he ordered her.

The man let us behind the counter, and we entered a back room so cluttered it looked like it was occupied by hoarders. Literally every single square inch of space was covered with layers of paper of all kinds: invoices, newspapers, dry-cleaner trade magazines. The woman gestured for us to follow her to a tiny office at the back. It had only a computer and monitor on a small desk, which was handy because that's all there was room for.

She punched some keys and asked us for the date and time. We gave it to her, and then she punched some more keys and sat back to let us watch.

The black-and-white images didn't allow us to discern any details, only gross movements. But we could clearly see John Doe reach for a woman in dark sunglasses who was walking in front of him. She spun toward him at first, then recoiled and tried to pull away. Seconds later, John Doe's arm fell, and the woman broke free. John Doe watched her for a moment, then sank down and dropped out of the frame. By that time, the woman was out of sight.

"So that's when he got stabbed," I said. "But it doesn't show the stabber."

"Because our John Doe's body was blocking him from view—at least from the angle this camera had."

"And I couldn't see what that woman did just before he went down, could you?"

"No," Bailey replied. She tapped the screen. "Would you mind replaying it for us?"

We watched again. "Look," I said, pointing to the monitor. "He grabs her, she stops, then somehow she gets free and turns away. But he's still standing."

"Right," Bailey agreed. "So he got stabbed after he let go of her."

"Could you please rewind a little and freeze it?" I asked.

She nodded.

I watched again as the homeless man grabbed the woman's forearm. At the moment the woman pulled away, I told the shopkeeper to freeze the picture.

I pointed to the screen, which showed John Doe still on his feet. "Makes it hard to believe that the stabber was just trying to protect her," I remarked.

"Though not impossible," Bailey said. "We need to find some surveillance footage from another angle."

"Ideally, one that shows the stabber," I agreed. "And it'd be good to find this woman. She had to have seen something."

"Right," Bailey replied.

"So why'd she split without reporting?" I asked.

Bailey shook her head.

We continued watching. Our John Doe dropped out of frame. Pedestrians walked by. Eventually a man stopped and looked down at the spot where John Doe had fallen, then walked on. Some minutes later, a young girl aimed her iPhone at the same spot, then continued down the street. Other passersby parted around an unseen obstacle, then rejoined and kept moving. I winced as, one by one, each of them walked right past my John Doe, most without so much as a second glance.

According to the time counter, John Doe lay on the ground for two and a half hours before the police arrived.

10

Chase sauntered into her office and dropped the flash drive on her desk with fake nonchalance. "We've got him," he said with a superior smile.

Sabrina flashed him a skeptical look. "We'll see," she replied. She didn't really doubt him, though. Chase wasn't a braggart. Tenacious and whip-smart, he had an almost perfect track record. Which was why she'd brought him in as her right-hand man. Well, that, and the fact that she'd always trusted him more than anyone else in the world. Though what that meant was somewhat murky, since she trusted no one else at all. Sabrina waited as Chase flopped down into the cushy sofa to the right of her desk and pulled off his "cover"—a wig and fake glasses. Sabrina wasn't usually a fan of disguises. Too often, they screamed "costume," which only managed to draw more attention. But she was forced to admit that for Chase, there was no other option. His long nose, piercing black eyes fringed by insanely long lashes, and thick curling brown hair presented a combination distinctive enough to make an impression on even a marginally observant witness.

"I take it my intel was good, then?" she asked.

"I don't know how you do it, but it's the best."

Sabrina plugged in the flash drive, then picked up the remote and pressed a button. The floor-to-ceiling metallic shades moved quietly across the wall of windows and shut out the afternoon sun. Now the only light in the cavernous office came from the glow of the cobalt-blue buttons on the remote in her hand.

She swiveled her chair to face the wall on the right and pressed another button. A flat screen descended and locked into place at eye level. Sabrina hit play, and the image of an empty bedroom filled the screen in gray scale. The colors were so muted, it was difficult to make out what was in the room. She adjusted the contrast for maximum definition, and the outline of a bed, a dresser with a television set, and two nightstands—typical hotel furniture—came into view. Seconds later, a man in his sixties—in slacks and shirtsleeves, his expensive suit jacket slung over one shoulder—entered, loosening his tie. He tossed his jacket onto a chair in the corner, lumbered over to the king-size bed, and sat down heavily, hands hanging loosely between his thighs. Sabrina smirked. The man was obviously more than a few drinks into his good time. He rubbed his face, then looked around the room. Sabrina hit pause and peered over at Chase.

"Can you enhance this? I don't want there to be any doubt."

"Yeah, of course. But, trust me, there won't be."

Sabrina turned back to the screen and continued the footage. The man went over to the minibar and pulled out two small bottles of champagne and two flutes. The door of the mini-fridge closed with a thunk, and when he set down the glasses, the clink gave a clear treble tinkle. Sabrina noted the clarity of the sound, pleased. A knock came at the door, and the man went to answer it. The visitor moved past him into the room and stopped dramatically at the foot of the bed.

She was tall and slender, with waist-length blond hair, and dressed in a classic trench coat cinched with a knotted belt. When she spoke, her words nearly boomed from the speakers in the silent room. "Pour the champagne, darling. We don't have all day."

The man obeyed, and the visitor undid the belt and dropped the coat to the floor to reveal a black sequined bustier and black fishnet stockings. She strutted over to the man. They clinked glasses and drank, and the man reached out with one hand and began to caress her breasts.

She drained her glass, sat down on the bed, and leaned back on her elbows, letting her hair cascade down her back. "Bring me any prezzies?"

"Just this," the man said, brandishing a clear baggie holding what looked like three grams of white powder.

"For the girl who has everything." She took the bag, dipped in a long plastic fingernail, and scooped out a nice little mound.

Sabrina hit pause, freezing the image of the woman holding a healthy snort of cocaine on her nail.

"Congressman Rankin, you dog," Sabrina said to the screen. "Or should I say *bitch*?" She gave a low chuckle. "If I didn't know better, I'd think this was fake."

"I couldn't fake it, man. Who could ever dream up stuff *this* crazy?"

There was that. A transvestite *and* a coker. *And* married with children. The rank, arrogant stupidity of it all was incredible, almost laughable. "Bless their pointed little heads—and Adam's apples," Sabrina remarked with a smirk.

"It was touch and go for a minute there. I lost him after the lunch break—somehow he melted into the crowd and got away from me. I panicked at first, but then I spotted his boyfriend there"—Chase gestured to the man on the screen—"the one you singled out in Miami. He was leaving the restaurant, so I followed him."

"And the rest, as they say, is history."

Chase gave a modest shrug.

Sabrina paused, then frowned. "How'd you get the camera in?"

"My old standby, the maintenance-man rig. Told the front desk I had to inspect the wiring and suggested they could give him a drink while he waited. They'll never check the maintenance logs. I mean, who's gonna complain?" Chase snickered.

Sabrina gestured to the flat screen. "I assume our lovebirds 'get down' after this?"

Chase's features twisted sourly. "You don't want to see it." He turned to the screen. "But the picture's good enough, right? And the sound. Couldn't be better, right?"

Sabrina nodded. "We got him."

"So when do we get paid?"

11

By the time Bailey and I thanked our store manager for his help and stepped out onto the sidewalk, lacy cirrus clouds had spread across the sky, covering the sun and causing the temperature to drop. I shivered inside my peacoat and looked longingly across the street at the Subway sandwich shop.

"You hungry?" Bailey asked, seeing the focus of my gaze.

"Kinda, yeah," I said, though I knew it wasn't just because my stomach was empty. I needed some comfort food. This case was making me feel sad and lonely.

"I'm with you," she said.

We headed back across the street and walked in. I'd just begun to read the menu on the wall behind the counter when I saw a familiar face.

I nudged Bailey. "That's the eyewit, the guy who pissed backward on the stand today," I whispered. His long, stringy hair was thankfully imprisoned by a hairnet, but there was no mistaking the face with that scraggly soul patch.

Bailey smiled. "Some things were meant to be, weren't they?" she whispered back. "What's the name again?"

I told her.

Bailey moved up to the counter and smoothly whipped out her badge. "Charlie Fern? We need to take a few moments of your time. If you don't mind."

Not that we cared if he did mind. It just sounded more genteel to say it like that.

"Oh!" he said, his eyes widening at the sight of the shield. "Uh, okay. Uh, sure. I've got a break coming up in about five minutes. That okay?"

"That'll be just fine," Bailey replied. "We'll be right over there." She pointed to a table against the wall.

Charlie nodded. We ordered our sandwiches from the young Latina standing next to him—a pastrami six-inch for Bailey, and a vegetarian six-inch, no mayo, for me. I vowed that after a couple of weeks at the gym, I'd be back to answer the siren song of the meatball and cheese.

I was about two surprisingly tasty bites into my sandwich when I saw Charlie lean in and say something to the woman at the register. She nodded, and he waved to Bailey and me and signaled that he'd be right out. He began to untie his apron as he turned and moved toward the kitchen.

I set down my sandwich and saw Bailey do the same. There was no need for discussion. Bailey and I jumped out of our seats and ran. Seconds later, we screeched to a halt at the side of the building—just as Charlie Fern burst through the back door. Bailey reached out, swiftly snatched a fistful of his T-shirt collar, and gave it a firm backward yank.

She held on to his shirt and shook her head. "Dumb,

really dumb." She looked at him with annoyance. "You made me leave my sandwich."

I contributed a tsk-tsk of disapproval. "You know, Charlie, it really hurts our feelings when witnesses dodge us like that."

Charlie's eyes darted between me and Bailey so rapidly I thought he was going to give himself a seizure. His voice came out in a squeak. "Look, man, I told the cops I din't see who stabbed the dude!"

"That's not how the cop remembered it," I said. "So let's hear the whole truth and nothing but. Did Yamaguchi do the stabbing or not?"

Charlie was breathing hard, and I could see he was facing a personal conundrum. Though I had a pretty good idea what it was, I decided to wait and see if he'd pop it out himself. We all stood there in silence for a few moments as Charlie weighed his options.

Finally he gave up, and his whole body drooped. Unfortunately, since Bailey still had a firm grip on his collar, this meant that the neck of his shirt dug into his throat, slightly strangling him.

Alarmed, he squeaked, "Okay! Let go and I'll explain."

Bailey looked at him impassively and didn't move.

"Please," he said beseechingly. "I promise I won't run."

Bailey gave him a stern look as she moved her hand from his collar to his forearm.

"Ever had a broken arm?" she asked.

"N-no." Charlie looked at her warily.

"Hurts like a son of a bitch."

He nodded and cleared his throat. "I'm on probation

for receiving stolen property," Charlie said. "But I wasn't guilty. I tol' my public defender, man. That stereo receiver was mine. That ass...uh...guy, stiffed me, so I just went and took it back. My dump truck of a PD said to just take the deal. I was scared of going to jail, so I did. I never shoulda listened." Charlie still looked aggrieved.

I wasn't buying the dump-truck story. My experience with public defenders, which was considerable, was that they'd happily fight a case that had any shot at all of winning. I'd bet good money our little Charlie was a thief. But I did buy the part about him being on probation.

"You're dealing out of here, and you got nervous about the cops watching your action, so you told them what you thought they wanted to hear," I said flatly.

Charlie gave me a wounded look. "No!"

Which meant yes.

"And you're in trouble with your PO," I said, sounding as bored as I felt.

I hate the predictable. Which, I guess, is one of the reasons I love my job.

Charlie sniffed. "It was a bullshit deal. I got caught with a little weed. But my PO said if I screwed up again, he'd violate me."

"So you figured you'd earn brownie points with the cops. That way, they'd leave you alone and maybe even help you out with your PO if you just happened to get unlucky enough to get busted again," I said.

Charlie nodded glumly. "I'm totally screwed now, aren't I? You're gonna bust me for lyin' ."

Bailey sighed. "Just give us the truth, Charlie. No more bullshit. What'd you really see?"

"I really did see that dude—whasisname? Yamashiro or something—"

"That's a restaurant, Charlie," I corrected with a sigh. "I take it you mean the defendant who was in court?"

"Yeah, him. He *was* there just before the homeless dude went down."

"You mean the victim?" I couldn't stand hearing one more person call him the *homeless guy*.

"Yuh, uh, yeah, the victim," Charlie said nervously.

"How close was Yamaguchi to the victim when you saw him?"

"Real close, like from me to her," he said, gesturing to Bailey, who was about seven inches away and still holding his arm.

He looked from his limb to Bailey, who ignored his silent entreaty and held fast.

"Was he still that close when the victim went down?" I asked.

"That's the part I don't know," Charlie replied, shaking his head.

Of course he didn't. That was the part that mattered most. "Try to picture how it happened," I said.

Charlie stared at a spot on the pavement and played out the images in his memory. "I seen the victim reach for that lady, then I saw the Yamashiro dude there—"

I didn't want to, but I had to stop him and ask, "And at that point, what was the lady doing?"

"I think she was moving away—"

"Are you sure?" Bailey asked.

"Yeah, pretty sure," Charlie replied, forehead wrinkled with the effort of replaying the incident.

"So the victim wasn't holding on to her anymore," I said.

"No, couldn'ta been," he answered, nodding to himself. " 'Cuz she was moving, and the homeless—uh, I mean the victim was still standing there. That, I'm sure about."

"And did you notice where the Yamashiro guy was at that point?" I asked. Having scored a major victory with *victim* instead of *homeless guy,* I decided to give up on the defendant's name.

"No. He mighta still been there, but I just din't see. Next time I saw him was after the cops came. He was standing with all the looky-loos, watching 'em do their thing."

"Can you describe the lady?" I asked.

"About so high." Charlie put his hand at chin level.

I estimated that would mean she was about five feet seven without factoring in what kind of heels she'd been wearing. So I guessed maybe five feet five or less.

"All I could see was long black hair, big sunglasses." Charlie paused and frowned, then shrugged. "It happened really fast, you know?"

Unfortunately, we really did. Bailey took his contact information and we thanked him for his time and generous cooperation. The sarcasm was wasted on our little doper buddy, who rubbed his arm, cast a wary glance at Bailey, and said, "You're welcome, man."

We'd turned and gone just five steps when Charlie called out to us. "Hey, wait! If that dude Yamashiro gets out, can I get some protection or something?"

"What for?" Bailey asked. "He's going to know you're the one who told us you never saw him do it. He'll probably send you roses. Besides, he's no gangbanger, Charlie. If he skates, the only one he's liable to go after is the city of Los Angeles. Make himself some money," Bailey said flatly.

Charlie stroked his chin. "Yeah. Guess you're right."

He waved, we waved, and he walked back inside the sandwich shop.

12

"**If this** case gets any thinner it'll fly away," I remarked. "I'd like to get ahold of the arresting officer. Find out how the defendant reacted when they popped him."

A defendant's reaction to the news of his arrest could tell you a lot. I'd had a case where a drug dealer had tied up his four rivals, put pillowcases over their heads, and then stabbed them all repeatedly. When the cops went to arrest him, he'd earnestly stated, "It was self-defense." Granted, it doesn't usually get that good, but inspirational tales like those keep the fires of hope burning.

I'd checked the paperwork before I left the office. "Arresting cop is Hank Aronofsky."

Bailey pulled out her phone.

"He's on patrol," she said as she ended the call. "He'll meet us at the Wells Fargo building at Second and Grand."

"You want to get your car?" I asked hopefully. It was an uphill hike for some long blocks, and I was wearing three-inch heels.

"No," Bailey said. "I don't want the hassle of parking."

"Since when did you start worrying about parking?" Cops do not have the cares and woes the rest of us mere mortals do when it comes to tickets and towing.

Bailey glanced at my shoes and sighed. "Fine, let's go."

We threaded our way through the briskly moving horde of office workers who were heading for their cars and trains, and finally arrived at the Police Administration Building, where we picked up Bailey's car. Minutes later, we pulled up behind a patrol car that was parked in front of the Wells Fargo building. Officer Aronofsky, whose uniform hung loosely on his wiry frame, met us on the sidewalk, and we all shook hands. I got down to business quickly.

"What'd you say when you first approached him?" I asked.

"Just that I wanted to talk to him about what he might've seen," the officer replied.

Smart move. Aronofsky hadn't given the suspect any hints. He'd just given him rope.

"You already knew the vic had a box cutter?" Bailey asked.

"Yeah. So I figured he might claim self-defense or defense of someone else. And if he did…" The officer shrugged.

Bailey and I nodded. The case would have ended with a manslaughter—at most.

"But he never said a word about the box cutter," Aronofsky continued. "Just said he saw the vic grab that lady's arm, so he pushed the vic off her and walked away—"

"Which didn't jibe with what your eyewit said," I remarked.

"Correct. So I told him he needed to come clean about what happened. But he just kept saying he'd told me the truth, he never stabbed anyone, yadda yadda. That's when I noticed the blood on his sleeve."

"And you busted him?" I asked.

"Told him he was under arrest for murder," the officer said, "and he went apeshit. Started yelling and screaming. That's when he got into a rant about how the homeless were ruining the city, destroying everything, they were a menace, and on and on. Looked to me like the guy was wrapped a little tight about the homeless, so when he saw this homeless vic grab the lady, he snapped. So I hooked him up and put him in the car and ran him. He's got a prior for ADW."

Assault with a deadly weapon. *Interesting.* "Was the assault victim a homeless person?" I asked.

"Don't think so," Aronofsky said, shaking his head. "Victim was listed as Robert Yamaguchi. So I'd guess it was—"

"A cousin or something?"

Aronofsky nodded.

Not as significant as if it had been a homeless person, but it was better than nothing.

"He ever change his tune, make any admissions?" Bailey asked.

"Not to me," the officer replied. "You talk to the eyewit?"

"Yeah," Bailey replied. "Very dicey."

"And the uni who took his statement?" Aronofsky asked. "You talk to him?"

"Not yet," Bailey said.

He sighed and leaned back against his patrol car. None

of us wanted to say out loud what each was beginning to think: this was already looking like an unsolved. We thanked the officer and went back to Bailey's car. She slowly pulled away from the curb, watching her side mirror for speeding commuters.

We'd done about all we could do today, and I figured now might be a good time to remind her of how winning and winsome I could be. "Got time for a drink?" I asked. "I'm buying."

Without a word, Bailey immediately made a U-turn and steered us toward the Biltmore.

"I'm thinking I should set up a meeting with the defendant," I said.

Bailey snorted and gave a short laugh. "Great idea," she said sarcastically. "Man, I'll bet he can't wait to have a heart-to-heart with the DA who wouldn't let his case get thrown out."

We stopped at the light, and I watched a pair of tatted and pierced boys in skinny jeans lope across the intersection. Their inky black hair was so stiff with goo that even in the gusty wind, not a strand moved. I turned to Bailey.

"You got a better idea?" I asked, knowing even as I said it that this was a bad question to pose right now.

"Yeah, but you don't want to hear it." Bailey pulled up to her favorite parking space, right next to a fire hydrant in front of the Biltmore. "But I'll tell you what: let's make it interesting. He talks to you, I'll buy the first round."

"Okay, but not here," I said warningly.

Bailey never paid for drinks at the Biltmore bar because Drew, the gorgeous bartender extraordinaire, was her boyfriend. The fact that they'd stayed together for the past year had surprised everyone who knew him. And her.

Drew was one of those men who'd always been catnip to women, and since I'd been living there, I'd seen a parade of hotties camp out at the end of the bar. But Bailey came along at just the time in his life when Drew was starting to think long-term—about everything. Now, he wanted to stick with one woman, and that woman was Bailey. Their only real challenge was finding time for each other. Bailey's hours were, and always would be, crazy, and Drew had gotten serious about fulfilling his dream of opening his own upscale bar.

"I'll tell Drew I'm paying," she said. "Will that do?"

"No."

"Fine, you name the place."

"I'll get back to you," I said.

"But before you start looking for the most expensive bar in town, remember: if you lose, you're buying."

That threat should've cooled my jets, but it didn't. It just made me even more determined to win.

I got the lawyer Walter Schoenfeld's number from Melia and punched it in. I got lucky; Walter was in. I briefly explained what I wanted and ended by admitting, "I'll be honest, it's a skinny case. If your guy hadn't popped off the way he did, I don't know that he'd still be jacked up."

Walter exhaled loudly and was silent for a moment. "You know, I can't even remember the last time I let a client talk to you guys."

"Well, sure," I said, trying to sound reasonable. "But this is me and Bailey. We're different—"

"No argument there," Walter interjected dryly.

"—as in, fair-minded," I said. "And you've got to admit, this is an unusual situation—"

"Yeah," he agreed somewhat hesitantly.

"Besides, how much worse off can he get if you're sitting right next to him?" I asked.

"I don't know, Rachel."

I ramped up my pitch. "Look, Walter. I can tell you really believe in your guy. If he impresses us as much, he's out of there. That's a pretty big upside."

"Yeah," he replied. "But I'm not so sure he needs to impress you. I don't think your buddy Charlie Fern's gonna go to bat for you, and I don't think you've got much else."

Time for my trump card. I did my best to play it with a little flourish. "No, not much else," I said. "Except the blood on his sleeve."

Walter fell silent. I held my breath.

He inhaled sharply. "Okay, listen. When I say it's over, everyone stops. Understood? No pushing."

I tried to keep the triumphant note out of my voice. "You've got my word, Walter. I'll be so civilized, you won't even believe it's me."

Walter sighed. "I hope I'm not making the biggest mistake of my career."

I reassured him he wasn't. And I wasn't lying. How should I know what mistakes he'd made in the past? There might've been some real whoppers. Surely this wouldn't be the *biggest*.

"And, Rachel, for what it's worth?" he said.

"Yeah."

"I really think this guy is innocent."

"Yeah, yeah, Walter," I replied lightly. "That's what they all say."

"So cynical, so young," he clucked.

We agreed to meet at Bauchet Street—the Men's Central Jail—at noon the following day. I ended the call, then turned a gloating face to Bailey.

She shook her head. "Damn. I cannot believe you pulled that off."

"Better work some overtime, Keller," I said, grinning. "This round's gonna hurt."

Bailey shook her head again and we got out of the car. I called Melia and told her I wouldn't be coming back tonight.

"Oh . . . yeah. You're out in the field, right?" she asked.

"I love how you put it all together, Melia. Especially since I told you I was going out to a crime scene before I left."

"Oh, right."

Fantastic. It was comforting to know that if I got nailed checking out a crime scene, no one would even know I'd left the office till some hiker found my body. There were wonderful secretaries in the DA's office. I wondered for the millionth time why we couldn't have gotten one of them.

13

Angel, the doorman, greeted us as he opened the heavy glass-and-iron door. "Evening, ladies."

"Hey, Angel," I replied. "Keeping warm?"

"Had to break out my thermals."

Though L.A. never got the kind of cold you'd find in the Midwest or on the East Coast, it could definitely get nippy enough to seep into your bones after a while. And unlike back East or the Midwest, builders out here never took heating and insulation all that seriously. This meant that the great indoors provided no real relief.

"I could lend you my Spanx," I replied. "That'll heat you up."

"Plus it'll smooth you out," Bailey observed.

Angel rolled his eyes and stepped back outside.

We made our way through the magnificently spacious lobby, our footsteps echoing on the henna-colored marble floors, then muted as we stepped onto the thick Oriental rugs. I reached the bar first and grasped the solid-brass handle to pull the door open. The electric fire in the brick hearth glowed warmly, casting an orange light on the forest-green-leather wingback chairs and mahogany tables. It was already fairly crowded with financial-district types and corporate lawyers—no cops or prosecutors, now or ever. Bailey and I took seats at the end of the bar. Drew looked, as always, like he'd stepped out of *GQ*, dressed in the usual white shirt and black vest that accentuated his broad shoulders and narrow waist, the diamond stud earring flashing brightly against his black skin. He poured from a silver martini shaker into four glasses on a tray, wiped his hands on the bar towel, and came down to greet us.

"The most beautiful women in the world have arrived," he said, somehow making the statement feel entirely plausible.

"And how are we tonight?" he asked.

"Tired," Bailey said.

They exchanged an obnoxiously sweet smile.

"And thirsty," I said pointedly.

"Graden joining us?" he asked me, referring to Lieutenant Graden Hales.

The common wisdom among female deputy DAs is *never fall for a cop.* Sure, they can be smart, handsome, sexy as hell. But they're almost guaranteed to be dogs who'll cheat on you with your sister and then tell all their buddies at the station. Lieutenant Graden Hales, whom I'd met when he got assigned to investigate the murder of my dear friend and fellow Special Trials prosecutor Jake Pahlmeyer about a year ago, seemed to be the exception. His hazel eyes; sandy-brown hair; wide, strong cheekbones; and full lips more than delivered on the handsome-and-sexy quotient. But as far as I could tell, there was no dog in him. He seemed to be an honest-to-

God decent guy who wanted a relationship with a real woman, not just some arm candy.

And unbelievably, to top it off, he was rich—filthy rich, to be exact. Though I didn't know much about his early life, I did know his wasn't family money. Before he figured out what he wanted to be when he grew up, Graden had worked a minimum-wage job for a construction company. As a hobby, just for the fun of it, he dreamed up video games. But once he got hired by the LAPD, he decided he didn't have the time or the desire for games anymore. So just before he finished the police academy, he put together one last game: Code Three— police jargon for a sirens-on emergency. Had it been up to him, that game never would've seen the light of day. But fortunately for Graden, his younger brother, Devon, a computer whizbang, saw the potential in this last creation and decided to write up the software and see if anyone was interested. Five years later, Code Three hit the gaming world like a tsunami, setting Graden and Devon up for life.

Graden and I had been dating for months, but I wasn't ready to pick out any china patterns. Toni likes to call me *commitment challenged.* I like to tell her that's the pot calling the kettle African-American. Though she hides it well, I know she finds this hilarious every time I say it.

I answered Drew with a shake of my head. "Graden's 'bonding' with his brother tonight."

Drew nodded, then favored Bailey with a slow, sexy smile. "How was your day, baby?" That voice had surely undressed enough women to populate a small country.

"Okay," she replied, her voice so silky, she practically purred. Hell, men at the end of the bar started loosening their ties. It was enough to turn your stomach. "And what about you? Did you talk to the bank today?"

Drew had been working on getting a small-business loan for his bar.

"I did," Drew replied. "So far, so good." He held up crossed fingers. "So, ladies, the usual?"

"Sure," Bailey replied, managing to give the word two syllables.

They exchanged another sappy smile.

"No," I replied. "I'll have a shot of Pepto-Bismol."

They both laughed.

"I wasn't kidding," I said.

They smiled, apparently unconcerned that their "sweet nothings" had caused a bilious "something" to rise in the back of my throat.

I fixed them with a steely glare. "I guess I'll let you pay off your bet now after all." I gave Bailey a smug look. "I'll have a Russian Standard Platinum martini, straight up with a twist." It was one of the most expensive vodkas in the house.

Bailey's expression turned dour. I smiled back sweetly. I take my revenge very dry and very cold.

14

The only downside to a meeting at the Los Angeles County
Men's Central Jail was that I'd have to go to the Los
Angeles County Men's Central Jail. Entering the dank,
sprawling concrete monstrosity, the largest county jail
in the world, always made me feel like I was walking
through the seventh gate of hell. The mixture of disinfec-
tant, sweat, and misery lingered in my nostrils for days,
and it took just as long to get the echoes of clanging metal
doors and gates out of my head.

"You find out what Stoner's done to identify our victim?" I asked Bailey. "I haven't had time, since I kind of
got stuck into this case headfirst—"

"It doesn't count as *got* stuck when you do it to yourself."

She was right, of course, so I ignored her. "You know
anything?"

"Stoner ran the fingerprints through all databases,
asked for DNA testing—"

"So we'll get those results about six months after we
get his killer," I said dryly.

The crime lab was notoriously backed up. It was hard to get fast results even when we had a suspect set for trial. Getting them to do testing just to identify a victim—a homeless victim, no less—would go to the bottom of the pile.

Bailey nodded. "Yeah. Especially because we probably don't even have his DNA on file. So far, his prints don't show up anywhere."

"A homeless person who's never been busted? You've got to be kidding me."

Usually there's at least a shoplifting or panhandling conviction. Either someone had dropped the ball and failed to print the guy, or this was one of the most unusual homeless people I'd ever encountered.

"Makes me wonder how long he'd been out on the streets," I remarked. "What'd the coroner say about his physical condition?"

"Don't know yet," Bailey replied. "Haven't had time to get the report since we 'got stuck into this case head-first.'" She shot me a meaningful look. I busied myself with a search for my badge at the bottom of my purse.

We crossed the lobby and held out our badges to the deputy sheriff behind the bulletproof glass.

"Drop 'em in the slot," she said. "You carrying?" she asked Bailey.

Bailey removed her service 9 mm Glock while I fished out my .38 Smith & Wesson. She passed us a key, and we locked our guns in one of the boxes lining the wall behind us.

I paused to ask the deputy, "Did a public defender by the name of Walter Schoenfeld check in?"

"What am I, your friggin' hostess for the day?" she

asked. She pushed our badges back out to us and buzzed us in. "You wanna know if he's here, go look."

We moved through the metal detector and found Walter sitting among a throng of defense attorneys in the waiting area. Bailey and I walked over to him.

"They tell you how long for an attorney room?" I asked.

"Said about ten minutes," Walter replied. He looked at his watch. "Twenty minutes ago."

I sighed. Typical. With only five attorney rooms, the wait could easily take hours.

"I'll go goose him," Bailey said, and walked off.

No one gets better service in county jail than a cop. Within five minutes, the jail deputy called out for us to follow him. I deliberately avoided looking at the other attorneys who'd undoubtedly been waiting there for hours as we passed by. The room was silent as we all read our reports and got ready for the interview. Ten minutes later, Ronald Yamaguchi was being escorted down the glass-enclosed hall toward us in waist and leg chains. He clutched a notepad in his hands, which were cuffed in front of him, but his expression was surprisingly serene.

"You guys going to tape this?" Walter asked.

"Yeah," Bailey said. She produced a small digital recorder from her jacket pocket and placed it on the table.

The door opened, and Yamaguchi was guided into the room and seated next to Walter, across the table from Bailey and me. I did a double take at the sight of Yamaguchi. I hadn't really noticed in court, but between the olive complexion, jet-black shoulder-length hair, and well-muscled physique, Ronald Yamaguchi managed to rock that ugly orange jumpsuit. I had to hand it to him—though not at the moment.

Before his client could speak, Walter warned him that he was being recorded and pointed to the device.

"Good," Yamaguchi replied.

An interesting reaction. I saw from Bailey's raised eyebrow that she thought so too. She calmly read him his rights and he waived them, and we got down to business.

"What were you doing in the area that day?" I asked.

"I work in Little Tokyo," he replied. "My bank's on the street where it happened. I made a deposit and was on my way back to work when I saw the homeless guy."

I made a mental note to get into the specifics of where he worked and banked later.

"What drew your attention to him?" I asked.

"What he did," Yamaguchi replied. "He, like, almost jumped at that lady, and then he grabbed her. I thought he might hurt her."

That wasn't exactly what he'd said when he'd been interviewed at the scene—at least, according to the arrest report. Then again, it wasn't completely different either. It was all a matter of emphasis, I supposed. Sometimes the truth can be elastic.

"Was she carrying a purse?" I asked.

Yamaguchi thought for a moment, then shook his head. "She might've been. I didn't get a good enough look at her."

"Could you describe what the man did when he reached for her?" I asked.

I was making sure to keep my questions open-ended so he wouldn't be able to claim later that I'd "confused" or cornered him.

Yamaguchi stared at the wall over my shoulder for a moment before responding. "I was on the sidewalk, just outside my bank. I caught a fast movement out of the corner of my eye. He kind of lunged and grabbed the lady at the same time," Yamaguchi said, frowning as he pictured the scene. "And he seemed pissed off—"

"Could you see his face?" I asked.

"No. But that's what it felt like to me, so I guess maybe it was the way he reached for her. He grabbed on to her elbow like this—"

Yamaguchi tried to shoot his hand out to demonstrate, forgetting it was chained to his waist. The motion jerked the chain taut with a loud clank but stopped just a few inches from his waist. His face registered shock for a brief moment.

"Did he actually manage to put his hand on her elbow?" I asked.

"Yeah. That's why I thought he might be trying to hurt her, so I knocked his arm down, like this."

Yamaguchi did his best to show us what he'd done. As he carefully lifted his hand and brought it down in a karate-chopping motion, I could see the muscles in his forearm bunch and move. That would've been one powerful hit.

"Did you see any weapon on the homeless man?" I asked.

"No." He shook his head emphatically. "For some reason, I never even thought about it. Stupid, huh?" he said, his expression puzzled. "The guy coulda shivved me right there. Matter of fact, I heard afterward that he had a box cutter—"

"But you didn't see any box cutter at the time?" I said evenly.

This was a critical point. If he admitted he hadn't seen the box cutter, he'd be hard-pressed to later claim that the killing was done in self-defense. I half expected Walter to jump in here and keep Yamaguchi from answering, but he sat quietly.

Yamaguchi said, "No, I didn't. I just saw the guy grab that lady's elbow, and I reacted. It wasn't like I had a chance to give it a whole lot of thought, it was just a reflex, you know?"

"You have any training in martial arts?" I asked.

Walter stepped in. "I don't see the relevance of that." He turned to his client. "Ronald, I'm advising you not to answer that."

Yamaguchi looked at Walter, confused. "Why? I thought the whole point was to be up front about everything. I've got nothing to hide."

Walter paused for a beat, then nodded and sat back. He waved his hand. "Go ahead."

Ronald continued. "I've got a black belt in tae kwon do."

"I had a feeling," I said. "Okay, so you knocked the guy's arm down. What did he do? Did he turn on you?"

I was giving him another chance to claim self-defense.

"No." He stopped and was silent for a moment. "I pretty much came at him out of the blue. He just stood there, like, in shock. But I don't know what happened after that, because as soon as I saw his arm drop and I could see the lady was out of reach, I took off."

If Yamaguchi was telling the truth, it meant that regardless of who the killer was, the stabbing certainly hadn't been done to defend anyone. This was a murder.

15

I moved in to nail down the point.

"What do you mean, 'the lady was out of reach'?"

"She took off running," he replied. "I remember thinking there was no way he was gonna get to her again. She moved fast, and the sidewalk was packed, you know?" He shook his head. "I can promise you I wouldn't have taken off if it'd looked like she was still in danger."

I heard the note of pride in his voice.

"The tae kwon do came in handy," I remarked.

He dipped his head and gave me a modest smile. "All those classes. I always hoped I'd get the chance to help someone."

And this was his reward. A cell in the county jail. But Ronald had uttered the words without a trace of irony. Though it definitely hadn't turned out well for him, he knew he had saved that dark-haired woman and he didn't regret it.

But that didn't mean he wasn't the stabber. I moved on.

"Did you see where she went?"

Again Yamaguchi stopped and thought. If he was pulling an act, I had to admit it was a good one.

"I don't know," he said. "It's all kind of a blur, it happened so fast. All I know is that after I hit his arm, he stopped, she moved away, and it seemed like everyone was okay. So I took off." Yamaguchi looked at me, his expression open, earnest.

There was something so...*off* about this case. The pieces weren't fitting into any logical pattern. Or at least not one I could see at this point. I rubbed my aching neck and shoulders, and moved on to the next subject.

"So the victim was standing and unharmed when you left the area?" I asked.

"Yeah."

"Where did you go?"

"Back to work," Yamaguchi replied. "I work at a spa in Little Tokyo on First near San Pedro Street. I'm a masseur—"

It wasn't conscious, but I guess my reaction showed on my face. I'd heard that some of those "spas" were just fronts for prostitution.

Yamaguchi continued, his tone firm. "It's a real spa and I'm a real masseur. And you could use some help," he said, nodding at my hand, which was at that moment kneading the rigid muscles in my neck. I dropped my hand, busted.

"But you went back to the scene. Why?" I asked.

Yamaguchi sighed and looked down at the floor. We all sat silently, waiting. Finally Walter spoke up. "Ronald, you've gone this far. There's no point in holding back now."

Intrigued, I leaned forward.

Yamaguchi nodded but pressed his lips together. After another minute, he spoke. "One of my regulars is a cop. He was on the table when the call came in on his radio, and when I heard the location I realized it might be the homeless guy I'd just seen. He ran out when he got the call, and I decided to go look." Yamaguchi held his hands out, palms up, as far as the chain would allow and shrugged. "Just curiosity, I guess."

His story was just weird enough to have the ring of truth. But we weren't quite done yet.

"First of all, I'd like the name of that cop," I said. "If he corroborates your story, it'll go a long way toward getting you out of here."

Yamaguchi shook his head. "If it gets out that he was getting a massage while he was on duty, he'll be in big trouble. He's a good customer. I can't do that to him."

I was impressed by his reluctance to dump out the cop—assuming it was the truth. What I'd need to do is talk to the officer on the down low, promise not to let anyone else know about his "afternoon delight," and see if he would corroborate Yamaguchi's story. But I'd need Bailey's okay first, because we'd be hiding evidence of an officer's dereliction of duty. That meant there was no point in pressing the issue right now.

"You know they found blood on the sleeve of your jacket," I said. "You have an explanation for it?"

The working assumption had been that it was the victim's blood, and Stoner had submitted the jacket for testing as soon as Yamaguchi was arrested, but the lab hadn't given us any results yet.

"I don't," Yamaguchi said, his expression distressed. "It couldn't have been much, or I'd have noticed it." He frowned to himself. "It was just a drop or something, right?" he asked Bailey.

Bailey shrugged, noncommittal. "Big or small, the point is, you don't remember cutting yourself at all that day, right?"

"I suppose it's possible," he replied. "But no, I have no memory of it."

It impressed me that he wasn't trying to give us a cover story. This was yet another answer that'd come back to bite him if he suddenly remembered at trial that he'd had a shaving accident. The fact that Walter was letting us pin him down this way told me he must really be thinking this guy is innocent. Still, Walter wouldn't be the first lawyer to be suckered by his client. I decided to continue with the last point.

"From what I hear, you had a lot to say about the homeless—none of it good. Want to explain the rant you got into with the arresting officer?"

For the first time since the interview began, Yamaguchi reddened and shifted uncomfortably in his seat. I waited without comment, letting the silence build. Sometimes silence is the best interrogator.

"That was…unfortunate," Yamaguchi said slowly, his eyes focused downward at a point on the table. "We've been having a real hard time at work because some of the homeless guys can be…pretty aggressive. They've been scaring off customers, especially the women." He paused. "This economy, things are already so tough. We lose many more customers, we'll fold." He shook his head. "When I went to the bank that day, I'd made the smallest weekly deposit ever. I was in a pretty bad mood." Yamaguchi stopped, realizing what he'd said, then looked at me steadily. "But I'd never kill someone. Never. And I didn't kill that guy."

I watched him as I returned his gaze. I decided to test the waters some more. "You willing to take a poly?"

"Sure," Yamaguchi immediately replied.

At that same instant, Walter erupted, "No! I do not trust those things, and I will not allow it."

Frankly, for my own reasons, I didn't trust them either. If Yamaguchi was a real martial artist, he might be able to control his breathing and galvanic responses enough to pass, or at least to give an inconclusive result. Maybe Yamaguchi knew that too. But if that were the case, I would've expected him to bring up the idea of taking a poly first, not to wait to see if I did. The fact that he hadn't, and that he'd readily agreed to take it, meant either he was the slickest con artist ever or he really was innocent and eager to prove it.

Yamaguchi gave his lawyer a perplexed look but didn't argue.

"Look, Ms. Knight, why don't you at least let me bail out?" he suggested. "Put a cuff on me, whatever. I can promise you, I'll stick around. I need to get back to work. Every day I spend in here, I'm losing customers. I lose enough customers, I get fired."

I was definitely leaning toward letting this guy go. The case against him was unraveling more and more by the minute. But I wasn't quite ready to cut him loose. Because if I let him go and he turned out to be the killer, both Bailey and I would have our necks in a noose.

"Seriously, Ms. Knight." Yamaguchi leaned forward, his body tense. "I won't run. I can tell you're reasonable.

Not like that other douche—" Yamaguchi stopped as Walter put his hand out.

I barely suppressed a smile, and I could see Bailey's lips twitch too. Brandon Averill *was* a douche.

"Tell you what," Yamaguchi continued, "you let me make bail, I'll give you a free massage. Hour and a half. You know you need it. What do you say?"

"I say you just added a count of bribing a public official," I deadpanned.

Yamaguchi stared at me, stricken.

I shook my head. "Kidding."

Yamaguchi blew his breath out through his mouth and sat back. "You guys have a sick sense of humor, you know that?"

"It's been suggested in the past," I admitted.

I looked over at Bailey, who nodded. We were on the same page.

"Tell you what, Mr. Yamaguchi, I need to check out a couple of things. I'll have an answer for you in no more than two days." I stood up to go. "Thanks for talking to us."

Yamaguchi replied, "I know you'll do the right thing."

I would, but that wouldn't necessarily be good news for him.

"What's the name of your bank?" I asked.

He gave it to me, along with the exact address, and I motioned to the guard that we were done.

"I'm going to stay a little longer," Walter said. "You'll call me?"

"Absolutely," I agreed, and Bailey and I walked to the door. As the guard opened it, Yamaguchi spoke again.

"Hot, wet rags."

I looked at him, puzzled.

"For the neck and shoulders. It'll do wonders," he said sagely. "At least until you can get in to see me."

My muscles were in such a bad knot, I was tempted to make the appointment right then and there. Then again, it might be a little soon. After all, he was still in custody for murder.

16

Maxwell Chevorin was flying in. Sabrina had called the lobbyist to let him know the package was ready. Give him enough time to get the two million in cash. And if he was smart, a hefty bonus to reward them for a home run of a job. Compared to the money Chevorin would make for delivering Congressman Rankin's swing vote on offshore drilling, even three million was pocket lint.

Sabrina stared out across the L.A. skyline from the balcony of her penthouse suite. The condos on the upper floors in downtown Bunker Hill afforded a view that made Catalina Island look close enough to swim to. But today the clouds hung low over a gray ocean, obscuring the line between sea and sky, and Catalina was only a suggestion in the misty gloom. Sabrina didn't notice. Her mind was racing to analyze the ramifications of what Chase had just reported. Though she couldn't yet formulate precisely why, alarm bells were sounding in every cell of her body. She knew that Chase would tell her she was being paranoid and obsessive, but her internal warning system had never failed her. She'd told him countless times over the years that he was too nonchalant. She turned to watch him now, hunched in a corner of the couch, typing furiously on his laptop. Sabrina walked back into the expansive living room, where smooth jazz played softly in the background, a counterpoint to her jangling energy.

"You're sure that was him?" she asked.

Chase lifted his hands off the keyboard and looked at Sabrina warily. "Yes. And I double-checked with the coroner's office. But don't worry, they've still got the guy in custody—"

"But they haven't dropped the case."

"No. But they will, trust—"

Sabrina stared him into silence. Chase never seemed to understand that threats ignored only came closer—they didn't go away.

Chase sighed. It was pointless to argue when she got like this. "What do you want me to do?"

Sabrina told him. His expression, as he listened to his marching orders, told her that he thought this was overkill. But she knew he'd do as she asked, just as he'd always done since they'd first met in the fifth grade, in that crappy prison of a boarding school.

When she finished, she glanced at her watch. "You'd better get going."

"Can I come back later?"

"I'll call you when we're done." Chevorin would be here soon, and she wanted Chase gone before he appeared. She'd never allowed the lobbyist to meet Chase or any of her other employees.

After Chase left, Sabrina moved quickly to her bedroom. The original walls that had divided the dressing room from the sleeping area had been knocked down to create one large space. The uncluttered, somewhat austere modern decor—spare lines, all fabrics in black and white, alleviated by the few splashes of red throw pillows on the bed and divan—made the room seem even larger, if somewhat impersonal. The choices were Sabrina's alone. She'd always favored that kind of simplicity, even in early childhood. Yet another way in which she'd presented a stark contrast to all the other little girls, who were covered in pinks, sparkles, and ruffles.

Sabrina checked her look in the mirrored wall next to the walk-in closet. The black V-necked sweater sat well above her cleavage. Good. But the black pencil skirt showed too much hip and thigh. She changed into wide-legged trousers and added a pair of four-inch heels to make her more imposing, then assessed her look again. The downstairs buzzer sounded. Sabrina quickly ran her fingers through her hair and, after one last critical glance in the mirror, went to the living room and checked the monitor. The lobbyist had arrived. She pressed the button to the outer door and punched in the code to let him into her private elevator. Then she went to the couch and slipped her hand under the far seat cushion. She felt for the .44 Glock and patted the cushion back down. Then she punched the button on the remote to turn off the music and went to answer the door.

After she'd played the footage of Congressman Rankin for him, Chevorin turned to her with a wide, sharklike grin. "Incredible. I never imagined anything like this." The lobbyist shook his head and chuckled. "We all knew he was a little loosely wrapped, but this? Pure gold. I'm gonna own this guy for life." He opened his briefcase. On top of the stacks of money was a bottle of champagne wrapped in a white cloth napkin. He picked it up and looked around the room. "Where do you keep your glasses?"

"I don't drink," Sabrina reminded him. Which was true. She didn't…anymore. Not that it mattered. There was no chance she ever would've shared champagne with Chevorin under any circumstances. Sabrina didn't mix anything in her life, let alone business with pleasure. "But I can get you a glass if you like."

His smile faded. "No thanks." He put the bottle aside and began to stack the money on the brushed-steel coffee table. "You want to count this?"

"I trust you."

They shared a grim smile at the obvious lie.

When the lobbyist had finished unpacking the money, he put the bottle back in his briefcase and snapped it shut.

"I have another job for you," he said. "This one's a CEO who's fighting a merger with a client. We need something to twist him with. I've tried to get dirt on this guy in the past, but I always came up empty. So this job might not be doable. But it's worth a lot to me, so I figured we may as well give it one more shot with you."

Sabrina gave him a cool and subtly contemptuous smile, seeing through the attempted manipulation. Telling her about his failure to get the dirt on this CEO was an obvious effort to amp up her motivation by adding the prospect of proving she could outdo him. What Chevorin didn't understand was that Sabrina had no desire to prove anything to him. She *was* better. In fact she was the best, and she knew it. If she didn't find anything on this target, it would be because there was nothing to find. But the past two years had taught her one thing above all: no one was completely clean. No one. There was always dirt somewhere. You just had to know where to look. "Give me what you've got on him. I'll see what I can do."

He handed her a file, and they negotiated the price. It was a brief negotiation that ended with an even higher seven-figure payout than the last job. The lobbyist left, and Sabrina kicked off her shoes, lay back on the couch, and opened the file. It didn't take her long to get through it all. The lobbyist was right: he hadn't made much headway.

When she'd finished, she locked the file away and reached for her cell, eager to get started. This one would be fun. She always loved taking down the Bible-thumpers.

17

"The bank?" Bailey asked as we walked out into a thin, gray afternoon that offered little contrast to the grim pallor we'd just left in the county jail.

I agreed and we got into her car. The postlunch wad of traffic forced us to inch along Broadway at a pace so slow it was maddening.

"Would've been faster to walk," I groused.

"Fine with me. I can park it right there." Bailey nodded to a steelworking yard that was dominated by a tower spewing out a river of smoke.

It wasn't the kind of place you'd leave your own car, but we were in a county car that hadn't seen better days in quite a while—it wouldn't be a tragedy if it did get stripped or stolen. But I looked down at my feet and shook my head. I'd worn a pair of new, *très* chic, black suede ankle boots I'd scored at a half-off clearance sale. I'd treated myself to them today as consolation for having to go to the jail. They were comfortable enough, but if they got messed up, I'd lose it.

"Never mind," I said.

But Bailey was fed up with the traffic too. She looked in her rearview mirror, then swung around to the right, passing the line of cars stopped at the light. She got to the limit line just as it turned green and flew through the intersection in a burst of speed. A man in an orange nylon jacket and work boots who'd been about to cross against the light jumped back onto the curb and grabbed the pole of the street sign as she roared past.

"But I'd still like to get there alive," I remarked. "If that's all right with you."

We'd just passed Temple Street when Bailey's cell phone rang. She fished it out of her jacket pocket, announced herself, and listened for a moment. "Okay, when's Newman going to have the blood?"

A few seconds later, she hung up. Her tight-lipped expression told me this hadn't been good news.

"Still nothing on our vic," she finally said. "He's never been printed for any job, and if he's ever been busted, it's not showing up in any database."

"Unbelievable. No ID on him and no prints on file. What are the friggin' odds?"

Not being able to identify a victim is a serious stumbling block in any case, but it was a particularly gnarly obstacle in this one, where there was no obvious motive and the suspect in custody was looking less suspicious by the minute.

"What's the coroner say about his physical condition?" I asked.

"Still waiting for him to return my call," Bailey answered in a voice that told me she was equally aggravated. "But we should be hearing about the blood on Yamaguchi's sleeve pretty quick."

Half good news anyway. I mulled over the situation.

"You don't have the autopsy report yet?" I asked.

Bailey shook her head. "Stoner told me the cause of death was 'sharp force injury,' known in English as a stabbing, but we don't have any details about what kind of knife was used or the nature of the wounds."

"Let me try Scott," I said. Scott Ferrier, the coroner's investigator, was a friend of mine who'd risked his neck to get me information in the past. My end of the bargain required that I reward his bravery with free meals at Engine Co. No. 28, his favorite restaurant. And since I loved the restaurant too, it was a win-win. I pulled out my cell and dialed, glad to have something to do besides fume over the gridlocked traffic. I got his voice mail and left a message.

"You know," Bailey said, "the bank will have a record of the time and date of Yamaguchi's deposit."

"And Yamaguchi might have a receipt with that information too," I said. "Corroborating that part of the story shouldn't be a problem. And if the bank has cameras outside—"

"Which I'd bet they do—"

"Then we might get another angle on the stabbing," I finished.

It was nearly three p.m. by the time Bailey pulled up in front of the bank, and downtown workers were already beginning to fill the streets, heading for home in cars, buses, and subways. By six o'clock, I knew the streets would be largely deserted, the crowded sidewalks of that afternoon a distant memory. Only the action in the bars and restaurants would show that this was a living, breathing city. The temperature had dropped at least fifteen degrees since the interview with Yamaguchi, and the cool air had a serious bite to it. I pulled up the collar on my peacoat and followed Bailey into the bank.

It never ceases to impress me just how damn useful a badge can be. Within three minutes, we were seated in front of the manager's desk.

"How can I help you, Detectives?" asked Andy Kim, one of the hippest-looking bank managers I'd ever seen, dressed in a smart, dark-green cashmere suit and paisley tie.

I figured I'd get more respect if he thought I was a detective, so I didn't bother to correct him. Bailey explained what we wanted.

"We certainly have footage, both inside and out. As you can imagine, in this neighborhood, it's a necessity." He gave us a little just-between-us smile. "It'll take them a few days to get you the footage, but I'll have the time of Ronald Yamaguchi's transaction brought in to you right now." He picked up the phone and made the request.

About ten seconds later, there was a knock on the door, and a young woman who looked pleased to be there came in and handed him a piece of paper.

Andy took it from her and scanned it. "Thank you, Ms. Daley," he said with a warm smile. He handed the paper to me.

"That's the hard copy. It seems Ronald Yamaguchi did indeed make a deposit at twelve fifty-seven p.m. on the day in question."

We thanked Andy, who promised to get us the surveillance-camera footage right away, and left.

"Well, part of Yamaguchi's story checks out," Bailey said as we headed for her car.

I got my cell and quickly checked in with Melia to make sure I hadn't missed anything. She said I hadn't, but that didn't mean much. If Melia had a new piece of pulp to read, the building could be seized by terrorists without her knowing it. We got into the car, and I checked my watch. It was four p.m. already. Amazing how time flies when you're having no luck at all solving a case.

"What're you doing tonight?" Bailey asked as she steered the car toward the Biltmore.

"Graden's taking me out," I replied. Then, because I knew she'd ask, I added, "To Yamashiro's."

Bailey whistled softly. "Someone's gonna get lucky tonight," she said with a lascivious smile.

I gave her a sideways grin. "Well, if it's only one of us, it's gonna be a bad night."

18

Graden was going to pick me up at six thirty, which meant at this point I had about fifteen minutes to pull it together. I whipped through my closet, looking for an outfit that would go with my beloved new boots. Black, stretchy slacks would work, and they were nice and long. I have a "thing" about short pants. I'd rather trip on the hems than wear "floods."

The black lacy top was sexy, but there was a chill in the air, and turning blue with cold would probably undermine the whole *sexy* thing. I settled on the cobalt-blue cashmere sweater with the roll-neck. Not exactly *wowee*, but better boring than freezing. A little eyeliner and blush later, I shrugged into my coat and patted my pocket to make sure I still had my .22 Beretta. But I was going to be with a cop and his .44. Did I really need the firepower? Then again, it couldn't hurt. I left it in my pocket and ran for the elevator.

By the time I got to the lobby, I found Graden standing next to the open passenger door of his darkly gleaming, freshly washed black BMW 750Li. He was talking to Angel, the doorman, who was looking at the car like it was Scarlett Johansson.

I hated to break up this lovefest, but nothing lasts forever.

"Hey, guys," I said.

Graden gave me an appreciative smile.

"Hey, Rache," he said, and gestured to the passenger seat.

I patted Angel on the arm as I got into the car. "How's it going?"

"Good, good, Rachel," he said. He tipped his hat to Graden and closed my door with a loving care that I knew had nothing to do with me.

Graden slid in and pulled the car around the circular driveway to the street. As he paused for oncoming traffic, he turned to me and said, "You look lovely, as always."

I smiled and squeezed out a thank-you with as much grace as I could muster. Compliments always make me uncomfortable.

"You too," I said, and meant it.

With his dark navy blazer and French cuffs, I knew that women's heads would be swiveling from the moment he entered the restaurant.

He'd been busy with what he'd briefly dismissed as "administrative matters" for the past few days, and I'd been pretty swamped myself, so we hadn't had a chance to talk.

"You want to tell me what's been on your plate at work this week?" I asked.

He sighed. "Maybe later. Right now I'd just like to forget about it for a while, if that's all right."

Having been in that head space myself, I didn't question him further. He'd tell me, if he wanted to, in his own time. We chatted about mutual friends, including Toni and J.D., but I broke off to enjoy the view when Graden turned up the narrow drive above Franklin Avenue and headed into the hills that would take us to Yamashiro. At the top of the hill, we entered the parking lot that wound around behind the famous restaurant and ended in front of the huge pagoda-style building that had one of the best views in town.

Yamashiro was an atmospheric landmark and a paean to old Hollywood. The dining room to the left of the entrance was formal yet lush and cushy, with white-table-clothed circular banquettes that gave views overlooking the city. The bar on the opposite side was romantically situated at the front of the restaurant and took advantage of the panoramic view with wall-to-wall windows that looked down on all of Los Angeles. Between the bar and the dining area there was a huge, high-ceilinged room decorated with waterfalls, gardens, and quaint red-painted bridges that spanned ponds of roaming brightly colored koi. Kitschy but charming.

The hostess took us to a table next to the window. I sat down and looked out at the glittering lights, neon signs, and vibrantly lit skyscrapers that outlined downtown L.A. From here, even the traffic looked beautiful, a moving river of red-and-white glowing beams. I exhaled with pleasure and saw that Graden too was entranced by the view.

"May I interest you in a cocktail?" asked the waitress, who appeared at our table within seconds.

Graden and I were both a little slow on the uptake, but the mention of drinks brought us back to earth. He looked at me.

"I'll have a Ketel One martini, very cold, very dry, straight up with a twist," I said. It didn't matter what the weather was like; there was only one way to have a martini, and that was icy cold.

"I'll have a Ketel One and soda with lime," Graden said.

"You don't have to do that," I said when the waitress left. "I'll have the vodka soda and drive tonight. It's only fair."

Graden waved me off. "I'm being impressively gallant," he said with a grin. "Now tell me what's going on with you."

I started to tell him about the John Doe case. But I'd gotten only a few words out when the waitress returned with our drinks. We gave her our dinner order: salads for starters, and a shared steak served on a heated salt plate. It's an Asian restaurant, but their steak is amazing. Then we toasted to ourselves and an amazingly clear night.

Now that we'd relaxed into the evening, I told him the story of my John Doe case.

Graden sighed. "I guess there's no such thing as an escape," he said.

I looked at him quizzically.

"That DA, Brandon Averill, beefed Stoner to the skies," Graden explained. "The whole chain of command is on the alert."

I shook my head and pressed my lips together in an effort to keep myself from saying what I thought. This wasn't the place to get loud and profane.

"Yeah," Graden said. "And some managerial type named Phil Hemet jumped into the mix too."

Hemet too? That was more than I could stand.

"Hemet is a talent-free jerkoff who brownnosed his way to the top, and Averill is a sniveling puke who thinks he craps flowers—," I snapped, unable to help myself.

"So what do you really think?" Graden said, laughing.

I gave him a little smile, though I really was angry. The waitress brought our salads, and I let mine sit for a moment, my appetite gone. But even in the throes of pissitivity, I was able to appreciate the fact that Graden not only understood my upset but felt the same way. It was one of the great things about being on the same side.

"What's going to happen to Stoner?" I asked.

"You can't talk about this," Graden said sternly. "Not even to Bailey."

"I promise," I replied. "Have I ever snitched?"

"No," he admitted. "That's why I'm going to tell you."

He took a bite of his salad and another sip of his drink. "I'm pushing to just let him off with some administrative leave. But there're some in the department who think Stoner's a hothead who needs a bigger paddling than that."

"Such as?" My stomach rumbled, reminding me that I hadn't eaten since...when? I couldn't remember. I dug into my salad.

"Maybe a transfer out of Homicide Special," Graden said, his voice stern.

"Seriously? Just for decking that asswipe?"

But I might be facing the same fate if Hemet decided to go after me. I filled Graden in on what Toni had told me about Hemet.

The waitress arrived and gave us steak knives and set the salt plate between us.

Graden started to say something, then stopped himself.

"What?" I asked.

A smile played on his lips. "I was going to say that it's not the same, and that you have nothing to worry about because Stoner has a way of speaking his mind that ticks off the brass an awful lot," he said wryly. "But it really is the same, isn't it? I mean, short of the fistfight."

I had to smile. "I guess it kind of is." I'd had more than my share of run-ins with both the office management and the judges. I called it "being direct." They called it "confrontational and insubordinate." Tomato, tomahto.

"One of the many things I love about you, baby," Graden said. He lifted his drink. "Here's to mouthy women."

"And hotheaded men," I said.

We drank, then tucked into our steak. Graden told me about a trainee who'd been caught smoking dope in his squad car after his shift ended. I topped him with a story about a DA who'd been caught shooting heroin in his car. On a lunch break. During trial.

After we finished, we turned to look at the view some more and sank back in our chairs, pleasantly relaxed. We rode to the Biltmore in a comfortable silence. Graden left the car with Angel and walked me to the elevator. I'd joked with Bailey about having sex with Graden, but the truth was, we hadn't yet slept together. Though we'd kissed enough to know it would be something great when we did take the plunge. We reached my door, and he pulled me in for a long, slow, romantic kiss. If I'd had one more martini, I would've opened the door and tackled him. But I managed to restrain myself. Just.

Graden stepped back and touched my cheek. "Call you in the morning?"

"Sounds good."

I opened the door and paused to watch him move down the hallway. He had a smooth, long stride and a strong, athletic build. I caught myself mentally undressing him and quickly stepped inside before he could turn the corner and catch me staring. I decided a cold shower would slow my revved-up jets, but it took only a few seconds before I was shivering and dreaming of nothing more X-rated than hot water. By the time I got into bed, I'd calmed down enough to feel how tired I was. I stacked the pillows to prop up my aching neck and opened the murder mystery I was forcing myself to wade through. The only thing I could say for it was that it never failed to put me to sleep. For some reason, no matter how much I hate a book, I can never manage to just stop reading—I have to see it through to the bitter end. And the end is inevitably bitter, because I'm always paradoxically irritated at having wasted the time to finish it.

The current offender that had the nerve to call itself a "thriller" lay open on my knees, but my mind wandered. Wasn't it time to get over my past and let Graden all the way into my life—not to mention my bed?

Maybe, finally, I was ready. If I'd had any energy left, that thought might've scared me. But exhaustion made my eyelids heavy, and my head dropped forward. I slid down and pulled up the covers, then turned off the light. As I moved onto my side, I vaguely heard the book fall to the floor. I left it there.

19

Sunlight streamed through the living room window. I'd forgotten to pull the drapes last night. I rolled out of bed, pulled on my plushy microfleece robe, and went out to the balcony.

The air was surprisingly balmy for a December morning. It would be a great day to get some fieldwork done, but I couldn't do it alone. One of the cardinal rules of investigation, especially for a lawyer, is never talk to a witness alone. A lawyer can't ethically testify in his or her own case. That means if a witness takes the stand and decides not to remember what he told you during a private interview, you've got no way to prove that he's lying. I opened my cell phone.

"Detective Keller, please. It's Rachel Knight."

After about five ominous-sounding clicks and an inordinate amount of time, a voice told me to "hold for Detective Keller, please," and I held some more. If I'd called the Kremlin it wouldn't have taken as long. It cheered me to know that the cops weren't doing any better with their support staff than we were.

"What?" Bailey barked.

"Feel like a massage?" I asked.

" 'Happy endings' included?" Bailey said, chuckling at her own joke.

"You can't afford me," I said. "I meant—"

"I'll be there in ten," she said, and then hung up.

I called Melia and told her I'd be out interviewing witnesses.

"Oh, uh…" Melia paused for so long I thought we'd been disconnected. "I think Eric wants to talk to you."

"Okay, have him call me on my cell," I replied.

"Uh, no. I think he wants to talk to you now."

"Then why don't you ask him and find out for sure?" I said.

This kind of lame exchange was vintage Melia. At least it wasn't in person. I walked over to the dresser and pulled out a pair of black jeans—a compromise that'd let me look presentable if I had to go to the office later.

"Um…hang on."

Seconds later, Eric's voice came on the line. "Rachel?"

"Hi, Eric. What's up?"

"You running on that John Doe case?"

"Yeah. I'm checking out the suspect we've got in custody," I explained. "It's pretty shaky on him from what I've seen so far."

There was a beat of silence, then I heard Eric sigh. "Okay, I'll give you today to get it sorted out. But if we have to cut this defendant loose, you're going to have to let the case go back to a regular trial unit. This isn't a Special Trials case, and your dance card's already pretty full."

Something was fishy. It wasn't like Eric to interfere with us about the cases we picked up. It took me a second, but I got there. "Hemet's on the warpath, isn't he?"

"For some reason," Eric admitted. "He got all worked up at the head deputy meeting last night. Said Special Trials deputies have been overstepping. We all knew he was talking about your John Doe case, so I told him it wouldn't have happened if his deputy hadn't dropped the ball—"

Go, Eric. This was one of the many reasons I loved him. "Which he took real well, I'm sure," I said dryly.

"Not so much. He said that since I didn't seem inclined to do anything about it, he'd talk to Summers."

"Which he was going to do anyway, Eric. It didn't matter what you said or did."

"Yeah." Eric sighed. "The feces is undoubtedly about to hit the whirling blades."

The only question was how hard and how fast. Fred Summers, the chief deputy, was officially the second in command to our fearless and witless leader, District Attorney William Vanderhorn. But in reality Vanderhorn was more political figurehead than boss. Summers was the real force to be reckoned with. And from what I'd seen and heard, he was generally a good guy with real smarts. Why he was giving an ear to Hemet was a mystery. I wondered if Hemet had some kind of dirt on him.

"This is such petty bullshit, Eric," I said heatedly. "It's not as though Hemet wants this loser."

"No," Eric agreed. "But I don't need to tell you how the rest of the office feels about our unit. Vanderhorn keeps us in Pampers because he knows he needs you trial monkeys to cover his ass on the heavy cases, but he's taken some heat about cherry-picking special unit deputies—"

"Anyone who wants to call this case a cherry should be disbarred for incompetence—"

"Of course, but the specifics won't matter. It'll be just another time he hears about a beef with a special unit—and this one in particular."

Because Special Trials got the most complex, high-profile cases, the deputies in that unit got all the "ink." Some were smart enough to know this was no gift, but many who weren't in the unit were bitterly jealous of the media attention.

Eric continued, "If Vanderhorn gets the sense that we can afford to pick up cases at random, he'll jump on the excuse to cut the unit down. And since yours will be the neck that's sticking out…"

I'd wind up trying meth-lab cases in Newhall for the rest of my career. "Okay. I'll get this wrapped up by the end of business today."

"I'm sorry, Rachel," Eric said. "But this is for your own good—and mine. I don't want to lose you."

"Thanks, Eric. I understand," I said. "And I appreciate it."

"You know it wouldn't happen if it were up to me. You did a good thing. We're prosecutors. We go after the bad guy no matter who the victim is."

Not that it mattered to petty bureaucratic asshats like Hemet. But I could tell that Eric was feeling guilty for having to give me grief about the case, so I tried to dial myself back.

"It's okay. I get it. I'll be in tomorrow, I promise."

We ended the call, and I grabbed my coat and purse and flew out the door. Bailey was probably fuming by now. Fortunately, when I ran out through the lobby and reached her car, I saw that she was swaying in her seat to the rap classic "Changes" by Tupac Shakur and seemed to be in a good mood. I slid into the passenger seat. "Sorry I'm late."

She waved me off. "It's all good."

"You're white, Keller," I said, pulling my seat belt on. "Deal with it."

She started to say something, then stopped herself. "You okay?"

I filled her in on my conversation with Eric.

"That was fast," she remarked.

"I take it you've already heard about Stoner?" I asked.

She nodded. "They made it official this morning. He's confined to quarters until they decide what to do with him."

"It makes me sick that a jerk like Hemet can rain crap on everyone for no good reason."

"Well, Stoner did deck that deputy DA," Bailey said philosophically.

"He had it coming," I replied, wishing I'd gotten in a good kick or two myself.

20

We pulled around the corner from the tiny storefront spa and parked in a loading zone.

"I've got the results on the blood on Yamaguchi's jacket," Bailey said.

"And?"

"It doesn't match our victim," Bailey replied.

"Huh," I observed brilliantly. "Is it Yamaguchi's?"

"Nope."

"Damn." I shook my head. "You ever find out how big the stain was?"

"Yeah, not big. About so," Bailey said, making a dime-size circle with her thumb and forefinger.

I thought for a moment, nursing a hunch. "Let's go talk to some spa workers, shall we?"

An oldish Asian woman with baggy eyes sat at the counter that was just three feet inside the door. Incongruously, a brightly colored parrot sat in a cage that hung from the low ceiling. If I hadn't believed Yamaguchi before, I did now: this definitely was a real spa. A curtain of hanging beads separated the counter from the rest of the business, but we could clearly see that the entire room was filled with massage beds—all out in the open, no closed doors. Several of those beds were occupied by customers who were clothed in at least tank tops and shorts, if not more, and were being attended to by white-coated massage therapists.

We stepped up to the counter that was just big enough to hold a register and a bowl of wrapped peppermint candies, and I pulled out my badge. "We're here to talk to you about an employee of yours, Ronald Yamaguchi."

The woman peered at my badge and the photo on the opposite side, then narrowed her eyes at me. "Hair look different," she remarked.

"Yeah, it was longer back then," I replied.

"Better now," she observed.

And maybe the parrot wanted to weigh in on my makeup?

"Were you here the day he got arrested?" I asked.

"Sure," she replied in a voice that quavered with a mixture of high and low notes. "He no kill that guy. Ronald no kill anybody."

"But he did go out to the bank that day," I said. "And the murder happened right outside that bank."

She shrugged. "I not there. I just know."

Fair enough. Everybody's entitled to an opinion, but I needed evidence.

"Is he friendly with any of the other therapists here?" I asked.

The woman turned around to look at the workers behind her. After a moment, she pointed to a small pony-tailed Asian woman at the back. "Wendy. She and Ronald friends. Eat lunch together."

"You know when she'll be done with her customer? We won't take long. We just have a few questions for her," I said.

The woman looked up at the '50s-style clock—probably less an effort at retro chic than simply the one she brought from home—that hung on the wall. "About fifteen minutes."

"Tell her not to leave when she's done with the customer," I said. "We'll be right back."

Bailey looked at me, puzzled, when we got out to the sidewalk. "Why aren't we waiting in there?"

"Because I didn't have time to order breakfast, and I'm starving," I said testily. "You can join me if you want." I pointed to the coffee shop on the corner.

"You're such a pleasure right now, why wouldn't I?"

I'd just placed my order with a tired-looking waitress at the counter when Bailey suddenly leaned forward and stared intently in the direction of the spa.

"What?" I asked.

A slow smile spread across her face. "Look," she said, pointing.

A patrol officer was staring into the newsstand machines in front of the spa, but after a few seconds I noticed that he wasn't looking at the papers; he was looking around the street as though checking to see if anyone—like us, I supposed—was watching. After one more quick glance, he entered the spa.

"Yamaguchi's customer?" I said.

The waitress was busy, so I headed for the register to

cancel my order. Bailey walked with me as she kept her eyes glued to the door of the spa.

"I'd rather be lucky than good," Bailey said.

"Who said you have to choose?"

I nixed my order, and we did a fast trot back to the building.

21

We caught up with him at his massage bed. He'd just leaned down to untie his shoes when Bailey badged him.

"Don't panic," she told him. "I just need a few minutes of your time."

The patrol officer stood up, his face—which had been red with the exertion of bending over—now white with fear. He opened his mouth to speak, then closed it and simply nodded. He shuffled out behind us, his shoes still untied.

"Detective Keller," Bailey said as she stuck out her hand.

"Harley Sahagan," he replied, taking it.

"And this is Deputy District Attorney Rachel Knight," she added.

I held out my hand, and Harley gave it a weak shake.

"I know this looks bad, but before you bust me, I want you to know I'm not just screwing off here. I got in a car accident on duty last year." Harley, having found his voice, was talking fast. "Felony evasion, the guy crashed into a wall and we couldn't stop in time. We rear-ended him hard. It messed up my back real bad. Riding in the squad car is killing me, but I used up all my leave, so I've gotta work. These guys"—he gestured over his shoulder at the spa—"saved me. I couldn't afford a fancy spa, and insurance won't cover a chiropractor. I was in really bad shape until someone told me about this place. I'm not cured, but at least I can deal."

"Harley, that's a lot of information, but I'm not here to bust you," Bailey said. "And I'm glad you're better. We just want to know if you have a regular masseur here."

"Uh, yeah," Harley replied uncomfortably. Then he nodded to himself. "So I guess he told you. Yeah, Ronald Yamaguchi was my masseur. Matter of fact, he was working on me when I got the call about that homeless victim." He shook his head, his expression perplexed. "I've got to admit, I never figured him for the type to do something like that." Harley sighed. "Guess you never know."

"Actually, in this case, you might," I said. "The way the evidence is shaking out, we're thinking he probably isn't the killer. And you just helped confirm that by corroborating his story."

"Good to hear," Harley said thoughtfully.

"And just FYI: he never did give up your name."

Harley acknowledged this with a little smile. "Heck of a guy."

I had a feeling Ronald's tips were about to get healthier.

"By any chance, did you interview any witnesses at the scene?" Bailey asked.

"Nah, just crime-scene control," Harley replied.

"Okay, we'll get back to you if we have any more questions," I said.

"Glad to help." He paused. "Uh...would you mind...?"

"Yeah, go ahead. Have a good one," Bailey said.

Harley went back inside and headed for his massage bed. We went in and returned to the front counter, where we found the ponytailed masseuse deep in conversation with the older Asian woman. When we walked over to the young woman, she looked pointedly at her watch.

I decided to play my hunch. It was a low-risk proposition at this point. I introduced myself and Bailey, then got right to it.

"Wendy, I understand you and Ronald Yamaguchi are close," I began.

"Yeah," she said, flipping her ponytail back. "So?" she asked with attitude.

"He ever let you wear his jacket?" I asked.

The question took her off guard, as it was meant to. She frowned at first, then shrugged.

"Sometimes he lets me, other times I just take it," she replied. "When I'm not working—it gets cold in here."

"Mind if I take a look at your arms?" I asked.

Wendy looked at me suspiciously for a moment before answering. "Why?" she asked in a bitchy tone. "You want to bust me for killing someone too?"

"Maybe," I replied. "Did you kill anybody?"

She rolled her eyes and gave an exaggerated sigh. "That's not funny."

"I wasn't joking," I said flatly.

She sighed again. "No. I didn't kill anyone."

"In that case, I just want to see your arms."

"Why?" she asked, her tone now belligerent. "I'm not a junkie or nothing."

This was getting truly annoying.

"Look, Wendy," I said in a stern voice, "I don't know many junkies who're full-time masseuses, but assuming you're one of the few, let me reassure you, I couldn't care less. I've got a homicide to deal with that has very little to do with you, and if you don't mind, I'd like to get on with it. So how about you show me your arms and we'll both get on with our day?"

Wendy didn't immediately respond, but eventually she rolled up the sleeves of her white uniform and showed me her arms, palms down.

"Could you turn them over, please?"

She complied, and there it was. A deep two-inch-long scratch on the inside of her wrist. "What happened there?" I asked as I pointed at the fresh-looking wound.

"I took that silly bird"—she gestured at the parrot—"out of his cage and he lost his balance. He scraped me with his claw."

"You remember when that happened?" I asked.

She thought for a moment. "Probably about two weeks ago."

"The day Ronald got arrested?"

"Right around there," she confirmed.

A young woman in tights and leg warmers came in. Wendy waved to her. "Go on back, Riley. I'll be right there."

Wendy watched her go, then looked at me. "You done?"

"I am."

She started to go, then stopped. "Ronald didn't do it, you know. You got the wrong guy," she said defiantly.

"I know," I replied.

This caught Wendy by surprise, and her eyes got big. "You know?" she asked, incredulous. "Then why don't you let him out?"

"We are," I replied. I glanced at Bailey, who nodded. "Today, as a matter of fact."

"Oh." She took a moment to regroup after the unexpected response. "Well, good," she retorted. "Never should've arrested him in the first place." And with another insouciant flip of the ponytail, Wendy went back to work.

Bailey made the call to the county jail. I was supposed to get in touch with Eric. Instead, I waited for her to finish.

"The minute I tell Eric we cut Yamaguchi loose, the case goes back into the hopper," I said.

Bailey agreed. "I'll probably have to give it up too. I only got it because we had a suspect in custody and they needed someone to babysit it through the preliminary hearing."

"So it'll wind up an unsolved, probably forever," I predicted.

Bailey nodded unhappily.

I couldn't drop this case into oblivion without a fight. John Doe deserved at least that much.

"Technically, Yamaguchi's still in custody, right?" I asked.

"Yeah," Bailey answered slowly, guessing where I was going.

"So technically I don't have to give up the case just yet." I glanced at my watch. "It's not even noon. That gives us a whole day and night to do...something."

"That's still not a lot of time. We need a tight game plan."

My loudly growling stomach told me what we'd do first.

Bailey heard it and smiled. "Since we need to regroup anyway, we may as well do it over lunch."

To save time, we went back to the coffee shop. I ordered a spinach salad with the dressing on the side, and Bailey, Queen Sadistica, ordered a cheeseburger and fries. They served us and we ate quickly. We had to pull a rabbit out of a hat in mere hours. At this point, we didn't even have a hat.

I finished my salad and began to pick at Bailey's fries—an endearing sign of trusting friendship, as I've explained to her on many occasions. Bailey says it really isn't so endearing, but I know she doesn't mean it.

"Other than nailing the perp, what's the one thing you'd like to figure out before we have to let this case go?" I asked.

Bailey thought a moment. "Why the hell you had to call me when you got it refiled?"

"Close, but no," I replied. "The burning question of the day is our victim's identity."

"Yeah, that too." Bailey took a deep breath, then blew it out. "But that's a tall order, Knight. This guy shows up nowhere. I've never seen anything like it."

"Agreed," I said. "But we have a clean photo of him from the coroner, don't we?"

Bailey nodded, knowing where I was headed. "Yeah. But showing it around and hoping for an ID is like trying to find the proverbial needle in a haystack."

"Except I just might happen to have a magnet."

22

Bailey raised an eyebrow. "Which would be?"

"Cletus."

Bailey blinked. "What's a Cletus?"

"My homeless buddy. Used to be a minor-league pitcher."

"And he wound up homeless, how?"

"He tore a rotator cuff and had to stop playing for a while," I said. "Then his wife decided it was a good time to find another man, and Cletus decided it was a good time to find a bottle." I gestured toward the street. "Now he lives out there."

"You know where to find him now?"

"On Wednesday nights, he's usually on Hill Street or Broadway."

"This is Thursday," Bailey pointed out.

"Thus, our dilemma," I admitted.

"You ever run into him on any other days?"

I thought back. Had I?

"I think I remember seeing him on Spring Street on a Monday. Or was it Main?" I shook my head. "I'm not

sure. But doesn't it seem likely that he'd be staying somewhere nearby?"

In my experience, the homeless aren't completely so.
They don't usually stray far from a familiar circumfer-
ence.

"So what're we going to do, just start walking up and
down the streets looking for Cletus?" Bailey asked.

"You got a better idea?"

"Yeah. Tell Eric you need a few more days and wait till
Wednesday, when you know where to find Cletus," Bailey retorted.

"Won't happen." I shook my head. "It's now or never."

Bailey sighed. "Okay." She threw down her napkin and
stood up. "Better get the lead out. We've got a lot of
ground to cover."

"And while we're at it, we can show around our photo
of John Doe," I said. "See if someone recognizes him.
Since this is our day for long shots, we may as well go for
broke."

"In for a penny...," Bailey agreed.

We decided to start in Skid Row, home to one of the
largest stable homeless populations in the country and
just a little more than four square miles. It was within
walking distance from the courthouse. Skid Row dwellers
aren't allowed to sleep on the sidewalks during daylight
hours, but the street is their home, so the area is always
filled with people sitting, eating, talking...surviving.

It makes me nervous to drive through there—I'm always afraid of hitting someone—but walking the area
is far worse, though for a completely different reason.
It's heart-wrenching to see so many human beings living
so hard. The streets are perpetually littered with crushed

cans, broken bottles of cheap alcohol, fast-food wrappers, cracked glass vials, and used needles. The stench of urine permeates the alcoves and sides of every building, and the air is thick with the mix of old grease, cheap food, unwashed bodies, and dirty clothes. The feeling in the air is more than abject poverty. It's the sense of overwhelming despair and defeat. On Skid Row, people didn't even aspire to living; they struggled merely to exist.

As we walked the streets, I fought to keep from sinking into the misery of it all. Back and forth we walked, up one street and down another, looking for the familiar pile of blankets I knew as Cletus, asking if anyone had seen him, showing the photograph of our John Doe to anyone who looked relatively alert.

We approached a short, squat woman of indeterminate age and race who wore a knitted cap with ears and unlaced army boots. She pushed a full shopping cart.

"Don't know no Cletus, and I ain't never seen that dude, nohow. Nohow, no way . . ." She wandered off, continuing to mutter to herself.

A middle-aged black man in glasses and a torn overcoat seemed fairly together, so we showed him the photograph of our John Doe. "Do you recognize this guy by any chance?"

He looked at the photo carefully. Hope rose in my chest.

"He doesn't look like any chance to me," he replied. "Does he look like a chance to you? I see no chance. No chance in France, and not in pants."

My heart sank back down. "Thank you, sir."

We walked on. After another two hours, feeling defeated, footsore, and tired, I was beginning to concede that this was a fool's errand. It was five o'clock and we were losing light. Pretty soon, it'd be too dangerous for two women—even two like us—to be out here.

"I'm sorry, Keller," I said. "It was a lame idea. I guess it's time to pack it in."

"It *is* a lame idea, but we knew that going in," Bailey agreed. "Let's give it another half hour down here, then head over to your usual meeting place with Cletus. It's on the way home."

It was times like this that I thought I didn't deserve a friend as good as Bailey. "Thanks," I said gratefully. Bailey waved me off.

In the next half hour, the sun sank along with our hopes of finding a lead on either John Doe or Cletus. Time to give up. "I'm pulling the plug, Bailey. It's getting really stupid now."

She nodded reluctantly. "I'm sorry, Rachel. We tried."

"Yep, we did," I agreed dejectedly.

We headed back down San Pedro to Fourth Street. At the intersection, I noticed an older man with a dog. The dog lay at the man's feet, his leash tied to the shopping cart. Maybe it was the dog, I don't know, but I decided to take one last shot and show him the photograph of John Doe.

"Nope. Don't know 'im."

"Do you know a guy named Cletus?" I asked.

The man frowned, creating a forest of eyebrows, and puffed on his stub of a cigarette. "You talking about the pitcher?"

I tried to keep the excitement out of my voice. "Yeah."

"He in trouble?"

"Not at all," I said. "He's a friend."

The man snorted. "Of yours?"

I looked at him steadily. "Yeah, of mine. You know where I can find him tonight?"

"Maybe," the man said, squinting at me through a haze of cigarette smoke.

I wasn't thrilled about pulling money out in this place, but I figured between Bailey's .44 and my .38, we probably had enough firepower to handle any comers. I fished out a ten-spot and held it up. "Take us to Cletus, and you'll get this."

The man took another drag on his cigarette and blew an enviably crisp smoke ring. Back in my smoking days, I'd tried to do that. My rings always came out wobbly and messy.

"Deal," he said. With that, he turned and headed up Fourth Street.

We followed, wary of ambush by the predators who come out at night to stalk the homeless. But I noticed we were moving toward Spring Street and Pershing Square. Safer territory by far than where we'd been. We crossed Spring Street and were approaching Broadway when the old man stopped and pointed. Sure as hell, there on the sidewalk in front of the Bradbury Building was the familiar pile of blankets. Close enough to his usual stomping grounds; far enough that, without help, I could've searched all day and night and never found him.

I thanked our guide, paid him...and threw in an extra few dollars for dog food.

He took the money, saluted, and walked off, a cloud of smoke floating behind him, his dog trotting alongside.

I slowly stepped up to the pile of blankets. As usual, they were crowned by a well-worn Lakers hat. "Cletus?"

A thick mop of graying hair poked up, and his eyes glittered in the darkness. "That you, missy? What you doin' here? What you doin' here?" The deep, ragged voice sounded as if it had scraped the words from the belly of the earth. It was music to my ears.

I smiled. "Yeah, it's me, Cletus. And I know it's not 'our' night. But I need your help."

With effort, he pulled himself up to a sitting position. "Cletus is always glad to help."

He coughed, an alarming hack.

"Are you okay, Cletus? You don't sound great."

He coughed again but waved his hand. "Just a cold. Always get 'em this time of year. What you need?"

"You recognize this guy?" I held out the photograph.

Cletus took it and stared for a long minute. I held my breath.

"No, missy. I do not. I don't. Sorry." He handed the photograph back to me.

Cletus had been my last hope. Deflated but grateful for his effort, I replied, "It's okay, Cletus. I appreciate you trying." I dug into my wallet and pulled out a twenty.

He looked at it. "I didn't do it for no money, missy."

"I know that, Cletus. I just want you to have it," I said.

He slowly took the twenty-dollar bill and tucked it into his pocket. "You know, I been around here a long time. If I haven't seen this guy, probably means he ain't living in this part. But you seen him here?"

"Yeah. So I thought..." I trailed off. It was truly hopeless if John Doe hadn't been living in the area.

Cletus fell silent.

"I got an idea," he finally said. "You heard 'a Johnnie Jasper?"

I looked at Bailey, who shook her head.

"No," I replied.

"Stays up in Boyle Heights. You ask poh-poh up there, they all know 'im. Good guy, good guy."

Poh-poh, as in police. "He a street person?" I asked.

Cletus nodded. "But he got a fine setup." He pointed in the general direction of Boyle Heights. "You go see ol' Jasper, he might help you out."

"Thank you, Cletus," I said, suppressing a shiver. The day had been mild, but the night air let us know it was still the middle of winter. "It's pretty cold out. Why don't you let me take you to a shelter? We can get you in."

He wagged a finger at me. "You promised me 'no grief,' remember?"

In the past, I'd tried to get him to come indoors several times until finally he'd put a stop to it and made me promise to leave him be. Reluctantly, since I had no other choice, I'd agreed.

"You go, you go. Go see Jasper." Cletus lay back down and pulled up the blankets. "Let an old man get some sleep. You go, you go."

23

"**I'll understand** if you want to pack it in," I said as Bailey and I headed back to her car. "But I've got to check this out. I know it's the mother of all Hail Mary passes, but I won't be able to live with myself if I don't take this one last shot."

Bailey looked at her watch. "I was supposed to meet Drew for dinner in an hour, but it's only about ten minutes from here, and since it seems all the local cops know this guy, it's easy enough to check out." Bailey shot me a warning look. "But I'm going to call Drew, and you are not allowed to give me any shit, no matter what I say. Got it?"

"Don't gag me out with your googly talk, and I won't give you shit," I said.

Bailey has a long, fast stride, and I was running to keep up. When we got to the car, she gave me a hard look over the roof. "I mean it."

"Fine." I got in and belted up.

But just to make sure a snarky remark didn't accidentally slip out, I put my fingers in my ears.

After she ended the call, Bailey pulled one of my fingers out. "It's safe."

"Thanks." I put my hands in my pockets to warm them. It was freezing, but Bailey hated the car heater, so I suffered in silence. "You know anyone at the Boyle Heights station?"

"I was just thinking that I used to know a patrol guy." She pulled out her cell.

"It's Detective Bailey Keller, Robbery-Homicide Division. Is Craig Andarian still working there?"

Bailey listened, then gave me the thumbs-up sign. I sat back, relieved. She chatted with her buddy Craig for a minute, then asked him about Johnnie Jasper. When she ended the call, I looked at her expectantly.

"So it's for real?" I asked.

Bailey nodded. "And I got directions."

Ten minutes later, we were looking through a chain-link fence at a wonderland made of castoffs. It had been a vacant lot, but someone, presumably Johnnie, had moved in and done some serious decorating. Shelves had been dug into the side of the small hill, and every inch was occupied by brightly colored toys, dolls, seashells, posters, and traffic signs. At the far end of the lot, under a peppertree, was an outdoor living room. Complete with rug, television, couch, generator, and propane oven.

The man himself, though, was nowhere in sight. I looked closer and saw a shack made of plywood to the right of the living room arrangement. It was practically hidden under the heavy, low-hanging branches of the peppertree.

"Hello! Mr. Jasper?" I yelled. "Are you there? Hello?"

I waited. I thought I saw the curtain over the makeshift

window move. "Johnnie Jasper? Hello!" I tried again.

A tall, slender black man stepped out of the shack and peered at us. Bailey held up her badge and pointed the flashlight backward so he could see our faces. "I'm sorry to disturb you, sir. We just need your help. It'll only take a few minutes of your time," she said.

The man looked at us carefully, then came out to the gate. "Lemme see that badge again, ma'am."

Bailey complied, and he looked from it to her, then at me.

"A'right, then," he said. He unlocked the gate. "Come on in." He ushered us inside.

When he'd locked the gate behind us, he turned to me and asked, "And who might you be?"

I introduced myself, and he led us to the far end of the lot.

"You're Johnnie Jasper?" I asked.

"I am." He gestured for us to have a seat on the sofa in his outdoor living room.

"You're quite a legend out here," Bailey said. "Is it true the cops bring you turkeys at Christmas?"

Johnnie nodded modestly. "They do. And I give them fresh strawberries and nectarines."

"You grow here?" I asked.

"Yes, ma'am," he said proudly.

I was impressed. I couldn't grow mold on cheese.

Whatever I had expected, Johnnie wasn't it. Intelligent and neatly dressed in a waffle shirt, jacket, and jeans, he could've been someone's father or boss. I was fascinated. I wished I had time to have a real talk with him and find out what brought him here, why he lived this way. But since I didn't, I came straight to the point and told him

Cletus had sent us because we were looking for someone.

"You a friend of Cletus?" Johnnie smiled. "He's a tough nut to crack, isn't he?"

I laughed. "I couldn't have put it better."

Bailey pulled out the photograph of our John Doe and handed it to Johnnie. This was it. I knew that if he came up empty, we were through. I tried to ready myself for the blow.

He stared at the photo. "No…I don't think…"

My heart sank for the millionth time that day.

Then he stopped and pulled the photograph closer. "Wait. This is…I think I do know him," Johnnie said. "Couldn't tell at first, he doesn't look so good in this." He gestured to the photo. Then he fell silent and examined the picture again. "He's dead, isn't he?"

"I'm sorry, Johnnie," Bailey said.

"Damn." He shook his head sadly. "He was a good guy. You mind telling me how?"

"Somebody stabbed him," Bailey replied.

Johnnie nodded. The death of a friend was not so uncommon among the homeless, though the way *this* one had died was certainly not the norm. I decided to spare Johnnie that knowledge.

"You don't have a suspect," he said.

"No," Bailey confirmed. "That's what we're working on. Did you by any chance know his name?"

"Simon," Johnnie replied.

"And his last name?" I asked.

The first name alone wouldn't do much, if anything, for us—especially because it might not even be his real name.

Johnnie shrugged. "Never did know that."

Damn. Another dead end. I was frustrated, but I refused to give up. Maybe if we kept him talking, he'd come up with something we could use.

"How long did you know him?" I asked.

"About a year. He'd stay here off and on—but when he was here, he was real good about helping out. Nice guy, but sad. Real sad." Johnnie paused, remembering. "And then, sometimes, just out of the blue, he'd get all fired up, be in a blazing fury. I'd tell him to let go of whatever it was." Johnnie looked at us. "It's not good to hang on to your anger like that, no." He shook his head.

"You ever know what he was angry or sad about?" I asked.

Johnnie's mouth turned down. "Simon wasn't much of a talker. But I do remember the last time he was here. Stayed for a few months that time, and he seemed a lot better. More upbeat and happy than I'd ever seen him," Johnnie said. "Matter of fact, he brought me something."

Johnnie got up and walked over to the bookcase next to the couch. He picked up a blue vase and handed it to me.

"He gave you this?" I asked, incredulous.

"Yep. Pretty, isn't it?"

It was beautiful, actually—an elegantly shaped flute, the kind that held just a few flowers, and the blue was a complex blend of shades that evoked the ocean. Not what I'd expect a poor person to own, let alone give away.

I turned it upside down and looked at the bottom. And there, etched into the clay, was the name.

Simon Bayer.

At last, our John Doe had a name.

24

Johnnie was reluctant to let us take the vase.

"Right now, this is our only link to his identity. We might need to show it to other witnesses, have it analyzed for prints, compare it to other pottery. Until we've got his identity nailed down, we have to hang on to it," I said. "I'll get it back to you. I promise." I looked at him intently, wanting him to understand how important this was.

Johnnie returned my gaze, then looked away. Finally, after a few long moments, he responded, "I guess if it'll help y'all find his killer…"

"I can't promise we'll get the killer—but I can promise we'll try."

"And I give you my word we'll bring it back," Bailey said.

Johnnie nodded slowly. "Then you go ahead and take it," he said quietly. "But no matter what happens, you bring it back, you hear? A man needs to be remembered. I believe Simon gave it to me because he intended for me to remember him." Johnnie lifted his chin and looked me in the eye. "That's what I mean to do."

The words, softly spoken, were powerful. I held his gaze for a beat. "You have my word."

Minutes later, we were speeding down the freeway toward downtown. It wasn't even eight o'clock, but it felt like midnight. I yawned, leaned back in my seat, and watched the lights in the skyscrapers grow brighter as we neared the Civic Center.

"You still going to make it to dinner with Drew?" I asked, glad I hadn't made similar plans with Graden for tonight.

"Yeah," Bailey said, sounding as tired as I felt. "But it's going to be a short one."

We rode in silence, both of us exhausted but happy. Bailey raced down the off-ramp at Broadway. "It's unbelievable how we pulled this off," she said.

"See?" I remarked. "We're good *and* we got lucky. Just goes to show ya…"

Bailey laughed and held up her fist, and I bumped it with mine as we pulled into the circular drive in front of the Biltmore. But one question nagged at me.

"It's a ridiculously long walk from Boyle Heights to downtown," I pointed out. "How did our victim do it?"

Bailey nodded in agreement. "Good question. But now that we have his ID, we just might be able to figure that out."

"And maybe this'll buy me more time on the case," I replied. "Not a bad day, huh, Keller?"

"It'll do," Bailey said with a grin. "I'll run Simon Bayer's name in the morning and call you with the results."

"Oh no, you don't," I said. "After all this, I'm going to be there when you find out. Call me before you do anything."

"Then get your ass up on time for once," she retorted.

"I will. Just promise—"

"I'll call. Now get out." Bailey laughed. "You're getting in the way of my love life."

"Give Drew my best," I said.

"I'll do better than that—I'll give him mine." She sped off.

I trotted through the lobby, got into the elevator, and ordered dinner from room service on the way up. Chicken breast with steamed broccoli. No bread. But that wasn't celebratory enough for the occasion, so I added a bottle of Deep Sea Pinot Noir.

The wine, which was delicious, made my virtuous dinner a lot more palatable. When I'd finished, I pushed the room service cart into the hall and took my glass of wine out to the balcony. The city lights cast a soft glow against the cloak of night that flatteringly covered the streets. Above, the stars sparkled in the cloudless black sky. For this one moment, all felt right with the world. I eventually put myself to bed and slowly drifted off, feeling as though I were falling through a cloud.

The next morning came sooner—and noisier—than I'd expected, with the jangling ring of the hotel phone. Only three people ever used this number. By the fourth ring, after my brain stopped swirling, I'd narrowed the possibilities down to one.

"Yeah," I said, doing my best to sound sharp.

"Don't bother," Bailey barked. "I know I woke you up. You want to be here when I run the name, get your ass over here."

"Jeez, put down the coffeepot," I groused. "I'll be there in—"

A loud dial tone told me there was no point in finishing the sentence. I glanced outside. It looked sunny, but I decided to do layers for safety's sake. It was unlikely I'd be out in the world for long, and I knew for sure that I had to go into the office to tell Eric about our latest break in the case, so I'd have to wear "real" clothes. I quickly threw on wool slacks and heels, a white blouse, and a black wool blazer.

Riding the high of having managed to identify our victim last night, I'd been optimistic about my chances of holding on to the case. Now I wasn't so sure. If Hemet was bound and determined to cause trouble, the fact that I'd been able to put a name to the face might not matter as much as I'd hoped.

I considered skipping makeup, then thought better of it. I might run into Graden. Hating myself for caring, I nevertheless took a few minutes to dust on bronzer and apply eyeliner and mascara. Never mind the lipstick—I was going to pick up coffee on the way, and it'd be gone before I even got to Bailey's desk. I pulled on an overcoat, dropped my .22 Beretta into the pocket, and at the last minute grabbed a cashmere muffler. I speed-walked all the way to the Police Administration Building, stopping only to pick up a cup of coffee from a churro cart, and jumped into a conveniently open elevator just before it closed.

25

All that running and jumping had warmed me up, and as I moved toward Bailey's desk, I had to unwrap the muffler. The room was relatively quiet, with just a few detectives in shirtsleeves working the phones.

"Let the games begin," I announced as I neared Bailey's desk.

"Here," she said, pulling a chair over, "have a seat."

I sat down and unbuttoned my overcoat. Bailey flexed her fingers and began to type. It took no more than five seconds before the screen filled with listings. She whistled softly, then frowned to herself.

"Hey, wait a minute...," she said, then stopped. For the next few minutes, she clicked and scrolled in silence.

Finally I could take no more.

"What?" I asked, agitated. "What?"

But Bailey held up a hand and continued to stare at the screen. From my angle, I couldn't see well enough to read it myself. I was about to shove her out of the way when at last she spoke.

"Sorry," she said. "Here." She turned the monitor toward me and clicked on a link, and an article came up.

I read the headline: "Brother of Murdered Cop Takes Case to Feds." *What the...?*

I read on:

Simon Bayer, brother of murdered Glendale police officer Zack Bayer, has declared his intention to take the case involving his brother's murder to federal authorities for filing. A jury acquitted the victim's wife, Lilah Bayer, in the state trial just two months ago, and the foreman stated it was the belief of most jurors that she was actually innocent: "It wasn't just that we thought she probably did it but they couldn't prove it. We really thought she was just plain innocent." Simon Bayer vehemently disagreed. "That jury got it all wrong," he fumed. "They fell for a pretty face and a slick defense attorney. I will not rest until I get my brother the justice he deserves."

There was more, but Bailey stopped me. "If I remember right, Zack Bayer was kind of a rising star in the department. He married this looker who was a young associate in one of those white-shoe law firms. They found Zack's body in the basement of his home. He'd been chopped up with an ax."

It was an unusually grisly killing style for any kind of female, except maybe a meth head. This woman didn't sound like one. "They got the murder weapon?" I asked.

Bailey nodded.

"Any prints or blood evidence?" I asked.

She stared off and knitted her brows. "We didn't handle the case, and it's been a few years, so I don't have the details. I just remember hearing that the jury acquitted her after about five minutes of deliberation. The Feds never did take the case."

"So Simon didn't get his wish."

Bailey shook her head.

I turned back to the computer and continued scrolling through the article. When I got to the end of the story, I hit a link that took me to the first published column. And came to a full stop. I stared at the image on the screen, a ripple of tension crackling up my spine. I barely breathed as awareness of the possible discovery—and its implications—spread through me. *How could this be?* I was so intent that I lost all sense of place and time. Then Bailey's agitated voice brought me crashing back to earth.

"Knight? Hey! Speak up, damn it! What's going on?"

I held my hand up. "Give me a second," I whispered as I looked up at the ceiling and concentrated on the memory that'd been conjured by the image on the screen. After a few more moments, I nodded to myself. I turned the monitor so Bailey could see it.

"Check this out," I said.

It was a shot of Lilah taken in court. She was sitting at counsel table. Though the photo was grainy and she was partially hidden by the shoulder of her lawyer, we could still get an overall sense of her appearance. Just enough to make the connection.

"Her hair's a lot shorter here," I said, gesturing to the screen.

"I'll be dipped," Bailey said, staring at the screen. "She's the woman in the video—"

I was relieved that Bailey'd confirmed my gut reaction.

"Can't say for sure yet, we can't tell her height or weight from this photo."

"But we can nail this one down easy."

That was certainly true. There'd be a number of people who'd be able to tell us whether the woman in the video was Lilah.

"If it *was* Lilah in the video—," I began.

"Simon's sister-in-law," Bailey said pointedly.

"Then Simon died trying to get to her."

"Looks that way," Bailey agreed. "But how did he know he'd find her right there, right then?"

Bailey and I exchanged a look as the question hung in the air between us. I again envisioned the surveillance footage of the stabbing. "The video showed that she'd turned away by the time Simon went down. There's no way she could've killed him."

"But someone who was with her might have," Bailey pointed out.

"Or, at the very least, she had to have seen something," I added. "She might be our best witness."

"One way or another, we need to find her..."

And I had an idea where we might get not only a lead on her whereabouts but some answers as to how she and Simon wound up just inches apart within seconds of Simon's stabbing.

"We're going to have to get into Zack's murder," I said.

Bailey nodded. She sat back and folded her arms, her expression sardonic. "Guess this means we'll be staying on the case."

She was right, of course. Now that the victim was "somebody," it was a Special Trials case. I didn't know whether to rejoice or break something.

26

Eric put his hands behind his head and leaned back in his chair as I gave him the update on our victim's identity.

When I'd finished, he sat forward and made a few notes on his legal pad before responding. "I can't say what Hemet—or, more important, Summers—is going to say about this, but given what you've told me, it's a Special Trials case now. And since you've been running with it from the start, it only makes sense for you to keep it."

I could see he wasn't sorry about this development. It gave him the right to keep the case in the unit and the chance to back Hemet down. But as much as I liked Eric, I didn't give a damn about management turf wars. It irked the hell out of me that it'd taken a development like this to let me keep the case. I looked out the window for a moment to stop myself from saying something I truly meant. Maybe that's exactly why head deputies like Eric had the best, most panoramic, views in the building.

"I know this pisses you off," he said, reading my mind. "And I understand. But all the same, you are getting what you wished for, aren't you?"

"I suppose."

"So just remember what they say about that."

I sure did. That's why my motto was *Never chase a case*. It invariably comes back to bite you. I hadn't chased this one; it'd fallen into my lap. But the result would be the same if it exploded in my face. And Eric knew as well as I did that if it all went south on me, Hemet would be right there to point an accusing finger.

"And given the connection to Zack Bayer's murder case, there's going to be a fair amount of press interest now. So how do the rest of your cases look?" Eric asked.

I shrugged. "I'll be fine."

"I'll leave it to you to manage your schedule. But if you're underwater, I expect you to be honest with me and let me reassign a couple of your cases."

I nodded to appear cooperative but knew there was no way in hell I was going to let him give away any of my trials. His phone rang, and I used the distraction to slip out.

Back in my office, I went through my calendar. I had ten pending cases, but I'd been right about the schedule: the month of December was relatively clear. This was no accident: December was a dicey month for jury trials. It was hard to know where a jury's sense of holiday charity might take them. They might feel sorry for a defendant (bad for the prosecution), or they might feel sorry for the victim (bad for the defense). Given that uncertainty, and lawyers' own holiday plans, little business got done in December. After that, things would get trickier. Because Special Trials cases were so newsworthy and so serious, it was rare to have cases plead out. So a caseload of ten usually meant ten "go" trials.

"Hey, stranger." I looked up to see a vision standing in the doorway, looking beautiful, as always, in a black gabardine suit with gold buttons and an off-white silk blouse.

"Toni! Where've you been?"

She came in and sat down. "Where've *I* been? I've been here. You're the one who's been gone. Is it time for a drink yet?" She looked out the window at the clock on the Times Building. "Just two thirty? How can that possibly be?"

"I know, right?" I chuckled. "You got plans tonight?"

"No, ma'am," she said. "So we can do whatever. But I'm not waiting till then to find out what's up with you. A little bird told me Hemet's after your ass, and you know I never pass up a chance to say 'I told you so.'"

"You sure did," I replied ruefully. I filled her in on the events of the past few days.

"This is definitely gonna chap Hemet's ass. Gotta love that," she remarked. "And you're right, the case is interesting as hell, but it's a real toughie." Then she added wryly, "Lucky for you, there's no pressure."

"Ugh," I said glumly. "Don't remind me. I just got an earful from Eric. I'm waiting for the bank's surveillance-camera footage and hoping it'll pop something out for us."

Toni nodded. "You mean, as in, make it an easy one?" She gave me an incredulous look. "You need to share what you've been smoking."

I laughed and shook my head. "A girl can dream, right?"

"Sure, whatever," Toni said with a dismissive wave of her hand. "You ever hear back from Scott about the victim's physical condition?"

"Not yet. But I'll keep after him. So catch me up with you—what's going on?"

Toni exhaled heavily, her expression dour. "I just got assigned to that geezer bank robber case."

"That eighty-year-old guy with the oxygen tank on his back?" I asked. "I didn't know they had a suspect in custody already."

"They don't, but we just had a press conference today," Toni confirmed. "I'm totally screwed on this one. The way he shuffles around on that surveillance tape, he looks like a geriatric tortoise," she said, shaking her head morosely. "The jurors are going to think he's just the poor little senior fighting back against the big, bad banks. It's got *not guilty* written all over it."

I bit my lips to keep from laughing. The geezer bandit was one for the books. He'd robbed all nine banks with an oxygen tank on his back, and after he got the money, he toddled out, slow as molasses. The case was ready-made for jury nullification. Boiled down to its essence, every jury trial is a popularity contest. And these days banks aren't exactly prom queen. The jurors would probably carry him out on their shoulders.

"You think the defense'll bring in the oxygen tank as an exhibit?" I asked.

"I know you think you're funny, I just don't know why," Toni replied flatly. "But I suppose I'd let you apologize for your insensitivity by buying me dinner."

I held up a hand. "I just spent about thirty dollars of my limited discretionary income on a couple of homeless guys. Take pity on a poor civil servant."

Toni relented, but we decided we deserved a splurge, so we agreed to try out Drago Centro, a relatively new restaurant in the financial district with an exotic menu and reputedly great service.

Toni took her leave, and I pulled out the Simon Bayer file and a legal pad. Having dinner plans always improved my focus. I started to work on my to-do list, but when I got to "canvass for more surveillance-camera footage," I stopped cold as my stomach twisted into a knot.

I immediately picked up the phone and called Bailey. After giving her the unsurprising news that I'd been assigned to the case, I got to the problem that had jumped out at me. "If it *is* Lilah Bayer in that surveillance footage, the fact that she never came forward to report the stabbing tells us at the very least that she's not interested in getting involved, right?"

"Yep."

"But we need her—badly—since we can't see the stabber on any of the footage we've found so far. The problem is, once I amend the complaint to show that the victim's name is Simon Bayer, the press will be all over it. Even a halfway-alert reporter will be able to figure out their connection and start looking for footage showing the stabbing—"

"They'll have that footage before the ink is dry on your complaint. 'Brother of Murdered Cop Zack Bayer is Stabbed to Death! Acquitted Wife, Lilah Bayer, a Witness! Film at Eleven!' "

"Exactly. And once that footage hits the airwaves, she'll *really* drop the shades and pull up the blankets. So the question is, how do we keep it under wraps?"

"You don't, Knight."

"Glad I asked. Okay, good talk. Later—"

"Hold on. I'm just trying to be realistic here. We can't ask the store owners not to share the footage—"

"Especially if someone shows up with money," I said. "And even if we got a warrant and seized everyone's footage, they've probably all got backups."

I stood behind my desk, holding the phone in a death grip as I mentally played out the options. None was foolproof.

"I could hold off on amending the complaint," I said. "There's no suspect in custody, so the correct name of the victim isn't critical just yet." But I couldn't legally use that gambit for long. I'd have to get my witnesses in hand fast. Especially Lilah Bayer. "And in the meantime, we're going to have to work under the radar. The press can't get wind of what we're doing."

Bailey gave a short bark of a laugh. "Good luck with that. The press lives on our doorsteps, and you know both our offices are sieves. Our only hope is to move fast, before the yakking has the chance to hit the wrong ears."

When you're skating on thin ice, your safety's in your speed. Bailey was right. Too many people already knew about this case: Chief Deputy Summers; Phil Hemet; my boss, Eric, who was certainly trustworthy, but also by extension Melia, the town crier, who certainly wasn't. And I hadn't even factored in the people on Bailey's side. I took a deep breath to loosen the band that had just tightened around my chest. I wrapped my arms around my torso and paced, still gripping the phone as I quickly calculated our first move. With time being of the essence, I'd have to prioritize carefully.

"Since Lilah was unquestionably on the scene, I'd say she's priority number one," I said. "And we hit the people who worked Zack's case for contact information on her."

"I'll reach out to the investigating officer and see if he has a line on her right now," Bailey said.

"I'll get ahold of the prosecutor and set up a meeting."

"They'll both be able to say for sure whether the woman in the footage is Lilah," Bailey said. "And I'll have to notify Simon's parents."

We fell silent. Death notifications were a miserable part of police work. And this family had lost *two* sons to murder. What a nightmare. I didn't envy Bailey. We hung up, and I started to chase down the prosecutor.

A few phone calls later, I learned that the prosecutor, Larry Gladstein, had transferred out to the Antelope Valley branch court—about as far away as you could get and still be in Los Angeles County. I vaguely remembered the area as the desert you crossed on the way to Arizona. I got Larry's voice mail and left a message.

Unable to make any other moves for now, I decided to get work done on my other cases so I could at least clear the decks. But in stray moments between phone calls and motions, I found myself thinking about Zack's murder. An ax killing in itself is rare—but an ax killing by a woman is rarer than a Republican at an NPR fund-raiser. I wondered what kind of evidence had persuaded Gladstein to file.

By six thirty p.m. Toni and I were more than ready to go. Although a brisk wind was blowing, we decided a little exercise would justify a lot of indulgence and hiked the several blocks to the restaurant. As we hurried in, the soft strains of a jazz trumpet greeted us, and I recognized it as Clifford Brown playing "Stolen Moments." The anxiety that had curled up and made a nest in my stomach began to unwind. By the time we reached our table, the rich smells wafting out of the kitchen had me ready to eat the air. The waiter brought black napkins so as not to—heaven forfend—leave white threads on our dark slacks, and took our drink order: Ketel One martinis, cold, dry, straight up with a twist. When our drinks came, we toasted to finally getting a night out together and took a sip.

"So how's it going with J.D.?" I asked.

Toni's eyes darted away before she answered. "Uh, okay."

"Gee, someone in space might actually believe that," I said. "What's up?"

"Really, nothing," she said with a sigh. "At least, nothing new. We've been getting along really great, but I can feel him starting to get nervous."

Graden had given me the skinny about this during our dinner at Yamashiro, but I'd been sworn to secrecy. For a moment, I was torn between my promise to Graden and my loyalty to Toni. But the moment passed and, as always, loyalty won out. It's a girlfriend thing.

I looked at Toni with a raised eyebrow. "That's funny, because J.D. said the very same thing about you."

"What?" she asked.

"You can never, ever admit you know this. Okay?"

Toni looked at me, curious.

"J.D. told Graden that you were the one always backing out and that he was the one always getting dumped."

Toni sat back, her expression stunned. "Huh." She looked away and frowned, trying to reconcile this new information with what she'd thought she knew. "*I'm* the one always backing out."

I spread my hands. "That's the skinny."

Toni looked perplexed but thoughtful. "I just find it hard to believe that I could've misread him so completely."

"Maybe it's not so complete," I observed. "Maybe it's just a matter of interpretation. He saw something in your behavior that made him think you were about to jump ship, so he got nervous. You saw him getting nervous and thought he was ready to bail."

Toni nodded slowly.

"Most of us are insecure in relationships, so when in doubt, we latch on to the most negative explanation," I added.

Toni gave me a lopsided smile. "Well, look at you, Sigmund Freud." She did that little head bob only she could pull off. "All jiggy with your analytical thing."

"Anna Freud, please," I said. "Sigmund had issues."

Toni rolled her eyes. "Whatever," she said. "You sure Graden didn't misinterpret something, get a little creative?"

"Men's imaginations aren't that good."

Toni had an impish grin. "At least not when it comes to that stuff."

We both laughed, and I raised my glass.

"To the other stuff," I said.

We clinked and drank.

27

With no avenue to pursue until I sat down with the prosecutor or the IO on Zack's murder, I had a lot of anxious time to fill. On Saturday, I saw Graden for a casual dinner at our favorite haunt, the Pacific Dining Car—a real railroad dining car near downtown that was converted into an elegant restaurant with fantastic food and one of the best bars in town. We'd had our first date there, and now we thought of it as "our place." On Sunday, my nerves propelled me to do something, *anything*, that felt like progress on the case, so I worked on my to-do list. After a few hours, feeling frustrated and stuck, I decided to schlep my sorry ass to the gym. It was sorry because I hadn't been in a while, and now it was dragging.

By Monday morning, I was ready to jump out of my skin. For all I knew, footage of Lilah was wending its way onto YouTube at that very moment. I'd just poured myself an unneeded third cup of coffee when my cell phone rang. The number on the screen was unfamiliar.

"This is Larry Gladstein returning Rachel Knight's call." The voice was gruff, the tone irritated and defensive.

A foul-tempered DA, first thing in the morning. Who says that's not fun?

"Hi, Larry, thanks for returning the call—"

"Look, let me save you some time here," he interrupted. "I've got nothing more to say about the case. Check with Media Relations if you want information. And maybe the IO."

Checking with the head of Media Relations, Sandi Runyon, wasn't a bad idea. She was as sharp as they come and she'd probably have some valuable insights as to why the case went belly-up. And Bailey and I fully planned to talk to the investigating officer, Rick Meyer. But neither of them could give me the lawyer's point of view, and that's what I needed right now.

"Larry, I'm not calling to talk about what you did or what went wrong," I said, knowing he'd probably been second-guessed to death. "I'm calling because we have another murder that seems to be related to your case, and we need the background information."

There was a beat of silence, then Larry asked me to explain. I filled him in on the stabbing murder of Simon Bayer.

Larry said nothing for so long, I wondered if we'd been disconnected. Finally he spoke.

"I'm real sorry to hear this," he said, his voice now low and sad. "I had a feeling Simon wasn't going to be able to move on. But this..." He fell silent again, then sighed. "Okay, we're instructing the jury on my child molest this morning, and I've got a prelim this afternoon, but I should be done by around four o'clock."

I agreed to meet him at four thirty and texted Bailey.

We left at two. Bailey took the Golden State Freeway

north to the 14 Freeway north, and within half an hour, stark, imposing mountains rose on either side of the road with small, isolated ranches sprinkled across the valleys. Above us, downy white clouds floated, creating patches of shadow and light as they moved across the sun. Hawks rode the air currents with graceful power in search of prey. Nothing about this place said "L.A." For all intents and purposes, we could've been in Montana.

I'd done a little homework on Larry. I'd known that he was reputed to be a good lawyer and a hard charger, but what I hadn't known was that in the twelve years before he picked up the Zack Bayer murder, he'd only lost one robbery case—an impressive record.

Mark Steiner, a buddy of mine who'd worked in the Van Nuys branch with Larry, told me that when Larry'd first caught the Zack Bayer case, there'd been more than the usual jealous carping by other prosecutors.

"Which was completely ridiculous on every level," Mark said heatedly. "Not only is Larry a great lawyer, but not one of those nimrods would've wanted to work that hard or deal with the pressure."

"Since when did that ever stop them?" I replied.

"Yeah." Mark sighed. "Anyway, Larry took that part in stride. What got to him was the shit he took after the verdict. He worked his ass off on that case, and I could tell that losing it just about killed him. So it was just a bridge too far when all the hallway hotshots went around bragging about how they could've won the case and made asinine claims to the press about what he did wrong. It was all bullshit, but you know how it is, DAs can be cannibals..."

I did. And they were.

"So Larry *asked* for Antelope Valley?" I said.

"Not exactly," Mark replied. "Larry asked for a transfer. What they gave him was Antelope Valley."

Nice. A man gives years of dedicated service, and his reward is to get planted out in the middle of the desert.

But that didn't mean the verdict had been wrong.

Thanks to Bailey's lead foot, we reached our destination with half an hour to spare. As she parked, I saw that the courthouse was the farthest outpost of civilization in the town. Just across the street, an unbroken expanse of Joshua trees stretched out to the horizon as far as the eye could see. An aged stucco building next door bore a faded sign saying KNIGHTS OF COLUMBUS. But the courthouse building was relatively new, and a lot nicer than the one I worked in. We made our way through the metal detector and upstairs to the reception area.

I introduced myself and Bailey to the secretary and told her why we were there.

She made a call announcing our arrival, then hung up. "He'll be right out."

I'd pictured Larry as a big barrel-chested guy in a tweedy jacket with full, ruddy cheeks. The man who came out to greet us was maybe five feet eight, on the slender side, with thinning brown hair and wearing a belt with a huge silver buckle and pointy-toed cowboy boots. So I was close.

"Come on back," he said, waving us in.

It was a nice office by county standards. Unlike mine, there was room for a normal-size person to walk behind the two visitor chairs that faced his desk, and he had a tall gray filing cabinet in the corner and two six-foot metal bookcases, all of which looked new, against the wall to the left of his desk. The view was great too—if you were into mountains and cacti.

We all sat down, and Bailey pulled out the still photograph taken from the surveillance footage that showed the woman in dark sunglasses. "Do you recognize her?"

The moment Larry saw the photograph, his mouth set in a grim, hard line and his jaw clenched. "I sure do. That's the defendant, Lilah Bayer."

Just to be on the safe side, I showed him the photograph of Simon.

He nodded. "That's Simon." He shook his head sadly. "What happened to him? I mean, other than the obvious. This is not the guy I knew during the trial."

"He'd been on the streets."

I explained what we knew so far about Simon's murder, then relayed the information I'd just gotten from Scott, the coroner's investigator, earlier in the day.

"According to the coroner, Simon's condition indicated he hadn't been living out there for years, but he'd been out long enough to show some wear and tear...obviously."

"I knew Simon took it hard. I just didn't know it got that bad," he said, gesturing to the photograph I'd shown him.

Larry's suffering was palpable, the air around him heavy with grief. He seemed to turn in on himself, his eyes, focused on a point outside the window, unseeing. We sat in silence for a long moment.

Larry continued to look outside as he spoke. "Simon was...a little too good for this world. What happened here would've been a lot to deal with for anyone, but for him..." He sighed heavily, the corners of his mouth turned down. "He wasn't exactly a flower child or anything, but he kind of had that softness, you know?"

I did. I shook my head sadly. The world seemed to grind up people like that.

Larry continued, "I remember when they read the verdict, he went a little nuts, almost had to be restrained." He paused a moment and kept staring out the window. "I gotta admit, I wasn't far behind."

"You know he tried to get the Feds to file the case?" I asked.

"Yeah. But I knew it was hopeless. They only take the slam dunks."

"Guess that should be a little reassuring to you, no?" I asked sympathetically. The Feds' refusal to file showed they didn't think they could win it either.

Larry shrugged. "Maybe so, but it doesn't help. If I'd had my druthers, the Feds would've taken it and won it."

I nodded. I would've felt the same. Of course, the other possibility was that the Feds might've refused to file because they didn't think Lilah Bayer was guilty.

"You think Simon was after Lilah?" he finally asked.

"It seems logical, since they were on the same stretch of sidewalk at the same time," I replied. "I don't like coincidences. And at the very least, regardless of why Simon was out there, Lilah was close enough to see who actually stabbed him. We need to find her, if only to question her."

"And she might very well be involved," Larry suggested, looking at me closely.

I returned his look. "Like I said, I don't believe in coincidences—"

"Neither do I," he agreed.

"I'm not committing to any particular theory yet," I

continued. "But the fact that both she and Simon and someone with a knife all managed to find their way to the same few square feet at the same time in a city as big as L.A. presents a strong likelihood that they're all connected."

"Well, if you can tag her for Simon's murder, you'll have my undying gratitude," Larry said. "So what do you want to know?"

"Was Simon close to Zack?" I asked.

"He was devoted to Zack," Larry replied. "Simon was about six years younger, so they didn't exactly share a childhood. But Zack was kind of a hero to him. You know, the cool older brother. Though with Simon, it seemed to be more than the usual."

"Because?" I asked.

Larry paused for a moment. "You'll probably get a better sense of this from the parents, but I got the impression that Simon had been a timid kid, probably got pushed around some in school. From what people told me, Zack was a lot tougher and much more social. He'd protect Simon when he could, though what with the age difference and all, he wasn't around a whole lot."

"What can you tell me about Lilah?" I asked.

Larry's expression, soft while reminiscing about Simon, suddenly hardened, deepening the lines in his face and giving his eyes a flat, dead look. "Lilah was a real looker and no dummy. Put herself through law school, eventually got hired in one of those big corporate law firms."

"A partner?" I asked.

"Nah, too young," he replied, shaking his head. "She was just a new junior associate when she killed Zack.

Though, from what I heard, she was on the partner fast track."

I paused, struck by Larry's reaction to Lilah. Whenever her name came up, everything in his demeanor changed—his voice, his features, his posture—the hostility, even rage, still burned through his pores. I'd expected him to be bitter. No prosecutor likes to lose. But Larry's attitude didn't strike me as the typical anger we all feel when a guilty defendant walks out the door. It was much deeper, much more personal. Now, I admit that I've occasionally run into defendants who made me want to run them over with a bus...repeatedly. But once the case was over, I let it go—win or lose—as we all do. Larry's fury, both in its magnitude and persistence, was unusual...and troublesome. "What was your take on Zack?" I asked.

Larry shrugged. "An ambitious guy on his way up. Popular with the troops, smart, good-looking." He turned and pulled out the murder book. He opened it to a page, put the book in front of us, and pointed to a photograph.

Zack was in uniform, and the photo looked like the kind taken to commemorate a formal event. Judging by how young he seemed, my guess was that it was taken when he graduated from the police academy. An open smile on a pleasant, even-featured face, warm brown eyes, regulation-length brown hair, a nose that might've been broken in the past and never set properly—not quite rugged, but fairly handsome.

"Was he a good cop?" I asked.

"Good, but from what I hear, more into the politics than the police work," Larry said.

"Think we'll have any problems getting his friends to talk to us?" Bailey asked.

A not-guilty verdict can make friends and family a little less than cordial toward the prosecution.

"I wouldn't think so," Larry replied. With a bitter note,
he added, "Unlike some in this office, they understood it
was a softheaded jury."

I nodded sympathetically, though since we hadn't
heard the evidence, I wasn't ready to commit to the
"crazy jury" theory yet. It was time to find out what kind
of case Larry'd had against Lilah.

28

"**So how** did this go down?" I asked. "Did the defense try to claim this was a burglary gone bad?"

"No," Larry replied. "They couldn't. There was no evidence of ransacking at all." He turned and pulled another binder out of the cabinet behind his desk. "Check out the crime scene photos."

He flipped to the section and turned the binder around so we could have a look. The house was as neat as a pin.

"I'll get you a copy of the murder books so you can see it all for yourself," Larry said.

"But if it wasn't a burglary, then the defense had to have claimed that someone targeted Zack," I said.

"Sort of," Larry replied. "You didn't read the news articles?"

"I figured I'd get a straighter story from you," I admitted.

That elicited a tiny smile. "Wise of you." Larry stared over my shoulder, collecting his thoughts, then he began.

"Lilah claimed they had breakfast together and he was still in the kitchen when she left for the office. It was

Zack's day off. We know he went down to the basement to work on one of his projects. He was an amateur carpenter, and he'd set up a workbench down there. Lilah claimed that as she was pulling out of the garage, she noticed a new gardener at the house across the street, someone she hadn't seen before."

"You verify that?" I asked.

"Didn't pan out," Larry replied. "Neighbors all denied having hired someone new, but gardeners sometimes bring in temporary help, so we had all the gardeners haul in all their workers, and we took photos. Either one neighbor or another recognized all of them." Larry narrowed his eyes, concentrating. "I think you have those photos in the murder books."

"You showed them to Lilah?" Bailey asked.

"Of course. Said none of 'em looked like the guy she'd seen."

Of course she did. If Lilah was the killer, it'd be pretty dumb to identify her straw man—what if he had an alibi?

Larry continued, "Lilah said that after she got to work, she realized she'd left a file she needed at home. She went to lunch, and when she came back for the file, she found the body." He paused, his eyebrows drawn together. "As I recall, Rick—the IO—nailed her on an inconsistent statement about that, but you'll have to ask him for the details. Anyway, she said when she saw it, she threw up." Larry's tone was sardonic. "It was a pretty grisly scene— if someone just stumbled on it without warning, that'd be a natural reaction." He nodded toward the murder book. "Check out the photos."

Of all the crime scenes I'd ever seen—and I'd seen plenty—this was one of the worst. The body lay on the basement floor in the middle of a sea of blood. The head was severed from the spine, the arms and legs had been chopped off at the joints, and the body was hacked up as well, leaving gaping mouths through which intestines extruded.

A wife throwing up at the sight of her husband's mutilated body tended to show she'd been shocked by the sight—an implicit indication that she wasn't the killer. She certainly could've thrown up after seeing what she'd done. But someone who has the stones to commit an ax murder doesn't strike me as the squeamish type. Or she could've made herself throw up to create the impression that she was innocent—but it would've been pretty sophisticated to even think of, let alone have the presence of mind to do.

"What did the crime scene analyst say?" I said.

"Crime scene analyst confirmed there was emesis on the floor that probably came from Lilah, and the coroner confirmed that they'd both eaten the same breakfast."

"Where'd the murder weapon come from?" I said, tapping the ax shown next to the body in the crime scene photograph.

"Their garage," Larry replied. "Which was usually kept locked. And, no, there were no signs of forced entry into the garage."

"Score another point for the good guys," I said.

"Just a half point," Larry said. "A neighbor—one who didn't particularly care for Lilah—said Zack sometimes left it outside in the backyard. The ax did have some rust and weathering, so that much was true."

"Did you get anyone to blow up her timeline for when she left for work, got to work, left work?" Bailey asked.

"That unfortunately came up equivocal." Larry sighed. "One neighbor swore she saw Lilah pulling out later than usual, at ten a.m., which would've been right after the murder. But another one was fairly sure she saw Lilah driving down the street at nine fifteen a.m."

"She could've driven out earlier, come back in time to do the murder, then left again," I pointed out.

"Sure, and I argued that to the jury, but the coworkers' testimony muddied the waters," Larry replied. He paused and stared at the wall behind me as he recounted the statements in impressive detail. "She was normally due at work by eight thirty a.m. Some of the staff swore she wasn't there until after ten a.m., but others were sure they'd seen her by nine at the latest." Larry tilted his head. "The testimony wasn't particularly helpful, but it didn't kill me either."

I tended to agree. Contradictory stories of that nature often canceled each other out in the minds of the jury.

"Blood? Hair? Fiber?" I asked. "Especially blood. I'd expect to find something on her clothing."

Larry nodded. "You would, but we didn't. It was my theory that she changed and dumped the clothes she wore when she killed him."

"Anything to back that up?" I asked.

"Now we come to the good part," Larry said, showing some enthusiasm for the first time. "We found fibers on the ax that didn't match what Zack was wearing. And given the way that ax had been wielded, anything that had been on it before the murder would likely have been shaken off or buried in the body."

"So they were most likely from the clothing worn by the killer."

"Correct. Our hair and fiber guy was a whizbang. He looked at the five or ten fibers we had and offered a few suggestions as to what kind of fabric and the color of fabric they could've come from. Wanna know what we found?" Larry now had a real smile on his face.

"Nah," I joked.

"A photograph of Lilah with Zack up in Lake Arrowhead, wearing what? A coat that fit the exact fabric and color description given by our whiz-bang analyst. And where was that coat?" Larry asked.

I had a pretty good guess but shook my head to give him the satisfaction.

"Nowhere. That coat was nowhere to be found."

"But that wasn't definitive," I said, plugging in the language fiber guys always used in their testimony. "The most he could've said was that the fibers appeared to be of the type that came from a coat like that or any other coat of a similar—"

"Blah, blah, blah," Larry interrupted, waving a hand. "Yeah. But there's more. We had evidence of forced entry at a side door they seldom used. A small—I mean a pin dot—of blood with skin was lodged in the splintered wood. We had just enough for DNA—it came back to her."

"But she could've scraped her hand on that spot before, or even shortly after, the murder—," I began.

"And that's what the defense argued," Larry said. "Except we had a neighbor with a colicky baby who woke her up at two thirty a.m. She was walking the floor, trying to pat the baby to sleep, when she noticed our girl Lilah standing at that side door at about two thirty-five a.m. Looked like Lilah was jiggling the door handle."

I sat back in my chair. Proof that Lilah had deliberately rigged up evidence of forced entry was pretty powerful stuff. *So how the hell?*

Larry watched my face and nodded. "Uh-huh. Well, first off, the neighbor went south on me when she took the stand. Said she was sure she saw *someone* at that door at two thirty-five, she just couldn't be sure it was Lilah."

I was perplexed. "What made her flip?"

Larry's face darkened. "I never could figure that one out. She seemed sure of it during the interview. And when she flipped at trial, I questioned her up one side and down another, but there was nothing to indicate that she'd been bribed or threatened."

"You don't think Lilah got to her somehow?" Bailey asked.

Larry shook his head. "We checked the neighbor out. Went back as far as her freshman year in high school. Couldn't find anything Lilah could've used against her, and I didn't ever believe Lilah would've tried to physically threaten her." He sighed. "Don't get me wrong, that devil's spawn wouldn't have hesitated if she'd thought she could get away with it; but she was smart enough to know better." Larry fell silent for a moment. "I guess I'll never know why that neighbor went belly-up."

Bailey was frowning. "They find blood anywhere else?" she asked.

"There was a small blood transfer on the wall next to the staircase that led up to the bedroom," he replied. "But not enough to do any kind of typing. We questioned Lilah about it, but she didn't take the bait. Said she didn't know how it got there."

Once again, an indication that Lilah was cool under

pressure. Suspects often can't resist the urge to explain everything in an effort to show how innocent they are, and those explanations can be the best gift the prosecution ever gets. A provably false story shows the defendant's not only guilty but also a remorseless liar.

"The way it sounds from the cheap seats, even with the neighbor dumping you out, the case wasn't a slam dunk, but it was there," I said.

"It was," Larry agreed. "But the defense had a helluva hole card." I could hear the anger in his voice. "Six months before Zack's murder, the Glendale Police Department had been targeted by PEN1, Public Enemy Number One, a skinhead group affiliated with the Aryan Brotherhood. A lieutenant in Glendale had targeted them after they shot one of his officers during a pursuit. The Glendale cops made a lot of busts, mostly for meth, and that really messed up PEN1's major source of income. So the skins declared war on the Glendale PD. They rigged a zip gun to the gate at the officer parking facility—just missed killing a sergeant. Redirected a gas pipe to shoot toxic fumes into the lunchroom, and then firebombed the evidence room."

That was big-time...and outrageous. How come I'd never heard a word about it? Bailey looked equally shocked. As much as anything, the fact that we hadn't gotten wind of this showed just how sprawling this county really was. But, intriguing as it seemed, I didn't see how this tied into Zack's murder.

"I get how the murder looked like the kind of overkill meth heads do," I said. "But I thought you said Zack was a political player, not a big gun out in the field—"

"Yeah. No reason to think he got up in anyone's face," Larry confirmed.

"Then why Zack?" I asked, perplexed. "And why in his own home? I mean, it's one thing to target the police at the station, but breaking into the man's home and chopping him up in his own basement—"

"Is another," Larry finished for me. "Which is, of course, what I argued."

"Did the defense come up with anything to back up the 'skinhead did it' story?" Bailey asked.

"Sort of." Larry sighed. "After they put the lieutenant on to testify about war with the skinheads, prison guards seized a kite between a couple of PEN1 inmates. Of course, the defense waved that puppy around the courtroom like it was their national flag. Which it pretty much was."

A note between inmates could be pretty compelling evidence.

"What'd it say?" I asked.

"That PEN1 was getting the 'credit' for the hit and no asshole Nazi Low Rider better try and claim it—something to that effect. Rick'll have the actual note if you want to see it."

"No names mentioned?" Bailey asked.

"Nope," Larry replied. "And it wasn't even in code, which you know their stuff almost always is."

That was significant. The white-supremacist gangs had an elaborate system of secret codes they used for all written communications. It usually took an FBI specialist to crack it. The fact that this note wasn't coded was some evidence that it was just a couple of jerks bragging, rather than a real admission that PEN1 was behind Zack's murder.

"And you let the jury know what that meant, I'm sure," I remarked.

"Oh yeah," Larry replied.

"Did you ever come up with any affirmative evidence to disprove that theory?" I asked.

"What was I going to do, put a bunch of skinheads on the stand to say they didn't do it?"

I shook my head. "Probably only make the jury believe it more. Was there evidence connected to the scene that pointed to someone else being in the house besides Lilah?"

"Not really, but it played that way to the jury," Larry responded. "There was a partial bloody print on the kitchen wall, but we couldn't pin it to her. Insufficient ridge detail to rule anyone in or out—including Lilah. Basically, that print could belong to anyone. The defense went crazy with that."

"Ouch," I said.

Larry nodded his agreement. "Yeah. It hurt us. I remember thinking we were in trouble when the jury asked about that print during deliberations."

A fingerprint in blood had the look of evidence that had to be connected to the crime. The failure to tie it to Lilah was a tough blow. That, plus the "blame the skinhead" defense, spelled big trouble for the prosecution. Then there was the neighbor who'd gone belly-up on the stand. No question about it, this was a tough case.

"Who represented Lilah?" I asked.

"Mike Howell. Know him?"

"Oh yeah."

Mike and I had been hired at the same time, did Planning and Training together. But after packing in about a hundred trials, he'd decamped for the greater financial rewards and flexibility of private practice. Mike and I were still friendly, and it would've been nice to get his personal take on the case. But the attorney-client privilege lasts a lifetime—sometimes longer—so I knew there wasn't much point in talking to him.

"The case had its problems, but even so, that defense probably never would've flown with another lawyer..." Larry trailed off.

We shared a look of understanding. Mike was one of the good guys who played it straight and fair, but he was unquestionably one of the best in the business. He knew how to zero in on every weak spot in the prosecution's case, and how to play the jury. To call him a formidable opponent was like calling Bill Gates "comfortable."

"And that's not all," Larry said. He reached out and flipped through the pages of the murder book in front of me to a single photograph.

Lilah's face stared up at me. Fair-skinned, with a shining cap of black hair and large, azure eyes, she wasn't just a looker; she was a stunner. I compared that photo to the woman shown in the surveillance video. The differences were subtle and, I had a hunch, deliberate: the woman in the footage had much longer hair, and she seemed to be a little thinner. But if you looked closely, you could see that the shape of the face and head was unquestionably the same. A jury had spent weeks looking at that face and trying to match it up with a decapitation ax murder. The skinheads gave the jury just the excuse they needed to resolve the contradiction.

"She take the stand?" I asked.

"Oh, you bet," Larry said bitterly.

"And she did well."

"Well enough." He looked out the window, and I saw his jaw muscles clench.

His grudging tone told me I should look elsewhere if I wanted to get an accurate read on her performance.

"Any idea where we might find her now?" Bailey asked.

Larry shook his head and stood, signaling the end of our conversation. "None. After she got acquitted, she pulled up stakes and took off. Hasn't even been a sighting." He laughed, a mirthless bark. "Until now anyway."

He escorted us out of the office and through the reception area, then stopped at the door to shake hands. "Hey, you want to hear the kicker?" Larry asked.

I stopped and met his gaze.

"Lilah clerked for about six months when she was in law school," he said.

"Why's that a kicker?" I asked.

"Because it was in the DA's office."

29

Bailey and I walked out to her car in silence. When we'd first arrived, I'd found the stark landscape soothing. Now it just felt desolate. We drove past the open fields of Joshua trees, heading for the freeway.

"A former intern. This is a proud moment for the DA's office," I said sarcastically. "So she actually had some experience in criminal law."

"Enough to know when to shut her mouth," Bailey agreed.

"I'll see what we've got on her," I said. "But interns don't do anything heavy or sensitive, so we don't spend a lot of time on their background checks."

Bailey nodded, but neither of us was in a talkative mood.

I could well understand Larry's reaction to the news of Simon's murder. Though no victim is ever just a chalk outline to me, the colors unique to each one fill in slowly, over time, painted layer by layer with the memories and feelings of their loved ones, until ultimately a picture with depth and nuance emerges. More than his words, the emotion in Larry's voice had shown me that Simon was a kind and gentle soul who'd been mortally wounded—long before his physical death—by his brother's brutal demise and the injustice of the verdict. The image of the vase he'd left with Johnnie, its simple beauty and innocence of vision, made my eyes burn.

The freeway again wound through the low mountain passes, but now that the sun had sunk below the horizon, the valleys were shrouded in darkness and had taken on an ominous, forbidding look. When Bailey finally spoke, I could tell her thoughts had been running in a similar vein.

"We're going to have to talk to the Bayers soon, you know."

I sighed my agreement. "Do you know if they had any other kids?"

"They didn't," she replied tersely.

So they'd lost their only children to murder within the last two years. I had some idea of what they'd gone through.

It was twenty-seven years ago. I'd been just seven years old when my older sister, Romy, who was eleven, had vanished. It felt as though my soul had been wrenched from my body. Not only had I lost my best friend, but I believed it'd been my fault. I've heard some families grow closer after such a tragedy, but mine didn't. We orbited farther and farther away from one another as we disappeared into our individual universes of agony. My father spiraled down into a bottle, and ultimately the oblivion he likely craved, when his car skidded off an icy bridge. My mother remained, but at first only in the most basic physical sense. For years after my father's death, her mind wandered off as the world fell out of focus for her. I can still feel the panic at seeing her vague gaze and constant state of confusion. Those were dark years. I felt so isolated that I used to dream I was treading water, exhausted and alone in the middle of the ocean and about to go under.

Losing both children, and to murder, had to be an unendurable and unimaginable agony. I wished we didn't have to ask the questions that would make the parents relive painful memories. But the story of Simon's downward spiral could provide information critical to solving the case, and his parents were likely to be the best source.

As we rode on in silence through the darkening hills, I mentally replayed the meeting with Larry.

"Larry never said anything about motive," I remarked.

"I noticed that too," Bailey agreed. "Any possibility it involved money?"

"I wouldn't think so," I said, frowning. "She was the moneymaker. She probably wasn't making a ton as a new associate, but if she hung in there, she stood to make a hell of a lot more than he did."

"In which case, she would've had to pay alimony," Bailey pointed out. "With Zack dead, she wouldn't have to worry about that. Plus, if there was an insurance policy, she'd get it all."

"I suppose," I said, unconvinced. "But if that's the way Larry went, you can see why it didn't work. If the criminal doesn't fit the crime, you've got to stick the landing when it comes to motive. He had a defendant who looked like a porcelain doll and a crime that looked like it was committed by Beelzebub on crack. So Larry had some serious explaining to do, and from the looks of things, he didn't get there. I'm starting to understand why the jury acquitted."

"That doesn't mean she didn't do it," Bailey replied.

"No," I said.

The mountains were behind us now, and the freeway forded a sea of ranch-style tract houses. The San Fernando Valley spread out around us, a vast expanse of low-rise suburban life. On my right, the sight of the familiar golden arches made my stomach rumble, reminding me that I hadn't eaten in a while.

"You in the mood for dinner?" I asked.

"I'm ready to eat my own hand," Bailey replied.

"How about the Tar Pit?"

"Perfect," she said with a smile. "We haven't been there in a while. It'll be a nice change of pace."

30

The cozy, art deco–style restaurant and bar on La Brea had great food and amazing drinks. Though I was kind of a purist when it came to booze, anyone who was even slightly more adventurous raved about their cocktails, like the Fashionista and the Warsaw Mule.

The waiter showed up the moment we were seated and asked what we'd have to drink.

"You go ahead," Bailey offered. "I'll be the designated driver tonight."

Still, friends don't let friends watch them get hammered all alone. I ordered a glass of the house Pinot Noir and chicken à la king, and made a mental note to use this sacrifice as leverage with Bailey at some later point. Bailey ordered an iced tea and the wild boar mushrooms.

"Chicken à la king?" she asked, incredulous. "Since when do you eat like a real person?"

The rich sauce was one hell of a splurge for me. "It's been a rough few days. I seem to be needing lots of comfort food."

"No need to sell me. I'm totally fine with it. For the

first time in months, I might actually get to have my meal to myself. Hell, I might even take a bite off *your* plate for a change."

"I wouldn't advise it," I warned, aiming my fork threateningly.

The waiter brought our drinks, and I tasted my wine. Nice and dry. I nodded at her glass. "Your iced tea all you hoped for?" I asked with a smirk.

"You think this is a good time to poke the bear?"

It was almost *always* a good time to mess with Bailey, as far as I was concerned, but I moved on to the second-most pressing issue of the evening.

"I was thinking about where to look for Lilah—," I began.

"I started the hunt this morning," Bailey replied.

I paused and looked at her with disbelief.

"You already knew she'd been an intern in our office and didn't tell me?"

Bailey smirked. "I wanted to drop that bomb on you myself," she said, taking a sip of her iced tea. "Damn Larry beat me to it. It was on her résumé that she'd clerked with the DA's office, but it didn't say where exactly. I figured that'd be an easy one for you—"

"I'll take care of it."

"Anyway," Bailey continued, "the law firm dumped her right after she got arrested."

"And didn't hire her back after the acquittal, I take it?"

"Not from what I could tell," she replied. "Big surprise."

It wasn't. A high-dollar corporate law firm couldn't afford even a whiff of scandal, let alone an associate who'd been on trial for murder—acquittal or no.

"Where'd she wind up after that?" I asked.

"That's the thing," Bailey said. "The trail dies there."

How could that be? A lawyer has to provide current contact information to the State Bar. "You check the State Bar website?"

"She let her bar card lapse—"

"Damn," I said, frowning. "Can't anything in this case be easy?"

"No," Bailey answered. "And she's not in any other database either—not under her married name or her maiden name." She sighed.

"It seems pretty obvious this woman doesn't want to be found," I observed.

Bailey nodded.

After the epic hassle we'd gone through to learn Simon's identity, this was the last thing we needed.

"Want to talk about our stabber?" Bailey asked.

"Please." I was glad for the change of subject. "I'd like to take another look at the video to make sure it's a man," I said. "But assuming it is, the guy could've been a Good Samaritan—"

"Who just happened to be armed and ready," Bailey interjected dryly.

"And didn't stick around to tell the police he'd been defending a damsel in distress. It is a little ridiculous," I agreed. "But it is possible he was just protecting her and didn't call the police because he had his own problems."

"Why take the risk if he can get away clean?" Bailey thought for a moment. "It's possible. Not likely, but possible."

"And if that's true, then it's also possible Lilah had nothing to do with the killing," I replied. "In which case it's iffy that she'd even be able to ID the guy...assuming we find her in our lifetimes."

Bailey frowned. "But from what I remember of the video, it seems to me the killer couldn't have known that Simon had a box cutter. Simon grabbed Lilah with one hand, the other hand was in his pocket."

"Right. In which case, the killer definitely targeted Simon—"

"Which means he and Lilah are in cahoots," Bailey said, finishing the thought.

"Cahoots?" I said with a pained expression.

Bailey started to defend herself, but at that moment the waiter brought our dinners, and the mouthwatering aromas wafting up from our plates brought an end to all rational thought. Silence reigned for the next several minutes as we ate, until finally I came up for air and took a sip of my wine.

"So, best guess, given what we know at this point, is that whoever killed Simon was with Lilah," I said. "That means he did it either because she told him to or because he knew Simon posed a threat to her."

"Physical or legal?" Bailey asked.

"Either one," I replied. "Simon was unhinged. If he'd given up on the legal system, he might've been willing to settle for street justice and take her out himself." I paused and thought a moment before continuing. "Or Simon might've uncovered something new on Zack's murder. Something good enough to get the Feds interested in the case."

Bailey looked skeptical. "As hard as Rick and Larry worked the case, I doubt Simon could've found anything that good."

"Probably not," I said. "But Lilah—or her buddy—couldn't be sure of that. Simon was Zack's brother. Who knows what he had access to?"

I paused to watch a group of hot-looking men pass behind Bailey on the way to their table. I decided they were too perfectly groomed and well-toned to be straight. I wondered why more straight men didn't take some of their cues from gay men—and looked back just in time to catch Bailey sneaking a bite of my chicken. I made no protest.

She paused with her forkful in midair. "Aren't you going to challenge me to a duel or something?"

"Nah," I said, waving her on. "I owe ya."

"Like that's ever mattered," she said, then put the fork in her mouth and chewed slowly.

I waved the waiter over.

"Can I get you something else?" he asked.

"Yes, thank you," I said, tossing Bailey a sadistic smile. "I'll have another glass of wine."

31

The sun had long since set—now only the pale moonlight glowed through the expansive windows of the loft. Sabrina sat at her desk, heedless of the darkness, her gaze fixed on her computer, her face bathed in the cool gray light of her monitor.

Chase, who'd fallen asleep on the couch, stirred and opened an eye. In one swift movement, he stood up and walked over to her desk, the sound of his steps muted by the thick carpeting. But the moment he drew near, Sabrina minimized the screen. Without turning, she spoke to him over her shoulder.

"You ready to talk about the CEO case?"

"Yeah," he replied. He moved closer and gestured to her computer. "You find anything on him?" It was a deliberate tweak. He had a feeling he knew what she was working on, and it wasn't the CEO case. It worried him.

Sabrina turned and fixed him with a stare. An effective KEEP OUT sign. Chase knew better than to ignore it. He stepped back, literally and figuratively. "No girlfriends or boyfriends, as far as I can tell at this point," he said. "No porn and no bad associates—now or back when. No kids out of wedlock and no early busts for anything. I was wondering whether you had any ideas…?"

Chase was a great wingman with great tech skills— though she was no slouch herself, both by training and by instinct. But the creative thinking was largely up to her. Unlike Chase, who loved only the money, Sabrina derived an erotic thrill out of gathering the information that would empower her to shatter a life forever. For her, the money was secondary. Though she admitted it was a close second. She leaned back in her chair and lightly drummed the armrests with her fingers.

"My sense is that our CEO has no sexual Achilles' heel. He's not the kind of narcissistic power junkie you get with politicians. But from what I saw, he made a lot of money in a relatively short time. Look into whether he got a little too 'lucky' with his investments."

Chase nodded. Her instinct for the jugular was so unerring that it was almost bizarre. He stood to go.

"You can crash here when you're ready to pack it in," she said. Sabrina knew he never slept as well in his own bed as he did in her office.

"You staying?"

"No."

"Then I'll probably head home after I'm done, but thanks." Chase left with a mock salute.

Sabrina turned back to the computer and clicked to re-open the window she'd been scanning earlier, but she'd lost focus. She closed the window and shut down. Neither she nor Chase knew how to sleep. For her part, she realized it'd started in very early childhood, with the fear of what she'd find when she woke up. What would she do wrong today? And what would be the instrument of choice—a broom? a shoe? a wire hanger? The latter was the worst. The wire raised ugly red welts, forcing her to wear long pants during the sweltering summer to hide the shame. And there was no one to appeal to. Her father saw none of it and didn't want to know. He wanted only a playmate in his little daughter—a refuge away from the wife he'd married but never knew, and whom he now both loathed and feared.

So, in a way, going off to boarding school at the ripe old age of ten had been a relief. Or so she'd told herself at the time. Because it was obvious even to Sabrina that she was heading down a road that could only end in disaster. In the year before she was shipped away, she'd been busted for an ever-escalating series of misdeeds—from fights on the playground to shoplifting, and finally to arson. Her egg donor of a mother had gleefully agreed with the counselors that the change of scenery and enhanced discipline of boarding school would help to straighten her out. And so she'd been thrown away, a broken doll no one wanted to play with. Boarding school hadn't been all bad, once she'd adjusted to the new order of things. But by the time she moved back home, in her sophomore year of high school, she was a "new girl"—a stranger in her own hometown. Tough as that was, after a few months, things seemed to be falling into place, she'd begun to feel like her life was getting back on track.

Until that one night. That night everything had changed.

32

I looked out through my balcony window, the steam from my coffee flowing up against the cold glass, creating a foggy circle that dripped watery tears. Outside, low-hanging storm clouds had gathered and were darkening even as I watched.

This morning, we were going to meet Simon's parents. It was as if the weather knew.

Not that I needed to be reminded of the sadness and pain they were feeling. In fact, I'd been thinking of nothing else since I woke up, and I'd been dragging from that moment on. I finished the last of my coffee and went to my closet. I scanned the rack for a warm but respectful outfit and landed on a dark-gray wool suit and cream-colored turtleneck sweater.

The Bayers lived in Burbank, a nice middle-class neighborhood. My .22 Beretta was probably enough for the burbs. I popped it into the pocket of my trench coat, where it sagged noticeably, but since, at Bailey's insistence, I'd finally gotten a license, I didn't have to worry about getting busted for carrying anymore. Not that the possibility of arrest had ever stopped me.

I had to force myself to leave my room, and as I headed for the elevator, I felt as though I were walking underwater. When I got to the lobby, I found Bailey at the front door, talking to Angel. One glance told me she was looking forward to this about as much as I was.

I patted Angel on the arm and told him to have a good day, and we both got into the car.

"Did you make the notification to the parents?" I asked.

"I did," Bailey said, swinging out onto Grand Avenue and steering toward the freeway. "But I didn't get into any real conversation with them at the time. Figured it could wait, since Simon hadn't been living with them for a while."

Smart. Usually you'd get the information first and notify afterward, because once you tell victims' families why you're there, no one's in any kind of shape to answer questions. But in this case, the parents hadn't witnessed the crime—all they could give us was background information, so we could afford to allow them time to absorb the shock and talk later.

We got lucky and made it to Burbank before the rain started, but only just. Fat, heavy drops slowly began to fall as we pulled up to the Bayer house, a beige variation on the theme of small stucco houses in the tidy middle-class neighborhood.

I hadn't noticed how close to the curb Bailey'd parked, so as I got out, I failed to notice that the mailbox was in my way. Off balance, I grabbed on to the nearest thing to break my impending fall—which turned out to be a painted metal rooster attached to the top of the mailbox. I didn't see that the rooster was on a hinge; it was meant to be pulled up to signal the postman that mail was ready for pickup. So, of course, when I took hold of the head, it immediately bent forward, and I tumbled backward off the curb.

Fortunately Bailey's car was right behind me, so I landed against the passenger door. Unfortunately Bailey saw the whole thing. I looked up to see her watching me, shaking her head.

"I meant to do that," I said, and righted myself with as much dignity as possible. "Thought I'd lighten the mood."

"It worked," Bailey said with mock sincerity.

As we crossed the sidewalk, a youngish woman wearing army-green cargo pants and a man's puffy nylon jacket, who seemed to be in the process of rolling out her garbage cans, stopped and gave me a sympathetic look. "That thing did me in once too," she said, nodding at the treacherous metal rooster.

I appreciated the show of support and gave her a rueful smile.

" 'Course I was five at the time," she added.

Seriously, she couldn't just stop while I was ahead?

Bailey covered a snort of laughter with a fake cough.

"You guys cops?" she asked, glancing from Bailey's car to us.

I nodded. Close enough. I didn't need to hammer home the fact that the doofus who'd just been nailed by the metal rooster had a law degree.

"You here about Zack?" she asked.

Something about the way she said his name made me pause. "You knew him?"

She settled the garbage can on the curb and brushed off her hands. "Grew up with him." She gestured toward the small house behind her. "That's my parents' place. I'm helping 'em get it ready to sell. They can't really manage it anymore. You know…" She trailed off.

I did know. It's painful to see your parents get older, though aging is preferable to the alternative. "Were you and Zack close?" I asked.

"Kinda," she said, staring over my shoulder into her childhood.

She seemed unwilling to take it any further, so I shifted gears. "Did you know Simon?"

"Not really. He was a lot younger. And then, after the trial, he…went a little bit off the deep end."

I nodded sympathetically. "Yeah, from what I heard, he took it pretty hard," I said. I decided not to tell her just yet that Simon was dead. She'd learn soon enough, and the fewer people who knew, the better. I extended my hand. "I'm Rachel Knight."

"Tracy Chernoff," she replied, taking it. Bailey introduced herself, and they shook.

"Well," Tracy said, "I'd better get back to it. Nice to meet you both."

"You too," I replied.

She put her hands into her jacket pockets and trudged up the walk, head down. I watched her for a moment, feeling her sadness…and something else I couldn't put my finger on.

"So…?" Bailey asked.

We moved briskly up the short walk that was lined on

both sides with healthy-looking rosebushes and rang the bell on the wall next to the screen door.

A tall, wide-shouldered man in a worn cardigan with wispy white hair answered the door. He called behind him, "They're here, Claire," then said to us, "Please come in."

He stepped back and gestured toward two matching gold-velour chairs that faced a marble coffee table and a gold-and-brown-plaid couch.

Bailey made the introduction. "Fred Bayer, this is Rachel Knight, the deputy DA."

As we shook, Claire came out wiping her hands on a kitchen towel. She nervously touched her brown hair, which was tucked into a short pageboy cut, and held out an arthritis-gnarled hand. "Claire Bayer. Nice to meet you..."

I took her hand. "Rachel Knight, DA's office."

She turned to Bailey with a small, forced smile. "Detective Keller," she said. "Good to see you."

I knew it wasn't, but I could already tell that Fred and Claire weren't the type to take their misery out on others. Polite, kind, considerate, they were the sort of neighbors who'd bring in the paper for you without being asked, bake extra cookies to share with you, and loan you their lawn mower. In short, the kind of people who should never be mired in so much bizarre tragedy.

"Can I get you some tea?" Claire asked. "It'll warm you up a little. I think I heard the rain start."

"It did," Bailey confirmed. "And I'd love some tea if it's not too much trouble."

Bailey actually hated tea, but I knew she was giving Claire something to do to help her relax. I took a glance around the room. There was an upright piano against the wall to my right, an entertainment center on the wall across from me, side tables on either end of the couch, and the obligatory coffee table. Other than that coffee table, every horizontal surface was covered with pictures of Simon and, I presumed, Zack, starting with their toddler years and climbing up through the milestones of games, graduations, and goals achieved. The coffee table was reserved for what I surmised were Simon's creations: a vase in the shape of a mother holding a child, a bowl that was two hands clasping, and a candleholder in the shape of a robed woman. They had the same simplicity of line and elegance as the vase Simon had left with Johnnie Jasper.

While we waited for Claire to return, I made small talk with Fred. I pointed to the piano. "Do you play?"

"No, no," he said. "That's Claire. At least, it used to be…" He trailed off.

"Arthritis?" I asked, wishing I'd thought for just one moment before opening my yapper and reminding them of yet another sad loss.

He nodded.

"Simon did those?" I asked, gesturing to the statuary on the coffee table.

That elicited a pained but tender smile.

"He started working with clay practically from the time he was born," Fred said. "He always had the gift."

"His work is beautiful," I said sincerely.

Fred cleared his throat. "Zack was good at making things too. I don't know if you knew that."

"I didn't." I did, but I wanted to let him tell me.

He nodded to himself. "Carpentry."

Claire came in with a tray bearing a teapot and cups on saucers. For most people, this is an unusual formality. For me, who lives on room service, it was Tuesday. I knew Bailey would find this observation disgusting, and it was.

Claire joined Fred on the couch across from us. I decided to ease into things and start with a topic that didn't directly involve the fresh loss of Simon.

"Do you know how Zack and Lilah met?" I asked.

Claire and Fred looked at each other for a moment, perplexed. Claire spoke first. "I'm not one hundred percent sure. I think at a party. Is that right, Fred?"

"That sounds right," Fred replied.

"What did you think of Lilah?"

"I never liked her," Claire said flatly. "From the very start, I thought she was a cold fish. I didn't know what Zack saw in her—other than the obvious. Isn't that right, Fred?"

"Claire never took to her," he confirmed.

"And you, Fred?" I asked.

" 'Course, now I think she should burn in hell, but at the time"—Fred shrugged—"I never really felt like I knew her, tell you the truth..." He paused and shrugged again. "And I'll grant you, she wasn't the warmest person I'd ever met, but I figured Zack saw more than just the pretty face."

"Well, pretty is as pretty does," Claire said in a firm voice. "And I never thought her 'pretty' went any further than her skin." She continued, a harder edge now audible in her voice, "That damn jury just fell for her act."

I nodded, though it seemed to me that calling Lilah "pretty" was like calling the Hope Diamond "shiny."

"I'd like to ask you about Simon's relationship with Zack," I said, shifting gears.

Claire hunched forward, and Fred put a protective arm around her.

I took a deep breath and prayed we'd get through this as fast as possible.

33

"**Were Simon** and Zack close?" I asked.

Claire's features softened. "Always," she said quietly. "There was a fairly big age gap. But if Zack was around, he'd always take care of Simon. Anyone ever hurt Simon, they'd answer to Zack."

"Did that happen a lot?" I asked. "I mean, Simon getting into trouble?"

"No," she admitted. "Simon was never one to mix it up with other kids. He was a dreamer, lived in his world of creations. But when he was little, there'd be the occasional bully who saw Simon as easy pickings…" Claire paused and teared up. "Zack would step in whenever he could. Simon…well, he just worshipped Zack."

I reached out to comfort her, and she patted my hand.

Claire continued, her voice shaking with the effort to hold back tears. "I remember how, when Simon was just in kindergarten, he'd sit on the stairs, waiting for Zack to come home from school so he could show his brother what he'd made."

I groped for something to say to ease her pain, but I

knew from my own hard experience that the wounds of loss would bleed for years to come. Then, one day, they'd find that a few seconds had gone by without some painful thought or memory; over time, the seconds would stretch into a minute, the minutes into an hour. Eventually they might be lucky enough to get a whole day. But that day would be a long time coming.

"Did Zack and Simon stay close as they got older?" I asked.

"As much as that was possible, living in different worlds," Claire said.

Fred cleared his throat again. "You know, what with Zack being a police officer and Simon being an artist, they didn't have the same group of friends or anything. But they loved each other."

"And was Simon still the younger brother, if you know what I mean?" I asked.

Claire nodded. "Oh yes. Zack remained the exciting older brother. I think being a police officer actually made him even more of a hero to Simon."

"So Zack's passing was pretty devastating for him too," I said gently.

"It completely destroyed him," Fred replied, his voice for the first time showing real signs of anger. "Until then, he'd been a pretty happy guy. Had a nice girlfriend—what was her name, Claire?"

"Angie," Claire chimed in. "She was an artist too. A painter. She hung in there with him for quite a while after Zack's . . . murder." She stumbled over the word, still unable to put it next to her son's name. She took a shallow breath. "Lord knows it wasn't an easy thing to do. Simon got obsessed with the case; it blocked out everything else.

Angie believed he'd get past it when the case was over. But when Lilah got acquitted, Simon totally shut down. For weeks, he didn't eat, didn't speak, wouldn't even get out of bed."

"And so she left him?" I asked.

"No, God bless her," Fred said. "She tried to stay and take care of him. It was Simon. He pushed her away, then he pushed her out."

"Only thing he'd do was sit in front of the computer. Got one of those LexisNexis accounts, read up on the law," Claire said, shaking her head. "That's when he came up with the idea of taking the case to the federal court."

"And once he latched on to that idea, he was like a man possessed," Fred said. "He'd write to the federal prosecutors every day. Took a while, but they finally wrote back. Thanked him for his interest, but said the case didn't fit their guidelines."

It wasn't high-profile enough and it wasn't a slam dunk. And it took only one of those problems to knock it out of the running.

"That set him off but good," Fred continued. "After that, he started going to the Federal Building downtown." He stopped and looked down at his hands, which were clasped together between his knees.

"How long did Simon keep that up?" I asked.

"I'd say a good six months," Claire said, her expression pained. "But then one day, he got a little too...agitated. We got a call saying he'd been arrested for causing a disturbance."

Bailey and I looked at each other. There was no record of this.

"Did they book him?" Bailey asked.

"We went down and spoke to the arresting officer," Fred said. "Explained the history, what had happened with Zack's case and all. Turned out the officer knew about the case. Felt bad for Simon. Just made him promise not to come back and cut him loose."

"So did he stay away from the court after that?" I asked.

"He stayed away from everything after that," Claire said, her mouth turned down at the corners. "One week later, he disappeared. No phone call, no e-mail. He left his studio wide open."

Fred coughed, covering his mouth with one big hand, then dropped it back into his lap. "We went crazy trying to find him," he said, his voice weary from just the memory of the ordeal.

"Did you file a missing persons report?" I asked.

"Of course," Claire said. "But they didn't find him. He came back on his own two weeks later, looking like hell. Filthy, sunburned, skinny; he looked half dead."

Her eyes welled up.

"We got him to a hospital, they fixed him up," Fred said. "It was mostly dehydration. We brought him home, got him to stay here for a little while. Even got him into therapy—"

"Then one day, he just up and left again," Claire said. "That time we were a little more prepared for it. But he was gone longer, for a few months, and we just didn't know if..."

"Did that keep happening?" I asked.

Claire nodded.

"And how was he"—I searched for a gentle way to say it—"mentally?"

"I didn't want to see it at the time, but the truth was, Simon wasn't himself from the moment Zack died," Claire said, shaking her head, her expression etched with grief. "He surely went downhill after the verdict, but by the time he went to the street, he was sliding fast—"

"His memory was all screwed up," Fred said, tapping his head. "He'd have days where he seemed okay, and then something would just…slip, and he'd make no sense. Talk gibberish, or not talk at all." He dipped his head and brushed away a tear.

"He'd rant about the government," Claire added. "Said you couldn't trust anyone, they were all liars, and on and on…"

"I know you're wondering why we didn't just commit him." Fred sighed. "We thought having him locked up like that would really be the end of him. And after that damn jury, and then the Feds turning him away…well, I guess he didn't seem all that crazy to me," he admitted. "I think he just lost all faith, you know?"

I certainly did know. I'd felt that way for a long time after losing Romy. It had a lot to do with why I became a prosecutor. Even if there was no justice for my sister, I could believe it still existed if I could find justice for someone else.

"And was that a consistent theme for Simon?" I asked.

Claire nodded sadly. "But the last time he came back, he looked better," she said, a smile passing briefly across her face, sun momentarily breaking through clouds. "He was still too skinny and leathery. But for the first time in two years, he seemed normal—almost upbeat." Claire turned and patted Fred on the knee. "We had a great visit, didn't we, Fred?"

Fred nodded silently, his gaze fixed on the coffee table.

"But a week later, he was gone again," she said. "A week after that, he..." Claire covered her eyes for a moment. "I know I should've been ready for this, the way he was living." Her voice trembled. "But..."

I could finish the thought for her. There's no way a parent can prepare for the death—let alone the murder—of a child.

Much less two.

34

It wasn't quite noon by the time we left the Bayers, but I felt like it was past midnight. I always come away from a session with a victim's family feeling a bone-weary exhaustion.

I buckled myself in and pulled my coat tight, knowing Bailey wouldn't allow me to turn on the heater.

"You know what I could use?" I asked.

Bailey raised an eyebrow. "A stiff drink? I know I could."

"I was thinking of a real distraction. As in some nice, intriguing, and—dare I say?—helpful evidence."

"What'll it be, DNA? Fingerprints? Just say the word, princess," Bailey replied.

I looked at her stone-faced. "I say it's time we go pound on the coroner," I said.

"Oh, good idea." Bailey steered onto the freeway. "I especially like the sound of that at lunchtime."

I folded my arms around my body for warmth and looked out the window at the nearby cars. As usual, we were doing all the passing. Driving with a cop is fun. We got to the coroner's and caught a double shot of lucky. Our pathologist, Dr. Sparks, was in, and he was free.

I could never look at Dr. Sparks without seeing Woody Allen: rail thin, no taller than me, with thick glasses, a beak of a nose, and a nasal, reedy voice. The first time I'd had him on a case, I'd been worried about his ability to connect with a jury. But his halting, careful manner on the stand had come across as thorough and precise. The jury loved him.

His tiny office was so cluttered we couldn't even find the chairs that I knew were across from his desk. But Dr. Sparks immediately picked up two sizable stacks of books and files and lugged them over to an already groaning table. He then scurried around behind his desk, adjusted his glasses, and opened the file on Simon.

"So our John Doe—," he began.

"Is now known to be Simon Bayer," Bailey interjected.

Dr. Sparks nodded vaguely without looking up from the file.

"Homeless, but not for terribly long," he said, scanning the paperwork. "Not that much to say about cause of death, other than it was sharp force injury. Not news to you, I know," he continued, putting the autopsy photographs on the desk and turning them toward us. "See how tight and clean that is?" He pointed to a photograph of Simon's upper abdomen that showed a neat, precise slit that looked more like an incision made by a surgeon in an OR than a knife wound inflicted on a city sidewalk. "That means he used a very sharp—"

"He?" I asked. "Couldn't the killer have been a *she?*"

Dr. Sparks studied the photograph again and frowned, then pursed his lips. "Well, I suppose it could've been a she. Though this...well...this happened out on the street, didn't it?" He pushed his glasses up the bridge of his nose and peered at Bailey.

"Yes," she replied. "And it happened fast."

Dr. Sparks shook his head. "See, that's...with this...well..." He sputtered to a stop, seemingly out of words.

I wanted to turn him upside down and shake him so a full sentence would fall out.

"You're thinking a woman is unlikely?" I said, trying to sound more patient than I felt.

"Um-hmm." Dr. Sparks paused again and pulled out more photographs. He stared at five photos in a row, holding each one within two inches of his face.

All the coroners seem to hold pictures that close. I don't know what that's about.

"See?" he said, tapping the photograph in his hand, which he held facing him, so we really couldn't—see, that is. He continued, "It's a quick, hard thrust straight into the aorta, right on target."

"So the victim would've died fairly quickly?" I asked.

Dr. Sparks nodded. "He would've bled out within minutes. Whoever used this knife either knew what they were doing or got lucky. And, like I said, the knife was sharp. That made quick penetration much easier."

He put the photograph down, and Bailey reached out and took it. I waited to see if she put it up to her nose. If she did, I was going to kick her.

"So," Dr. Sparks continued, "it could be a female. I mean, a woman is capable of inflicting that wound—especially with a knife like that. It's just, oddswise, less likely."

"What can you tell us about the kind of knife that was used?" I asked.

"Other than being sharp," he said, looking down at his report again, "the wound track was three inches deep, wound width...very narrow. Steven would know more, but..." Dr. Sparks turned through several pages in the file. "I see he did do the wound cast, but I don't see his report. Give me a minute, it should be in here."

I was happy to give him several minutes if it meant getting one of Steven Diamond's reports. Steven was the criminalist for the L.A. County Coroner, and he was one of the best in the country. I call him the "everything man," because he can literally do everything except the autopsy. Gunshot residue, drug overdose, poison—you name it, he knows how to test for it. Come to think of it, he could probably do autopsies too, but the man can only stretch twenty-four hours so far. Steven had compiled a database of blunt and sharp force injuries by taking impressions of wounds with red silicon material—kind of like the stuff a dentist uses. When there's a known murder weapon in a case, he can use the wounds to tell him what kind of tool marks that weapon makes.

If we got lucky, he'd be able to match Simon's wound to a particular kind of blade. Although he wouldn't be able to say that it was made by one knife to the exclusion of all others, if our blade type was distinct enough, it'd be a nice piece of evidence.

"Oh, here you go," Dr. Sparks said. He read from the report, "Double-edged blade, likely with a three-inch cutting edge, total length of blade likely three and five-eighths, one-eighth of an inch thick—"

"Pretty small," I remarked.

"It is surprising, but we don't mess with Steve." He continued to read. "Fits specifications for a combat knife. Very concealable, lightweight, very lethal."

"Could it be automatic? A switchblade?" I asked, picturing the surveillance footage of the stabbing.

"I...uh, wouldn't be able to tell that because...it was obviously in the open position when it was used to inflict the wound," he replied. He adjusted his glasses as he pulled out the autopsy photographs. "But they don't usually sell those types of combat knives to the public—at least from what I know."

"He could've gotten an automatic on the black market," I suggested.

"Or a gun show," Bailey added. "But they're not cheap."

"Well...I wouldn't know about any of that," Dr. Sparks said, frowning.

He was one of those rare experts who'd never stretch to offer an opinion that was even an inch to the left of his precise field of study. A maddening but credibility-grabbing trait.

"Did the victim's clothing get sent to the crime lab yet?" I asked.

Before he could respond, Bailey jumped in. "Yes," she said, looking at her notebook. "Stoner took the clothing over himself the day after the autopsy." She snapped the notebook closed and pocketed it.

Dr. Sparks blinked rapidly a few times, then checked his own file. "Yes. That is correct." He looked up at us. "Is there anything else you'd like to discuss?"

Bailey shook her head. We might come up with more questions later, but for now we were done. We thanked Dr. Sparks and took our leave.

"I take it we haven't heard anything from the crime lab yet about Simon's clothes," I said.

"I would've told you about it already," Bailey replied. "I've got it on my list."

"A combat knife," I said, thinking back to Steven Diamond's conclusions about the murder weapon. "And if it was an automatic, which I bet it was, our stabber was not only well-trained but might be a vet or a former cop."

"God forbid it's a former cop," Bailey said grimly. "We don't need any more help in the bad-rap department. But what made you ask if it was an automatic-opening blade?"

"I was just thinking about how fast it happened. Even if someone's really good, I couldn't see how he—or she—could manage to pull a knife out of the sheath and make a direct hit on the aorta as fast as it looked on that surveillance footage. It's possible the stabber was carrying an open knife, but it'd be hard to have it at the ready and avoid getting cut pretty badly with a blade that sharp. And there was nothing in the crime scene reports showing any stray blood drops. But if the knife was an automatic, it'd be easy for the killer to carry and stab someone without nicking himself too badly. All he'd have to do is press a button."

We got into her car and belted up.

"Nice work, Sherlock," Bailey said.

"Nice enough for you to buy me lunch?"

"I would," Bailey said, "had I not already thought of the automatic myself. I was just waiting to see if you'd figured it out."

"Truly pathetic, Keller," I said.

But in all fairness, she probably had.

35

As it turned out, no one was buying anyone lunch that day. By the time we got back to the courthouse, it was almost one thirty and there was not only a depressingly large stack of messages but also a full in-box that reminded me this wasn't my only case. Ordinarily I might've taken lunch anyway and worked late, but I had to leave on time tonight. I had a date with Graden.

It'd been a busy and emotionally draining day, so I was more than ready for an escape. Graden had suggested we hit the Catalina Jazz Club. It'd moved several years ago from its old digs to a much bigger—and more comfortable—space on Sunset. All the bigs in the jazz world played there. I was up for something new, and listening to good jazz was one of the best antidotes I'd found for the sadness and misery that was an inevitable part of every case. By six o'clock, I'd whittled down enough of my stack to stave off panic and headed back to the Biltmore.

It wasn't raining at the moment, but it was still cold, and there were clouds hanging around that might yet decide to douse us again, so I dressed warmly in black leggings, a long sweater, and black over-the-knee boots. And, just in case, I slung a raincoat over my shoulder, then headed downstairs.

As usual, Graden looked gorgeous. Tonight's attire was a simple black crewneck sweater and jeans, but he made it look like an ad for *GQ*.

"Hey, Rache," he said warmly as I walked through the door.

"Hi," I said.

"Don't you look fantastic," he said with a smile, leaning in for a quick kiss and a hug, which gave me the chance to notice that he not only looked great but smelled great too.

"It's so helpful that you work with men all day," I replied.

On the way to the club, I gave him the rundown on the events of the past few days. I'd told him during a brief phone call that Bailey and I had wound up with the Bayer case but not what we'd learned since then.

"I have a vague memory of Zack's murder," he remarked. "From what you've said, it sounds like the evidence was good enough for a conviction. I guess the jury just didn't want to believe a woman—"

"Especially one who looked like that—," I interjected.

"—could do something that heinous," he finished. "My theory about why women get a pass from juries is that men don't like the idea that women can be that cold-blooded. Wrecks our little fantasy about female helplessness."

"Hard to believe that fantasy survived Lorena Bobbitt," I said.

"We're a stubborn species," Graden said as he pulled into the parking lot at the back of the club and found a spot right outside the door.

"Yet, surprisingly, you're not extinct," I observed. "But I'd guess you're at least partially right. I think that's why Lizzie Borden got acquitted."

"She did?" he asked incredulously as he opened the door for me.

"She walked, and no one else was ever charged."

Graden shook his head as he followed me into the bar. "Juries."

"I'll drink to that," I said.

We ordered Ketel One martinis and a basket of fries. A great quartet that featured a smoking tenor sax had already started the first set. When our drinks came, we toasted to a great night, and I felt my engine slow as the vodka did its work. I leaned back to enjoy the music. The band swung into a slow, moody rendition of "One for My Baby." Out of the corner of my eye, I saw that Graden was looking at me. We exchanged a slow smile that made a warm glow start in my chest and spread out all over. Would tonight be the night we made love? I thought I might finally be ready to go there—that is, I thought with a rueful inward smile, if Graden was in the mood. It wasn't something I felt comfortable taking for granted. I'd discovered during my relationship with Daniel that although teenage boys were ready even if they were in a coma, grown men occasionally had down days. Not often, but they did happen.

Then the band started to play "Jordu," and I let all thoughts float away as I sank into the music. The evening passed, warm, relaxed, and intimate. But as Graden and I got into his car, he seemed a little distracted.

Our conversation was minimal, but he reached out to hold my hand on the console between us—an unfamiliar gesture. What was going on? I'd been seriously considering inviting him up to my room, but by the time he'd pulled off the freeway and headed down Temple Street, I wasn't so sure.

"Rachel, I don't want you to take this the wrong way, but I'd like to talk to you without a crowd around," Graden said seriously. "Would it be okay if we talked in your room?"

I would've made a joke about it being an obvious line, but his tone told me he wasn't in the mood. What the hell was going on? A breakup? Had there been a death in the family? Did he have a fatal illness? An evil twin? My mind filled with questions, none of them good.

"Sure," I said. "Of course."

Naturally, since I was dying to get this over with, the elevator took forever. When the doors opened, he put a gentle hand on the middle of my back to guide me inside, and when they closed, he left it there and looked down at me with soft eyes. I briefly returned his gaze, then looked away, more confused than ever.

We walked toward my room at the end of the corridor in silence. Barely conscious of my movements, I let us in, picked up the remote, and turned on the radio, which was permanently tuned to Real Jazz. The strains of Stanley Turrentine playing "Little Sheri," one of my favorites, softened the brittle silence. I put my purse on the chair near the window and unbuttoned my coat as I walked to the couch. Graden took my coat and laid it down, then held my hand as we sat on the couch. When he finally spoke, they were the last words I expected—or wanted—to hear.

"Rachel, I want to talk to you about Romy."

36

Hearing him say my sister's name made my heart lurch painfully, and suddenly my throat tightened. For a panicked moment, I forgot how to breathe. When I finally drew air, I found myself light-headed and unable to hear over the rushing in my ears. Graden, his expression concerned, was saying something.

"What?" I said, momentarily confused and disoriented.

How could he know about Romy? I took some deep breaths and forced enough calm for the sounds to take the shape of cognizable words.

"...wanted to know more about you. I guess I should've just asked you directly." He paused and stared out the window. "But then I thought, the case doesn't have to stay unsolved. I know the local police up there did all they could, but we've got more resources. Hell, I know I could get some help from the FBI on this..."

I mentally curled inward, trying not to let his words conjure the pictures, but I knew it was hopeless. The wheels began to turn, pulling me under, and the day that perpetually lurked just beneath my consciousness replayed for the millionth time in heart-clutching detail.

It was my seventh birthday. Romy, an unusually sedate eleven, was cautious and patient from birth, a counterpoint to my more impulsive and reckless nature. And, unlike my friends' older siblings, Romy almost never got annoyed by my constant bids for attention. I hadn't needed my parents' reminders that I was lucky to have Romy for an older sister.

Our little two-bedroom home in Sebastopol, north of San Francisco, stood on the outer perimeter of the relatively new development of unimaginative stucco ranch houses that repeated the same three styles throughout all ten square blocks. Young as I was, I nevertheless had a dim awareness that money was scarce. My mother's job as a bank teller didn't bring in much, and my father, who'd just finished a stint in the army, was in his first year in college, pursuing his dream of becoming an airline pilot. But ours was a neighborhood filled with young families struggling to get a leg up, so we never felt deprived.

And it was a kind of heaven for us. Young children poured out of every house at all hours of the day, shooed outside by overworked mothers who needed some peace and quiet. And in that place, there was plenty of "outside" to play in. Our neighborhood had been carved out of a broad expanse of woods and fields that still surrounded our development, so a child's paradise of wilderness was just steps away.

For most of the kids, the biggest draw was the old abandoned house that stood in a clearing in the middle of the woods. The ramshackle hut burned a fire in the imaginations of all the neighborhood children, its hauntingly vacant windows staring out like sepulchral eyes. Rumor had it that the owners had been murdered and/or abducted by aliens...or was it that they'd been arrested for having killed, skinned, and eaten children...exactly our ages?

But that house hadn't intrigued me. For me, the big thrill lay a half mile away in the decidedly unmysterious chicken ranch that filled the air with feathers, stench, and the squawks of roosters at all hours. It had horses, which I, being a typical young girl, loved, as well as pigs, cows, and one surly-looking bull. The owners would sometimes let me ride the older mare with the bushy forelock that looked like a teenage girl's overgrown bangs. But I daydreamed about sneaking a ride on the bull—though even I knew enough to keep that particular goal to myself.

The day of my seventh birthday dawned bright and early, the August sun already intense by ten a.m. I'd woken up filled with joyous anticipation. Romy had declared that for my birthday present, she'd do whatever I wanted for the whole day. I'd given the matter a lot of thought and come up with a list of the things that were usually the hardest to get Romy to do: double-Dutch rope jumping (she'd grown tired of it), play Monopoly (Romy hated board games), play hide-and-seek (she thought it was "dumb"), and visit the chicken ranch.

I'd known that the ranch owners were on vacation, and that by the afternoon the caretakers who came to water and feed the animals would be gone. That's when I'd planned to realize my dream of riding that bull. I told myself that I wanted to do it when Romy was there so I'd have a witness to my triumph. I didn't admit that I might also have wanted Romy there to rescue me in case the bull wasn't on board with my plan. Of course, I kept this part to myself, because I knew Romy would stop me if she knew in advance. So I devised a strategy to spring it on her. I was going to suggest we play hide-and-seek around the ranch in the afternoon, and when it was my turn to hide, I'd make sure Romy did her counting near the bull pen. Then I'd sneak over to the pen, climb up, and call out just in time for Romy to see me swing a leg over the bull's back.

We'd begun the morning with double-Dutch rope jumping and moved on to Monopoly. By then, I was feeling more than slightly guilty for what I was secretly planning to do, so I called off the game halfway through and said we could end my birthday early with a game of hide-and-seek at the chicken ranch. Romy had gratefully leaped at the offer.

We made our way across the open field that separated our little suburban community from the ranch and the wilds that surrounded it. I let Romy be the first to hide, knowing that would give me the right to stake out where "home base" was, and I purposely positioned myself in front of a big oak tree right next to the bull pen. I'd only counted to seven when I heard the crunch of tires on the dirt road and looked around to see that a pickup truck was slowly approaching. Most of the ranch workers drove those trucks, so when the dusty red pickup rolled toward me, I shielded my eyes from the sun and prepared to wave. But as I lifted my hand, I saw that the driver was a stranger. A big black dog was on the seat next to him. The man wore the battered cowboy hat favored by a lot of the ranch hands, and as he drove by, he smiled and lifted it, showing closely cut dark hair and a round, open face.

It was a pleasant smile, and I gave him one of my own before turning back to the tree to resume counting.

When I got to one hundred, I knew exactly where to look. Romy always chose the same spot, and I ran straight for it. Sure enough, there she was, in a large hole in the trunk of an oak tree.

"Come on, Romy!" I complained, forgetting that the game was just a ruse for my planned bull ride. "Pick a real hiding place!"

Romy made a face, but she conceded. "Okay, okay. Jeez, Rache, aren't you ever going to get tired of these baby games?"

I shrugged, embarrassed but stubborn. Even though I had a bigger goal in mind today, I didn't think it was such a baby game, and I wanted to play it right. Romy reluctantly trudged back to home base. I turned to face the trunk, closed my eyes, and began to count again. Behind me, I heard Romy run toward the woods.

"Twenty-one, twenty-two . . . ," I counted, and then stopped. Something felt wrong; there was a bad energy in the air. A wave of apprehension rippled through me. I didn't want to cheat, but the feeling was so strong, I couldn't ignore it. I opened my eyes and looked around.

The pickup truck had stopped just fifty feet down the road, and it was pointing into the woods. The driver's door was standing open, and the truck looked empty. I stared, sensing danger, but unsure of why or what to do.

Suddenly I heard a sharp yelp from somewhere in the woods, then abruptly the sound was cut off and there was a distant rustling noise. Terrified but disbelieving, I whispered, "Romy."

I began to walk toward the woods, stiff-legged, face frozen, unable even to name a reason for my fear. I walked faster and faster, an instinctive terror growing and solidifying with every step, forming a hard ball in my chest. Finally, too overwhelmed with dread to wait another second, I took the deepest breath I could and screamed, "Romy!"

Silence. Romy had to have heard me. Now the ball of fear rose up from my chest and into my throat. I tried to call out again but choked; nothing came out. I stopped and gathered all the breath in my body and was about to call out to her again, but at that moment the man in the cowboy hat appeared. He was jogging out of the woods, toward his truck. An object I couldn't identify was draped over his shoulder. I stopped breathing and stood dead still, paralyzed with fear. Then, heart pounding and without conscious thought, I started to run toward him, screaming over and over again, "Romy! Romy!"

But though I was pushing my body as hard as I could, my legs felt leaden, as if I were running through quick-sand. Some part of my brain realized I couldn't make it in time. I watched, mute with terror, as he threw the object that'd been on his shoulder into the passenger side of the truck. I stopped, and with every ounce of strength in my body, arms and legs shaking, I screamed out, "Romyyy!" The man looked up and, for just a moment, our eyes met. Then he jogged around to the driver's side, slammed the door, and drove off, his tires kicking up a cloud of dirt and rocks. "Romyyy!" I screamed again.

I ran after the truck. "Noooo!" I sobbed in a high, keening wail. "Romyyy! Romyyy!" I screamed in help-less desperation as the truck became a pin dot in the distance and the graveled turn of its wheels faded into silence.

I kept running and screaming long after the truck had disappeared, until a sharp, stabbing pain in my side made me crumple to the ground. I lay there, panting, trying to catch my breath as tears streamed down my face. Finally I pulled myself up, hiccuping and still breathless. It couldn't be true—I refused to acknowledge what "it" was, stopping the thought before it could complete itself. I began talking to myself—my old baby habit—telling myself that maybe Romy was still in her favorite hiding place. Then I told myself she *had* to be there. I filled my heart with conviction and began to limp toward Romy's tree. As I moved, clutching my side, I spoke out loud. One long stream of consciousness: "Romy, please be there, please, oh please, I promise I'll never make you play it again, I promise, Romy, please, please oh please be there! Please be there, Romy!" My breath was ragged, my voice rasping and hoarse.

The tree was empty.

I have no memory of what happened next, but I was told that I'd been found by one of the ranch hands, stumbling around in the woods, sobbing, filthy, my clothing torn. I either couldn't or wouldn't speak, and when the man tried to lead me out of the woods, I'd kicked and bitten him until he'd backed off and gone for the sheriff. I couldn't explain it at the time, but in my child's mind, I believed that as long as I stayed in the woods, there was still a chance that Romy would be there, that somehow she'd appear and everything would be okay.

I never saw my sister again.

Eventually her disappearance—I still refused to accept

the possibility of her death—claimed both my parents. When my father died, the small light that had continued burning in my mother's eyes flickered and went out. She slipped into a clinical depression that left her virtually immobile for weeks at a time. When her health insurance ran out, she'd managed to rally and go back to work and put food on the table, but I knew she only did it for me. Up to that point, I hadn't thought it possible to feel any guiltier than I did.

As for me, not only had I lost my family but I'd also lost my friends, for whom I'd become the object of pity and fascination. The story of Romy's disappearance made the local news. There was no place I went where someone didn't point and stare or outright ask me about the day Romy went missing.

As much as I came to hate my life, it didn't occur to me that there was anything to be done about it until I was in my junior year in high school. And then one day, for no particular reason, it hit me: why not move? In a new city, my mother could get away from a town that held nothing but agonizing memories, and I could become someone else—someone who wasn't the local freak. I'd never again have to see those hellish woods.

It took some time and effort to convince my mother, but I was relentless. I'd chosen Los Angeles. Big, anonymous, and not so far away as to be daunting. Slowly we learned together how to navigate an entirely new life. My mother found her smile again, and I found a fresh identity as a normal person. Those were sweet years, when my mother and I discovered a closeness we'd never known before. Then, three years ago, she was diagnosed with melanoma. Six months later, she was gone. I know, because she told me, that she'd never expected to have any happiness in her life after losing Romy and my father; the joy we'd found in these years was an unexpected gift.

My mother's death was a crushing blow. I was truly alone. What got me through that terrible time was the support I had from Toni and Bailey. But even they never knew about Romy.

When I moved here, I'd very deliberately decided never to tell anyone. Carla the Crone, my lifelong shrink, says it's an unhealthy sign that I still suffer guilt for my sister's abduction. She also says that a true friend will neither judge nor pity me, nor treat me like a freak. I say, why take the chance? And besides, what's the relevance? Romy's been gone for more than twenty years. I don't see why a relationship should require all parties to divulge their entire life histories.

I think adults get to decide what to share and when . . . and what to keep to themselves.

37

That philosophy fits well in Los Angeles. What I hadn't known when I'd chosen to move here is that Los Angeles discourages intimacy. Unlike other cities, Los Angeles, with its vast sprawl, forces you to get into a car to go anywhere. That means you won't be making any new friends on your daily route from here to there. In fact, it's damn unlikely you'll ever run into anyone you know without an appointment. Natives are a rarity—most are transplants from other parts of the country, if not the world. And though you'd think that kind of diversity might make personal histories a common point of interest, I'd found the opposite was true: people seldom asked questions about my past, and when they did, my minimalist answers were accepted without follow-up.

I'd happily crawled into that cocoon of anonymity. At first, I'd been consumed with guarding its walls. But after years without challenge, I'd come to believe there was no cause for fear. I'd found security in the knowledge that I'd never have to worry about a breach because no one cared. And so I was caught off guard. Hearing that Graden had

dug into my past without ever asking my permission left
me stunned. But within seconds the surprise gave way to
fury.

"How dare you?" I asked, breathing hard.

"What...what do you mean?" Graden asked, his expression shocked and perplexed.

"What the hell were you doing snooping around in my
life without asking me? I'm not some jerkoff perp you
'run' at will."

My voice was low and steady, but I was shaking with
rage. Graden's eyes widened.

"Why wouldn't you tell me about Romy?" he asked.
"We're supposed to be a couple—"

"And a couple shows respect for each other's boundaries! They don't go stomping around, digging up dirt just
because they can!"

I roughly pushed my hair back from my face, getting
angrier by the second.

"Digging up dirt?" he retorted. "Your sister's abduction isn't dirt! It's a life-altering event. I care about you.
Don't you think I deserve to know about it?"

"Deserve!" I shouted. "I most certainly don't! You deserve to know what I want you to know and not one thing
more! It's *my* life," I said, pointing to myself, "and it's
my choice what to tell." I stopped a moment to catch my
breath, then added, "And since we're on the subject, what
exactly have you chosen to share with me about *your*
childhood?"

Graden was silent, his face now stony with resentment.
"I would've been glad to tell you anything you wanted to
know. All you ever had to do was ask me," he replied.

"But I didn't ask. I gave you time and space to tell me

whatever you wanted—whenever you wanted. And I sure as hell didn't go scurrying around behind your back."

"I wasn't *scurrying around,* I just…" His voice trailed off, and he fell silent.

Graden took a deep breath and looked at the floor. I waited till he raised his eyes and held my gaze.

"I meant well, Rachel," he said, his voice now calm, apologetic. "I can see it was a mistake, but I just wanted to know more about you. And I didn't run your rap sheet." He said it with a little smile that died when he saw I wasn't softening. "All I did was google you." He paused again. "But when I saw the story about Romy, I got upset. I couldn't understand why you wouldn't tell me about something like this. At the very least, you'd have to know I'd understand. I might even be able to help—"

"Understand? Why? Because you've handled millions of *victims?*" I was so angry my breath was coming in sharp, rasping gulps. The old childhood wounds had been torn open and were bleeding out.

Graden shook his head.

"And help?" I continued. "It's been over twenty years! Do you think in all that time I've just been sitting on my hands, waiting for Sir Galahad to ride up and slay the dragon?"

Graden gave me a hard look. "I'm not a plumber, Rachel. I've got fifteen years on the force, I've worked thousands of cases, and I've got friends and connections all over the country. So while it might be optimistic to think I could come up with a new idea, it's not inconceivable that I might be able to help."

I returned his gaze, feeling ice-cold inside.

"But that's not really what this is about, is it, Rachel?"

I looked at him. "What are you talking about?"

"We were getting too close, weren't we?" he asked, his voice heavy.

"Don't use that fear-of-intimacy crap on me," I said. "This is about the fact that you can't respect my privacy. This is about *your* issue, Graden. Your need to know everything about everyone, regardless of how they might feel about it—"

Graden, who was almost as computer savvy as his propeller-head brother, had confided to me in one of those private, vulnerable moments of closeness that he had "researched" not only all his partners on the force but also his competitors for every single promotion, including the lieutenant's position. And yet I never once suspected that he'd do the same to me.

My using this knowledge against him now was below the belt; in a more sane state, I wouldn't have done it. Graden's eyes widened.

"Haven't you ever thought about the fact that your need to know everything about everyone is a serious control issue?" I asked. "And stupid me for ever thinking I might be exempt," I said bitterly. "Clearly, I'm not. So maybe you need to consider the possibility that it's not my problem with 'intimacy.'" I paused to do air quotes, to give my words an extra sting. "It's about your need for control."

I hadn't even known I was thinking those things until I said them. But in that moment, as heated and over the top as it was, I knew I'd hit a core truth about Graden. And about *us*.

At my last words, he physically drew back away from me and fell silent.

"I'd be willing to consider that, Rachel," he said seriously, then looked me straight in the eye. "But I'd ask only that you return the favor: consider the possibility that you've got survivor's guilt over Romy. And that means you can't really let anyone into your life."

The mention of Romy's name shot a red flare off in my brain, ending the possible reentry of rational thought.

"Now you think you're going to psychoanal—"

"Oh, so you can dish it out, but you can't take it!"

He wasn't wrong, but I'd had enough.

"You'd better go," I said. I heard a quaver in my voice at the end that I didn't like. I refused to break down in front of him. I pressed my lips hard against my teeth and held my body rigid.

Graden glared at me. "Finally, we agree about something."

He walked to the door, then stopped, his hand on the knob. He blew out his breath and shook his head.

"I'm sorry, Rachel," he said as he stood looking at the floor. "I thought we were going to be great together," he added quietly, then left.

I was still shaking and cold with fury, and yet it was the leaden feeling in the pit of my stomach that scared me the most. A tiny voice from deep inside me asked, *What have you done?* I let the anger envelop and squash it. I opened the mini-fridge, poured myself a tall Russian Standard Platinum neat, and took it into the bathroom, where I drew myself a steaming-hot bath. I drank until I was warm and the water was cold. Then I got into bed. And cried myself to sleep.

38

I woke up at the obnoxiously early hour of six thirty a.m. with an aching throat and a monster of a sinus headache, the aftereffects of too much booze and too many tears. I crawled out of bed and rinsed my face with warm water. After a few splashes, the congestion started to clear, and I felt marginally better. But my brain still seemed foggy, so I doused my face with cold water—a painful but effective remedy. Then I threw on my robe and, although I had little appetite for food, ordered a bagel and cream cheese to soak up the acid of the large pot of coffee I intended to slug down.

The day was blustery, and a thin, stinging rain spattered against my windows. I appreciated the fact that the weather had decided to work with my mood. Though I still felt fully justified in my fury at the way Graden had violated my privacy, self-righteousness is a cold form of comfort.

And the one thing that really would've helped was the one thing I couldn't have: the shoulders of my buds Toni and Bailey. I'd definitely have to explain why Graden wasn't around anymore, but I couldn't tell them the truth, because I'd never told them about Romy. It would've been different if it'd just been a fight. I would've made excuses for his absence until we made up. But this was a breakup, not just a fight. Graden had violated my privacy once, and that meant it could happen again. Like a crack in the windshield, the damage caused by this breach of trust would only spread over time. I couldn't see a way to patch this up—ever.

A depressingly familiar isolation wrapped itself around me, bringing back the old feeling of inhabiting a separate plane, peering in through life's window at a party to which I'd never be invited. My throat tightened, and hot tears sprung to my eyes as the memories of my child-hood after Romy's abduction flooded through me.

Abruptly I shook my head to stop the thoughts. Enough. I wasn't that little girl anymore. I had a new life, wonderful friends, and a career I loved. And I detested self-pity parties. I resolutely swallowed and blinked until I'd forced back the wave of emotion.

Luckily, it was only Wednesday. That meant I'd have three days to dive into work and put some buffering be-tween my breakup with Graden and the now-unclaimed "freedom" of the upcoming weekend—a looming black hole of unwanted solitude that offered too much time to ruminate on my once-more single state and, more impor-tant, the reasons that led to it...again.

Stop it. I tightened the belt on my robe and deliberately picked up the Bayer file and flipped to my to-do list, then called Bailey.

"Since when are you up and at 'em this early?" she asked.

Without even thinking about it, I defaulted into white-lie mode. "Since I went to bed early. Want to know what I had for breakfast too?"

"No," Bailey said flatly. "It's too early to be that bored."

"I'd like to get back out to the scene and see who else has surveillance cameras on the sidewalk," I said. "See if we can get a different angle on the stabbing."

Bailey agreed to come by and pick me up at eight fifteen, and I pushed out my room service cart and headed for the shower. I'd finished dressing and still had an hour to kill. Since the meeting with the prosecutor, Larry Gladstein, I'd found my thoughts returning again and again to Lilah. I wasn't quite as sure of her guilt as Larry was, and even he couldn't explain why she did it. Whether she was guilty or not, I needed to know who this woman was if I was going to track her down. I started my own private to-do list entitled LILAH. Engrossed, I lost track of time—until the jangling of my room phone made me jump out of my chair. I looked at the clock: eight twenty. *Rats.* I picked up the phone. "I'll be right down," I said.

"Or I'm leaving," Bailey said, and hung up.

By eight thirty, she had found a parking space next to a fire hydrant. It was early, so there were other legal spaces to park, but Bailey's devotion to her job perks bordered on the religious.

"Am I right about you saying Detective Stoner never got to any of these places?" I asked as we got out of the car.

"Sort of," Bailey replied. "He did get to the Subway, but the camera wasn't working."

"The bank video come in yet?" I asked.

"No," she replied. "But any day now."

I looked up and down the street. "Okay, we got the check-cashing place already. That leaves the dry cleaner, the liquor store, and the travel agency."

We decided to hit the dry cleaner first and work our way down the street.

An older heavyset woman with crooked red lipstick and hair that'd been dyed a metallic rainbow of blond hues stood behind the register, talking on her cell phone in what sounded like Russian. A bell tinkled as we opened the door, and she looked up. She said something into the phone before addressing us. "Yes?" she said, her tone annoyed. "You have something to pick up?" she asked impatiently in a heavy Russian accent.

I guess business was so good she could afford to treat customers like a nuisance. Glad to be able to disappoint her, I replied, "No, we're here on a murder investigation."

This information impressed her not at all. She gave us a stony expression. "What murder investigation? I don't know what you're talking about."

I reminded her.

"Hmmph," she replied. "I can't tell you anything. I was working, I don't have time to be looking all around. Anything else?" she asked in a tone that heavily suggested her preferred answer.

"Yes," I answered. "We'd like to see the footage on your surveillance camera from that day. So maybe you should tell your friend you'll call back."

"You have some ID?"

We flashed our badges.

The woman exhaled heavily and all but rolled her eyes,

but she signed off with her friend and motioned to us. "Follow me."

She led us to a back room, behind the motorized racks of hanging clothes in plastic bags. We gave her the exact date and time, and she tapped some keys on the computer on her desk.

"Would you mind starting it an hour before so we don't miss anything?"

Bad choice of words. Of course she minded.

"I can't sit here for an hour," she replied. "I'll miss customers."

Suddenly she's Ms. Customer Service? I raised an eyebrow. "That's what the bell on the door is for, isn't it?"

She gave me another of her stony looks, then tapped some more keys. Grainy black-and-white images of the sidewalk began to play on the screen. It took almost the full hour for Simon to appear. He was walking toward the camera. The woman I now knew to be Lilah was five feet ahead and almost out of frame. Because there were so many people on the sidewalk, it was hard to tell who, if anyone, in the surrounding crowd might've been with her. I told the woman to slow the footage.

Simon moved toward Lilah in jerky frames. His hands were both out and visible. "No weapon in either hand," I said.

Bailey nodded. "And he's, what, five feet behind her?"

I stared intently, hoping to get a view of the stabber and maybe a clearer view of Simon at the moment he grabbed Lilah. The latter would tell me definitively whether Simon had pulled out the box cutter at the critical moment. But as Simon closed in on Lilah, he moved out of frame. That was the last frame that showed Simon. No stabbing. No stabber.

"Damn it," I said, frustrated. "And we can't even see what happened after Simon grabbed Lilah."

"Yeah," Bailey acknowledged. "But it helps as far as it goes."

I shook my head. "If the bank video doesn't give us a view of the killer, Lilah's our only hope."

Bailey and I exchanged a look. The prospect of having to rely on Lilah was not a promising one.

Just then, the bell chimed.

"You're done?" the woman asked.

It was tempting to say no just to irritate her, but I didn't want to waste the time.

"For now," I said.

We followed her out to the front of the store, where a young man in jeans and a big parka was waiting, bopping to the beat playing through his headphones. I hoped he paid her with a bad check.

"Make sure you hang on to that footage," Bailey ordered her. "And don't go anywhere. We may need to talk to you."

"What for?" the woman asked.

"You've got a customer waiting," Bailey pointed out, deliberately evading her question. She gave the woman an insincere smile. "Have a nice day."

As we hit the sidewalk, I had one happy thought: if she gave *us* that much grief, she wouldn't be so quick to co-operate with reporters. It didn't take much to cheer me up these days.

39

The liquor store was farther away from the action, but we checked out the footage anyway. Nada. The travel agency two doors down didn't have anything for us either, though the owner was a charming sort.

"I'm so sorry I couldn't be of more help," he said, sounding like he meant it. "But have you considered a trip to Costa Rica? It's beautiful there this time of year," he said eagerly. "I could get you a great deal."

The mention of Costa Rica made me think of Graden. On our first date, he'd casually mentioned his ten-day trip to Crete and the Greek islands. At that point I'd already begun to wonder how a cop could afford a top-of-the-line, late-model BMW, so when he mentioned that vacation, I started to entertain the possibility of drug money. He'd laughed, seeing the suspicion on my face, and explained about the video game that'd set him and his brother up for life. The memory did nothing for my mood, but that wasn't the travel agent's fault.

"Sounds wonderful," I said. "Maybe some other time."

We walked out to Bailey's car.

I yawned as I buckled the seat belt. The adrenaline of last night's fight now largely burned off, I was feeling the effects of too much stress and too little sleep.

"Thought you got to bed early," Bailey remarked.

Caught in the lie, I was forced to stick with it. "Happens that way sometimes. The more you get, the more you want."

"I've heard that's true about a lot of things." Bailey smirked. "Speaking of which, I meant to ask if you guys had a good time last night," she said, then added with a lascivious grin, "though from the look of you today, I guess I've got my answer."

Now what? I knew I wouldn't be able to put off telling her about our breakup for long, but I wasn't in the mood to get into it right now. Maybe more to the point, I had no idea what I'd tell her about why we'd broken up. I nodded noncommittally and changed the subject.

"You got the bank footage?" I asked. At this point, neither Bailey nor I held out much hope that the bank video would give us anything new. My question was a stall, and it didn't fool Bailey for one minute. She gave me a long look, but she knew better than to push.

"Yeah, I meant to tell you, it just came in," she replied. "Want to go check it out?"

I was about to say yes but stopped myself just in time. Going back to the police station might mean a run-in with Graden. I had a hunch neither of us needed that right now.

"I've gotta get back to work. Mind dropping me at the office?"

Bailey raised an eyebrow, but she wisely left it alone.

"Sure, no problem," she said.

"I'm not optimistic about it. But on the off chance we finally get a shot of our killer, let me know," I said as we pulled up in front of the courthouse.

"Good to see you so excited," Bailey said dryly.

I trotted down the steps and badged my way past the metal detector. When I got to the bank of elevators, I found Toni there, waiting impatiently as she looked from her watch to the lighted panel above. It brought back fond memories of our early days, when we'd place bets on which elevator would hit the lobby first. The sight of Toni was comforting yet unnerving. In all our years of friendship, I'd never managed to get anything by her. The chances of my being able to hide my upset about the breakup with Graden from her for more than five minutes were virtually nil. I was going to have to dream up a plausible story—fast.

I forced a smile and called out, "Tone!"

"Hey, girl," she said, returning my smile. "Been out to lunch with that hunky lieutenant of yours?"

Did everyone suddenly have Graden on the brain? Or was I just now noticing it because I wanted to avoid the subject?

"No," I replied. "I was out with the hunky Bailey Keller on that John Doe case, now known as the Simon Bayer case."

The smile abruptly fell from her face. "You see the *Daily Journal* yet?"

I shook my head. I read the weekly version of the legal newspaper only to catch up on the recent appellate decisions.

Toni looked around to make sure no one who'd care was close enough to hear us.

"Hemet gave 'em a quote about you," Toni said in a low voice.

The set of her jaw told me it wasn't a paean to my legal prowess.

"Said you're just another cherry-picking special unit deputy and you only picked off the homeless-guy stabbing to grandstand in front of the judge."

"What? That's bullshit!" I said, truly shocked.

"Keep it down," Toni said, glancing around us again. "You know you're preaching to the choir," she whispered harshly, her voice drenched with disgust. "But this is exactly what I warned you about, isn't it?"

The elevator dinged its arrival, and we crowded in with the rest of the herd. We had to wait until the fifteenth floor for it to empty out.

"I didn't expect even Hemet to stoop that low," I said.

"Look, if you had any doubt, now you know: it's on," Toni said, her eyes flashing with anger. "So what're you going to do about it?"

I shook my head slowly. We got off at the eighteenth floor, and I punched in the numerical code on the security door to our wing. As we headed to my office, I pondered my options. None was great.

"If I call the reporter and give him a response, I'll make it a bigger deal. You know what they say—"

"You wrestle with a pig, you both get down in the mud, but the pig likes it," Toni finished for me. "Kinda late for that. The mud's flying, and some of it's already on you."

"But there's more to it here. The last thing I need is attention from the press." I explained about having to find Lilah Bayer before the press got its hands on the surveillance footage and spooked her into running.

"So you're trying to outrun them?" Toni shook her head. "Good luck with that."

She sat down in front of my desk and put her feet up on the table by the window. I dropped my purse into my bottom drawer and looked longingly at the bottle of Glenlivet, then quickly slammed the drawer shut and plopped down into my majestic judge's chair—the one I'd proudly corralled after finding it abandoned in the office hallway late one night. On brighter occasions, Toni and I'd tried to picture the scenario that caused it to roll off a judge's bench on the fifteenth floor and into a corridor in the DA's office on the eighteenth.

I slipped off my shoes and curled my feet under me.

"You really think Vanderhorn's going to care what an idiot like Hemet says?" I asked.

"Vanderhorn cares about what makes him look bad," Toni replied. "Hemet's mudslinging about you has 'bad for Vanderhorn' written all over it." She paused and raised an ominous eyebrow. "Especially if anything goes wrong with the case."

"So your advice is, what?" I asked irritably. "Don't let anything go wrong?"

Toni shrugged. "Yeah, pretty much. Just don't lose, and everything'll be fine."

I rolled my eyes. "Gee, thanks, Tone," I said sarcastically. "Why didn't I think of that?"

It came out a lot snarkier than I'd intended.

"Gee, Rache, I don't know," Toni replied. "Maybe because you're too busy jumping my shit?" She stared at me. "What's going on? You are not yourself."

More than her words, Toni's expression of concern brought me to a screeching halt.

"Or, apparently, anyone better," I admitted. "I'm sorry, Tone."

"You want to talk about it?" she asked softly.

Her gentle tone unlocked the angry shell I'd built around the pain of losing Graden, and against my will, I felt tears leap to my eyes. But the middle of a workday was no time to lose it. Mutely, I shook my head and pressed my fingers to my temples as I willed the tears back.

"Okay," Toni said. "You let me know when you're ready."

I nodded.

Her cell phone rang, and she looked down at the number and sighed. "The IO on my geezer bandit case—I've gotta take it."

I waved her off. "Go. And don't worry, we'll talk."

Toni smiled as she opened her phone and headed out to her office.

I tried to lose myself in the work that'd piled up on my desk, but my thoughts kept wandering back to my fight with Graden. Was my need to keep Romy a secret really all about my feelings of guilt? Not just my desire for privacy or an escape from my past? And even if it was guilt, I knew I wasn't just imagining Graden's control issues. So maybe we'd never have made it anyway—Romy or no. The truth was, we'd probably always been doomed. My need for privacy—obsessive as it might be—would always clash with Graden's need to control and know all. Better to accept that it had always been hopeless than believe the lie that we'd ever stood a chance of making it.

I pushed away from that depressing conclusion and found my thoughts returning to Lilah. I pulled out my "Lilah list" and went to work.

I was on my cell, wrapping up a call with my contact in the public school system, when my office phone rang.

"DA's office," I said.

"We got something on the bank video," Bailey said.

"Something—as in a view of the killer?"

"No." Bailey sighed.

"Then we're stuck with Lilah."

"Yeah. We've hit every place within camera range."

I was already in a lousy mood, and this news didn't help—even if I hadn't really expected the bank video to give us the stabber. "Why don't you bring it over?"

"Thought you might want to come watch it here," Bailey replied. "It's on your way home, and we could grab a drink after…"

It *was* on my way home, and ordinarily I'd have been on board with the plan. But now I was suspicious. Was she purposely trying to get me into the station? This was the second time she'd suggested it today. On the other hand, both occasions made sense, so maybe I was just being paranoid? Either way, I wasn't taking the bait.

"I need to finish up some work here," I replied tightly. Even little lies didn't come easy with Bailey or Toni. "Why don't you bring it here and then we can go back to the hotel for a drink?"

I knew that over drinks, I was going to have to tell her about Graden. For all I knew, he'd already jumped back into the dating pool. I didn't want Bailey to find out from someone else. Of course, this meant I had to come up with a decent reason for the breakup, and so far I hadn't thought of anything that'd float. Or, to be completely accurate, anything at all.

Bailey paused a beat, but she agreed. "Be there in ten."

40

It actually took her twenty minutes, but I didn't mind. For some weird reason, I got more work done in those twenty minutes than I'd managed to do in the last two hours.

"What took you so long?" I asked when she appeared in my doorway.

"Ran into Graden on my way out," she replied.

How unlucky could I get? But I didn't think he'd talk about anything personal during work hours, so I was fairly sure he hadn't said anything to Bailey. And I knew he'd never tell anyone about Romy—not after the way I'd reacted. As angry as I was, I still knew I could trust him not to deliberately do anything to hurt me.

I fought to keep my voice even. "Oh?"

Bailey shrugged. "He looked a little rocky, but I guess everyone's entitled to their off days."

She peered closely at me, then looked away. The moment of silence stretched on while I tried to decide whether to just tell her now. Ultimately she made the decision for me.

"Here," she said, producing a disc. "Pop this in your computer."

From the moment the image came up on my screen, I could tell this was a sharper picture than any of the other surveillance footage. It figured that a bank would have better equipment. The camera captured Simon from the front, so that meant it was behind the stabber. We watched as Simon approached Lilah and grabbed her arm, then got shoved off. I paused the disc and pointed.

"Looks like a side view of Yamaguchi, doesn't it?" I said.

"Yep. Confirms his story," Bailey agreed. "Push forward a little way, and you'll see..."

I did and saw that Yamaguchi immediately stepped back, then turned and moved out of range. "Simon's still standing," I said.

"Right," Bailey agreed. "Now put it in slo-mo."

I hit a key, and the disc moved frame by frame. I watched as a hand protruding from a long-sleeved shirt or jacket stretched out toward Simon. The hand was closed; I couldn't tell what, if anything, was in it.

One second later, the hand made a rapid, forceful thrust straight into Simon's abdomen, then quickly withdrew. But as Bailey'd said, the camera hadn't picked up the stabber's face or even his body. Whoever it was immediately moved back and out of range as Simon sank to the ground.

I played it again. This time, as the hand extended, I froze the image and stared.

"So this is all we're going to get on our stabber as far as surveillance footage goes," I said.

Bailey nodded. "We need Lilah."

We exchanged a look. A tough case had just gotten exponentially tougher.

I turned back to the computer screen. "It's a man's hand, no question. Let's get a still blowup and see what we can see. Be nice to find a tattoo or something."

"Be nice to find anything," Bailey groused.

I replayed it three more times, noting the brief glimpse of Lilah's arm and then its complete disappearance. The second time, I concentrated on Simon. The third time, I focused again on the stabber's hand.

"No faces," I said. "But it does get us closer to some answers." I paused the video and pointed to the stabber's wrist. "See that watch?"

"Yeah, I noticed that too," Bailey said. "Looks kinda special."

I nodded. "I'd say it—"

Bailey cut me off. "Say it over drinks and food. Because, speaking of watches"—she glanced at her wrist—"mine says it's time to get out of here."

It was almost seven p.m. Ordinarily this was the shank of the evening for me, when I did my best office work. But I knew I wouldn't be able to focus tonight. And, besides, I couldn't stall much longer. I decided to get it over with and tell Bailey and Toni about my fight with Graden tonight. I'd figure out what to say on the way over…I hoped.

"Want to see if Toni's available?" I asked.

"Always."

I called her on her cell.

"You couldn't walk down the hall and ask me in person?" Toni laughed.

"What if you said no?" I asked, incredulous. "I'd have walked all that way for nothing."

"I need a few more minutes to wrap up. I'll meet you over there."

Fifteen minutes later, Bailey and I walked into the bar at the Biltmore, and I steered her over to a booth near the electric fire.

"Since when do we sit in a booth?" she asked.

We always sat at the bar, in part so we could talk to Drew—the other part so Bailey could check him out when she thought we weren't looking. But Drew was off tonight—one of the reasons I'd wanted to meet here. It'd be hard enough to bear up under a grilling by Toni and Bailey without having Drew chime in too. Before I had the chance to answer, Toni walked in.

"What's up with the booth?" she asked as she slid in next to me.

I signaled to the waiter to bring our "usuals": three Ketel One martinis, straight up with a twist.

"I wanted some privacy," I admitted. "And as soon as we get our drinks, I'll tell you why."

They both raised their eyebrows at me, but they capitulated and caught up with each other while I frantically searched for a believable explanation for my breakup with Graden. In the end, as the waiter approached our table with the tray of drinks, I decided on a version of the truth. As they say, the truth is always the best lie.

We toasted to ourselves and took a sip. Mine was long and hearty.

When everyone had put their glasses down, I said simply, "Graden and I broke up."

Neither of them looked shocked. I was relieved. And a little insulted.

Bailey nodded. "If I hadn't seen him today, I'd have been blasted by this news. But given the way he looked…it figures."

Toni stared pointedly at me. "And you—"

"Have been really special too," Bailey chimed in.

"I know," I said. "And I'm sorry—"

"You don't need to go there," Bailey said. "I get it. But what happened? You guys seemed so great together."

I admit, I was momentarily thrown at hearing the very words that Graden had used last night. Last night? It was hard to believe that only one day had passed, not even twenty-four hours.

"I think he just...got a little too controlling," I said, staring down at my drink. I looked from Bailey to Toni. "You know?"

After a beat of silence, Bailey replied, "Bull."

Toni looked perplexed...and unconvinced. "Was that really news to you, Rache? I mean, look what he does for a living. Isn't that part of the job description?"

I thought about what she'd said. "Probably so," I agreed. "But it's one thing on the job, and a completely different thing when it comes to a relationship."

Toni still looked confused. "But again, you didn't know that to begin with? So why all of a sudden? What happened?"

Damn. Toni was a good lawyer. And so, like any good lawyer, she spotted the flaw and went straight at it. I knew she wouldn't let go until she got an answer she could believe.

"I guess I just didn't see how much it would get under my skin at first," I said. And that was the truth—even if not the whole truth. "Sometimes you can't know how things will play out until you've...played with them awhile." My lame attempt at a joke didn't work. The table remained silent. Neither Bailey nor Toni looked convinced, but they knew better than to press for an answer that simply wasn't coming. At least, not right now.

"So how're you doing, Knight?" Bailey asked gently.

"I'm okay," I said, the words somewhat undermined by my wobbly voice. I quickly swallowed to push down the lump in my throat and added, "Well, I *will* be okay."

I tried to sound confident, if only to convince myself.

"Saying it won't make it so, Rachel," Toni remarked as she looked at me closely. "And this time . . . I don't know." She fell silent.

Bailey's expression told me she agreed with Toni.

"Are you sure it's for good? Everyone has their rocky times." Bailey gestured to Toni. "Just ask the queen of the bumpy road over here," she said with a little smile.

"I have no idea what you're talking about," Toni replied with mock indignation. "But you can't tell me you and Drew don't get into it," she challenged. "You got so mad that one time you threw his boxers into the blender."

Bailey gave a small smile and shook her head. "He had it coming."

"No doubt," Toni replied. "And what happened?"

Bailey shrugged. "New boxers, new blender, we moved on."

"And they're still together," Toni said with a pointed look.

I shook my head, a leaden weight in my chest. "Not happening for us."

The table fell silent, and we all took a sip of our drinks to cover the awkward moment. As we put our glasses down, I saw Bailey and Toni exchange a look I couldn't—and maybe didn't want to—decipher. Telling them about the breakup was almost as stressful as withholding the real reason for it. And I worried that now that the story of Romy had been brought into the present, by consciously withholding it I'd create a distance between us. But I wasn't ready to tell them and wasn't sure if I ever would be. Not knowing what to do, I went for my default mode.

"Mind if we talk about that bank video for a minute, Bailey?"

I was gratified to see the look of relief on their faces at the change of subject. We filled Toni in on what we'd seen.

I concluded by observing, "I watched Simon just before the stabbing. He never pulled the box cutter."

Bailey shook her head. "Didn't have the chance," she agreed.

"From what I saw," I said, replaying the footage in my mind, "by the time Simon got stabbed, Lilah was completely out of his reach."

"No way our stabber can claim self-defense—," Bailey said.

"Or defense of another," I added.

"Then from what I just heard," Toni observed, "your stabber had to have been with Lilah."

"I'd say we can let go of the theory that he was just an unrelated Joe Blow helping a damsel in distress," I agreed.

"So fill me in on Zack's murder," Toni said. "I never did get the full story."

We gave Toni the rundown. When we finished, she sat back and looked from me to Bailey. "Who *is* this Lilah woman anyway? I have never heard of a female killing that way."

"That may be the point," I said.

I explained that assuming she'd committed the murder, Bailey and I believed she'd deliberately done it in the most gruesome manner possible. For just that reason.

"I get it, but still," Toni replied. "Even if she did it to throw off a jury...that's one ice-cold bitch."

Bailey and I nodded. No argument there.

41

Sabrina left the top two buttons on her emerald silk blouse undone. Just enough to intrigue but not advertise. She twisted her hair into a loose bun at the nape of her neck and chose the silver chain earrings to add a little sparkle. She glanced at her watch. She had an hour before Chase was due. More than enough time for what she had planned.

She stopped the taxi at Second and Spring and walked the rest of the way to the Redwood Bar & Grill. Minutes later, she pushed into the darkened lounge and paused just inside the door to let her eyes adjust. After a few seconds, she spotted him. He was sitting alone, a glass with ice and the remains of a drink in front of him. She stood there, watching, getting the lay of the land. He didn't appear to be expecting company. She walked over to the bar and slowly climbed onto the chair two seats to his right. As she settled in, she surreptitiously glanced in his direction. He was staring straight ahead. He did not look happy.

The bartender, who'd been serving two mustached

men in shirtsleeves at the other end of the bar, stopped in front of the man. "Another Glenlivet?"

The man looked down at his glass. "Make this one a Russian Standard Platinum."

"Thought that was your prettier half's drink." The bartender turned and pulled the bottle out of the refrigerator and scooped ice into a glass, then poured a generous shot and set it down. "She coming?"

The man clenched his jaw a moment before answering. "No."

Sabrina leaned in. "Russian Standard Platinum?"

The man seemed not to hear her, but the bartender, who'd been wiping his hands on a towel, turned to Sabrina. His eyes widened and for a moment his mind went blank as he stared. Finally he found his voice. "It's terrific. Would you like to try it?"

"Why not?" she replied, annoyed that the bartender had been the one to answer.

Sabrina took a sip and gave her approval, then stole a look to see if the man was paying attention. He wasn't. She crossed her legs and turned toward him. "I'm Sabrina. And you're Detective...?"

He looked at her out of the corner of his eye without turning.

"I can always spot a cop," she said with a smirk.

He continued to stare straight ahead. "Since this place is two blocks from the Police Administration Building, your odds were pretty good." He took a sip of his drink.

She tried again. "I would've known anyway. I interned with the DA's office, I know the look." She sipped her drink and waited for his reaction.

He sighed and took another sip but didn't respond.

Sabrina finished her drink. "This *is* smooth." She jiggled her glass at the bartender, who, like the men at the other end of the bar, had been staring at her. But if the man next to her had noticed all the attention she was getting, he gave no sign.

The bartender poured her another shot, which was more like a double. She favored him with a smile and he nodded dumbly, gratefully.

The man lifted his glass for another shot. The bartender, still transfixed by Sabrina's smile, took a moment before the order registered.

"Here's to trying new things," Sabrina said, lifting her glass.

Graden Hales exhaled and finally faced her. His expression gave no sign that he was affected by the view. "Look, if you're trolling for cop love, you've got plenty of other opportunities here. And if you don't mind them being married, your odds just doubled."

Sabrina took a long pull from her drink. "You might find it refreshing to have a woman who can pay her own way. And yours. That 'opportunity' will never happen with a county lawyer. Have another one on me, Lieutenant."

Sabrina slapped down a one-hundred-dollar bill, then slid off the bar stool in one fluid motion and walked out. Graden Hales stared after her as he absorbed the import of what she'd just said. Disturbed, he got up and went to the door to see where she was headed. But when he looked outside, she was gone.

When Sabrina stepped off her private elevator, she found Chase sitting on the floor outside the locked door of her office, his head back against the wall, eyes closed.

He took in her cocktail attire and updo, his expression puzzled.

"Just needed a walk." She unlocked the door and looked down at him. "You coming?"

But her eyes glittered with a distant energy. Chase wanted to press her for the truth. Instead, he silently followed her into the office.

42

Bailey and I headed out early for our meeting with the investigating officer on Zack's murder, Rick Meyer.

I hadn't known there was such a thing as an upscale trailer park, let alone one that had gated security, until Bailey described where Rick lived. Rick had bided his time until his dream lot came up for sale: a sweet spot on a bluff overlooking the ocean in Point Dume, Malibu. His small but charming one-bedroom semipermanent trailer had a view of the Pacific unrivaled by the multimillion-dollar properties that crowded the coastline. Now retired at fifty-eight, he was one of the oldest surfers in the water, and probably the happiest. It was too cold in December to sit out on the deck and watch the dolphins, but we could see the ocean from his living room, and that view, plus the sea air, was so relaxing I wanted to ask if I could crash on his sofa for a few months.

Rick himself had gone native in a big way. In his Teva sandals, a torn T-shirt, and faded baggy jeans, no one would ever guess he'd been a homicide detective for the past twenty years—unless they looked closely at his eyes.

They still had the sharp glint of skepticism, the result of hearing too many lies from too many people—only some of whom were in handcuffs.

We spent the first half hour reviewing the evidence in Zack's case, just to make sure we hadn't missed anything in our interview with Larry. I ended by asking about the communiqué between the inmates who were members of Public Enemy Number One.

"Do you have the kite that passed between those skinheads, by any chance?" I asked.

"Got a copy," Rick replied. He leafed through the folder in his lap and handed us a page in a clear plastic sleeve.

We read the note. *PEN1 Ruehls! We nailed that pig in his own pen. NLR suckasses, don't even try to claim this one!*

"Just two punks bullshitting," I said.

Rick nodded. "Way we saw it."

"You looked into Zack's life-insurance policy, I assume?" I asked.

"SOP," Rick confirmed. He looked away for a moment. When he turned back, his jaw was set, but his expression was pained. "Named his brother, Simon, as the beneficiary."

"No shit?" Bailey remarked.

That was significant. Spouses and children are the named beneficiaries on life-insurance policies almost 100 percent of the time. The fact that Lilah wasn't Zack's beneficiary was more than odd. And problematic. Lilah's motive to kill was getting more remote by the minute.

"And what about the house?" I asked. "Who'd it go to?"

"His parents," Rick said. "But that seemed a little less strange—Zack's parents gave it to them in the first place."

"Did you ever look into any of the cases Lilah worked on, the clients she handled?" I asked.

"You mean, did Lilah have a hot prospect for the high life, so she killed Zack—?"

"Or maybe had a client who'd arrange it for her?"

Rick shook his head. "I went there too. But from what I could tell, since she was a junior associate, she didn't have much contact with the clients." Rick shifted in his chair. " 'Course that didn't mean the firm didn't dangle her around to pretty up the landscape now and then."

"And that's all it would take to introduce her to a 'hot prospect' worth killing for."

"Only three problems with that theory," Rick said, holding up three fingers. "One," he said, ticking off a finger, "the playing field was too wide. The partners brought her in on meetings for at least fifty clients. Two," he said, ticking off the second finger, "none of them admitted to having seen her outside those meetings. And, three, I had no proof that any of them were lying."

"But you must've been able to eliminate at least some of them, no?" I asked.

"Tried to," Rick replied with a shrug. "But it was mostly based on supposition, not hard evidence. Like, for example, I started by ruling out the female clients—"

I started to argue, but he held up a hand to stop me.

"You're right," he said with a little smile, "that's biased and maybe wrong. Lilah might've been willing to swing that way—or maybe that's the way she really did swing. But I had to play the odds. Odds were, since we didn't have any indication she had girlfriends, and she'd been married to a man, she'd go for a male client. And I ruled out the smaller fish, the ones making less than five million per."

"That means you ruled out the possibility that Lilah might've actually had feelings for one of these guys," I said, though without much conviction.

"Way I saw it," Rick replied, "someone cold-blooded enough to kill like that probably wasn't looking for love. But like I said, I was just playing the odds, because I had to narrow the field."

"What were you left with?" I asked.

"About thirty-five big players. CEOs, entertainment types, a pharmaceutical company, a lobbying firm, an accounting firm—"

I held up a hand. "I get it. Any of them run or owned by a single guy?"

"A few," Rick replied. "But there was no evidence— and I'm including office gossip here—that Lilah had an inside track with any of them."

I frowned. Since she was that beautiful, and probably that interested in money—I was willing to buy, for now, Rick's theory that Lilah wasn't the type to give it all up for love. But with so much access to big rainmakers, how could she not have found a likely prospect?

Seeing my expression, Rick nodded. "All that big game grazing around her, you'd think she could've bagged one. But every single person I talked to at the firm said she kept 'em all at arm's length. Not a whiff of personal interest. From what they all said, I got the impression Lilah had zero concern with becoming *de*pendently wealthy."

At a seeming dead end on this angle, I moved on to Rick's personal observations of Lilah. Rick had the chance to observe her for the duration—from the moment the case first broke to the very bitter end. A sharp detective can tell you a lot about a suspect that you'll never find in a murder book, and from what Bailey'd said, Rick had been one of the best in the business. I asked him to tell us what he knew about Lilah personally.

"Maiden name Rossmoyne," Rick said, leaning back on the overstuffed, nubby cotton reclining chair, the case file open in his lap. "I think she may've been the smartest I've ever seen...they usually blow it at the crime scene: either act too smooth or act too crazy. Not her, though. Acted pretty much like you'd expect a young wife to act," he replied thoughtfully. "Made only one mistake that I could catch—"

"The inconsistent statement," I said. "At first, she said that she stopped for lunch before she went home."

"Right," Rick confirmed. "A few minutes later, she changed her story and said she'd gotten her days confused. She actually didn't have time to stop for lunch."

"So the defense said it was the natural confusion of someone who'd just seen her husband all hacked up," I surmised.

"Yep," Rick agreed. "I predicted the jury would buy that, and they did. But my opinion? She wanted to say she'd stopped for lunch because it'd put more time between the murder and her finding the body. But she threw up at the scene—"

"So she realized you'd have the emesis analyzed, and that'd show she hadn't eaten anything since breakfast."

"That's my take," Rick said.

"You said she wasn't too smooth or too rough," Bailey said. "Did she cry real tears?"

"Oh yeah," Rick replied. "And out of the ten or fifteen cops around at the time, I was probably the only one who didn't buy her act."

That was definitely saying something, though not necessarily what he intended. I was getting the feeling that both Rick and Larry had been a little too quick to believe that Lilah was guilty. And if that had been the jury's take, the verdict had just gotten a little easier to understand.

"She try to work you?" I asked.

Lilah wouldn't be the first beautiful woman to think she could play up to a detective. And if she had, that would've made a shrewd customer like Rick doubly suspicious.

"Not even a little," Rick replied.

"She have any support people in the audience at trial?" I asked.

"No friends or coworkers," Rick replied. "Just her parents. You talk to them?"

"Not yet," Bailey replied. "Getting ready to, though."

The parents of a defendant are never going to be the most cooperative of witnesses. And with hostile witnesses, it's best to gather information before talking to them. That way, if they try to lie, you have a shot at catching them at it. Hopefully that inspires them to tell the truth—at least some of it anyway.

"They didn't testify for her at trial?" I asked.

"Didn't have to," Rick replied. "They couldn't help with her alibi, and the lawyer was sharp enough to see he had a winning hand with the 'skinheads did it' defense."

"But they were on her side?" Bailey asked.

"Daddy for sure," he said. "He never for one second believed she was guilty. Mommy...I never knew what she really thought." Rick shook his head. "Pam was a piece of work. I gotta admit, I never heard a mom talk about her daughter that way. Ice must run in the family."

"What way is that?" I asked.

"Well"—Rick paused and stared out at the ocean for a long moment—"probably jealous," he finally said. "You saw Lilah's picture?"

I nodded.

"I got the feeling it was about more than looks, though," Rick said, his tone thoughtful, subdued. "Pamela didn't strike me as someone who chose motherhood. More like someone who got stuck with it. And here's Lilah, an attorney with a big, fancy career ahead of her. She had the life Pam wanted and never had a shot at."

Women got to break out of the housewife mold in the '60s, but what they hadn't anticipated was that the bright promise of that iconoclastic time would only lead to a new mold every bit as pernicious as the old one. Because instead of society accepting the fact that some women could do without the 2.3 children, the new group-think was that a woman who wanted a career not only could but *should* do it all—raise a family, run a household, *and* have a career. That was one hell of a daunting to-do list, and if a woman had the baby first, the demands of a new family left very little time—or energy—for career ambitions. But now that women were "allowed" to have careers, there was no sympathy for those who didn't go out and get one, regardless of the obstacles. And so someone like Pam would feel not only stymied in her ambitions but blamed for not achieving them. I found it very easy to see how that could make for one frustrated and jealous mother.

Rick suddenly looked toward the tiny kitchen. "Hey, I'm a hell of a lousy host, aren't I? Can I get you something? Hot tea? Iced tea? Water?"

"No, I'm good," I said. "Bailey?"

"I'm fine," Bailey replied. "Was there anything specific you saw happen between Lilah and her mother?"

"It was little stuff, really," Rick said slowly. "Her tone of voice when she talked about Lilah...kind of negative and...dismissive. Even when she'd say something complimentary, it came out backhanded."

"The parents talked to you?" I asked.

"We hadn't made the arrest yet, so the parents were still somewhat cooperative," Rick replied. "I asked her how Lilah had gotten the interview with that law firm. She had good grades, made dean's list and all that, but she went to a local law school, and I knew that firm only hired from the Ivy Leagues. She said, 'Oh, Lilah always gets whatever she wants.' Technically it was a compliment, but not the way she said it..."

I could hear the bitterness and envy lying just under the words. It said a lot that, even when she was talking to a cop who was trying to nail her daughter for murder, Pamela couldn't keep the resentment at bay.

Seeing my expression, Rick nodded. "There was definitely something 'off' there," he said. "And watching her in court every day...her daughter was maybe going to prison forever, and I don't recall ever seeing her sad, worried, pissed off—nothing."

"But if she felt that way about Lilah, why go to court?" I asked.

"I'm sure the lawyer told the parents it'd look much better if they came. Shows the jury her family's in her corner. And if Daddy came every day and she didn't, she'd look bad."

"To whom?" Bailey asked.

"Didn't matter. The jury, the press—there was some media attention," Rick pointed out. "What people thought was real important to Pam."

"And Lilah's father?" I asked.

Rick pressed his lips together, then exhaled heavily. "Acted tough, and maybe he was tough—with anyone but Lilah. He had a real soft spot for his little girl." Rick shrugged. " 'Course that's just my impression. Dad didn't want much to do with me once he figured out I wasn't going to back off."

So Lilah was Daddy's favorite. Yet another cause for Mommy to be jealous. I stared out at the ocean. Even on this gray, forbidding day, it was beautiful in a wild, austere way. A pelican plunged headlong into the water, then soared back up and flew to an outcropping packed with others. It opened its beak to the sky as though in victory. Its size and angularity made it look prehistoric. I remembered the question our interview with Larry had raised for me.

"Lilah took the stand at her trial," I said. "How'd she do?"

Rick's expression hardened. "Best I've ever seen. Usually when you have a cop for a victim, the jury's a pretty hard sell. They don't like cop killers. But Lilah? She had 'em eating out of her hand. Larry never laid a glove on her." Rick paused and shook his head. "Between you and me, he kinda lost it with her during cross. Never a good thing to get mad like that—makes the DA seem desperate, out of control, you know? Especially with someone who looks like her."

I did know. It was pretty rare to have a defendant testify. Rarer still for one to make a seasoned prosecutor lose his cool that way.

"If you had to guess, you think that's when you lost the case?" I asked.

"Seeing the looks on those jurors' faces when Larry got done, I'd have to say...probably so."

"Any contacts who might know where to find Lilah now?" Bailey asked.

"I never had anyone who claimed to be her friend," Rick said, frowning. "All I ever had were law-firm people and neighbors, and you've already got their statements in the murder book."

Bailey nodded.

"Not much help, I know." Rick shrugged apologetically. "So she dropped off the map, huh?"

"It's like she vanished into thin air," Bailey said, frustrated. "Didn't even give one postverdict interview."

"Not surprising," Rick said, his expression sour. "She got away with killing a cop. She was smart enough to know better than to push her luck."

We all fell silent, pondering where in the world Lilah Bayer might be. The pelican—I thought it was the same one—again took flight and began circling a patch in the water. Meanwhile, seagulls patrolled the coastline, searching for leftovers. One of them suddenly dived toward a bag that'd been left in the sand. When it soared back up, I saw that it had a french fry in its beak.

I had one last question for Rick.

"Did you know Zack?" I asked.

"No," Rick said, shaking his head sadly. "You going to ask me how those two wound up together?"

I smiled. "Pretty common question?"

"Most definitely," Rick confirmed. "But I never did get a good answer."

43

It was early evening by the time we finished with Rick. I hadn't wanted to leave his charming aerie, but we'd run out of questions. Bailey navigated through the narrow streets of the trailer park and pulled onto Pacific Coast Highway, heading toward town. The highway ran parallel to the ocean, and I stared out the window, mesmerized by the vast expanse of gently undulating water that stretched to the horizon under the gray, cloud-filled sky.

"Hungry?" I asked. I didn't have the energy to return to work, and I wasn't keen to get back to my room, where I'd have too much time to think about Graden.

"Funny you should mention it," Bailey said. "How about Guido's?"

In our last murder case, the body of the rapist/suspect had been found in his car, impaled on a tree branch, at the bottom of a ravine in nearby Malibu Canyon. One of the crime scene techs had told us about the warm, familial Italian restaurant that was just minutes away, on the land side of Pacific Coast Highway, but we hadn't had a chance to get there at the time.

"Perfect."

Five minutes later, Bailey pulled into the parking lot. Strings of white lights hung from windows facing the small inlet of water next to the restaurant, giving it a festive holiday feel. At six o'clock the dining room wasn't yet busy, but the small, intimate bar near the entrance was packed with regulars, some talking, some watching the basketball game on the television that hung from the ceiling. The atmosphere was relaxed and convivial, and the manager greeted us like we were his favorite cousins.

He guided us to a booth that overlooked the small inlet. A waiter, who introduced himself as Aris and talked as though we used to get stoned together in high school, brought us water, bread, and a plate of olive oil, and left us menus. I watched a family of ducks paddle serenely across the water as twilight gave way to the silvery luminescence of moonlit clouds. Beautiful.

A busboy carrying a pitcher of water stopped by the table. "Want me to top you off? Or you afraid you'll rust?" he asked, chuckling at his own joke.

"Thanks, we're good," Bailey said.

I smiled as I watched him move down the aisle to another table. "What is up with the staff here? I don't know whether to invite them to the next family reunion or ask to borrow money."

Aris came back, and I ordered an arugula salad and grilled tilapia. Bailey chose the grilled salmon and vegetables. We ordered a bruschetta appetizer and a glass of Pinot Noir for each of us, figuring we'd be here long enough to burn through the alcohol. The second glass would determine who was driving back.

"So," Bailey said after the waiter had brought our wine, "how're you doing?"

Exactly the question I wanted to neither contemplate nor answer. "Okay," I said, taking a sip of wine. I savored the rich, peppery flavor and hoped that'd end the topic.

"I don't know what exactly happened between you and Graden, and I'm not saying it's any of my business."

"Here comes the *but*," I said, leaning back in the booth.

"Yeah, here it comes," Bailey agreed. "But your welfare *is* my business. That means I'm supposed to at least say something when I think you're making a big mistake. This breakup is a mistake. You are not yourself, girlfriend." Bailey paused and looked at me meaningfully. "And, just for the record, neither is Graden."

I wanted to say I didn't care what Graden was, but I knew Bailey would catch the lie. I said nothing.

"You two were really good together and good for each other. You owe it to yourselves to make sure there's no way to work it out—"

"Please believe me, Bailey," I said, my voice brittle even to my ears. "There isn't."

"Rachel, a man can screw up once, learn from his mistake, and never do it again. I know you don't believe that right now, but do me a favor—give yourself a date to think about it again, say, a week from now," Bailey suggested. "Can you at least promise me that?"

"Will you drop it then?"

"Yes," she replied.

"I promise." I picked up the bread basket, took a piece, and offered the basket to her.

Bailey accepted and we both dipped our bread in the olive oil.

"Do we have appointments with anyone tomorrow?" I said, liberally salting the plate.

"Thanks for the side of hypertension," she said, grabbing the saltshaker from me. "I've got us set up to see the hiring partner at the law firm."

"We'll hit the younger associates on the fly?"

Bailey nodded. "And the secretaries."

She took another piece of bread and swiped it around the plate of salty olive oil, then popped it into her mouth and chewed with relish.

Bailey thought a moment, then reached across the table for the saltshaker. "Needs more."

44

Chase closed his laptop and pocketed the flash drive. "Bottom line? You were right. Our esteemed CEO got his start by selling nonexistent homes."

Sabrina nodded absently but didn't immediately reply. Chase frowned. Her increasing distraction over the past few days had begun to worry him. He saw her pull her attention back to him with effort. Yet when she spoke, it was clear she'd heard and analyzed every word he'd said.

"No one ever exposed his bullshit excuse about the construction company having stolen the money."

"Not as far as I can tell."

She drummed her fingers on the arms of her chair. "Find out why no one sued or took their claims to the police. There's a fix in here somewhere, and I'd bet the fixer is higher up on the food chain. I want to bag the CEO *and* his fixer. We'll save the evidence on the fixer for future use."

Chase nodded, relieved that, wherever her mind had been—and he had a feeling he knew—her priorities were still in place.

Sabrina pushed away from her desk, stood up, and stretched. She hit the button that opened the window coverings, and they parted to reveal moonlit clouds in a night sky. She shivered.

"You cold?" Chase asked.

"I've just been sitting too long. I'm going to get a sweater."

Chase waited until she left the room, then quickly went to her desktop and tapped some keys. He'd meant to sneak a quick look before she came back, but what he saw was so upsetting, he forgot the time. She caught him red-handed.

"What the hell—?"

Chase gestured angrily to the monitor. "We agreed *I'd* handle this, Lilah!"

"Sabrina!" she hissed.

"We're alone, Lilah! You've got to stop it. We can't afford to leave a trail."

"Back off, Chase."

He heard the steel in her voice and knew he'd get nowhere with her tonight. He shook his head, his shoulders sagging with defeat. "I just... worry..."

"There's nothing to worry about," she said coldly. "Go home. Get some sleep. You've got a lot to do tomorrow."

A thick knot in his gut told him there was trouble brewing. Big trouble. But he knew that when Lilah obsessed, there was nothing he could do to stop her. She'd do what she wanted to do. He'd just have to hope for the best. Chase slid his laptop into the case and left.

Lilah walked over to the window. She usually found the lights of the downtown skyline soothing. Not tonight. Not any night since Chase had told her they were looking for her. It felt like her brain had gone into a sort of hyperdrive, and her body vibrated constantly with a nervous jangling energy that gave her no peace. Only action gave her some momentary relief.

Like in her encounter with Lieutenant Hales. Lilah hadn't particularly wanted to get Hales into bed. There was no reason—nothing she needed from him. She'd just wanted to reach in and touch something in Rachel's world. Lilah'd considered the possibility that Rachel might be there with him. If she had been, Lilah had planned to fade into a corner and watch them from a distance. But she'd gotten lucky. Graden Hales was alone and seemingly miserable, which was probably why he'd shown so little interest in her. And that had irritated her. That's likely what made her take the risky step of tipping her hand with that last line. But she'd needed to get a reaction out of him, even if she couldn't stick around to see it.

And she knew she'd succeeded. Hales was too smart to miss the little heat-seeking missile she'd fired. At first, she'd been annoyed with herself for letting her temper make her pop off that way. But the more she thought about it, the more certain she'd been that there was no downside—in fact, there was a considerable upside. Because once the import of it all hit him, he'd tell Rachel. And then Rachel Knight would begin to have some idea of who she was dealing with. It couldn't have been more perfect.

Her Rachel Knight campaign had just begun. And it promised to be even more satisfying than the destruction of Brenda Honesdale.

Not even Chase knew about Brenda. The "best friend

ever," the girl who made her feel like she belonged when she'd come home from boarding school in her sophomore year and entered the local high school, a loner and a stranger. Lilah'd experienced for the first time what it was like to have a crowd of friends who were normal kids, and to be accepted as one of them. It was something Lilah'd never known before, and she'd believed her new friends would be hers forever—especially Brenda.

Until the night of the party. When Brenda and all her minions were revealed to be liars and traitors—and Brenda a monster. Lilah never did know what they put in her drink. She only knew that she'd woken up sick and battered, inside and out. She'd stumbled home on wooden legs, clutching her blouse together. Her mother had stared at her coldly—the unspoken accusation heavy in the air. Lilah'd declared that she was never going back to that school. And Pam—Lilah never again called her Mother—was happy to let her earn her GED with a home tutor. The sooner Lilah graduated, the sooner she'd go to college and get out of the house.

Lilah spent years planning and waiting. Waiting for Brenda to have something she cared about, something to lose. Something Lilah could take away. Eventually she got her wish. Brenda married William Sharder, a successful local politician from a wealthy family. And they had a baby. Brenda and William enjoyed a sparkling life filled with luxury, privilege, and power.

Lilah moved in slowly, and—patiently, bit by bit—she began to dismantle Brenda's life. Rumors of Brenda's blackout drinking and prescription-drug abuse began to circulate. No one knew how or when they started. And at first the rumors were just a vague worry—no one really believed them. But on more than one occasion Brenda was seen staggering home, with no memory of where she'd been. Then she got into an accident while driving home from a fund-raiser. The police received a tip that a person driving a car similar to hers had been weaving erratically, so they took her in for a blood test. Though she claimed she'd only had one glass of wine, the drug test showed high levels of OxyContin in her blood. She denied having taken any drugs. By that point no one believed her. On the advice of her lawyer, Brenda pled guilty to drunk driving.

And while Brenda was doing community service picking up trash on the freeway, Lilah just "happened" to run into Brenda's husband, William, at—of all things—a prayer breakfast. They'd gone out for mimosas afterward and wound up in Lilah's bedroom. In the warm afterglow, Lilah told him that she'd lovingly preserved the memory of their tryst on videotape. A young politician with big dreams can't afford scandal, and Lilah kept her demand simple: give her a junior associate position in his white-shoe law firm. He'd been happy to oblige.

The rumors of Brenda's alcohol and drug abuse were now rampant and largely believed. The following year, she was shopping in the local mall when a security guard, acting on a tip, found drugs tucked into the bedding in her toddler's stroller. That led to a felony conviction for possession of methamphetamine. By then Brenda's husband, who was aiming for state office, found he could no longer afford to be married to her—or leave her alone with his child. He left with the baby, taking with him everything in the world Brenda had lived for.

Lilah had been gearing up for the next round and

would likely have gone on for many rounds to come, but Brenda thwarted her. She drew a bath and slit her wrists.

Lilah sat down at her computer and pulled up the screen she'd been viewing. Rachel Knight would be a much more challenging target than Brenda. Lilah began to read. It was an obituary. As she scrolled to the end of the obit, she found a photograph. Lilah stared with gritted teeth at the image of a smiling Rachel Knight, arm in arm with her adoring mother.

45

The next morning dawned gray and brittle, a perfect accompaniment to the day's planned festivities: a visit to Lilah's law firm. Spending the day in a law firm—any law firm—was not my idea of fun. But I hoped someone could give us a line on where Lilah might be now, or at least tell us something more that would help us find this cipher of a woman. So far all I'd managed to do was add to the list of questions about her that'd been running through my mind on an endless loop. I put on my "lawyer clothes" and reluctantly left my firepower at home.

It was a typical white-shoe law firm, occupying the upper floors of a skyscraper in Century City. An elevator dedicated solely to the law office opened onto a glass-encased lobby with thick carpets and window treatments in earth tones. The obligatory modern art hung on the wall behind the predictably coiffed mannequin of a receptionist. She was seated at the epicenter of a semi-circular marble counter. "May I help you?" she asked skeptically.

Neither Bailey nor I had the down-at-the-heels look

(i.e., scuffed-up shoes and dull, boxy suits) of the stereo-typical civil servants. I wore a gray cashmere turtleneck sweater and black blazer, and Bailey wore a black turtle-neck and slacks under her camel-hair midcalf coat. Not bad, but not nearly luxe enough to be clients of this place. And the receptionist's greeting showed she knew it.

"We've got an appointment with Lyle Monahan," Bailey said, handing the woman her card. I handed her mine as well.

"Have a seat, please," the receptionist said dismissively.

She waved her hand at the plush beige leather sofa that was as far away from her desk as you could get without falling through the floor-to-ceiling window.

"I feel banished," I told Bailey after we'd crossed the ten feet to our destination. "Did you see that look she gave us?"

"I think Botox has something to do with her expression," Bailey said. "Don't take it personally."

We cooled our heels for a good fifteen minutes before a baby-faced young man in an expensive navy-blue suit and wing-tip shoes ushered us into the sanctum sanc-torum: a huge corner office with windows that spanned two walls, providing a commanding view of the city that stretched all the way to downtown. It was sparsely fur-nished with a high-tech glass table mounted on a steel sculpture at one end of the room; at the other was an ivory-colored leather sofa and matching barrel chairs. A putting green would've fit nicely between the two group-ings. The young man planted us in the ergonomic ecru leather chairs that faced the desk, said that Mr. Monahan would be right with us, and left.

"Notice how he didn't even ask us if we wanted anything to drink?" I remarked.

"You thirsty?" Bailey asked.

"No," I admitted. "But it's the principle. I think we should threaten to take him downtown for questioning."

"We just got here. I don't feel like going back downtown," Bailey pointed out. "Besides, I don't think that kid knows anything."

"I meant Lyle Monahan," I said with an exasperated sigh. "I think we should make him sweat."

"You watch too many cop shows," Bailey said as she took a leisurely look around the office.

"Tell me you don't sweat people."

"I don't sweat people," she replied, deadpan.

Clearly I'd have to do the sweating myself.

The desk was sparklingly free of anything that resembled work. However, there was a miniature Japanese Zen garden on the desk. The pretension of this tickled me, and I'd just picked up the tiny rake to draw a very un-Zenlike message in the sand when the man himself strode into the office.

"Sorry to keep you waiting," said Lyle Monahan.

His tone told me the sentiment wasn't entirely sincere.

He was a beefy Irishman with thinning reddish hair who was trying very hard to look like a Calvin Klein model in a black silk V-necked sweater, charcoal blazer, and slacks. Looking at him was like seeing Beverly Sills sing hip-hop.

He extended his hand, first to Bailey, then to me. It was a professional handshake: just enough squeeze and pause to make you feel noticed but not so much that you'd get the idea you were actually friends.

"I understand you want to talk to me about Lilah Bayer," he said evenly as he rounded the desk and sat down in the ivory leather chair that I'd bet was custommade for his very special derriere. "I've got a meeting in"—he glanced at his watch, a Patek Philippe, of course—"ten minutes, but that'll probably be enough, because there isn't much I can tell you. The extent of my knowledge of Lilah was that she did excellent work and was particularly good with the complex contract cases. A very bright young woman."

"But bringing her into this firm was pretty unusual, wasn't it?" I asked. "You only hire from the Ivy League schools."

Lyle gave me a cold look.

"Actually, it wasn't that unusual," he replied. "We make it a point to integrate young lawyers of diverse backgrounds in this law firm in order to offer a more comprehensive breadth of life experience—providing they have the grades."

"But your other non–Ivy League hires were all minorities," I said. "Lilah was the only 'white hire' who didn't come from an Ivy League school, wasn't she?" Naturally I already knew the answer.

"I wasn't aware of that, quite frankly."

Bailey could see I was spoiling for an unproductive fight, so she stepped in. "When did you last have contact with Lilah?"

"I personally had my last contact with her some time before her arrest," Monahan replied. "I can't at this time remember exactly when that was. But once she was arrested, we let her go, and I had no further contact with her after that point. I doubt anyone else did either—"

"You didn't personally fire her, then?" Bailey asked.

Monahan shook his head. "No, it was handled by one of the junior partners."

"Do you have any idea how to contact Lilah now, or where she might be?" I asked.

"None," Monahan said with finality.

His tone told me he was glad to give this answer. I had no reason to doubt the truth of it.

"Did you ever meet her husband, Zack?" I asked.

Monahan shifted back in his seat and put his hands on the armrests. "No," he replied, his tone displeased. "In fact, I never even knew she was married."

"It wasn't indicated on her application?" I asked.

"As far as I can recall, she was single when she applied," Monahan said.

I'd be willing to bet a month's paycheck that when she was hired, he'd made it his business to find out.

"And she never updated her information to indicate she'd gotten married?" I asked, intrigued.

"She should have," Monahan admitted. "But if she wasn't trying to get him health-insurance coverage, it wouldn't have been a pressing concern."

"And she never brought him to any office functions?" I asked.

Monahan shook his head. "The firm has only one or two office-wide parties a year. There isn't much opportunity for young associates to bring in their significant others. And they often choose not to. Office talk is boring."

The explanations were plausible enough, I supposed. But for some reason I wasn't convinced. Then something else occurred to me.

"Did you ever mention to the detective that you didn't know Lilah was married?" I asked.

Monahan cleared his throat, the first sign of discomfort. I enjoyed the sight.

"It never came up as far as I can recall," he said.

He was starting to sound like Oliver North. Memory failure, done right, can be the most effective way to avoid getting pinned with prior inconsistent statements. All lawyers know this.

"Really?" I asked skeptically. "It never occurred to you to tell the detective in charge of the case that you had no idea the suspect was married to the victim?"

Monahan looked down his beaked nose at me. "No, it didn't, Counsel," he said coolly. "I had very little interaction with Lilah, and even if I did, I'd have no reason to ask her about her marital status. So the fact that I didn't know of her marriage was of no import whatsoever."

Though I was itching to get into it further with this pompous ass, it was a waste of time. The fact that Lilah may have kept her marriage a secret was interesting and possibly germane. But the fact that Monahan had failed to tell the police about it was, at this point, irrelevant.

"Do you have a human-resources type who keeps track of personnel information?" I asked.

Monahan looked annoyed, but he nodded reluctantly. "We do," he said. "I'll have someone take you to Audrey's office. I've got to get to my meeting."

46

CRITI BY DEGREES 279

But Audrey Wagner, the paralegal in charge of human resources, hadn't known about Lilah's marriage to Zack either.

"Don't the lawyers usually keep you up to speed with their personal information?" I asked.

"Usually," she said, peering at me through hip-looking black-framed glasses.

She pushed a stray hair back into the bun twisted at the nape of her neck with brisk efficiency. That hair had some nerve.

"Did she have health coverage through the firm?" I asked.

Audrey scrolled through the file on her computer. "Yes, the standard employee deal. Individual, no spouse, no children."

"Did she leave you any contact information after she got fired?" I asked. "Any place to forward her mail?"

"I never heard a word from her after she got arrested. So, long story short, no." Audrey thought for a second. "Matter of fact, I don't even know that I ever had any kind

of backup or emergency contact information for her."
Audrey scrolled further, then tapped a few keys. "Well,
she did provide her parents' address." She frowned at
the screen, then looked up at us. "I'm not sure I'm allowed…"

"It's okay," Bailey said. "We've already got it."

"Good. Anything else I can help you with?" she asked.

Audrey really seemed to mean it. I appreciated that.

"Can you tell me if anyone else got hired around the
same time as Lilah?" I asked.

Audrey peered at the monitor and jotted something
down on her notepad, then punched some keys.

"Phyliss Blankmeyer and Joel Carstone," she read
from her screen. "You can find them one floor down." She
gave a wry smile. "Where we keep the 'help.' I can give
you their numbers," she offered.

"That'd be great," Bailey said.

Audrey wrote the information on her notepad, tore off
the page, and handed it to Bailey.

"Audrey," I said, "you're a breath of fresh air. Thank
you."

"Actually," she said, shooting a careful look over my
shoulder at the hallway, "I'd much rather work with criminal lawyers. So much more interesting. You're in the
DA's office, aren't you?"

"I am," I replied. "And you're right, we are more interesting."

Why be modest?

"Do you mind telling me what they pay senior parale-
gals?" she asked.

I told her.

"Oh," she said, her eyes widening for a moment. She

adjusted her glasses. "Well, good luck. Let me know if you need anything else."

Once again, the promise of meager financial reward had choked the life out of a budding career in criminal law.

Bailey and I made our way downstairs. Exercising our superior investigatory skills, we quickly succeeded in locating our targets. The nameplates on their office doors did help.

"I haven't known anyone named Phyliss in a long time," I remarked.

Bailey nodded. "It fell off the 'cool baby name' list a while ago."

We found uncoolly named Phyliss just as she was pushing away from her desk. No doubt getting ready for the only physical exercise she and all the other young associates would get that day—a trip to the cafeteria for a fast lunch.

"Knock, knock," Bailey said from the threshold as she held out her ID.

Phyliss, a short-haired, no-nonsense, athletic-looking type, involuntarily stepped back a few feet when she saw Bailey's badge.

"Whoa," Phyliss said, holding up her hands. "I know I was a little late with my parking tickets, but isn't this kind of extreme?"

"Parking is no laughing matter, Ms. Blankmeyer," I said sternly.

"And you are?" she asked me, looking alarmed.

I pulled out my badge. "Rachel Knight, DA's office."

"You've got to be kidding me," she said, looking from me to Bailey.

"Yeah, I am," I said with a little chuckle. "Just a little law-enforcement humor. Crushing crime one lame joke at a time."

Bailey shot me a look. "We'd like to talk to you about Lilah Bayer."

Phyliss sighed and shook her head. "Okay. But I can't tell you any more than I told the first guy—"

"Rick Meyer?" I asked.

Phyliss squinted. "I think so . . . yeah. I haven't seen Lilah since she got arrested. Man, that was gnarly."

"You have any idea where she might be now, or how to reach her?" I asked without much hope.

Phyliss shrugged. "Once she got arrested, she was untouchable. All of a sudden, everyone had amnesia. 'Lilah who?' I've got to admit, I felt a little sorry for her. I mean, we all know it's bull, but still, whatever happened to innocent until proven guilty?"

"Was there any talk of rehiring her after she got acquitted?" I asked.

"They might've talked about it—if she'd ever asked to come back," Phyliss said.

But she hadn't even tried. It was somewhat surprising, and it was significant. Her old law firm was the most likely place to forgive her past—and, granted, those odds were long. But any new place where she hadn't already proven her merit wouldn't want to take a chance on someone who'd been on trial for first-degree murder. She had to be doing something—and whatever it was had to be way off the radar, because we couldn't find any trace of it.

"You ever hang out with her when she was an associate?" I asked.

"Yes and no," she said. "Lilah'd go out with us after

work every once in a while." Phyliss stopped so abruptly, I got mental whiplash.

"But?" Bailey prompted.

Phyliss stared past us, her gaze unfocused. "I never really felt like she was there to hang. It was like she just wanted the latest dope on office politics. Lilah was super-ambitious." She quickly added, "Not that we all weren't, but…"

Phyliss again paused suddenly. It was a dramatically effective gambit that both she and some rather famous actors overused. But it could be handy in a closing argument.

This time, I did the prompting. "She was more so?" I asked. "How?"

"No wasted motion," Phyliss said. "She was totally focused on the bottom line one hundred percent of the time. Lilah did the work, no question about it. And she was good. But she worked the personal angle just as hard—"

"You mean schmoozing with the partners?" Bailey asked.

"Yeah," Phyliss replied. "She had the looks, and she used them. Bent the men around her little finger like they were pipe cleaners."

I detected more than a tinge of jealousy in Phyliss's voice. I couldn't say I blamed her.

"She ever have an affair with any of the partners?" I asked, thinking that our buddy Lyle Monahan, the senior partner, was a likely conquest. "Or a client?"

"Clients, I wouldn't know about," Phyliss said. "We didn't work the same cases. Partners…not that I ever heard. And I would have, because that kind of news travels fast around here." She paused, then added, "I really don't think Lilah did have anything happening on the side. She was smart enough to know better than to play favorites. Lilah never let anyone in too close. Not us, not the partners—nobody."

"Did you know she was married?" I asked.

"None of us did. And that was a shocker. Believe me, Lilah being married to a cop was not something any of us would've guessed."

This appeared to be a popular sentiment. Since we seemed to have come full circle, I asked Phyliss if she had any other observations or information to add. She didn't.

"We need to talk to Joel," I said. "Do you know where his office is?"

"Two doors down," Phyliss replied. "Though he probably left for lunch by now. Come on, I'm on my way out. I'll show you."

We followed Phyliss down the hall. Before we got to Joel's office, a young male voice called out to us.

"Can I help you with something?"

The voice belonged to a male secretary in a shirt and tie who was eating an obnoxiously healthy-looking sandwich of sprouts and avocado at his desk in one of the partitioned cubicles. The nameplate next to his computer said he was Teddy Janeway.

"Joel Carstone?" I asked.

"May I ask what this concerns?" Teddy inquired, his tone polite but firm.

Why oh why couldn't I get a secretary like this instead of Melia? Then I remembered Audrey's reaction when I told her the salary range at the DA's office.

Bailey identified us, then explained, "We want to talk to him about Lilah Bayer."

"Really?" Teddy remarked, looking at us with interest. "Let me see if I can find him."

He picked up his phone and punched in numbers.

Phyliss gave us a mock salute. "Since my duty seems to be done here, and I've got about seven minutes left for lunch—"

"No worries, Phyliss," I said. "You've been great. Thank you."

"Not a problem," she said.

She moved in long, fast strides toward the elevators, and Bailey and I went over to Teddy Janeway's desk. He hung up, shaking his head. "Joel's not answering for some reason."

"Do you know how long he'll be gone?" I asked.

"Twenty minutes, tops. None of these juniors get a real lunch."

So the cliché about slave labor in the big law firms was true. On the other hand, I had little cause for celebration. My hours were no better and my pay was a heck of a lot worse. I pushed away this irksome train of thought and considered what to do next.

I didn't want to wait. Based on what we'd seen so far, it seemed unlikely that Joel would give us anything new. Plus, I hated waiting—for anything.

"Did you happen to know Lilah?" Bailey asked Teddy.

"As Lilah Rossmoyne," he replied. "And if you're wondering whether Joel knew her well, the answer is no. He was just a junior associate, so he didn't have any clout. And he's not the political type, so he didn't have any juicy information either. Therefore, Lilah had no use for him whatsoever." Teddy's tone implied he had uniquely confidential information.

"How well did you know her?" I asked, intrigued.

"We didn't hang," Teddy replied. "But I keep my eyes open, so I notice things. And from what I saw, Lilah really didn't have any friends."

I nodded. "Which is why no one knew about her marriage to Zack."

"Exactly," Teddy replied, then looked around the near-empty office. He wiped his mouth neatly, dropped the napkin into the wastebasket, and stood up. He leaned toward us and spoke in a low voice. "But when the case first broke, I saw a picture of her husband on the news."

Teddy again scanned the room quickly before continuing in a voice barely above a whisper.

"I *recognized* him," he said. "You can ask anyone around here. I'm one of those people who never forget a face, even one I've only seen for a few seconds."

Pattern recognition. Some have it, some don't.

Teddy had stopped to let a beat of silence build the suspense. Seriously, what was it with the people in this law firm and their addiction to the "pause for dramatic effect"? If I'd worked here, I'd have smacked someone by the end of the first week.

"And?" I prompted.

"It was just a few months before the murder," Teddy said. "He was here—"

"Here?" I asked. "In the office?"

Teddy shook his head. "No, he was sitting in a car, parked out in front of the building. But in a regular car and civilian clothes."

"What made you notice him?" I asked.

People sitting in parked cars couldn't be that unusual

around here. The area was filled with twenty-story office buildings.

"The fact that I saw him out there on at least three different days," Teddy said. "And the way he just *sat* there, watching the front entrance, not doing anything. Something about the way he looked just…bothered me."

It bothered me too.

"Why didn't you tell the police about this?" I asked.

"I did," Teddy said, his tone peevish. "And I can't remember which cop I told, so don't ask me for a name," he said, anticipating my next question. "I just remember that when I told him, the cop looked at me like, 'Uh-huh, *sure*,'" Teddy mimicked and then sniffed. "He didn't believe me—thought I was one of those fools who'll say anything to get his name in the news."

Bailey and I exchanged a look.

"We believe you, Teddy," I said.

47

Bailey and I thanked Teddy and left the plush confines of Lilah's former employer.

I thought about our next move. Especially after having heard what Teddy had to say, I wanted to get a better sense of who Zack was.

"Want to hit Glendale PD?" I asked.

"May as well," Bailey replied.

Glendale was only twenty minutes from downtown, but it still felt like the older, middle-class suburb it'd been back in the '50s. The Glendale Police Department was smack-dab in the middle of the residential section of town. It struck me that this would've made the skinhead attacks on the station that much scarier for everyone involved. Which, of course, would've made Lilah's defense tactic that much more effective.

I'd hoped to talk to the lieutenant who'd testified at the trial about the attacks by the skinheads, but he wasn't in. We settled instead for Sergeant Paul Tegagian, a jovial, slightly pudgy man who seemed happy to have the distraction of chatting with us.

"Call me Paul," he said when we'd introduced ourselves and the reason for the visit. He gestured to a couple of metal-framed chairs in his tiny office and plunked himself down in the secretary's chair behind the small, cluttered desk.

I started out with the most pressing but least likely to be productive question. "Have you had any contact with Lilah since the verdict?" I asked.

"Nah," he replied. "And I can promise you, no one else has either. She's a stone-cold killer. You won't find any fans in this shop." Paul's voice was hard with anger.

"What can you tell us about Zack?" I asked.

Paul relaxed back into his chair.

"Zack was pretty well liked around here," he said. "He was a good cop, and a smart one. Always had his eye on the ball and a nice word for everyone—"

"So he was popular with the troops?" Bailey asked.

"Definitely," Paul replied. "Plus, Zack wanted to make captain, and you know what they say about more flies with honey than vinegar." He laced his hands behind his head. "Not to say it wasn't genuine, but he was a pretty sharp guy, politically speaking."

"How'd he meet Lilah?" Bailey asked.

Paul looked up at the ceiling. After a brief pause, he shook his head. "You know, I never knew, and never really thought about it." He added, with a sour twist of his mouth, "With someone as hot as Lilah, you don't wonder about something like that."

"Did you know Zack before he met Lilah?" I asked.

"It's a small department—everybody knew each other."

"Did you go to his wedding?"

At that, Paul frowned. "They eloped. Didn't want to waste money on a big wedding." He shrugged. "Made sense to me at the time, though now I wonder...about everything."

"Like what?"

"Like she was on track to be a big-time, fancy lawyer—not like you guys, no offense—"

"None taken," I said, wondering how many more times I could possibly be reminded of my lowly civil-service status in a single day.

Taking me at my word, Paul continued. "I mean, what was she doing with a cop—even if he did manage to make captain? I could see why they'd hook up for a while. But married? It just didn't fit. Don't know why, but I never questioned it before." Paul looked down at his desk, then added quietly, "Wish I would have."

It probably wouldn't have mattered if he had. When it comes to sex and romance, people are going to do what they want, no matter how ill-advised. Yet another topic I didn't need to dwell on.

"Did you get to know Lilah at all?"

"No," Paul replied. "Zack only brought her to a couple of the bigger wingdings, where no one really had a chance to talk."

"Did they socialize with any of the other cops as a couple?"

"Nope," he replied firmly.

"You know why that was?"

In my experience, especially in the smaller departments, officers tended to hang together when they were off duty. That usually meant the wives did too.

"Lilah wasn't into it, you could tell," Paul said. "On

the rare occasion when she showed up, she'd be polite, but it was an effort." He fell silent for a moment. "But to tell you the truth, I never heard of Zack trying to schmooze around with anyone either. He'd hang out with the guys, especially if any brass was around, but he didn't go drinking, and as far as I know he never invited anyone over to his place."

So Zack was a loner and a climber too. He and Lilah did have something in common after all, and it was not insignificant. Ambition had fueled the fire of many marriages—which made it only harder to see what Lilah's motive was for murdering Zack. What Paul said next made it harder still.

"Got to say, it really rocked my world when I heard about them starting a family," he said, shaking his head.

"What?" I asked, sure I hadn't heard right.

"Yeah," Paul said, his expression perplexed. "Came out in some article during the trial that Lilah had been seeing a fertility doctor. I'm sure the defense leaked it on purpose. You know, 'How could she possibly have killed him if they were trying to have a baby?' But it was the first we'd ever heard about it."

This did not fit the profile for either of them, but especially not for Lilah. Babies and the partner fast track don't mix.

"Did you believe it?" I asked.

"Article gave the doctor's name," Paul replied. "So I'd guess there had to be records to back it up."

It was easy to check. Paul remembered that the article had been in the local Glendale papers, which explained why we hadn't run across it during our first, cursory search. Bailey accessed the news archives and found the article. The doctor's office was in Glendale. A phone call got us an immediate appointment with the doctor's record keeper.

The promise of a formal subpoena duces tecum got us an informal chat with the nurse.

Sure enough, she confirmed that Lilah had been getting injections of Clomid, a fertility drug.

48

Bailey drove down Alameda Avenue toward the Golden
State Freeway, which would take us back downtown.
I'd wanted to interview some of Zack and Lilah's
neighbors who'd lived nearby, but it had been a long
day and we'd both run out of steam. Not to mention
the fact that the likelihood of finding a neighbor at this
point who'd add anything of substance was pretty low.
Door-knocking the 'hood was Standard Police Proce-
dure 101, and Rick had hit every single house within
a five-block radius. In short, the neighborhood interviews would keep.

But I did want to get a look at the murder house. I always had to see crime scenes for myself. Even in cases
like this, where the crime was already years old and the
exact site of the murder no longer existed—the new owners had filled the basement with concrete in an effort to
wipe out all memory of its bloody history—I liked to at
least see the area. It put the events in context for me.

"How about if we go to the house?" I suggested. "Just
a quick drive-by."

Bailey looked at her watch. "May as well. It's already rush hour, so we're screwed anyway."

She made a U-turn, then took Glenoaks Boulevard to Louise Street and pulled to the curb across the street from the house. It was completely unremarkable. Roughly two thousand square feet, it had a fresh-looking coat of white paint and green shutters that framed the two paned windows facing the road. I could see that all the lots on the block were narrow but ran deep, providing a decent backyard for planting or playing. A great house for kids, as the minivan in the driveway attested.

"Did you know that real estate agents are required to tell prospective buyers if a violent crime was committed on a property?" I asked Bailey.

"Do now."

"Would you buy a house if you knew someone had committed a murder in it?"

Bailey looked in her rearview mirror for traffic, then pulled away from the curb. "Doubt it."

Bailey? Afraid of ghosts? "Bad vibes?" I asked.

"Nah. I just wouldn't be able to stop looking for evidence."

Of course.

Bailey merged with the barely crawling traffic on the freeway, and we inched along in silence as the weak gray light of day faded into darkness.

"I don't know what to make of that fertility-drug business," I said. "Even if she decided she didn't want kids, there are a lot less drastic ways to avoid pregnancy than killing the guy."

Bailey nodded. "But I also don't buy the claim that it shows she didn't do it either."

"Not because of that, no."

"'Not because of that'?" Bailey asked. "You're thinking she didn't do it?"

"I'm just wondering," I said. "The harder we look, the less I see. Seems like the evidence gets less and less compelling—at least from where I'm sitting."

It was like watching the sand flow out from under your feet when the wave recedes.

Bailey sighed. "It does, doesn't it?"

It was a relief to hear that I wasn't the only one having doubts. "I'd like to come up with one rock-solid piece of evidence that'd make me sure—either way."

"Yeah. I keep going back and forth in my head. 'She did, she didn't.' The jury's verdict seems less and less crazy."

I agreed. It was maddening. I felt as though no matter how I twisted the lenses to bring Lilah into focus, her image stubbornly remained blurry. I watched the downtown buildings grow as we drew closer to the city and pictured myself going back to my room and ordering dinner, knowing there'd be no call from Graden. An icy chill spread inside my chest, and I reflexively wrapped my arms around my middle.

"Hey, would you mind dropping me at Checkers? I need a change of scenery."

The restaurant was near enough for me to walk home, and being alone wouldn't feel so bad in a different place.

One minute later, she pulled over to let me out.

"I'll call you," she said.

"Good deal." I got out, patted the roof of the car, and nodded to the doorman, who welcomed me inside.

I could've eaten at the bar but decided to give myself a

solitary fine-dining experience instead. The dining room was spacious but not so big that it lost warmth, and the decor of soft, warm colors, gentle lighting, and white tablecloths was soothing. I asked for a corner seat against the wall.

A waiter who really knew how to work his fitted vest gave me a menu and took my drink order. I decided to splurge on a bottle of Ancien Pinot Noir.

A few minutes later, he returned and poured a taste for me. Delicious. The waiter filled my glass, and I ordered a grilled-artichoke appetizer. Then I took a long sip of wine, sat back, and felt the rough edges of the day begin to smooth out. I looked around the restaurant. From my relatively hidden corner, I could be subtle about watching my fellow diners.

An older woman in her seventies, dripping with heavy diamonds and also dining solo, imperiously gave her waiter one of the most detailed critiques of a bread basket I'd ever heard, added an elaborate order that included how each dish was to be prepared, and capped it all off by commanding that her food be brought "right away." The waiter took it all in stride with a courteous bow. I'd done a few stints as a waitress during undergrad and law school, and I couldn't remember anyone being as high-handed as this lady.

The waiter brought my artichoke, and as I pulled off the first leaves, I heard the woman talking. I turned to see that she was in animated conversation, hands flying, expression lively, laughing and gesturing...to an empty chair. Riveted by the bizarre scene, I didn't notice that anyone was nearby until I heard my name.

"Rachel?"

The familiar voice startled me. It was out of place, so I couldn't immediately make the connection. But when I looked up, there he was, smiling.

The former love of my life.

49

Daniel Rose was a lawyer's lawyer. When attorneys talked about the best in the business, his name was always front and center. He'd turned that considerable reputation into a niche business by becoming a Strickland expert—a lawyer who gives expert testimony on the competence, or lack thereof, of other lawyers. It was a job that took him all over the country, both for testimony and for lectures. But we'd begun dating during his slow season, so I hadn't known how much time he actually spent on the road. We had six blissful months before the other shoe fell. When it did, my old fears of abandonment and commitment came flooding back and ultimately drowned our love. Of course, at the time I didn't have enough insight to realize that that was the problem—understanding came later. It'd taken me a long time to get over him, and there'd been many nights when I'd thought it'd never happen. Eventually, though, the wounds became scars and the scars thickened and grew tough. I moved on. And with Graden in my life, I'd thought my feelings for Daniel had finally ebbed away. But seeing him now, twinkling eyes behind wire-rimmed glass, thick salt-and-pepper hair—now a little more salt than pepper—I wasn't so sure.

"Daniel," I said, trying to force my throat to open. "What are you doing here?"

His smile was warm. "I'd guess the same as you."

I glanced behind him but didn't see anyone.

He saw me looking. "I'm alone," he said. "You too?"

I nodded, aware that my answer applied to more than just dinner.

"Would you like some company?" he asked. "Please feel free to say no. I don't want to intrude."

"No, not at all," I said, feeling a smile spread across my face. "Sit. Try this wine."

After he sat down, I leaned in and whispered, "And don't look at that lady behind you."

"Now I *have* to."

"I know, but be subtle."

He managed to be graceful about it, turning just a hair farther than necessary when the waiter came to take his drink order. Daniel said he'd share my wine, then took another moment to watch as the waiter responded to the woman's peremptory wave. Daniel turned back, chuckling softly.

"She's drunk as a skunk," he observed. "And still manages to be imperious."

"But her imaginary friend seems like fun," I remarked.

"Lucky her," Daniel said. "Mine are all pissed-off judges."

"They're not imaginary. And they're not your friends."

"That explains a lot," Daniel said with a rueful smile.

"What brings you downtown for dinner all by yourself?"

"I've got a trial of my own for a change," Daniel replied. As opposed to being a witness on someone else's case.

"What've you got?"

"Civil case. I'm suing an insurance company for denial of benefits."

"Doing the Lord's work. Here's to that." I raised my glass, and we clinked and drank. I'd finished my wine, and Daniel picked up the bottle to pour.

"Empty," he said, examining the Pinot Noir in the light. "This is unacceptable. I deserve more toasts for my display of valor against the forces of darkness—"

"So we're not counting your hefty contingency fee?"

"The one I don't yet have and may never get?" he replied, flagging the waiter over.

I raised an eyebrow. "Yes. That one."

I knew he'd win the case, but we don't jinx each other by saying things like that. The waiter appeared, and Daniel ordered another bottle. We both asked for the Colorado rack of lamb with osso buco ragout.

"So you're driving downtown every day?" I asked. "That's a hell of a commute."

Daniel had a home in Hidden Hills, near Calabasas. It was a beautiful, horse-zoned, very pricey neighborhood, but it was at least an hour from downtown. With morning commuter traffic, it'd take him closer to two hours.

"I know, that's why I'm not doing it," Daniel replied.

The waiter returned with the bottle and poured a taste for both of us. We approved, and he poured us each a glass.

"You're not?" I asked when the waiter left.

Daniel shook his head. "I'm staying downtown in a condo for the duration. You still in the Biltmore?"

I nodded.

"I'm about six blocks away from you," he said, smiling.

I managed to stretch a polite smile across my face and say something like "That's great." Then I picked up my glass of wine and gulped it like it was a Slurpee.

50

Though I was definitely enjoying myself, it was also stressful trying to have a friendly chat with a man who'd once been my most significant other, and for the first half hour, I'd avoided Daniel's eyes, afraid of the intimacy. The discovery that he was living just a short walk away didn't help matters any.

But bit by bit I relaxed as we fell back into the effortless conversation of two people who'd shared their lives and still shared a world. By the time we called for the check—I insisted on splitting—I was sorry to see it end.

"You heading back to the Biltmore?" Daniel said as we stood and pulled on our coats.

"I am." I hoped he wouldn't ask to join me there for a nightcap. It'd been a great evening, but I was still emotionally wobbly, and in that condition, more alcohol plus Daniel might equal doing something really stupid.

"I've got my car," Daniel said. "Let me drop you."

I wasn't sure that being alone in a car with Daniel was my best move either. Actually I *was* sure. It wasn't.

"Thanks, but I need the exercise. I've been cooped up

in a car all day with Bailey." I smiled and added, to ease the moment, "But I'll wait for your car with you. The more air I can get, the better."

Daniel responded with a tight smile, aware of the unspoken message behind my words. It was a vivid reminder of the heaven and the hell of him: he missed nothing. It'd been a real source of stress in our relationship, because he never bought my bullshit excuses—even when I, in my usual self-deluded state, believed them.

"Okay," he replied. "I'll meet you outside."

"I'll give your ticket to the valet."

"Great, thanks," he said, and loped up the stairs in the direction of the restroom.

I stepped outside into a blast of cold air and buttoned my coat as I handed the ticket to the valet. The doorman wasn't around, and when the valet trotted off to get Daniel's car, I was alone on the sidewalk.

The street was dark and empty at ten o'clock, even on a Friday night. Suddenly a feeling of menace crawled up my back. My heart gave a thud as I peered into the darkness, trying to find a shape or silhouette that was out of place. I stepped off the curb to get a better view as I pushed my hand deeper into my pocket, reaching for the reassuring feeling of my gun. It wasn't there. I remembered I'd decided not to take it this morning. It figured. I stared into every doorway and alcove but saw nothing. Still, the sense that someone was watching, waiting, stayed with me. It'd be a stupid place to attack someone, but people got killed in stupid ways all the time. I edged back up onto the sidewalk. Just then, something brushed my back. Electric with fear, I jumped and opened my mouth to scream.

"Hey," Daniel said.

I froze and clamped my mouth shut. Before turning to face him, I quickly blinked to rid my eyes of the panic I knew was written there.

"You okay?" he asked.

"I'm fine."

I could feel Daniel's skeptical look, so I pulled my head down into my coat and made a big show of huddling against the cold to cover my nerves. He started to say something, but thankfully at that moment the valet pulled up to the curb. I looked up Grand Avenue toward the Biltmore and envisioned the walk ahead. What had seemed like a brief, refreshing jog now felt like a treacherous gauntlet.

I turned and patted him on the chest, aiming for a playful note. "You know what?" I said. "I'll take you up on that ride after all."

Daniel looked at me closely and nodded. "Good."

He opened the passenger door for me. As he rounded the car and paid the valet, I again searched the darkness. Nothing.

"So when did you move in?" I asked as Daniel drove down Grand Avenue.

"Just a few days ago. We start trial next week, so I wanted to give myself time to get acclimated."

We talked about places to buy groceries and how to manage a few of the other mundane but necessary life activities downtown, and within two minutes, we were idling in the driveway of the Biltmore.

"Thanks for the ride, Daniel," I said, my hand on the door.

"Yeah, you owe me large for this major hassle," he

joked. Then his tone turned serious. "Listen, I'd like it if we could have a meal now and then. Is that a possibility?"

"Of course," I said, my smile bright with the effort to reassure him. The truth was, I didn't really know how I felt about that. I said good night and stepped out of the car.

Angel tipped his hat. "Evening, Ms. Knight," he said. He threw a pointed glance at Daniel's car, which was pulling away, then opened the lobby door for me.

"Just an old friend, Angel. Nothing else," I said. I loved having people around who cared, but at the moment my Biltmore family was feeling a little intrusive.

Back in my room, I took a long, hot shower, then poured myself a glass of Pinot Noir and settled on the couch with my feet up.

Daniel and I hadn't broken up because I'd stopped loving him. No one cheated or did anything really shitty. I just hadn't been able to handle his frequent and sometimes protracted business trips. But I'd no more share that information with him than I'd tell him about Romy. So the relationship had foundered largely because of a "failure to communicate." Mine, that is.

That admission led me back to Graden. That breakup too was about my past. Or was it, rather, my inability to deal with my past? No—I wasn't going to put it all on me. Graden had gone behind my back and violated my privacy. My history was mine to tell, not his to ferret out on a whim. I felt myself bristling again, the spring inside me winding up for battle. If I kept this up, I wouldn't sleep all night.

I took my glass of wine and a magazine that featured an interview with Johnny Depp to bed with me. I'm a big fan of his, but it'd been a long day and a lot of wine. Within minutes, my eyes had closed and the magazine slipped off my lap.

It was only as I turned out the light that I briefly remembered the sense of danger I'd felt standing in front of Checkers. But I was an old hand when it came to dealing with fear, and I knew better than to try and figure it out in the middle of the night. Promising myself to think about it all in the morning, I fell back on the pillow and into a deep but turbulent sleep.

51

On Monday, I was sitting in court, waiting for my last case to be called, when inspiration hit me. We'd gone about as far as we could trying to find Lilah by conventional means. No one she'd known in her previous life had any idea where to find her, and all of Bailey's efforts had failed to turn up any trace of her under either of her known legitimate names.

But maybe there was another way in. I'd been noodling around with a theory about Zack's case, and it might just dovetail with our search for Lilah.

"People v. Reynolds," the judge announced.

Finally my case was called. The defense attorney jumped up, eager to get it done and get on the road to his next appearance. We picked a trial date, and I headed to the snack bar to grab a water.

As I rounded the corner, I spotted Melia. She was standing near the elevators talking to a short man who was obviously trying to alter that perception with hair that was gelled to reach for the sky. I kept moving as I tried to figure out why he looked so familiar. Then it hit me. I nearly stopped dead in my tracks. He was a reporter for one of the syndicated news agencies. Melia, aka Gossip Central, talking to a reporter spelled nothing but trouble in general. But for me in particular, it might mean total disaster. If the press was onto the Simon Bayer case, I was hosed. I quickly ducked into the snack bar and pretended to browse. When he got on an elevator, I started to head over to Melia, but when I saw that she was moving toward the snack bar, I stayed put.

The moment she walked in, I pulled her to the back corner. "What did that reporter want?" I asked.

Melia made a face and eased her elbow out of my grip. "What's your damage? I didn't tell him anything."

"I didn't ask what you told him," I said. "I asked what he wanted."

Melia looked at me sullenly. "Since when am I not allowed to talk to people?"

I took a deep breath to keep from choking her. "He's not 'people,' Melia. He's a reporter. And that can be a problem—for all of us." I looked at her pointedly, but her expression told me I'd have to spell it out for her. "You included."

Melia gave an exasperated sigh. "He was asking about you guys—"

"Us guys?"

She rolled her eyes. "Special Trials deputies. What hours you worked, how many cases you carried. Like that, okay?"

"And what'd you tell him?"

"Nothing," she said. "I told him to ask Eric."

The subject was just boring enough to make me believe her. "He ask about anything else?"

"Like what?" she said, finally interested.

Like I'd tell her. I shrugged. "No idea. I was just asking." I was pretty sure I knew what the reporter was after, and it wasn't good. But the fact that it wasn't the Bayer case and, even better, that Melia didn't know the case was gossipworthy was excellent news. Relief made me magnanimous. "I'm getting water. Can I get you something?"

Back in my office, I called Bailey on my cell phone so she'd see it was me and pick up. On any given day, this might or might not be a winning strategy. On this day it was—either that, or she hadn't looked at the number.

"Yeah?" she said.

"I've got two good reasons why we should celebrate over lunch. We just dodged a big bullet, and I have a hot new plan for finding Lilah."

"The bullet-dodging, maybe. The hot idea…we'll see," she said dryly. "Where?"

"How about Engine Company Number Twenty-eight?"

"Meet you downstairs in fifteen," Bailey said. "Toni coming?"

"I'm waiting to see. But if she's not here by then, we'll let her know what she missed."

Ten minutes later, I heard the *kee-koo* of Toni's stiletto heels hitting the linoleum down the hall. I jumped out to intercept her and told her about our lunch plan.

"Fantastic," she said, pushing her bangs off her forehead. "I can't wait to get out of here. Just let me drop this junk." She gestured to a thick file in her arms.

I waited in the hallway, and we trotted out to the elevator together.

"What was that?" I said, referring to the file she'd been hauling.

"Old arson case. Judge kept jurisdiction to impose restitution, and it took a while to get all the paperwork in to prove up the losses."

"Which I'm sure the defendant's going to pay, making all that dough on license plates," I said sarcastically.

Toni nodded, her expression fatalistic. "It's the principle, you know?"

I did. As we stepped out of the elevator, I whispered, "I had dinner with Daniel on Friday."

Toni stopped and stared at me, her eyes huge. "You what?"

I pulled her by the arm through the crowd, knowing Bailey was probably already waiting outside.

"I'll explain in the car," I said.

"You bet you will, honey," she replied.

Our timing was perfect. Bailey pulled to the curb just as we got to the top of the stairs, and we jumped in.

"Did you know this girl had dinner with Daniel?" Toni said the moment we'd closed our doors.

"You what?" Bailey said, echoing Toni's response.

I explained how it'd all happened, but I admitted that I'd had a good time.

Toni shook her head.

"What? Daniel and I can't be friends?"

"You certainly can," she said. "But you're still pissed off at Graden, which makes it a dicey time to strike up a friendship with an old boyfriend. Tell me I'm wrong."

I couldn't, so I said nothing. Engine Co. No. 28 appeared on our right. Bailey deliberately picked a parking space in the loading zone to the left of the entrance.

We got a good booth toward the back of the restaurant, and when we were settled, I told them about my Melia-with-reporter sighting. "My guess is he's running with Phil Hemet's vendetta against Special Trials," I said.

"Not good," Toni replied, frowning.

"But not as bad as it could've been," Bailey said. But I could see that the close call had made her as nervous as it'd made me. She leaned forward, her arms folded on the table, expression intense. "Let's hear your genius idea."

"I never said it was genius," I replied. "I just said it was...new."

"I believe the term you used to bribe me was *hot*," Bailey said.

"Try this on," I began. "It's fair to assume that Zack told Lilah about the skinhead attacks on the police station?"

Bailey nodded. "I'd say so."

"Then that's where Lilah got the idea to finger the skinheads as Zack's killers."

"Or maybe even hired one to do it?"

"It'd be risky," I admitted. "These guys aren't choirboys. She'd have to know that the minute a guy like that got busted, he'd start yapping about who hired him—"

"But who're the cops going to believe?" Toni pointed out. "Some skinhead asshole or a lawyer who was married to a cop? Especially the way this murder went down—"

"Exactly," I said.

"But if she did hire a skinhead to do the murder, how did she get to him?" Toni asked.

"I have an educated guess," I said. "Remember Larry said she'd interned in the DA's office? We had a hiring freeze. She wound up working in Orange County—"

"Lots of skinhead activity down south," Bailey interjected.

"Right. So even if she didn't work on skinhead cases herself, she had access to all kinds of information."

"Names, addresses, phone numbers, and who the heavy hitters were," she said. "It's a definite possibility."

"So I'm thinking that we run down Public Enemy Number One," I said. "I'm not saying she hired one of them to do the hit on Zack, but it's worth looking into the possibility that she's got some kind of connection to them. Who knows? She might be using one of them as a bodyguard—"

"To protect her from Simon," Bailey finished. "She had to be worried that he'd come after her, the way he went off in court. And it was in the news that he was trying to get the Feds to file on her."

"Right," I said. "And don't forget, there was a whole police department that thought she did it and took the verdict very friggin' personally."

"So if your theory plays out, Simon's killer might be a skinhead," Bailey observed.

I shrugged.

"But if not, at the very least one of those clowns might know where to find her," she finished.

"And if we find her, we might be able to convince her to give up the stabber—"

"Because if she doesn't, she looks good as an aider and abettor to the murder," Bailey said. "I buy the logic. I'm just not sure about the 'how' of it. As in, how we're gonna get a skinhead to talk to us. We'll need to have some serious leverage on whoever we grab."

"Come on," I said. "How many of these guys *don't* have a tail of some sort?"

The odds were good that most of the gang members would be on probation or parole for something. And finding a violation to bust them for wouldn't challenge a kindergartner.

Bailey nodded. "The trickier part will be figuring out who we can talk to without earning ourselves a toe tag. So how do you propose to find a way in with these jokers?"

I gave a self-satisfied smile. "This is where you thank me for my interpersonal skills." Bailey just looked at me.

"My buddy Luis Revelo," I said. "The shot-caller of the Sylmar Sevens."

52

Bailey and I met Luis Revelo during our last case, when he was a rape suspect and was thought to be targeting yours truly. When I proved he wasn't guilty of either crime, he became a helpful, if somewhat unorthodox, ally.

Toni looked from me to Bailey. "Uh, hello? Luis is Hispanic. Last time I checked, these skinhead guys don't do swirl."

Back in the day, before the Aryan Brotherhood—the granddaddy of white-supremacist prison gangs—got locked down on a 24-7 basis, Toni would've been right. No dealings, business or otherwise, were tolerated with anyone but whites. But the Feds had moved in with a vengeance to shut them down, bringing a series of criminal charges against dozens of the major players and instituting the most draconian lockdown conditions in prison history. As a result, the AB lost significant mobility, which should've meant operations—at least the ones guided from behind bars—were at an end. But being the resourceful, enterprising group they were, the AB followed the lead of many large corporations: they outsourced and recruited more junior groups whose movements in prison weren't so restricted. Groups like Public Enemy Number One, whose younger members hadn't had the chance to rack up lengthy rap sheets and still had the "yard privileges" that let them move freely about the cabin.

"Ever since the AB brought in the youngsters, there's been a bit of an attitude shift about dealing with the mud people," I said.

"When it comes to money, the new kids go a little color-blind," Bailey said. "They'll deal to blacks—"

"Or date Latina girls," I added.

"Sex and money," Toni concluded. "The great integrators. See? We *can* all just get along."

The waiter took our orders.

"I'm going to call Luis," I said, getting out of the booth. "Well, realistically, leave him a message and get the ball rolling."

I had to move outside to find a space quiet enough to use the phone.

As predicted, I got his voice mail.

" 'S Luis, leave a message, I'll get ya back."

I did. But as I hung up, I felt it again: a presence, hidden and menacing, watching me. I tried to look over my left shoulder without turning my head, hoping to catch someone off guard. Running valets and brisk walkers, a woman with bright-orange shoulder-length hair the consistency of steel wool deep in conversation with a young, sullen-looking—is there any other kind?—teenage girl. No one who gave a damn about me. Unsettled, I went back inside the restaurant, my appetite gone.

We were heading up Broadway when my cell played "FM" by Steely Dan.

I opened my phone. "Knight."

"Nah, 's daytime. You sittin' in a box or something?" Luis said, then laughed, cracking himself up.

"Luis," I replied, a smile in my voice. "How've you been?"

"I ain't complainin'—I mean, *I'm not complaining.*" He corrected himself with a sigh. "Whassup with you?"

"Can you spare us a half hour or so?" I asked. "We need some information."

"You still hangin' with that hot blonde?"

"Detective Keller, yes. And I'll tell her you—"

"Aw, come on," he interrupted. "You know I was jes' jokin', Miz Knight. You ain't—damn, *aren't*—going to tell her I said that, are you? Jeez."

Luis sounded truly aggrieved.

"No, I won't," I said. "What's a good time?"

Luis gave a protracted yawn. I turned to look at the clock on the Times Building. Nearly three o'clock, and he was just now joining the world.

"How about five?" he eventually answered. I heard him whisper to someone nearby, *"No. No más ahora."*

Not wanting to know what he didn't want *más* of, I quickly agreed. "Five, it is—"

"You're buyin', right? 'Cuz I'm gonna need to eat about that time..."

Of course he would. Luis knew how to work it with the best of them.

"How about Les Sisters?" I suggested.

"Les Sisters, yeah," Luis said with a satisfied sigh. "That's what I'm talkin' 'bout."

I told Bailey the plan as she turned onto Temple Street and pulled to the curb to drop Toni off.

Luis got busy—with what, neither of us wanted to know—later in the evening. He was, as they say, a mixed bag. Well on his way to earning a GED and aiming for college and an MBA, he fully intended to leave the gang life behind. And, no question, he'd provided invaluable help on our last case. But there was no sense denying that he still had a foot planted on the less-than-savory side of the street.

"I sent in our latest video footage to get a still blowup of our stabber's hand," Bailey said to me now. "It's supposed to be in. Why don't you come back to the station with me and we can check it out?"

I was dying to see that photo. A blowup might show some identifying detail on the stabber's hand. But that could also mean a possible run-in with Graden.

Bailey looked at me. "You can't avoid it forever."

Toni added, her voice warm, sympathetic, "And believe me, we'd both be feeling the same if we were in your shoes."

She opened the door and stepped out onto the curb, then leaned down and pointedly looked at my feet as she spoke through my window. "Though I'd have better shoes."

She would've too.

53

When we got off the elevator, my palms were sweaty. I put my hands in my pockets, forced a long, slow exhale, and kept my eyes fixed straight ahead on Bailey's back. We got to her desk without a Graden sighting. Making it look casual, Bailey carefully scanned the room.

She whispered, "I don't think he's here."

"Thanks," I said.

"He's a lieutenant with a job. It probably eats into his mooning-over-you time."

"It's heartwarming the way you go that extra mile to comfort me."

I pulled a chair over and sat down while Bailey sifted through her in-box. She pulled out a single piece of paper and a manila envelope fastened with a string on the back flap.

"Well, whaddaya know," she said. "We got the crime-lab report on Simon's clothes *and* the photo."

She quickly scanned the page. "Ha!" she exclaimed as she flicked the paper. "They've got a small speck of blood on one of the buttons on Simon's shirt. Preliminary tests show it doesn't match his."

I moved next to her and scanned the report over her shoulder.

"But that doesn't necessarily mean it came from the stabber," I said. "Simon was homeless. Who knows where that shirt's been?"

Looking deflated, Bailey reluctantly agreed. "You're right. The crime lab won't even bother to put it through the database. Even if it matched up to someone..."

"It might not mean anything," I said.

"So it's a low priority for them," she replied. " 'Course if we get someone in custody who looks good for it—"

"They'll jump right on it," I finished. "Perfect. Now all we need is the stabber. Gee, we're almost there."

"A journey of a thousand miles must begin with a single step," Bailey said.

"Thanks, Lao-tzu. Let's see the photo."

She removed two eight-by-ten grayscale photographs and set them on the desk. Together, we pored over the images. The tech had done a nice job of zeroing in on the area of interest. I'd hoped to find an unusual tattoo or some kind of deformity, such as webbed fingers, or a hook. We didn't get either of those. But we did get something.

"See, that's what I thought when I saw this view the first time. Look at the watch he's wearing." I pointed to the large dial with what seemed like chronographs inside it. "What do you know about men's watches?"

"Not much," Bailey admitted. "But I'd say it looks expensive."

I was no expert, but that seemed right to me.

"This might help ID our stabber in the video if we catch him wearing it. We should get an expert who can testify to the type of watch, how rare it is, yadda, yadda," I said, thinking out loud.

"I agree," Bailey said. "Want to keep this, just to have?" She held out one of the photos.

I took it. "You got a spare envelope, so I don't mess it up?"

Bailey found one in a drawer, and I tucked the picture in. For some reason, looking at the photograph gave me a chill. Reminded me of that creepy sense I'd had that someone was watching me.

"We'd better get going," Bailey said. "Your buddy Luis has got people to do and places to meet."

Distracted, I slowly stood and picked up my purse. As we moved toward the elevator, Bailey looked at me. "Stand down, Knight, he's not here."

I shook my head. "That's not it. I'll tell you in the car."

When Bailey'd finally navigated us onto the freeway and threaded her way through the tightly woven traffic into the fast lane, I told her about my creepy feeling of being watched.

She frowned. "Without something more concrete, I won't be able to justify a security detail for you."

"I'm not asking for one," I replied. "I'm just sharing."

"A little out of character for you, isn't it, Knight?" Bailey smirked. "This 'sharing' thing?"

The offhand remark hit home. I stared at the carpet of red lights that spread out before us. My seat belt suddenly felt too tight. I pulled it away from my chest and took a deep breath. I didn't want to tell her about Romy and the real reason for my breakup with Graden, but I hadn't anticipated that I'd feel this bad about keeping it all from her.

Soon it'd be Christmas, then New Year's Eve. A bad time to be dealing with a recent breakup for anyone. For me, that misery landed on top of the agony that always burned tight and furious during the holidays over the loss of Romy, my mother, and my father.

"Bailey...," I began, and had to stop. My throat was swollen with emotion, and the strangled sound made her turn to look at me with alarm.

"Yeah? What? You okay?"

Suddenly the air around me felt like deep space; I was floating alone and untethered through a dark, endless sky. Desperate to escape the icy purgatory, without having made a conscious decision, I began to talk.

"There's something I have to tell you. I had an older sister, Romy..."

The clot of humanity that filled the freeway ensured that I had plenty of time to tell the whole story, including the fight with Graden.

I stared straight ahead as I spoke, eyes fixed on the sea of cars ahead, aware in the back of my mind that I'd have hell to pay for keeping this secret after so many years of friendship. Bailey let me talk without interruption.

"Bailey, I'm sorry," I said when I'd come to the end. Finally I turned to face her. "I know I should've—"

What I saw brought me to a full stop. Bailey's cheeks were wet with tears. I couldn't remember ever having seen her cry. After a moment, she spoke.

"Telling me this when I'm driving, you're lucky you didn't get us killed." She wiped her cheeks with the back of her hand.

"So that's why I broke up with Graden."

"I get it." Then, proving she knew me all too well, she continued, "And, no, I don't think you're nuts. I wouldn't like the idea of someone tromping around in my past trying to find out shit about me either."

The relief was almost dizzying. Bailey wasn't angry. Not only that, she understood. Until this very moment, I hadn't realized how much it'd cost me to keep this secret from her.

Bailey nodded to herself. "So I get it. But all he did was google you," she said quietly. "He didn't do a deep background check." She paused. "You don't think you overreacted...just a little?"

I folded my arms around myself and stared out the window. The moon was just a ghostly apparition in a sky still infused with the last stubborn rays of sunlight. Exhausted by the emotional strain of the past half hour, I let myself get mesmerized by the sight for a moment. But when I tried to rationally consider Bailey's question, I couldn't come up with an answer. I didn't know how to measure my reaction objectively.

"Obviously, googling me isn't the same as running a background check. But you didn't do it, and neither did Toni...did you?"

"No, I didn't. And neither did Toni. But we're not Graden—"

"Exactly my point," I said emphatically. "That's the problem. This was about his need for control, not his concern for me."

"Can't it be both?" Bailey continued. "Graden's need to know everything and your...issue with boundaries is a challenge. But it doesn't have to mean the end. Unless you say it does."

"Or he says so," I added.

"He doesn't," Bailey replied.

I turned to look at her.

"I didn't talk to him," Bailey said. "I didn't have to. I've seen him. That's enough."

Bailey never lies, so I believed her when she said she hadn't spoken to Graden. But whether she was right about him not wanting to break up . . . that was another matter.

Not that I cared.

54

We were fifteen minutes late getting to Les Sisters, which meant we were still way ahead of Luis. The New Orleans–style restaurant in Chatsworth, at the northern tip of the San Fernando Valley, had been around for twenty-five years. Famous among those in the know for serving up some of the best Southern-style cooking this side of the Mason-Dixon Line, it would fit the bill for us in more ways than one. Aside from the killer food, the prices were reasonable, the people were great, and it was way off the beaten path, so we wouldn't risk being seen together, which would've been bad for the shot-caller of a gang and not so great for a prosecutor either.

We took a table against the window in the tiny café and picked up the menu. Fried chicken, chicken creole, crawfish jambalaya, baby back ribs...I wanted to eat it all. Watching the waitstaff bring out steaming-hot plates heaped with all of the above didn't help. We ordered the "hush pups" and Cajun popcorn for appetizers, and I told myself I'd order only a green salad for dinner. I tell myself things like that a lot.

I was on my fourth hush pup when Luis swaggered in and shuffled over to our table with a lazy grin. Dressed in a black leather coat, baggy jeans, and skull-stud earrings, he appeared more debonair than usual. Which wasn't to say he didn't look like a gangbanger—just one who was slightly more upscale.

"*Hola,* Ms. Prosecutor, Ms. *Policía,*" he greeted us, folding himself into the padded metal chair and stretching out his legs.

Luis always managed to look like he was kickin' it in his living room. Even when he was cuffed in the back of a squad car.

The waitress's smile told me it hadn't been long since Luis was last here. So did his order. Without even looking at the menu, he ordered the rib combo with corn muffins, black-eyed peas with rice, and another plate of hush pups.

Bailey got the fried chicken and creamy slaw, and I ordered a green salad…and the fried chicken. Screw it, I was under stress.

"You still working on your GED?" I asked.

"Finished it." Luis sniffed with pride. "Got into Los Angeles Community College. Startin' in January."

"That's fantastic, Luis," I said, truly impressed. I'd known he intended to earn his high school diploma and get into college, but sometimes intentions and reality don't mix.

"Din't think I could do it, huh?" he asked, his head tilted back, looking down his nose at me.

"Oh, I knew you *could* do it," I replied. "I just didn't know if you *would.*"

I smiled at him and raised my glass of water. He and Bailey lifted theirs, and we all clinked. "Congratulations,"

I said. Luis looked pleased with himself as he nodded, then took a sip of water.

"So does this mean you're not in the life anymore?" I asked.

Luis looked away, then back again. "Don' you think it's a bad idea for me to be talkin' to you about that?" he said, an eyebrow raised.

"Usually," I admitted. "Though if I was going to make something of it, I wouldn't do it in this place, would I?"

"Hard to say what you might do." Luis looked at me out of half-closed eyes.

I couldn't tell whether his pose was meant to be seductive, threatening, or wary. I decided it didn't matter.

"You have any connects with PEN1?" I asked.

This time both eyebrows shot up, and Luis pulled his head down into his jacket and leaned forward. "Why you wanna talk to them"—he sighed with exasperation and corrected himself—"I mean *those . . . pendejos* for?"

"We're trying to find someone who might've hired them to do a hit," I replied. "This person might still be using them."

Luis snorted. "Usin' 'em as what? A piñata?"

"As protection," I said.

"Huh," Luis said derisively. "Mus' be *un gilazo,* usin' a skinhead for somethin' important like that." He shook his head in disgust.

I looked at him impatiently. "Anyway . . ."

"I don' know nobody in PEN1, but I got a connect with the Low Riders. Guess I could hook you up." Luis turned back to me. "You sure you wanna meet with that *pinche* fool?"

A Nazi Low Rider could still work. He might be able

to give us the leads to get to someone higher up in PEN1. And it wouldn't take long. They all swim in the same cesspool.

"I don't want to marry the dude, Luis," I said. "I just need some information."

"Whatever...," he replied.

The waitress brought our food, and we all dug in. Between wolfing bites of ribs, Luis gave us the name and description of the "*pinche* fool."

We'd finished dinner and walked out to Bailey's car when Luis asked, "How's your ride?" His grin was wide.

My car had been severely vandalized during the case that'd caused our paths to cross. Not only had Luis put my car back together, but he'd spiffed it up with a midnight-blue-sparkle paint job, new rims, and, among other amenities, a slamming sound system.

"It's still way out of my league," I said, smiling. "But I'm loving it."

"You lemme know if you have any pra'lems, right?" he said earnestly.

"I absolutely will," I said. "And thanks for the hookup, Luis."

He muttered something that included *pinche cabrón* as he rounded his freshly polished green Chevy. He paused to wipe the chrome on the side-view mirror with his sleeve, then got in, fired up the engine, honked, waved, and slowly pulled away.

I waved back and couldn't help smiling.

"He is one of a kind," Bailey said, a little smile on her face too.

"Which is a good thing," I replied. "One of him is plenty."

55

"So we pay a visit to Butch Adler, aka Glass Man," I said, trying to picture the guy Luis had described. "I'm sure that means he replaces windows," I added dryly. *Glass* was common slang for *methamphetamine*.

"Undoubtedly did some home-renovation projects for Luis," Bailey agreed.

"You think he still works at the Pep Boys in Simi Valley?"

"With the economy the way it is, and jobs the way they are, I'd bet he's still in pocket," she said. "Want to hit him tomorrow?"

"Definitely." It'd be a good starting point. We needed to get to the heart of PEN1, and that probably meant its head, to see if they had any connection to Lilah. But you don't hit the target first—you hit the outer periphery and gather information as you work your way in and, hopefully, up. That way, by the time you're talking to someone in power, you sound like you know what you're talking about; and with a little luck, you've found something to threaten them with. So I didn't mind the fact that Luis's connection was at a lower rung of a different skinhead group.

It was eight o'clock by the time Bailey dropped me off at the hotel, which gave me plenty of time to get to the gym and work off those hush pups. I did some serious ab work, pushed myself for half an hour on the treadmill, and wrapped it all up with a combination of machines and free weights to work my upper body. By the time I dragged myself up to my room, I was drenched with sweat and virtuously tired.

One hot shower and a glass of Pinot Noir later, I was tucked in bed with a new, and hopefully better, murder mystery than the one I'd been slogging through. Five minutes later, I was asleep.

I hit the snooze button four times the next morning—one more than usual—which meant I had no time for breakfast. More important, no time for coffee, and on a day like this—cold, glittering, and with air so fresh it cut through me like a razor—I badly needed my hot caffeine fix. At least the wardrobe choices would be easy. I could go casual today, since I doubted the Glass Man, aka Butch Adler, or the Pep Boys where he worked enforced a dress code. Jeans, boots, and a forest-green pullover sweater would do the trick. And I decided to take along the manila envelope containing the photograph of the stabber's wrist. Bailey and I could look it over again if we had any downtime waiting for our soon-to-be new buddy Butch. I stuffed my .38 Smith & Wesson into the pocket of my peacoat, threw on a black muffler, and headed out.

"There's a Coffee Bean on the corner," I said as I got into Bailey's car.

She gave me a look but knew better than to argue. She

pulled over. The line was long and slow. Ten annoying minutes later, I trotted back to the car.

"Here," I said, handing Bailey a cup. "And I brought us provisions for the long trek ahead." I held up a bag with bagels and cream cheese.

"It's Simi Valley, not Idaho," she said.

I raised an eyebrow. "You sure?" Simi was a very white enclave.

"Well, maybe a little bit," Bailey said as she enjoyed a long sip from her cup.

"What do we have on Glass Man?" I asked, spreading cream cheese on a piece of bagel with the tiny plastic knife.

"Probation for drunk driving. He got one year suspended—"

"That's not much," I said, worried.

Most of these guys could do a year standing on their heads.

"We work with what we've got," Bailey replied philosophically.

"I hate to waste the time if he's just going to tell us to pound sand," I said sourly.

"Got a better idea?"

"Not at the moment."

"Then suck it up and think positive," Bailey said.

We made it to Simi Valley in relatively good time. It was a study in contrasts, as we had just left the funky, multiethnic mix that's downtown L.A. Wide, flat streets with neatly trimmed trees lined the sidewalks, and everything was suburban clean. Even the bus-stop bench, adorned with a real estate ad that bore the grin of a cheesy-looking blonde who wanted to sell YOUR home, looked safe enough to sleep on. But unlike downtown, I'd bet no one ever did.

Bailey navigated us to the Pep Boys in the middle of a vanilla strip mall. Two muscular-looking young guys in crew cuts and long-sleeved waffle shirts under short-sleeved uniforms conferred beneath the hood of a red Ford pickup truck that was in a front parking space. As we passed them on our way into the store, I steeled myself for the usual macho review.

Except there wasn't any. The guys just kept talking about the alternator, whatever that is. I didn't know whether to be relieved or depressed.

Bailey asked the cashier, a remarkably wholesome-looking girl with a single blond braid that hung down her back, where we could find the manager.

She directed us to a man in a dress shirt and black polyester pants wearing a name tag that said TOMMY.

Tommy was on the phone, so while we waited, I looked around. All manner of gadgets designed to fix or shine up a motor vehicle were stacked neatly on shelves throughout a cavernous store. I was never into cars, but the array of products had me looking around for something to buy. I can shop anywhere. A young dark-haired man with a wispy mustache brought a car cover to the cashier. He took his time counting out his money, giving himself a chance to flirt with her. I heard him ask her whether she liked working around all that car stuff. She gave him a sweet smile, flicked back her braid winningly, and said, "Sure," in a perky voice. *Liar.*

I'd just decided I had to have that attractive set of spark plugs on the shelf to my right when the manager finished his call and looked at us.

"What can I do for you ladies?" he asked.

I hate being called a lady. It makes me think of white gloves and fussy teacups. And women who simper. It's a patronizing word that shrinks you, makes you inconsequential and easily dismissed. Or it could just be me.

Bailey stepped in closer and held her badge down at her waist where only he could see it. We didn't want Glass Man to get a glimpse and take a powder. Tommy's eyes got big, which I found satisfying. *Still want to help the* ladies, *pal?*

"What can I do for you…uh…"

"Detective Keller," Bailey said. "And this is Deputy District Attorney Knight."

He nodded politely. "Pleased to meet you."

Respectful. Better. I supposed this was one of the upsides of Simi Valley. Quite a contrast to the 'tude we usually got downtown.

"We're looking for Butch Adler," I said.

"He's here." Tommy looked around the store. "Might be helping someone outside. Is he in trouble?"

"No," Bailey said. "Not at all."

Not yet anyway.

Tommy looked relieved. "Come with me."

We followed Tommy to a service bay, where a bald man wearing a Pep Boys uniform shirt and heavy black motorcycle boots was rolling a tire. "Butch," Tommy called out. "Can you come over here a sec? Got someone who wants to see you."

Butch narrowed his eyes at Bailey and me. Unlike Tommy, our friend Butch knew how to spot a cop at twenty paces. "Let me just get this out," he said, gesturing to the tire. He rolled it to an older man standing next to a green Honda Civic, said something to him, and walked over to us, rubbing his hands on a blue kerchief.

Tommy introduced us, but Glass Man didn't offer to shake. Just kept rubbing the kerchief between his hands and sizing us up.

"Thanks, Tommy," Bailey said. "We'll take it from here."

Tommy gratefully excused himself and went back inside.

"I didn't test dirty and I haven't been busted," Butch said. "So you got nothing on me."

"You sure about that?" Bailey said, bluffing.

Butch said nothing, showing his street smarts. When in doubt, clam up.

"I'd prefer not to bust you, tell you the truth," Bailey continued. "Just want to have a little chat."

Butch's eyes got narrower. Now that I was up close and personal, I could see that he had a tattoo on his neck of a death's-head wearing a Nazi helmet. *Très* chic. He folded his arms.

"I don't talk to cops," he said. "Guess you better bust me."

Tough guy. I decided to try another tack.

"Aren't you a little curious to know what we want to talk about?" I asked. "Maybe we want to ask about your golf handicap, or your pick for *American Idol* this season."

Butch just looked at me, then turned to Bailey. "You got something, bust me. You don't, let me get on with my day. I got work to do."

Out of patience and pissed off at having lost all this time for nothing, I snapped, "We just want to know what you heard about PEN1 hitting that cop Zack Bayer in Glendale."

Butch's eyebrows shot up, making his whole scalp move back on his head. "You wanna talk about PEN1? Those pieces of cow shit." He snorted. "Whyn't ya say so?"

56

Butch was more than willing to talk but not out in the open. He led us into the manager's office at the end of the store.

"Those PEN1 punks all try to act like they're hard cases, but they're just a bunch of little punk-ass bitches," Butch said in a voice that sounded like a rusty muffler being dragged over a bumpy driveway. Too many cigarettes smoked during meth-fueled all-nighters will do that for you.

"So you don't believe they did Zack?" I asked.

Butch made a face as though he wanted to spit. "They don't got the stones."

"You ever hear of anyone working for the wife, Lilah?" I asked.

"That the hot chick they got for it?"

"The one they *tried* to get," I corrected. "She walked."

"Yeah," Butch said, nodding to himself. "You askin' if someone from PEN1 did it for her?"

I nodded.

"No fucking way," Butch said emphatically. "Like I said, they don't got—"

"—the stones, I know," I said. "You ever hear about anyone doing bodyguard work for her? I mean, now—not back then."

Butch frowned, then folded his meaty arms across his chest. "Why'd she want to hire one o' them?" he asked, his tone genuinely curious.

"Same reason anyone hires a bodyguard," I said.

"She'd be stupid."

My expression told him the wisdom of hiring those fools was of no interest to me.

He added, "No. I never heard that."

It was looking like we'd hit the bottom of this particular well. I wanted to walk away with something more than Butch's antipathy for all things PEN1.

"I have to talk to them," I said. "We need names."

"You're not going to put out any paper, are you?" he asked.

I shook my head. "No reports. This conversation never happened."

Butch reeled off a list for us.

"Who's the highest up of this bunch?" I asked.

"Dominic—no one's farther up the chain than him," Butch replied, a note of respect creeping into his voice.

"Who's just below him?" I asked.

Butch thought a minute. "Lonnie," he finally said.

"He in the PEN1 death squad?" I asked.

"Last I knew."

"This Lonnie have a last name?"

Butch shook his head slowly. "I never knew it. But he used to hang down in San Berdoo."

"San Bernardino's a big county, Butch. I'm guessing

there's more than one Lonnie out there," I said. "How about a description? Any tatts?"

"Yeah," Butch replied. He paused and squinted. "Had a snake on one arm. Something else on his left...a dagger? Yeah, I think that's it. A dagger on his left."

We tried a little longer, but we'd exhausted his repertoire of PEN1 lore.

We headed out of the office. "Hey, Butch," I said, "how long were you in PEN1?"

Butch stopped and acknowledged my deduction with the faintest of smiles. " 'Bout five years."

"Right up until they busted you for selling to Hispanics." I made it the statement of fact I was sure it had to be.

Butch nodded, his expression showing he was impressed. "Nice catch, Counselor," he said. "Pretty smart, lady."

This time *lady* didn't bother me.

We headed back to Bailey's car.

"You got enough on Lonnie to locate him somewhere in the Inland Empire?" I asked.

"I'm going to call it in and see," she replied. "In the meantime, you ready for lunch?"

"May as well," I said. "Just make it someplace where I can get a salad. Please."

Bailey gave me a superior smirk, but she found us a Marie Callender's.

Once we got seated, Bailey called in the description of Lonnie, and I took out the photograph of the stabber's wrist. The watch looked thin and light, the way the most expensive ones often do, though the chronographs gave it a sporty appearance. The glint of metal barely protruding between the fingers of his left hand told me which hand he favored—or at least that he was ambidextrous. That might help narrow it down—that is, if we ever found any suspects. Bailey interrupted my already dead-ended musings with a sharp snap of her cell phone.

"I found a Lonnie Wilson in Costa Mesa who fits the description," she said.

"Costa Mesa has its share of skinheads," I remarked. "Sounds good so far. Got anything on him?"

Bailey grinned. "If he's our boy, we've hit the jackpot. There's a warrant out for his arrest. Probation violation."

"Means no bail." I smiled.

"And he's looking at a ten-year fall."

"So how do we find him?" I asked.

"Finally an easy one. They already picked him up— Men's Central Jail, Bauchet Street."

We bumped fists. Then it dawned on me: that meant I was going back to that dump. Again.

57

The bloated concrete mushroom squatting in the middle of Bauchet Street soaked up the brilliant sunshine like a black hole. Somehow, no matter how bright the day, the Men's Central Jail in downtown Los Angeles always felt like it sat in the darkest bowels of the earth. Smelled that way too. We got out and walked toward the entrance. I was glad Lonnie Wilson was within reach, but I wasn't glad to be in this hellhole—*again*.

"I deliberately avoided defense work so I wouldn't have to come here," I grumped. "Now it feels like I'm here more than my own office."

Bailey tried to suppress a chuckle...and failed.

We checked our guns and passed through the metal detector, then waited in the claustrophobia-inducing attorney room for Lonnie Wilson.

The filthy windows of our glass bubble filtered the already dim light, adding to the sense of being in a dungeon. Which, I guess, it was. Five minutes later, I saw our quarry approach. He was tall, somewhere between six feet one and six feet three, and solid like a linebacker—probably 250 pounds at least, and most of it muscle. The chains at his waist, wrists, and legs dangled off his body like jewelry; his hair was slicked back with not one piece out of place. But as he approached, I saw that his features were surprisingly delicate: a small nose, a rosebud of a mouth, and china-blue eyes. It was an eerie combination.

The guards brought him in and sat him down, then locked both hands and legs to the metal chair, which was bolted into the concrete floor. One of the guards left; the other stayed just outside the door. A nice, cozy gathering.

Bailey introduced us. Lonnie looked from her to me.

"What do you want?" he asked. His tone was calculating and faintly superior.

"Information," I said. "And maybe an introduction, if you're lucky."

"Lucky?" he replied, jerking his head to point out where we were.

An unexpected surprise: a skinhead who knew the meaning of irony. But I was in no mood to play with this jerk.

"Things could get worse." I paused and looked at him steadily. "Or they could get better."

Lonnie exhaled through his nose. "I'm listening."

"A good word from a cop and a DA," Bailey replied. "The judge might find that interesting, since you got violated for resisting arrest."

Lonnie drew a breath, about to argue his side of the case, then thought better of it. "I asked around about you two. They say you're straight." He pressed his lips together and narrowed his eyes. "We'll see. Ask me."

I brought up Zack's murder.

Lonnie nodded. "I remember that."

"Yeah, I figured you were the type to keep up with current events," I said.

Lonnie snickered.

"I heard PEN1 did it," I said.

He smiled slowly, his china-blue eyes as cold as ice. "Can't say we did, can't say we didn't."

"Actually, you could," I said, unimpressed with his obnoxious swagger. "You could say, 'Oh, we had nothing to do with that.' Or, 'Yes, we did do that.' See how easy it is?" I tried to rein in the sarcasm—and my growing desire to grab something heavy and smack him upside his head. Lonnie glared at me but somehow managed to keep his fear at bay.

"What do you know about Lilah Bayer?" I asked.

"She the piece they hooked up for it?" he asked.

I nodded.

"Less than you do," he said, his voice diffident.

I had to tread carefully. This cretin had reason to lie and pretend to have information to feather his own nest. The more I let him know I wanted something, the more likely I was to get a bullshit answer. His posturing about Zack's murder meant nothing either way—someone from PEN1 could've done it...or not. But his attitude about Lilah told me he really didn't have a line on her.

"I want a meeting with Dominic," I said.

Lonnie chuckled coldly.

"It's good to see you have a sense of humor. It'll come in handy while you're serving your ten-year sentence." Which is probably what he'd get no matter how good a word we put in for him.

Lonnie favored me with a flinty gaze. I returned it, and

we continued the stare contest until he finally gave up and shrugged.

"I can't promise anything," he said.

"Try," Bailey said as she pulled out her cell.

Lonnie looked hard at Bailey as he recited the number. She punched it in.

"I'd like to speak to Dominic," she said.

Bailey and Lonnie had a stare-down while we waited to see who, if anyone, would come to the phone. After a few more moments, Bailey spoke.

"Dominic? I've got someone who wants to speak to you." She got up, walked behind Lonnie, and held the phone to his ear.

It was fun to watch Lonnie kiss some ass. He was surprisingly good at it.

"I know you don't like this, Dom, and I want you to know I'm sorry to do this to you, but I need you to talk to some cops. I guess you know I'm looking at ten—," Lonnie began, then stopped and listened. "No," he replied. He listened some more. "Just some old case." Lonnie nodded. "I will. I owe ya, and you know I'll find a way to—" He stopped and listened. "Will do. And really, thanks, man, I—"

Lonnie stopped abruptly. "We're done," he said to Bailey.

She snapped the cell shut.

And Lonnie gave us directions.

58

I couldn't get out of there fast enough. Even Bailey had to make an effort to keep up as I trotted out to the car, taking deep breaths of cold air to get the stench of the jail out of my nose. When we got to the car, I rolled down the window and stuck my head out, but after a couple of minutes I got too cold and quickly rolled it back up. Bailey headed for Vignes Street.

"What a waste of flesh," I said.

"A real gem," Bailey agreed. She glanced at her watch. The clock in her department-issue car had never worked. "It's just about seven o'clock. We should hit Dominic tomorrow."

"That'll work."

"I might hang out at the bar with Drew for a while," she said. "Want to come?"

That didn't sound bad. A nice dry martini, some laughs with Bailey and Drew. The perfect combination to wipe out the foul smell of the Hellmouth and the stench of that white-supremacist pig. She parked on the street in the ten-minute drop-off zone and ignored the thunderous looks from Rafi, the valet.

"I'm going up to the room to bleach myself and burn my clothes, but then I'll be down."

Bailey laughed. I didn't.

She headed for the bar, and I hit the up button for the elevator. It'd been a full day and I was glad to have the elevator to myself, as there were no annoying stops along the way. I walked down the hallway toward my room, plotting the questions I'd ask skinhead kingpin Dominic when we saw him tomorrow.

As I passed the narrow corridor that led to the fire escape, I felt a rush of cold air. I stopped to see if someone had left the door open when something slammed against me with the force of a steel wrecking ball. I flew a few feet until I hit the far wall and fell to the floor. Before I could push myself up or get my bearings, a heavy boot landed a vicious kick to my kidney. I reflexively curled up to protect my head, but a gloved hand grabbed me by the hair and banged my head on the ground with so much force the impact reverberated through my brain. The color red filled my eyes. Then everything went dark.

I didn't even know I'd been unconscious until I came to. When I cracked open my eyes, I saw that I was still lying on the floor. My head was throbbing so badly I couldn't lift it, and my stomach was seesawing, making me afraid to stand up. I felt around for my purse but couldn't find it. I tried to open my eyes further, but the light stung. I decided to lie there a little while longer since I didn't seem to be able to do anything else.

I must've blacked out again, because the next thing I knew, paramedics were strapping me onto a gurney and

Bailey was hovering nearby, looking worried. As they began to roll me down the hall, I spoke to her.

"It's okay," I said. But she didn't respond. Maybe I hadn't said it out loud? I opened my mouth to try and speak louder, but the blackness closed over me again.

When I woke for the third time, I was in a hospital bed, and Bailey and Toni were on either side of me—bent in weird positions on uncomfortable-looking orange plastic chairs.

I slowly pulled myself up into a sitting position—a victory. Then the world began to swim, and I vomited. Victory may have been an overstatement. My head felt like someone was using a hammer to drive sharp metal rods through it, and I involuntarily groaned. Bailey and Toni were at my side in an instant.

"I'm fine, really," I said, my voice barely a whisper. Sounds were going to be difficult for me, I could tell. "Just a headache."

"Sure," Toni said. "Just lie back and take it easy. You're lucky to be alive."

"Does anyone else know about this yet?" I asked.

"No," Toni replied. "But they're going to—"

I reached out to grab Toni's arm, but it was too much movement, too fast. I fell back against the pillows.

"No, Tone," I said weakly. "Not yet."

I knew my condition wasn't helping my cause any, so I tried to put a little more force in my voice.

"They might take me off the case," I said. "Give us a couple of days to figure out what this is. What if it's just some random purse snatch?"

Toni looked at me skeptically, then at Bailey.

"What do you say?" Toni asked her.

Bailey looked torn.

"It may not be related." She paused. "You think they'll take her off the case if we report?"

"It's possible," Toni admitted.

"*She* can hear you," I said, annoyed enough to momentarily forget how lousy I felt.

Neither of them seemed fazed. I closed my eyes but could clearly imagine the expressions on their faces: Toni eyeing me skeptically, Bailey frowning her disapproval.

After a few moments, Bailey sighed. "Hold off for a day or so, until we sort it out."

I opened my eyes, relieved. Toni started to object, but Bailey looked at her pointedly. Toni nodded and said nothing.

"Did you get a look at him?" Bailey asked.

I shook my head, which hurt, so I stopped. "No." I closed my eyes to try and visualize the attack. "But I did see a hand. It was in a glove, but I could tell it was a man's hand."

That little speech ended my limited energy reserve. My eyes stayed shut and didn't open again until morning. By that time, the doctor said I was in good enough shape to go home. I called Toni and Bailey, who were in the hospital cafeteria, and told them I was released.

"You are not going back there by yourself," Bailey said. "I'm staying with you. You've got the space. And besides, I could use some room service."

"And if she gets busy with Drew, I'll be there," Toni said.

"Fine," I said.

Though I wouldn't admit it, I liked the idea of having them there. Bailey drove us all back to the Biltmore.

When we got to the room, they tucked me in and shook out my prescribed happy pills.

"I'm not taking these," I said, putting the pills on the nightstand. "They'll knock me out and I'll be out of it all day tomorrow. We don't have that kind of time to lose."

Bailey and Toni exchanged a look.

"What?" I said. "It was a bump on the head, not a brain tumor."

"Take one pill so you can sleep tonight—which means I'll get to sleep tonight—and we'll hit it tomorrow. Okay?"

I took one pill and within minutes drifted off.

When I woke up the next morning, I was hurting all over. I looked at my alarm clock. Only 7:30 a.m. I had a whole day ahead of me if I got my ass in gear. Gingerly, I moved out of bed one limb at a time. One leg, then the other, then an arm—pretty soon, I was sitting up with my feet on the floor. I stood up slowly, one hand on the bed for balance, then let go. I was standing. I looked in the mirror. The right side of my torso was covered in dark bruises, and my right cheek and shoulder were both bruised and badly scraped. My eyes were swollen and there was a big, ugly lump on my forehead. It'd hurt, but I'd have to do a serious makeup job if I didn't want to scare small children.

I slowly inched my way out to the living room. I looked into the spare room and saw that Bailey was still in bed. She wouldn't be for long. I called room service and ordered us breakfast and two large pots of coffee, then painfully shuffled to the bathroom and took a long, hot shower, stretching carefully under the warm spray to try and loosen up.

"How're you doing?" Bailey greeted me when I came back out to the living room, dressed and ready for the day. "You look good for someone who got clocked like that."

"I'm fine," I lied. "A little wobbly, but not bad."

Room service had come and set up our breakfasts. Bailey gestured for me to sit down and poured us both coffee.

She took the silver cover off her plate and inhaled the rich sweetness of her French toast. "Room service," Bailey said with a look of supreme satisfaction. "So good to be here." She took a sip of coffee, then added, "And, you know, to be here for you too."

I was going to take issue with her priorities but figured that coming in second to room service was probably a step up. I savored my first bite of my ham-and-cheese omelet splurge and tried to replay the attack in my mind.

"Did he take my purse?" I asked. The paramedics had found my gun in my coat pocket. A lot of good it'd done me.

"Good news and bad news," Bailey said, digging into her hash browns.

"Bad news," I said.

"He took your wallet."

"Good news?"

"He left your purse; we called and canceled all your credit cards already, and from what I remember, you didn't have much cash on you."

That's right. I'd offered to leave a tip for the waitress at Marie Callender's and didn't have enough. And I was going to have to get another driver's license. Worse, I'd have to get another driver's license photograph.

"I've never had any problems here before, and I haven't heard of anyone else having a problem like this either," I said.

"I know," Bailey agreed. "And even though there's no such thing as 'can't happen here,' this has got me thinking."

I'd been thinking about it too. In fact, from the moment I woke up in the hospital.

There was nothing near that fire escape but my room. "He was waiting for me."

59

We sat in thick silence, contemplating who the attacker could've been.

"We just got done talking to two skinheads from warring factions," I said. "And we squeezed Lonnie pretty hard to get to his boss."

Bailey nodded. "So PEN1 issued a warning?"

"That's the last rock we looked under."

Bailey shook her head. "For all we know, one side might be using you to set up the other side."

That made a kind of twisted sense, given who we were dealing with.

"Then I can't think of a better time to have a chat with their Grand Wizard, what's-his-name...Dominic," I said. "If it was one of his minions, he had to have given the order." Hitting a prosecutor was too big a move to make without getting executive approval.

"Grand Wizard's the Klan," Bailey corrected.

"Thank you," I deadpanned. "I appreciate you saving me from the mortifying experience of referring to some douche-nozzle skinhead by the wrong title."

Bailey dropped her napkin on the table, then put on her shoulder holster and checked the magazine of her Glock. Taking her cue, I went to the dresser where I kept my firepower and pulled out the biggest gun I had—the .44-caliber H & K. My recent assault had given me a whole new perspective on self-defense. I would've taken a bazooka if I'd had one.

"I'd go easy on the douche-nozzle too," Bailey said, picking up her overcoat. "At least until we're off the compound."

Compound?

"Dominic Rostoni lives on a compound in Calabasas," Bailey said. "He's a skinhead *and* an entrepreneur."

"Great," I said. I popped the magazine into my .44, checked to make sure the safety was on, and put it into my purse.

"We're going to have to leave these in the car," Bailey said, gesturing to our guns. "There's no way they're letting us in if we're strapped."

We shared a long look. If our chat with Dominic didn't pan out the way we hoped, safety was going to be an issue for both of us.

I did what I could with makeup and concealer and presented myself to Bailey.

"What do you think?" I asked.

She looked at my face and shrugged. "It's as good as you're going to get."

With those encouraging words, we headed out to Bailey's car. I had to move slowly at first, which frustrated me. I didn't want to hobble into this meeting like a ninety-year-old—especially if it was one of his minions who'd attacked me. I pulled myself up straight and forced myself to walk as normally as I could. It was pretty slow going, and I'd have to remember not to wince, but I thought I pulled off a pretty good semblance of normal.

While Bailey drove, I surreptitiously tried to stretch and work out the kinks. I wanted to keep my little rehab efforts on the down low, because if Bailey saw, she might cancel the meeting and hustle me back to bed. I could not let that happen. The possibility that this cretin Dominic was behind my attack had me good and mad, and I was spoiling to confront this son of a bitch.

We'd picked a good time to travel. At 10:30 a.m., the northbound traffic on the 101 Freeway was light. We flew up through Hollywood, Studio City, Tarzana, and Woodland Hills. As we headed toward Calabasas, stores and strip malls gave way to rolling green hills and the Santa Monica Mountains. Calabasas itself was once a bucolic one-horse town with open fields and a hitching post in front of the post office. But in recent years, developers had seen the possibilities of catering to the newly moneyed families who wanted a quiet place to raise their children. Now it was an upscale suburban enclave filled with gated communities, McMansions, and plush estates. But there were still rural pockets where the roads were barely paved and the animal population outnumbered the humans.

Dominic's compound was nestled in one of them.

Bailey got off at Las Virgenes and headed west, toward the Santa Monica Mountains. If we stayed on that road, it'd take us to Malibu in minutes. But our destination was on the Calabasas side of the mountain. Bailey turned left onto Mulholland, then made another left onto a wide country road.

The air was clean and crisp, and the sky was a cloud-less cornflower blue. In a fenced pasture on the right, beautifully groomed horses galloped and played, their manes flying, and in a large open stable on the left, equally well-kept horses stomped their hooves and whin-nied to one another. Goats and sheep grazed on the hill-side above the pasture, and a family of cows huddled on a hill just beyond the stables. Giant oak and maple trees that undoubtedly provided welcome shade in the summer but were now bare-limbed lined both sides of the road. We stopped to let two ranch hands holding the reins of a pair of gorgeous platinum-gray mares cross the street. It was hard to believe that just forty minutes ago, we were surrounded by concrete and skyscrapers.

Bailey turned right, into a driveway that was closed off by ten-foot gates with cameras mounted on the posts. A concrete wall of equal height surrounded the front portion of the property. The back abutted rolling, wooded hills. From what I could see, the residence was a single-story ranch-style home of about seven thousand square feet that sat on at least an acre and a half of land. Bailey pushed a button below a speaker on the right side of the gate and gave our names. There was no response. We waited thirty seconds, but just as she'd reached out to push the button again, the gates slowly swung inward.

The driveway led us onto a road that wove through lush shrubbery and mature trees and ended in a horseshoe driveway. We pulled to a stop at the apex of the arc, where two muscle-bound six-footers in blue do-rags guarded the front door. I'd call them a welcoming committee, but they didn't look all that welcoming. I decided not to let this hurt my feelings.

"We're about to get frisked," Bailey said. "Try not to give anyone your phone number."

We exchanged a "here goes nothing" look and got out of the car.

The thug on the right spun his finger in a circle, gesturing for us to turn and "assume the position"—i.e., face the car, with our hands on the roof. We complied, and they ran their hands across our arms, down our sides, and all over our legs and ankles. Then they patted our torsos, front and back. It wasn't rough, but it was thorough, and in my current condition, any touch hurt like hell. I clamped my jaws together to keep from wincing.

I considered making the standard joke about at least buying me a drink but rejected the idea. What if they took me up on the offer?

We followed them into a foyer with dark-wood floors and walls lined with photographs of gleaming motorcycles of all shapes, sizes, and colors. The sign in the background of one of the photographs told me what had built this mansion. Motorcycles—exquisitely customized ones—were big business. Our escorts gave us no time to linger and steered us directly into a room that would ordinarily be called a study, except no one was ever going to study anything in here. Instead of the usual dark leather and mahogany, the room was carpeted in a champagne-colored low-pile topped off with burnt-orange throw rugs. A latticed window gave the sunlight a gentle glow, and the biggest flat screen I'd ever seen presided over a grouping of soft, cushy burnt-orange couches and reclining chairs at the other end of the room. I noticed that our host was already seated on one of the reclining chairs, and we were steered to the couch nearest to him. I lowered myself onto the farthest spot on the end of the sofa slowly, hoping it would make me look cool and defiant rather than stiff and sore.

Dominic Rostoni did not look Italian. With shoulder-length white-blond hair, ruddy, pitted skin from an early siege of acne, and dark-brown eyes, he looked more Nordic than Neapolitan. And although it couldn't have been more than fifty degrees outside, he was wearing just a wifebeater, jeans, and flip-flops.

"You're the cop." He looked at Bailey. "And you're the DA," he said to me.

"And you're PEN1's CEO," I replied, just to show I'd prepared too.

"It's not a crime," he replied, his voice relaxed, conversational.

This was true. It wasn't a crime to belong to a gang. It was only a crime to do crimes with a gang.

"You remember the case where the Glendale cop got murdered in his own basement?" I asked.

Dominic frowned a moment and stared out the window.

"That the one where the wife cut off his head with an ax?" he asked.

Not much I could add to that, so I nodded.

"That's what you want to talk to me about?"

"The defense said you guys did it," I said. "Part of the whole war you had going with the Glendale PD." I stopped and watched his reaction.

"I did hear something like that, now you mention it," he said with little inflection.

He gave no indication of any concern, and his answer made it clear that he wasn't going to give up one more word than he had to—the cagey type. Or the type who'd learned from his previous encounters with law enforcement.

"There're some in your crowd who say it's true," I remarked.

Dominic didn't answer immediately. He looked at me impassively.

"From what I remember, that case was over a while ago," he said, looking at me through hooded eyes. "So I'm gonna guess that you're here about something else."

"We are," I replied.

"Then shouldn't you be reading me my rights?"

"You're not in custody," I said. "And you can refuse to talk, but we're not looking at any group…activity you need to be concerned about."

Though I wasn't entirely sure PEN1 hadn't done Zack's murder, I tended to agree with Larry that a gang hit didn't fit with the nature of the crime. And there was no reason to believe that Lilah's protection was a gang priority. So if one of these guys was helping her and had killed Simon in the process, it was likely a private arrangement. But private or no, any PEN1 member would be foolish not to get Dominic's approval before taking the job. It wouldn't be good for the guy's health to look like he was sneaking around, doing private money gigs on the side.

Dominic peered out the window again for a few moments, then turned back to me and stared straight into my eyes.

"Go ahead," he finally said.

"Did PEN1 do Zack?" I asked.

Dominic shook his head once. "No."

"You're sure?" I asked, though I knew the answer.

"No one makes a move that big without my approval," he replied flatly, as though I'd asked whether the sun always rose in the east. Then, as if reading from a script, he calmly added, "Not that I'd ever approve an act of violence."

"No, of course not," I said.

He continued, "Anyways—"

"Anyway," I corrected. I could feel Bailey mentally rolling her eyes and telling me to shut up, but I couldn't help it. I never can. Shit like this drives me nuts.

Dominic looked at me, perplexed, but obediently repeated, "Anyway...doing a cop in his own home is just plain stupid."

"Then why'd some of your people seem to think it was PEN1 business?" I asked, bluffing a little.

" 'Cause some of our people are dipshits who like to act tough and don't have the brains God gave a kickstand."

Heavy is the head that wears the crown.

"You or any other PEN1 member ever have any dealings with Lilah Bayer?" I asked.

"That the wife?" he asked, his tone genuinely curious.

"Right."

He frowned, then gave me a puzzled look. "Why would we?"

"Does that mean no?" I asked.

Dominic sighed. "Lawyers," he said, shaking his head. "Yeah, that means no."

I was out of questions. I looked over at Bailey, who shook her head.

"Thanks for your time, Dominic," I said.

I stood as quickly as I could, subtly using the arm of the sofa to push myself up. At least I'd thought it was subtle.

"What happened to you?" Dominic asked.

Oh well.

"Nothing," I said, trying not to grimace as I turned my head.

He nodded sagely. "Ice'll help that *nothing*," he said. "Or a cold gel pack."

"Thanks."

We were escorted out to the car and followed by our two guards until the gates closed behind us.

We stopped for a red light at the intersection on Mulholland. A biker on a Harley in leather chaps with a baby carrier strapped to his chest rode by, heading for the ocean. A tiny white poodle was snuggled happily into the baby carrier, its ears flying in the wind. Poodle was going to the beach with Biker. At least it wasn't in someone's purse, dressed up like a ballerina.

We drove in silence until Bailey got to the freeway on-ramp. The traffic was starting to back up with lunchtime travelers.

"We had to check it out, but I'm just not feeling this whole Lilah-skinhead connection," she said.

I nodded. "But it was worth it to make all those fun new friends."

"You still think it might've been one of those fun friends who jumped you?" Bailey asked.

"No," I replied with certainty.

I'd given this a lot of thought since we left the compound.

"What makes you so sure?"

"Because I just remembered one very salient point," I said. "That guy didn't just take my wallet. He also took the photo—the one of the stabber."

"Shit," Bailey said softly.

My sentiments exactly.

60

Lilah gestured to Maxwell Chevorin to have a seat on the couch. "I'm having green tea. Can I get you anything?"

"That sounds good," the lobbyist replied. He watched her move to the kitchenette, enjoying the view. It was a nice perk.

Maxwell once again congratulated himself on his luck, and his instinct. His luck, because it'd given him state senator William Sharder for a buddy. His instinct, because when Sharder confided that Lilah'd blackmailed him into getting her a junior associate position with his law firm, it'd told him that she was cut out for this line of work. So when she was acquitted of her husband's murder, he'd recognized the golden opportunity and immediately made her an offer. Personally, he'd never believed she was guilty, but it wouldn't have mattered if she had been. If anything, that would only have made her more attractive to him. Someone smart enough to get away with murder was someone he could use. The lobbyist had never feared for his own safety. He understood Lilah. She needed him as much as he needed her. She was, in some respects, his female counterpart: ruthless, brilliant, and obsessive.

Lilah set down two big-handled mugs and sat in a chair across the coffee table from him.

"The CEO job is largely completed," she said. "I just want to take a few more days to make sure we've bled every source dry." Which was why she hadn't wanted to take this meeting today. But Chevorin had been insistent. Not that she blamed him—she probably would've felt the same in his position. Since they only communicated about cases in person, he had no other way of knowing whether they'd made any progress.

"Here's where we stand right now." Lilah described what they'd found on the CEO but didn't tell him about the bonus dirt they'd dug up on the CEO's "fixer." She intended to keep the fixer for herself. He was worth much more than the lobbyist would ever pay.

At the other end of the spectrum, she'd also caught a minnow in her net. The bookkeeper of the company, a devoted family man with two daughters, was apparently engaged in a very lusty affair. Along with dozens of steamy love letters, Chase had found a photograph of the man's paramour: a well-endowed twentysomething young man dressed only in a bolo tie and cowboy boots, signed, "All my love, Bryce." Lilah had taken all the letters and the photograph and personally shredded every single item, then fired off an anonymous letter to the bookkeeper, warning him to cover his tracks better in the future. She had no use for him, so why bother to ruin him?

"Amazing," Chevorin said with undisguised admiration. "Can you deliver the final package by next week?"

"I'll call you." Lilah stood, indicating the meeting was at an end.

After the lobbyist was gone, she summoned Chase and told him to get there immediately. She needed an update of her own and was hoping it'd be as good as the one she'd just given the lobbyist. It wasn't.

"Why the hell didn't you take care of it yourself?" she asked when he finished describing what had happened at the hotel.

"I couldn't take the chance," he replied, taken aback by her display of temper. "My face might already be on that surveillance footage."

"So you sent a moron? It was a very simple order: find out what they have. How does that translate to 'put a DA in the hospital'? That idiot just made the case priority number one."

Her anger stung—in no small part because she was right. He should've known better than to give the job to a new hire.

"He grabbed her wallet too," he said. "Maybe they'll just think—"

Lilah froze him with a look.

"You're right," he said. "You're right."

Her voice now quiet and much more ominous, Lilah outlined what she wanted him to do.

When he left, she took a deep breath and went over to the window. Her head had begun to throb and the sunlight pierced her eyes. As she pushed the button to close the shades, she noticed that her hands were shaking. The attack on that prosecutor was exactly the kind of bushleague mistake that could ruin her. She was getting that familiar, hated vulnerable feeling—the sense that events were spinning out of her control. That feeling always brought on the towering rage that had fueled so many of her murderous nightmares.

Action typically made her feel better, but it was too dangerous to make a move now, without a plan. She pressed her hands together to stop them from shaking and went to the kitchenette. She found the bottle of Xanax and popped three milligrams, then threw ice into a towel, held it to her forehead, and lay down on the couch, willing the fury to abate. A fury that, if ever unleashed, would make those murderous nightmares a reality.

61

"If he took the photo, then whoever attacked you—," Bailey began.

"—is involved somehow in Simon's murder," I finished. "Whether it was the stabber himself or a cohort, it's clear now: somebody's tracking us. *Has been* tracking us."

Which explained that creepy "being watched" feeling I'd been having. Though it was a relief to know that I hadn't been hallucinating, the knowledge that someone, likely a murderer, was following me was less than wonderful. A lot less.

"He could've killed you—but he didn't."

"Killing me makes it a bigger deal. I'd bet his first choice was to break into my room, but those doors are built like a vault's."

"Still, the attack on you shows he'll go as far as he has to—regardless of what his first choice is," Bailey said, looking worried. She pulled up in front of the courthouse. "Call me when you're ready to leave, and I'll come pick you up," she said. "Got it?"

I sighed. "Fine," I said. "But I'm leaving early." I looked at her challengingly.

"See you in a couple of hours," she said.

I got out and swam upstream against the wave of lunch-bound hordes. When I got back to my office, I saw that I had a message to contact Eric. Melia was at her desk, but her eyes were glued to the tabloid rag in her lap. It was a pleasure to interrupt her.

"I'm here to see Eric," I said.

Her head popped up, mouth open. "Huh? Oh, uh, yeah." She buzzed him and told him I was there. "He says you can go on in," she said, then immediately dropped her attention back to her lap.

Eric stood up when I walked into his office.

"I just heard about what happened," he said.

"Who told you?" I asked.

"Hotel security," he replied. "They wanted to coordinate your protection. Naturally, I said we'd be glad to work with them." Eric gave me a pointed look.

Uh-oh.

"But first, are you okay?" he asked.

"I'm fine," I said, lowering myself slowly into one of the chairs in front of his desk.

"Yeah, you look great," Eric said dryly, watching my descent. "Any idea who did it?"

I shook my head. "Someone connected to Simon Bayer's murder. Could've been the murderer himself."

I told him about the missing photograph.

He looked down at his desk, pensive. "This worries me a great deal—"

I cut him off. "Don't even think about reassigning the case." I tried to collect myself and speak in a rational tone. "It won't be any less dangerous for any other deputy. And I've been in on it from the start—"

Eric held up a hand and looked at me for a long moment. He slowly nodded. "You're right." He sighed and frowned. "But I'm assigning you security. We're putting DA investigators on your tail and in your hotel. Starting now." He gave me a stern look. "And you'll be fully co-operative with them."

"Got it," I said, knowing it was no use to protest even if I'd minded. Which, at the moment, I had to admit, I didn't.

"And now, I have to give you a heads-up," Eric said. "I hate to give you anything else to worry about, but Phil Hemet's been in the chief deputy's ear, claiming you've been out playing around when you say you're in the field. He came to tell me personally that someone saw you and Bailey partying it up at Guido's—"

I protested hotly. "This is complete bullshit, Eric!" I'd known Hemet was up to something, but this was just an out-and-out lie. I told him about Melia's encounter with the reporter.

Eric nodded. "It figures. Hemet's got someone in the newsroom who's all fired up to do an article on how special unit—and especially Special Trials—deputies screw around on company time. Apparently he's got quite a few buddies in the news business." Eric's voice was low, but the underlying anger was palpable. "And I know what he said is horseshit, Rachel. But Hemet's out for blood, and I don't think he cares what's true anymore."

I tried to control my voice despite the rage and frustration boiling in my gut. "So what're we going to do about it? We can't just let him spread these lies around," I said.

"No, but there's nothing we can do at the moment," Eric replied. "Just give him as little fodder as possible. I understand you had to be out of the office to get this case rolling. But just be careful from here on out about what you do and when you do it when you're in public."

I tried to console myself with the knowledge that at least Hemet hadn't tipped the press to the Simon Bayer case, but it didn't help much. Now that Hemet had promised a mudslinging insider exclusive, the press would be watching. I'd known that someone was bound to figure out what I was working on sooner or later, but now, thanks to that asshat Hemet, it would be sooner. Much sooner. I'd have to move faster—if that was possible. I sifted through my in-box and got the most pressing business on my other cases out of the way. To avoid the fun and hilarity of lowering myself into my chair one inch at a time, I did it standing up. Then I pulled out my Lilah to-do list and did what could be accomplished at a desk, but by four thirty I'd hit a dead end. Again. I was ready to pack it in. But after my chat with Eric, I knew it wouldn't look good to leave that early.

The fact that I had to worry about that infuriated me all over again. I put in so much overtime (unpaid, of course) that my hourly wage was about a dollar and a quarter. And I never had a chance to take my comp time. So now, not only was I being stalked by a murderer but I'd been targeted by a dickhead middle manager with a petty grudge. Adding insult to injury, the very same manager who was the number one supporter of that useless sack Brandon Averill—the prosecutor whose slipshod, lousy work got me into this mess to begin with. I eyed the bottom drawer of my desk where I kept the Glenlivet but didn't want to waste good scotch on bad lawyers. I made myself work until five o'clock, then called Bailey.

"I'm pulling the plug," I said.

"Thought you were leaving early."

"I am," I said testily. "Should I see if Toni's around?"

"Sure, why should I get your great mood all to my-self?"

I hung up and dialed Toni's extension, too tired to walk down the hall. No answer. I tried her cell.

"I'm still in court, believe it or not," Toni replied. "Hang on." I heard her whisper to someone nearby, then she came back on the line. "I'll meet you downstairs in ten."

My security detail, which was comprised of district attorney investigators, was waiting in Eric's anteroom. DA investigators are basically cops who work exclusively for the DA's office, and plenty of them used to work for police agencies. They handle specialized investigations and all security details. District Attorney Vanderhorn has investigators assigned to him as security on a full-time basis. That's no easy job, because the biggest threat to his safety probably comes from those of us who work for him.

A well-built man with a crew cut and kind eyes stepped forward from the group and put out his hand. "Gary Schrader, senior investigator," he said. "I'm the team leader." He gestured to the three other men with him. All were wearing the navy-blue nylon DA investi-gator Windbreaker. Gary gave me a sympathetic look. "I was sorry to hear about the incident, Ms. Knight. But we plan to make sure it doesn't happen again."

His manner was old-school, courtly and respectful yet

warm. Though I'd grudgingly admitted I didn't mind having security around, the idea of being followed 24-7 hadn't exactly thrilled me. But now I felt not only well-protected but honored.

"Thank you," I said, shaking his hand. "And please call me Rachel."

He nodded. "Gary," he said.

He turned to gesture behind him. "This is Stephen." A stout young man with slicked-back brown hair gave a little wave. "James." An impressively tall, fair blond with light eyebrows and eyelashes nodded. "And Mario." A slim but muscular Latino with thick black hair and a sexy smile saluted me.

I shook hands with each of them. "I rate four investigators?"

"They'll usually rotate in teams of two," Gary said.

I told them my plans, and we all trooped out to the elevator. My own private retinue of navy-blue nylon Windbreakers and running shoes.

I found Toni already outside at the curb, and one of the investigators went to get his car while the other three waited with us. Toni looked from the investigators to me and nodded.

"Good," she said.

Thirty seconds later, Bailey drove up, and Toni and I piled into her car. The investigator who'd gone to get his vehicle pulled up behind her, and one of the guys got into the passenger seat. The other two saluted and promised to see us tomorrow.

As we headed down Spring Street, Bailey said, "The Biltmore? Or somewhere else?"

"Let's hit my room," I said.

"Your room?" Toni echoed, looking puzzled.

My room was often the place where we eventually crashed, but it wasn't usually our destination for evening entertainment.

"I'll explain when we get there," I promised. "Besides, I already told my dates"—I jerked my thumb at the investigators behind us—"that's where I was going, and I'm trying to be cooperative."

Toni and Bailey snorted almost simultaneously.

The DA investigators tailed us into the hotel and went to their posts in the hallway when we entered my room.

"How'd you wind up with protection?" Bailey asked.

As we took off our coats and dropped them on a chair, I explained how Eric had found out about the attack. "So you're off the hook now," I told her.

"I'm here for the duration. I don't care how many of those guys are hanging around."

I was too tired and frazzled to argue. I held up a bottle of wine and a chilled bottle of Russian Standard Platinum vodka.

Bailey picked up a barrel glass. "Vodka."

"I think I'm in the mood for wine," Toni said.

I opened the bottle and filled glasses for her and myself, and let Bailey do the honors with the vodka. "Want to order room service?"

"Not yet," Bailey said. "At least, not for me."

Toni shook her head. "I'll take some snacks, though."

I put out the nuts and pretzels, then sat down on the couch and held out my glass for a toast.

"To a terrific week," I said sarcastically.

"It's almost over," Toni said. "I'll drink to that."

We all took a long sip.

"Now, what are we doing in your room?" Bailey asked.

I told them about Phil Hemet and his latest quest to trash me and all of Special Trials. When I finished, Toni was fuming. She poured herself another glass of wine and hunched over it, tapping one finger on the glass.

"You know what we need?" she asked.

"An unregistered gun?" I said helpfully.

Toni stared at me. "No," she said. "Dirt. On Hemet."

"That's good too," I said. I ran my hand through my hair and winced as I accidentally touched one of the many sore spots on my head. "But how?"

"Leave that to me," Toni replied.

62

We never did make it out of my room. In fact, Toni never even made it home. She crashed on the couch.

The next morning dawned bright and sunny. I got up and felt the window. It seemed warmer today than it had been. Maybe that would help ease the aches and pains. I still felt like I was about ninety years old. I heard Bailey moving around in the other bedroom. Did I smell coffee?

I quickly showered and inventoried the damage to my face and torso. Better, though not good. But now some yellow was peeking through the purple. Progress. I threw on some jeans and a sweater. Well, not *throw* exactly. I inched my way into them. When I reached the living room, I saw there was indeed coffee. And pastries. And bagels. With Bailey for a roommate, I was going to wind up wearing bedspreads to court. I poured myself a cup of coffee and pulled off half a bagel.

Toni sat up, yawning, then sleepwalked to the bathroom. Two seconds later, the shower began to run.

"How you feeling, sunshine?" Bailey said, looking perfect in her brown pencil slacks and short boots.

"Better." I took another sip of coffee. "Thanks for ordering."

Bailey smirked, knowing I wasn't entirely pleased with the selection. "Come on, it won't kill you, and your security might put up with you longer if you give 'em a bear claw."

"On second thought, pass me that Danish."

She passed me the plate. "That's the spirit," she said.

I put most of the remaining pastries on a spare dish and stepped out into the hall. Gary was standing closest to the door, and I could see Mario at the end of the hall. I held out the plate to Gary.

"I thought we should all get fat together," I joked.

"You have nothing to worry about, Rachel," Gary said, taking the plate from me.

If someone else had said it, the line might've sounded a little bit lecherous. But Gary just made it sound reassuring.

"Your wife is probably the luckiest woman on earth," I said.

"So I've been telling her for the past ten years," he replied. "But feel free to call and back me up. A little corroboration never hurts." He held up the plate. "And thank you for these. Mario'll love it."

"My pleasure."

I went back into the room, picked up the remaining Danish, and took a big bite. It was fresh and delicious. "It's time to hit up Lilah's parents." We'd been hoping to have enough information on her to keep them honest before we had the meeting, but it looked like we had all we were going to get.

Bailey nodded. "I know we've talked about it for a

while," she said. "But I'm not sure what we expect to get from them. They're on her side. Even if they don't know we're looking at her possible involvement in Simon's murder, they've got to know she's flying under the radar and using an alias. I don't see them helping us."

Bailey sat back and folded her arms over her chest. Her thinking posture. I got up and paced. My thinking posture. One of us had a more annoying thinking posture than the other.

I thought out loud. "You couldn't find any trace of her under any of her known names—"

"I've checked every database in every city, county, and state in this country. I've checked banks, jails, prisons, hospitals, even the morgue, I've checked—"

I held up my hand. "Enough. I get it. But she can't just be No-Name. She must've gotten a new ID, right?"

"Right," Bailey said. "Though that may not necessarily mean she's up to no good. She's got every reason to want to change her name and erase her past."

True enough. "But even if she is into something shady, she can't get by with no ID."

And Lilah's new name was the least of the unknowns that'd been plaguing me. Was she a cold-blooded murderer? Or was she the victim of a misguided investigation—someone whose life had been ruined by being falsely accused? If the latter, then what was she doing now? Why was she seemingly in hiding? I had a hard time believing she was cowering in a corner somewhere. I'd studied her on that surveillance footage too many times to count, and one thing was clear to me: that strong, confident stride didn't fit with someone who'd disappeared out of fear or shame. But that single conclusion, based only on my intuition, left a world of questions unanswered. Every time I thought about Lilah, I wound up on this same circular path.

"No one gets by in this world without ID," Bailey agreed. "And I didn't see anything in her past that was helpful. Though I did think it was weird that she got a GED instead of finishing high school."

"Especially since she'd just come back home after years of getting stellar grades in a boarding school."

Bailey sat up. "When'd you come up with that?"

"A little while ago." I shrugged. "Checked out her school records, talked to a few people. Seems she got into enough trouble to make the counselor recommend a boarding school for 'problem children.'"

"She have a juvenile record?"

"No. And it seems the boarding school did straighten her out. By the time she left, she had a four-oh."

Bailey looked at me intently. "You pulling all-nighters working on this woman, or what? And elementary school? How on earth's that supposed to help us find her now?"

Until that moment, I hadn't thought to question it. But now I wondered: What *did* I hope to gain by delving into Lilah's personal history—especially that far back?

"I just wanted to fill in some blanks," I said. "I needed to get some answers for a change, instead of questions that only led to more questions. It's been frustrating, you know?"

Bailey nodded. Her puzzled look told me she wasn't entirely convinced, but I didn't have any better explanation.

I paused to look out the window at Pershing Square. The small park in the middle of downtown always sets up

an ice rink in winter. A young girl wearing lighted rein-
deer antlers stumbled blindly around the oval rink. She
couldn't have been more than fourteen. Her wet jeans told
me her efforts to stay upright hadn't been a total success.
Suddenly she slip-slided her way off the ice and into a
roped-off area, where she dropped heavily onto one of the
folding chairs. A rink official glided over and appeared to
order her out of the area. When she unsteadily followed
his directions, he sat her down at one of the public tables.
Was she stoned? Or just new on skates?

I brought my thoughts back to the matter at hand and
gave voice to an issue that'd been dancing around in my
mind.

"How did Lilah and Zack meet anyway?" I asked.

"No one knows," Bailey replied. "Even Zack's parents
were vague. At some party or something."

I nodded, frowning, and turned back to the window.

The girl with the antlers duckwalked her way back
onto the rink and began to bounce off the low wood barri-
ers. This time, a tall, strong-looking rink official quickly
skated up behind her, grabbed her under the arms, and
steered her off the ice, then motioned for a nearby patrol
officer. Stoned. Definitely not the skates.

I began to pace again. "If they did meet at a party, then
how come no one has any details? Like when or where it
was, or who threw the party?"

Bailey shrugged.

"It bugs me that they have no logical point of intersection," I said. "Work? School? Church?" I turned another
circle, thinking.

"Your pacing is making me nuts," Bailey warned.
"And dizzy."

She had a point. The room was pretty small, so my circles were tight and fast. "Sorry," I said. I resumed pacing but tried to make it look like a casual stroll. "Zack didn't go to law school—"

"—so they didn't meet there," Bailey said. "And they didn't meet at work. When she interned for the DA's office, she was down in Orange County."

"And no one ever said they were churchgoers—"

"She'd immolate on the threshold." Toni emerged from the bathroom looking like a magazine cover.

Makeup, flawless. Hair, perfect. Clothes, chic. And if circumstances required, she could even do it fast. I was no slouch, but I was a mere grasshopper next to Master Toni.

I resumed pacing. "She went to law school, interned at the DA's office, and got hired at a fancy law firm. None of that explains how she and Zack crossed paths."

Bailey refolded her arms and stared down at the table. After a moment, she looked up. "If she did kill Zack, it wouldn't be a big strain to believe Lilah had a shady past."

I stopped pacing and looked at Bailey. "A hotshot corporate lawyer with a shady past? Impossible," I said with a sarcastic smile. "So maybe they met at Zack's workplace."

"As in, Zack busted her for something?"

I shrugged.

But Bailey was frowning. "I don't know. Men think with the little head and all that, but hooking up with a suspect..." She shook her head. "It's a career wrecker if anyone finds out. And from everything we've heard about him, Zack was an ambitious guy. Cops who want to be captain—or more—don't take those kinds of chances."

"I agree," I replied. "And if he did bust her for something, he must've hidden it, because she's got no rap sheet, right?"

"None," Bailey said. "But then again…we're pretty sure she's got an alias now, right? Maybe she had an alias back then…"

No cover-up would've been required.

"Or maybe he didn't bust her," Toni chimed in. "Maybe she was a witness."

I nodded. "That might've given her a legit reason to have an alias…"

"Such as?" Bailey asked.

"She was hiding from an abusive boyfriend," Toni said.

"If she did have an alias back then—for whatever reason—it'd be a lot easier to go back to it now than to get a whole new set of fake IDs," I said.

Bailey sighed. "This means we've got to go through Zack's arrest reports and see if we can find a witness or suspect who fits her description. Needle in a haystack."

I nodded glumly. This time, I had no magnet.

63

"**Records show** they were married for two years, and according to witness interviews, they dated for about six months before that," Bailey said.

"Then let's go back a year before the marriage to be on the safe side," I said. "Where was Zack working back then?"

"I'll check," Bailey replied, pulling out her cell.

"Well, I'll leave y'all to it," Toni said, giving her makeup a final check in the mirror next to the entry. When I'd first moved into this suite, I'd thought that was a weird place for a mirror. Toni showed me the error of my ways.

She looked outside and set aside her coat. "Got an extra scarf?" she asked. "Preferably gray," she said, gesturing to her pale blush-colored blouse.

"Oh yes, ma'am," I replied jokingly. My neck is my weak spot when it comes to cold, so I've got a pretty impressive array of scarves, pashminas, and mufflers. Toni, of course, knows this. I went to my closet and dug out a charcoal-gray wool-fringed number for her approval.

"Perfect," Toni said. With one deft movement, she had it wound around her neck and looking better than I'd ever managed.

"You going to be around this weekend?" I asked.

"I am," Toni said. "J.D.'s got a conference to go to. Want to do something?"

"Definitely," I replied. I looked at Bailey.

"Drew and I are going up to Ojai on Sunday."

"You're dead to me," I said.

It was actually for the best. I'd been looking for a chance to tell Toni about Romy anyway.

"Call me," Toni said, and glided out the door.

Bailey had already pulled out her phone to find out where Zack had been assigned before his marriage to Lilah.

I went to finish my makeup and hair, and finally admitted that I was preparing myself in case I ran into Graden. Telling Bailey everything had had a calming effect. Seething done in private can keep anger burning, but like a pot of boiling water, once you take the lid off, the heat dissipates and the boil turns to a simmer. I was still angry with Graden, but there was a small part of me that was beginning to consider the possibility that I'd overreacted. Just possibly.

"Hollywood," Bailey said, snapping her cell phone shut.

It was Bailey's old stomping ground before she'd been assigned to Robbery-Homicide, so she got a hero's welcome.

"Look what the cat dragged in," said the Hollywood station desk sergeant, a rotund, apple-cheeked man with thinning brown hair and big, dark eyes.

"Gomez, how come they haven't fired you yet?" Bailey asked, grinning.

He shrugged. "Guess they keep forgetting," he replied. "Come on back, we'll get you set up."

Five minutes later, we were parked in front of a computer and scrolling through all the crime reports signed by Zack Bayer.

"Could be any kind of crime," Bailey said.

"As long as there's a female involved somehow," I said. "Either as a suspect, witness, or victim. Anyone who might be Lilah, using an alias."

"That narrows it right down," she said sarcastically. But it wasn't a completely useless filter. We weeded out a bunch of drug busts that involved no females right off the bat.

"Hmmm, domestic-violence call," Bailey said, pointing to the screen.

She read aloud, "Victim: Latasha McKenzie, five feet one, one hundred ten pounds, African-American—"

"Okay, probably not the victim," I said. "Suspect?"

"Boyfriend, Lamar Washington, six feet, two hundred pounds—"

"Any witnesses?"

"None," Bailey said. "We move on."

I watched as she scrolled. "Hey, what about that one?" I said, pointing to a robbery.

Bailey clicked and read. "Victim: Oren Abnarian, male...whatever. Suspect: Abner Clarence, male... whatever. Witnesses: Starla Moreno, no description, but she's female for sure, and two males. Checking on Starla."

"Interesting name," I replied.

Bailey clicked for the full report. "Yeah," she said, continuing to read. "Even more interesting than you thought. Starla's aka is Stanley. Description is six feet one and two hundred pounds with a skull-necklace tattoo."

"She sounds lovely."

Bailey sighed. "This is going to be a long night. And I'm spending it with you."

By ten p.m., the morning-watch crew—who worked ten p.m. to six a.m.—was heading out for duty. I stood up and stretched. "I hate to have caffeine after breakfast, but if I don't, I'll do a face-plant. Want some?"

"Yeah. And make it black," Bailey said.

As I walked out to the vending machine, I saw that our investigators had already tanked up. The table was littered with paper cups and sugar packets. I came back bearing our doses of caffeine, and we rolled on.

"Prostitution bust, suspect name, Brandy."

"Isn't it time to retire that name?" I asked.

"It's a classic," Bailey said. "Seems the right age." She continued to read. "Hispanic—"

"Could be faked."

"She's five feet ten," Bailey said.

"Next."

We sorted through a dozen more without finding anything worth exploring further.

I was leaning on the desk, head propped up on one hand, rubbing my temple with the other to keep myself awake. I was trying to think of a faster way to do this when Bailey elbowed me, pointed to the screen, and read aloud.

"Res burg—owner/victim's a white female, no witnesses, no suspects."

Residential burglary and a promising-looking victim. "Apartment building or house?" I asked.

It was unlikely that someone as young as Lilah was at that time could've afforded a house. The residence needed to be an apartment to make the case a real possibility.

"Apartment," Bailey replied. "Victim: Nina Klavens, no DOB."

"That's a keeper."

By four a.m., we'd gone through the entire year of crime reports and come up with two other distinct possibilities: a car theft in Los Feliz, and a purse snatch on Sunset Boulevard.

We called it a night and dragged ourselves back to the Biltmore. I fell into bed. My last thought before I dropped off was that Phil Hemet didn't put in this many hours in a month. How come there was no reporter tailing me now?

64

I woke up energized and hopeful about the leads we'd found last night. We were finishing breakfast and I was looking through my to-do list. I poured another cup of coffee for myself, but Bailey waved me off.

"I'm good," she said. "I'm going to see if I can find out where our burglary victim is now."

"If she's still at the same location, she's probably not our girl," I replied.

Bailey nodded and opened her cell. She gave the victim's name and address, and while she waited for a response, I slinked my fork over to her plate of hash browns and speared a mouthful. Bailey shot me a look.

"What?" I whispered. "You were done."

She pulled her plate closer and returned to her call. "Yes," she said, taking out her notebook and pen. She scribbled the information. "Thanks. Can I run a couple of other reports by you?"

Bailey gave the information we had on the purse snatch and car theft. While she waited for an answer, I went back to my bedroom to finish getting dressed.

When I returned, Bailey was standing and finishing her coffee.

"And?" I asked.

"Our burglary victim has moved."

"So far, so good," I said.

She nodded. "The purse snatch is a bust. Victim was a tourist who got groped and robbed on Sunset Boulevard by R2-D2—"

"Funny, you ask me, I would've picked C-3PO to be that guy," I said.

Costumed impersonators of famous figures, both fictional and real, had become a thriving business on Sunset Boulevard. On any given day, Darth Vader, Spider-Man, or the Hulk could be found strolling back and forth in front of Grauman's Chinese Theatre. Unfortunately some of them were tweakers—speed freaks—who targeted unsuspecting out-of-towners.

"Our victim was an Aussie, and she went back to the Land Down Under," Bailey said. "She declined to return to prosecute, and we've got no information on her current whereabouts. Suspect was a male."

"Doesn't sound like Lilah anyway, so no loss."

"No," Bailey replied. She checked the magazine on her .44 Glock and slipped it back into her shoulder holster, then put on her coat. "Let's go see if Nina Klavens is our girl."

Nina was now living in Studio City. According to her DMV record, she had a small house on Valley Vista Boulevard.

"That's a pretty nice neighborhood, isn't it?" I asked.

"Nice enough," Bailey replied. "But remember, Lilah used to be a corporate lawyer, so she's got skills. She could make enough money for a nice little place."

Bailey assured our security detail of DA investigators that we could go it alone today. We'd be in her car and in decent places when we were out in public. A tail wouldn't make us any safer. They checked in with their lieutenant, who'd agreed. I felt their despair at having to miss out on more time with us, but I was confident they'd console themselves with a second choice—say, for instance, clogging.

By the time we left, it was almost noon. That should've meant smooth sailing down the 101 Freeway, especially since we were heading northbound. But for some reason the traffic was even worse than usual. Getting stuck in traffic on a Saturday afternoon never ceases to confound and irritate me. *What the hell is everyone doing out on the freeway on a Saturday?* For the next half hour, in typical L.A. fashion, we crawled northbound, inch by inch.

We rode in silence until Bailey cleared her throat. "Have you said anything to Toni about...?"

"Not yet," I said.

"Are...ah...are you going to tell Drew?" she asked, uncharacteristically hesitant.

Because they were going to be alone in a quiet place for a while and she didn't want to slip and tell him anything I didn't want him to know. There was so much to appreciate about Bailey.

"I'll tell Drew pretty soon."

"And don't worry," she said. "I'll never tell."

"I know."

"I'd never waste my time with Drew talking about you." She grinned.

Bailey exited the freeway and headed west on Ventura. Ten minutes later, we turned onto Valley Vista and drove up the winding road, watching the address numbers. Halfway up the incline, I saw it.

"There." I pointed, indicating a little brick house with white shutters on the right.

Small yet meticulously maintained, it was on a fairly secluded plot, set at least fifty feet back from the street and partially blocked from view by mature peppertrees. I could definitely see how this place would be a perfect fit for someone who wanted privacy.

Bailey parked and we followed a bricked path to the front door. A tasteful, well-polished brass knocker was placed just above a tiny eyehole. Bailey stood within view of the peephole and banged the knocker twice. At first, I heard nothing. But as I concentrated, I thought I detected Beethoven's Seventh playing somewhere inside the house.

Bailey looked toward the driveway, and I followed her gaze. A red Prius was parked there. A likely indication that Nina, or hopefully Lilah, was home. Bailey banged the knocker on the brass plate a little harder this time. I leaned in to listen. I thought I heard the low thump of footsteps approaching on a wood floor. Seconds later, the thumping stopped.

"Who's there?" said a woman's voice, muffled by the heavy-looking door between us.

Bailey pulled out her badge and held it up to the peephole. "Bailey Keller, detective with the LAPD."

"You alone?" the woman asked.

"No," Bailey said, moving to the side.

I stepped in front of the peephole. "Deputy District Attorney Rachel Knight. We're here to talk to you about the burglary," I said.

The door swung open.

"Well, it's about damn time," said the woman.

Nina Klavens, who, it turned out, really was Nina Klavens. And ninety years old if she was a day.

65

Thirty minutes later, after getting an earful of the slipshod job the police had done investigating her burglary, we were finally released from Nina Klavens's clutches.

"Assuming we did find her Hummel collection in some report, how'd we be able to tell it was hers?" I asked. "Don't all those little kids holding umbrellas and watering cans look the same?"

"Ask me, because I'm a collector," Bailey replied dryly. "Besides, I wasn't the one who offered to look for it."

We got into the car and belted up. "If I hadn't, we'd still be in there."

"So we're down to the auto theft," she said. "Give me the info."

I pulled out the report. "Victim, Alicia Morris. No description, no DOB. Address in…Hollywood, on Fountain Avenue, east of Fairfax. Apartment J."

Bailey turned right and headed toward Mulholland Drive. Eventually we landed on Benedict Canyon, which would take us from the San Fernando Valley to the west side of town. The canyons are older roads where trees and greenery have had plenty of time to mature, creating a canopy that filters what little sunlight penetrates the hills. The homes lining the road range from overbuilt and grandiose to charming and rustic. Though the ride was more picturesque than the freeway, it took just one slow-moving car to back up traffic for miles. Luckily, today we were the ones out in front. We flew all the way down to Sunset, where we headed east, then took La Cienega south and ended up on Fountain Avenue. When we passed Fairfax, Bailey slowed and I watched the numbers, searching for the address, listed as 7300 Fountain Avenue.

"Wait, slow down," I said as we neared Fountain and Martel. I read the sign on the building at 7300 Fountain. "Morman Boling Casting?" A casting agency. Not Alicia Morris's—or anyone else's—residence.

Bailey and I exchanged a look. "Maybe the numbers go down and then up again," she suggested.

We continued east, but by the time we'd passed Kat Von D's High Voltage Tattoo at La Brea, the numbers were still descending.

"Fountain dead-ends just past Gower and picks up again at Van Ness. If the numbers don't start going up by then, we'll call it quits," she said.

We hit the dead end, made the jog, and picked up Fountain at Van Ness. The numbers continued to fall. When they kept falling after we'd passed the La Fuente Sober Living facility, I'd seen enough.

"Give it up, Bailey. It's a bogus address."

"How long ago was the report made?" she asked.

I looked at the date. "Four and a half years," I replied,

knowing what she was thinking. "We can confirm this with the permit office, but I didn't see any building that looked like it'd gone up in the last four years or so."

"Agreed." Bailey sighed. "It's bogus."

She pulled over and parked. There was a fire hydrant and a tow zone right ahead of us. But she wasn't even an inch over the line. She was that distracted.

I tossed out another possibility.

"This wouldn't be the first victim to give a bum address for personal reasons," I suggested. "Maybe she was growing pot in her closet and didn't want the cops to show up unannounced."

"She'd still have given a phone number," Bailey said. "There wasn't one."

I checked the report again. She was right.

"Maybe she wanted the car to stay stolen so she could collect on the insurance," I offered. I beat Bailey to the punch and looked to see if an insurance company was listed. "No insurance shown here, but that doesn't mean anything."

Bailey was silent, her expression intense. "Except it does," she said. "I checked with the DMV, and there was no insurance on the car. It was kind of a junker. An old Audi."

"Probably wasn't worth insuring," I remarked.

The traffic light just ahead of us turned red, and I watched the line of cars come to a stop. The closest was a red Ford Focus with a bumper sticker that said, NAMASTE, BITCHES. A sticker on the rear window added, I DON'T DO NICE. I looked inside the car to see the badass who was advertising. It was a soft, round-looking woman in her fifties.

"Are there any cars registered under Lilah's maiden name?" I asked.

Bailey nodded slowly. "An Audi," she said, her voice stretched tight. "But the license and registration don't match."

A no-match on the license and registration should've ended the matter, but Bailey kept staring out the windshield.

"Then what's the big deal?" I asked. "There must be thousands of old Audis out there."

"Yeah," Bailey said. "But I wrote down the license and registration of Lilah's car." She pulled her notebook out of her jacket pocket, flipped to the page, and handed it to me. "Check it out."

I looked at the numbers written in her notebook, then pulled out the report. Then went back to the notebook again.

The license and registration for both cars was just one number off. It could've been a coincidence. The hairs on the back of my neck told me it wasn't.

"What happened to Lilah's car?" I asked.

"I just got the report back," Bailey said. "According to the DMV records, a guy named Conrad Bagram reported it stolen—"

"Stolen?" I sat up.

"Yep."

"So he bought the car from Lilah, and then it was stolen?" I asked.

"He had it on consignment," Bailey replied. "Bagram owns a gas station and body shop on Sunset Boulevard near Highland and sells cars on the side. The 'King of Sunset.'"

"When'd the King report it stolen?"

"Two days after Alicia Morris reported her car stolen," Bailey said.

"So Alicia Morris doesn't want the cops to know her address or phone number," I said.

"But she does want them to know her car was stolen," Bailey replied.

I frowned. "So the car exists, but Alicia Morris doesn't?" I wondered.

66

We let the possibility sink in for several moments.

"The similarity between Alicia's car and Lilah's is beyond chance," I said. "Let's work with the hypothesis that Alicia Morris may be Lilah's alias." When we'd started the search for Alicia, I'd been feeling tired and flat. But now the possibility that I was about to enter Lilah's world had energized me.

Bailey looked at her watch. "Six thirty," she said. "Probably too late to pay Bagram a visit."

We were on a roll and I didn't want to call it a day, so I considered what else we could do tonight. I checked the report—and smiled. "Seems the car was stolen near La Poubelle. Alicia said it'd been parked on the block behind the restaurant."

Bailey read my mind. "Gee, what a bummer. We're going to have to check out La Poubelle." She pulled away from the curb and headed for Sunset Boulevard.

"You cops are always leading us hardworking deputies astray," I said.

"You can watch me while I eat," Bailey suggested.

"Save your sterling reputation. But you better give your security detail a call, so they can watch you watching me eat."

I pulled out my cell and arranged for them to meet us at the restaurant.

Traffic was heavy, and even though we were just a few miles away, it was seven o'clock by the time we got there.

La Poubelle was in the middle of a block of very hip, funky stores and restaurants that were big on character—and characters—and low on fancy. A few doors down from La Poubelle was a place called Birds that served up barbecue and had a human-size birdcage where people who got drunk enough to make it seem like a good idea could dance.

The bar at La Poubelle was already doing a brisk business, and customers stood three deep as the bartenders rushed to fill orders. I took a few moments to let my eyes adjust to the dim light so I could get to a table without doing the lambada with strangers. We slowly inched our way into the dining area in the back. The restaurant catered to a late-night crowd, so there were still a few empty tables to be found.

Our waiter sauntered over with a desultory air that told me our service tonight was not a given. His hair, dyed completely white, sloped straight up on one side and dipped precariously over the other to cover his left eye, which was adorned with the longest fake lashes I'd ever seen. His spandex capris were bright pink, which went brilliantly with his silver-sequined V-necked shirt.

"What are we in the mood for *ce soir?*" he asked in a bored voice.

He looked around the room, and I knew we'd lose him

midsentence if we didn't make it snappy. I gave my drink order so fast it came out as one word.

"A Ketel One martini, straight up, very dry, very cold, olives on the side."

He inhaled, looked down his nose at me, and turned to Bailey. "And you?"

"The same."

Our waiter wandered off. I had no faith that he was going to place our orders, so I watched to see where whim would take him. He glided slowly through the tables, but eventually I could see he was headed for the bar. Victory was mine. Sort of: there was no guaranteeing he'd take as direct a route back to our table.

"You got the photographs?" Bailey asked.

I patted my oversize purse. "Want to start with the manager?"

"Probably should," Bailey replied. She stood up. "I'll go find him."

Five minutes later, she returned to the table with a handsome man in his forties, wearing jeans, expensive leather loafers, and a shirt opened down to his sternum, very European-looking. Bailey made the introductions, and then I started to pull out Lilah's photograph.

He put his hand on my arm. "I have to tell you that I'm not the best person to ask. When I'm here, I'm usually in my office or in the kitchen, so..."

He had a French accent, but it wasn't overpowering. Just sexy as hell.

"Got it," I said, then showed him the photograph.

His eyes got 50 percent wider, and he whistled softly. "I'd surely remember a woman like *that*," he said. "But"—he shrugged—"I'm sorry, I do not recall ever seeing her here." He took another long look at the photograph. "I must say, I wish I had."

"No problem," I said. "Can you tell me who was working here about four years ago?"

The manager frowned and stared at the table, then looked toward the bar. "The bartenders, I don't think so. But you can certainly ask. And maybe Jessie." He gestured to a slender waitress in black tights and a long, clingy sweater. "I think Chris, for sure—"

"Chris?" I asked.

At just that moment, our waiter appeared with our drinks. I suspected the speed of service had something to do with the fact that we were sitting with the manager. But that's just me, ever the cynic.

The manager stood and gestured to our waiter. Voilà. "Chris," he said, "these ladies have some questions for you."

The manager bowed gracefully. "Let me know if there's anything else I can do for you," he said.

I took a moment to enjoy the view as he left the table, then got back down to business.

"Chris, I want to—," I began.

"Oh no, you don't," he said, holding up a hand. "I didn't see a thing."

"You don't know what we're going to ask."

"Exactly," he said, staring at me to make his point.

"I just want to know whether you recognize the person in this photograph," I said, pulling out the picture of Lilah.

Chris gave an exaggerated sigh and dipped his neck, swanlike, to look. After a few moments, a little smile spread across his face.

"Why yes, I believe I do," he said, his voice mildly surprised. "I think she was here a few times."

"Recently?" I asked.

"Mmm, no," he said. "A while ago."

"Could it have been around four years ago?" I asked, holding my breath.

"Four years ago?" Chris put a finger to his cheek and tilted his head. "That would've been my first year here." He held his tray against one hip and thought a moment more. "Yes, I believe that *is* when I saw her."

I couldn't take the chance that he might waver after calmer reflection. "Are you sure?"

"Oh my, but yes." He tapped the photograph. "Not a face you see every day. Or forget once you do."

67

"**Thank you** so much, Chris," I said.

"Just so you know, I'm willing to do my civic duty...to a point," he said. "But don't put me on the witness stand, Ms. Prosecutor." He gave me a stern look. "It's not my thing."

"I'll try," I said, smiling. But I wouldn't promise anything. A character like Chris would have the jury eating out of his hand.

"Try hard," Chris replied, giving me a mock glare. "Now drink up. There's nothing more disgusting than a warm martini."

He sashayed off to the next table.

"Nothing?" Bailey asked.

"No," I replied. "Nothing." I held up my glass for a toast. "To one gi*nor*mous break in this damn case."

"And may they keep on coming," Bailey said.

We clinked glasses and took a long sip.

"You have an address for Conrad Bagram's place?" I asked.

"Yeah," she replied. "Want to drive by?"

"Just to get a look," I said.

Not wanting to blow our security's cover, I texted them the address of our next destination.

Dinner was tasty. I had the penne alla vodka, and Bailey had the croque-monsieur. Pleasantly full, warm, and probably more stoked by Chris's identification of Lilah than we should've been, we paid our bill, left Chris a big tip—those eyelashes weren't cheap—and headed out to Conrad's Auto Body and Repair. We made it there by eight thirty. It was a fairly large operation, with three repair bays and a big fenced-in area that held several cars with FOR SALE signs. Surprisingly the lights in the office next to the service bays were on. We pulled in and parked in one of the spaces at the side of the station. When we got out and approached the office, a man I assumed was Conrad Bagram came out to meet us.

Five feet one on his tallest day, thin, and hyper, he clapped his hands and rubbed them together. "What can I do for you ladies?" he said with a toothy crocodile grin.

I could tell by his expression that he was hoping we either were in the market to buy a car or needed ours repaired—preferably in a big hurry that would put us at his mercy. But when he peered over our shoulders and saw Bailey's car, his smile dimmed.

"Police?" he asked with little enthusiasm. He forced a smile back onto his face and nervously extended his hand. "Conrad Bagram. What can I do for you?"

Bailey shook his hand perfunctorily. "You had a car stolen off your lot about four years ago," she said. "A red Audi."

"No disrespect, Officer," he replied. "But it's hard for

me to remember that long ago. I've had more than one car stolen from here. Especially back then."

I looked at the fence that surrounded the cars and the cameras that were mounted around the perimeter. Three red LED lights glowed in the dark. Conrad Bagram caught my glance.

"Back then, I didn't have as good security," he said. Then he lowered his voice. "And those cameras are just for show."

Bailey pulled out a printout and presented it to him. "What can you tell us about this car?"

He took the paper and scanned it. After a moment, he said, "What is there to tell? It was there, then it was gone. I called the police."

"Did you know how long it'd been gone when you reported it?" I asked.

Conrad shrugged. "Honestly, I can't recall. It wasn't one of my better cars, so I didn't keep such good track of it. And like I said, I didn't have very good security measures back then." He shook his head.

"Did the police ever tell you they found it?" Bailey asked.

Conrad's hefty brows knitted, creating a forest of unibrow. "No. *That* I would have remembered."

"You make an insurance claim on it?" I asked.

"The car was here on consignment, so I didn't carry insurance on it. You'd have to ask the owner about that."

"What do you remember about the owner?" I asked.

"Whatever it says on that paper," he said, nodding toward the printout.

"You remember whether it was a man or a woman?"

"Like I said, whatever's on that paper," Conrad said, his voice edgier. "I sell a lot of cars. You ask me about one, but it was nothing special, so..."

So I wasn't going to get anything out of this guy. Whether he had it to give or not.

Conrad looked down at his watch. "Look, I'm always glad to help police, but it's past my closing time, and my wife made dinner. She's going to kill me if I'm late..."

"Okay," I said. "But if we come back..."

"You'll be welcome," Conrad said quickly. "You know where to find me."

"Yeah, we do," Bailey said.

Conrad tried and failed to hide the look of alarm that crossed his face, then rallied and managed to wave to us before hurrying back to his office.

Bailey and I exchanged a look, then quickly walked to the car. She drove a half block away and parked on a side street. Less than a minute later, we saw the office lights go out and Conrad walk briskly to a late-model Mercedes that'd been parked at the side of the station. He got in and drove off, heading eastbound on Sunset Boulevard.

Bailey alerted our security to fall back, and we followed Bagram at a discreet distance. When he turned left onto Camino Palmero Street, she hung back in the shadows at the corner. Conrad pulled into the gated driveway of one of the apartment buildings, and Bailey drove past it so I could see the address. I gave it to her and she called it in, then we headed downtown.

Two minutes later, Bailey snapped her cell phone shut. "It's legit," she said. "He lives there."

"But something's not right with him," I said. "He's

nervous." I replayed the conversation we'd just had. "But he's not worried. Whatever the story is with that car, he's pretty sure we can't figure it out."

Bailey nodded grimly.

We were getting closer. I just didn't know to what.

68

On Monday, I had an appearance on a double homicide that'd been languishing while the defendant played "musical lawyers," hiring and firing them to delay the inevitable. Bailey went to the station to work the phones with a contact at the DMV and check out Alicia Morris and the stolen report on her red Audi.

The judge let the defendant substitute in his fifth new lawyer but put his foot down. "This marriage is going to last, Mr. Hamlin. No more divorces. Got it?"

Glad to have a go-date for the trial but worried about my burgeoning caseload, I hurried toward the courtroom door, too distracted to notice that someone in the gallery had stood up to intercept me.

"Rachel?"

I stopped and turned. Graden came out to the aisle. "Could I talk to you for just a second?"

My pulse stuttered at the sight of him. There was no denying it, the attraction was still as strong as ever. But the courthouse, where the whole world could see—and gossip—was not the place to hash anything out, even if I'd wanted to. Which I didn't.

He saw my expression and shook his head. "It's important."

Not trusting myself to sound as cool as I wanted to, I nodded mutely and headed out to the corridor. We moved to a corner that was relatively quiet.

"I . . . first, how are you?" he asked.

Standing this close was distracting—the smell of his cologne, the warmth of his gaze . . . it was an effort to wall off my feelings. "I'm okay, and you?"

Graden looked at me closely. "I've been better. Look, I came to tell you about a weird thing that happened the other night."

He told me about a woman who'd gotten "friendly" with him at a bar and tried to buy him a drink. At first I thought maybe he was trying to make me jealous. But by the time he'd finished, I stared out at the crowded hallway with eyes that were filled with the image of Lilah. There was not a doubt in my mind that that's who had chatted Graden up at the bar, and I told him so.

"It fits." He frowned. "But it's very weird. And very dangerous." He looked at me with a puzzled expression. "You don't seem all that shocked."

I wasn't, though I couldn't explain why. I shrugged. "She's a strange duck—nothing she does would surprise me."

But I had to admit, what she'd done made no logical sense. The woman had an alias and obviously didn't want to be found. But she was stalking me, mucking around in my life? Whether she'd hoped to seduce Graden or not— and I had to admit I was impressed that he hadn't taken the bait—somehow I knew her goal was to get at me. And though I wasn't surprised, it did creep me out. The danger was less of a worry, thanks to my trusty security detail. How to let Graden know about bodyguard investigators without telling him I'd been banged up? But the conundrum solved itself.

Graden peered at my face, his expression worried. "What's going on? Did something happen to you?"

It was on the tip of my tongue to deny it, but for some reason I couldn't. I told him about how I'd been ambushed.

Graden raked his fingers through his hair and took a deep breath. "Jesus, Rachel. Why didn't you…" He caught himself—we both knew why I hadn't told him. "Please tell me you have security."

"Oh, I'm loaded for bear." I smiled. I told him about the investigators who'd been assigned to me and how they were dogging my footsteps. Seeing him smile and nod his approval reminded me of how good it'd been to be with someone who understood my world, because it was his world too. I'd missed him. But that didn't mean we were good for each other.

"Will you promise to let me know if I can do anything?" he asked.

"Of course," I lied.

Graden's expression told me he didn't entirely believe me.

"Well…thanks for the heads-up," I said.

"I…sure." He paused and gave me a searching look. He seemed to want to tell me something. I braced myself for whatever that might be, but then he said simply, "Take care of yourself, Rachel."

I nodded and headed for the elevator. When I got back to my office, I found Bailey there waiting for me. I started to tell her about my visit from Graden, but when I saw the dark expression on her face, I changed course. "What happened?"

"The car registered to Lilah was found in Griffith Park about two weeks after it was stolen from Conrad Bagram's lot." Bailey paused and examined her notes. "The car had rolled down an embankment and crashed into a tree," she said. "Young guy named Tran Lee was found in the driver's seat. Dead. Lee was a meth head who presumably stole the car while he was high and crashed it."

"And we would've known that if we'd finished running down the records on Lilah's car before we hit Bagram," I said.

We both fell silent. Something about this latest development didn't feel right.

"I wouldn't mind shaking out any paperwork Bagram had on that car," I said. "At the very least, he must've written up some kind of consignment agreement."

"Agreed," Bailey said. "Rick Meyer must've investigated this at some point when he was getting ready for Lilah's trial."

"I would too," I said. "There's one way to find out..."

Bailey nodded, but she didn't look happy. She abruptly shifted gears. "First, let's get all we can on Tran," she said. "The reports should be at the Hollywood station."

We threw on our coats, and Bailey went to tell the DA investigators they could take the day off. Five minutes later, we were in Bailey's car and rolling. I told her about Lilah's move on Graden.

Her eyes widened. "Oh man. Who *is* this psychobat?"

More than ever, that question burned in my mind. I'd spent more time researching her than I'd ever spent on any defendant. What I'd learned in terms of concrete facts was precious little. But I had a growing intuitive sense of her, especially after hearing about her interaction with Graden. It wasn't something I could quantify or put into words, though, so I shorthanded my answer to Bailey. "She's like no other. Nervy, nuts, and obsessive. A bad combination."

"But now we know: she is still in town."

"And can therefore kill us both at close range," I said.

"You are such a buzz kill, Knight."

I supposed I was. I sat back and tried to relax, but the morning traffic was brutal, and our halting progress was making me want to jump out the window, so I fished out my headphones and punched up "Soul Food" featuring Cyrus Chestnut on piano and James Carter on tenor sax, one of the finest players ever to lift the instrument. I defy anyone to feel bad when they listen to that song. I was swaying to the music when Bailey nudged me.

"Uh, excuse me, Ms. Daisy," she said, annoyed. "There's a way you could actually be useful."

I hit pause and took off my headphones. "Already did it," I said.

"You don't even know what I was going to say."

"Yeah, I do," I replied, enjoying the moment. I don't often get the jump on Bailey. "While you were talking to the investigators, I called Scott and asked for Tran's autopsy report."

Unlike other recent requests I'd made of coroner's investigator Scott Ferrier, this one hadn't put him in the position of risking his job to smuggle out confidential material. I'd thought he sounded a little disappointed about that, but I could be wrong.

Bailey stared at me. "Put your headphones back on," she said flatly.

I gave her a smug grin and returned to James Carter.

Back at the Hollywood station, it took very little time to find Tran Lee's accident reports. The car had rolled down an embankment and hit a tree at the bottom. Tran Lee had been thrown through the windshield. A crack pipe had been found on the dashboard, and the coroner's toxicology report showed his blood tested positive for methamphetamine. Cause of death was massive blunt force trauma. It'd been two weeks since the car was reported stolen, and the condition of the body indicated it had been lying there for some time when two hikers finally stumbled upon it. The coroner's report would tell us how long.

"No witnesses," I said, disappointed.

"And no next of kin," Bailey added. "At least not in this country." She continued to scan the final report. "But here's something." She read for another moment. "Tran Lee's friends said he was supposed to meet them for dinner but never showed. And he didn't turn up at the restaurant where they all worked as waiters either, which wasn't like him. Apparently he was a pretty reliable employee. When no one had heard from him for a couple of days, they filed a missing persons report."

I took the incident report from her with no great enthusiasm. It looked like another dead end. Some tweaker stole a car, got high, crashed it. Sad, but not all that remarkable. I set it aside, then picked it back up. Something had caught my eye. I scanned through the report again.

And then I saw it.

"You happen to notice where the dead guy was supposed to meet his buddies?" I asked Bailey.

"No, where?"

"Birds," I said. "Mr. Lee stole a car on his way to dinner at a restaurant that's just a few doors down from La Poubelle."

69

According to the witness statements, Tran Lee and his buddies all worked at a diner on Fairfax called Josie's. Although it was a little early for lunch, I'd learned from hard experience: better too early than too late. We got back into the car and headed for Josie's. I called my security people and reported our destination.

"When can we get crime scene photographs of the crash site?" I asked.

"This is Robbery-Homicide," Bailey said pointedly. "We'll have 'em by this afternoon."

"Can we pull the original paperwork on the consignment of Lilah's car to Bagram?" I asked.

"Already requested it," Bailey replied. "If there's something off, I'm betting that's where we'll find it."

"Could be he just fudged on the sales price to save sales tax," I suggested.

"He wouldn't be the first," Bailey agreed.

She pulled to the curb in front of Josie's, a small, no-frills restaurant with a counter on one side and wooden tables and chairs in the remaining space. Waiters were taking the chairs down off the tables and getting the place ready for lunch. When Bailey knocked on the glass door, one of them, a skinny kid in black jeans with short blond hair, held up his hands and shouted, "Not open yet!" Bailey showed her badge, and he shielded his eyes with his hand to see, then trotted over to the door. After fumbling with the lock for a few seconds, he managed to get it open and let us in.

"C-come in, Officers," he stuttered anxiously. "What's going on?"

"Nothing recent, so don't worry," Bailey reassured him. She introduced herself.

I did the same and showed him my badge. I didn't have to do that, but people take you more seriously when you have a badge. A gun'll do that too, but I've found that sometimes a gun makes them take you *too* seriously and they forget how to talk.

The young man said his name was Duncan Friedkin.

"Did you happen to know someone who used to work here, name of Tran Lee?" I asked.

The young man's face fell. "Tran," he said, and sat down heavily in one of the wooden chairs. "Yes."

"What can you tell us about him?" I asked.

"Tran was a good guy. I mean, you probably already know he was kinda into drugs..."

I nodded.

"But he wasn't a thief," Duncan said sadly.

"So you don't believe he stole that car," I said.

"No," he replied, then sighed. "But I guess nothing's impossible. Not if he was high."

Duncan stared off.

"He didn't have a car of his own?" I asked.

"No," Duncan replied. "He didn't have a license."

"What about an ID card?" I asked. An ID card would have his photograph and personal information.

"I don't know," he answered. "Maybe."

On a hunch, I pulled out Lilah's photograph. "Ever see her before?"

Duncan's eyes widened. "No. Wow." He recovered himself, then repeated, "Uh, no. Why?"

I didn't have a good answer. "Just checking into some possibilities."

I wasn't 100 percent sure where I was going with this, so I hoped he wouldn't ask.

We bumped around like that for a few more minutes, but we really didn't have any more questions. All this kid knew was that his friend went missing and then his friend was dead.

"You have a picture of Tran, by any chance?" I asked. I wanted to see what he'd looked like when he was alive, just in case he didn't have an ID card.

"No, sorry," Duncan said.

Bailey and I stood. "Thanks for your help. If you—"

"Oh, wait," Duncan said. He fished his cell phone out of his pocket and scrolled through an impressively large collection of photographs. "Yeah, here you go. It's our Christmas photo. We take group pictures here every year." Duncan pointed to a young man in a photograph featuring a small chorus line of waiters and waitresses in their uniforms. "That's Tran."

I saw a young Asian with a wide smile and bangs that jutted straight out from his forehead. He didn't look like a tweaker, but he might not have been at it long enough for the damage to show.

"Do you know anyone else who was friendly with Tran?" I asked.

"A couple of the other guys who worked here," Duncan replied.

Bailey jotted down the names and as many phone numbers as Duncan could remember. We thanked him and left.

Back in the Hollywood station, I parked myself at the vacant desk we'd been using and waited while Bailey went to see if the crime scene photographs had been found. When she came back, she was smiling and carrying a manila envelope.

She sat down next to me and pulled out a stack of photos. The first pictures were establishing shots of the area. It looked vaguely familiar to me.

"Is this near the Griffith Observatory?" I asked.

Bailey nodded.

We sifted through the photographs. The embankment wasn't all that high, but it was steep. When the car drove off, it had gathered enough speed to hit the tree with real force. Tran had been propelled straight through the windshield and rolled down to the bottom of the ravine.

I stared at the report for a few moments, then went back to the crime scene photographs and pulled out the ones that featured Tran.

"Remember the photo Duncan showed us?" I asked.

"Yeah."

"Notice anything different here?" I pointed to the crime scene photographs of Tran.

Bailey looked for a moment. "No glasses. He was wearing thick ones in Duncan's photo."

"They could've been thrown when he crashed."

"But then they should've been found at the scene," Bailey replied. "Evidence report," she muttered to herself, then shuffled through the papers again and pulled out a two-page report. We carefully scanned the pages, going entry by entry.

No glasses were listed.

"Do we know if he had an ID card?" I asked.

Bailey nodded and gestured to one of the reports. "It was in his personal effects."

She woke up the computer and began tapping keys.

Thirty seconds later, Tran was staring back at us. The same wide grin, the same firecracker bangs.

And the same heavy glasses.

70

Hoping we were on a roll, I called Scott. "Hey, Scottsky," I said. "How're we doing on the autopsy report?"

He loved it when I called him Scottsky.

"You know I hate when you call me that," he said. Then he sighed. "I've got it. But it'll cost you."

I knew the drill. "You say when."

"I'll leave it for you at the desk."

I picked up my coat and purse. "Autopsy report's ready."

This time we got lucky and hit the freeway between traffic snarls. We made it to the coroner's office in just thirty minutes. We were back in the car with the report open on my lap in another three. Although reading while the car's in motion usually makes me queasy, I couldn't wait.

"Degree of decomposition indicates Tran was there for about two weeks," I said.

"So he stole the car and nailed himself on the same day."

"Yeah…cause of death, blunt force trauma…tox report shows meth in the bloodstream...personal effects...clothing, wallet..." I stopped.

After a few moments, Bailey turned to look at me. "What? What?" she said impatiently.

"No glasses," I said. "No cell phone. And only one shoe."

"He got thrown through a window," Bailey said. "Everything went flying. Maybe they just didn't find it all. And some stuff could've been dragged off by critters."

"I suppose...but coyotes don't use cell phones, and I don't know of anything that eats shoes." I shifted in my seat, agitated.

Bailey sighed, recognizing the signs. "Okay, what're you thinking?"

I took a moment to collect my thoughts.

"We've got a bogus theft report for Alicia Morris made from La Poubelle, which was taken by Zack Bayer," I began. "Lilah'd been sighted there around that time. We have an Asian kid on his way to meet buddies at Birds, just a few feet away from La Poubelle, on the night he goes missing..."

Bailey nodded. "Then we have an auto-theft report by Conrad Bagram that says the car registered to Lilah was stolen off his lot about the same time Tran Lee goes missing," she chimed in. "And two weeks later, Lee's found dead in that car in Griffith Park—"

"Missing his glasses, a cell phone, and one shoe," I added.

"Stoned and with a crack pipe," Bailey said.

I frowned. Something about this was bugging me. "Bagram's shop. How far is it from Birds and La Poubelle?"

"About two miles," Bailey said.

"So why would Tran hit a place like Bagram's on the way to meet his buddies?"

After a few moments, Bailey replied, "Maybe took a bus to Birds, rode past Bagram's place, got inspired…"

We could check possible bus routes, but I didn't like it. "If Tran was going on a joyride, wouldn't he have called his buddies and invited them to join? Or at least tell them he wasn't coming? According to Duncan, he wasn't the type to just flake out."

Bailey stared at the road. "Unless he was that high."

I shrugged. "Pretty strained, don't you think?"

"So…what? You don't think Tran stole Lilah's car off Bagram's lot?"

"No." I paused to collect my thoughts. "None of the contact information about Alicia Morris checks out, but Tran Lee definitely wound up in Lilah's car—"

"And he didn't take that car to Birds—"

"And he never contacted his buddies to say he wasn't coming," I said. "In fact, he wound up several miles away from there, up in the woods in Griffith Park."

"Pretty hinky," Bailey agreed. "And then there's the bogus info on Alicia Morris."

"Who reported her car stolen about the same time Bagram reported Lilah's car stolen. Which, by the way, just happened to be six months before Zack and Lilah got married—"

"And Alicia's car happened to have a VIN only one digit off from Lilah's. So the VIN wouldn't be an obvious mismatch with the year of the phony car."

"Lilah is Alicia Morris," I said. "That's how Lilah and Zack met."

Bailey considered what I'd said, then nodded. "Why

would Lilah give Zack a fake name, address, and VIN?"

"I don't think she did."

Bailey turned to look at me before refocusing on the road. I could see the implications of what I'd just said settling in. "The only other way that report gets dummied up like that is if Zack…"

I said nothing and let Bailey fill in the blanks. We drove in silence for the next few minutes. By the time she parked behind the Criminal Courts Building, her expression was stormy. We didn't speak again until we'd fought the surging homebound crowds and reached my office. I dropped my purse and took off my coat, and Bailey settled into a chair in front of my desk.

"Lilah hit Tran and took the body up to Griffith Park," Bailey said.

"She covered up a hit-and-run."

"It did bug me that Tran Lee's supposed to meet his buddies at Birds and somehow winds up solo, driving off an embankment in a stolen car."

"When someone calls in a stolen car, there's a record of time, date, and place the call was made, right?" I asked.

Bailey nodded. "And a recording of the call—"

"So you could hear the voice—and tell whether it's male or female, young or old, right?"

"Yeah," Bailey replied. "It's probably not clear enough to match up a voice to a person in a court of law, but it's good enough to rule out a voice that obviously doesn't fit. And if your theory holds, then Lilah called it in herself—"

"So there was no hiding the fact that a female made the stolen report, and said it'd been stolen from the area near La Poubelle. Zack knew whatever he put in his report would have to match that call. Hence, he put down Alicia Morris, white female, a close VIN, and the location as La Poubelle. So then the question becomes, why would Zack bother to dummy up her stolen report? He's basically burying her connection to the car Tran ended up in, right?"

"Right. And she'd get a copy of the report at some point and be able to see that all her personal information was bogus. So she had to have gone along with it."

"My take? Lilah's report was a lie to begin with. Her car was never stolen," I said.

We fell silent. I played it all out again in my mind, looking for flaws, but I was pretty sure I'd figured it out. At least some of it.

"But if Lilah drove up to Griffith Park and then sent the car off the hill, that means she would've had to drag Tran's body into the car. She's no weight lifter," Bailey said.

I looked at the coroner's report. "Tran Lee was barely five foot two, weighed one hundred and ten pounds. A woman could drag a body that size into a car. Especially with this kind of motivation." I opened the bottom drawer of my desk and put my feet up.

"So if we think Detective Rick knew about Lilah's car being reported stolen, how come he didn't catch this bogus report listing Alicia Morris as the victim?" Bailey asked.

I'd thought about this too. "Why would he?" I replied. "Zack was a murder victim. The only reason that report gets a look is if you're doing what we did. Even if he did do a search through Zack's past reports—and he might have—he would've done it for a different reason."

"To find suspects who might've had motive and means to kill Zack," Bailey said. "With an emphasis on skinheads."

"Right," I agreed. "So why would you look at an auto-theft victim—a female at that—as a suspect for Zack's killing?"

"You wouldn't," Bailey agreed.

"And who'd ever care about that report? The VIN and license plate listed on it don't tie in to any other crime."

Bailey nodded. "Then that means two things: one, Zack figured out that Lilah's story about the auto theft was bullshit very shortly after he took her report, and two, he got Bagram to cover for Lilah by saying her car was stolen off his lot."

"It's not hard to imagine that Bagram had a relationship with a cop who was willing to cut him slack now and then," I agreed.

"How did Zack know there'd be a body to find?"

I stared out the window, then spoke slowly, considering the plausibility of my theory as I laid it out. "I don't think he did. Even Lilah, with her considerable superpowers over men, couldn't count on getting a cop to cover up a homicide. No, she made a phony stolen report and hoped it'd stick. I think when Zack checked out the scene, he found evidence that showed Lilah *might've* done a hit-and-run and dummied up his initial report, put in a fake name and fake VIN and license plate number—"

"Just in case a body turned up," Bailey finished.

"That way, he's got a report to show for the auto-theft call that came in that night and it won't come back to Lilah's car," I said. "And then he covered for the possibility that her car would turn up with evidence that it was in a hit-

and-run by getting his buddy Conrad Bagram to report that Lilah's car was on consignment and got stolen off his lot."

"So, even if Zack was wrong about the hit-and-run, or the car never turned up again, it wouldn't matter," Bailey said.

"And six months after all this business with the stolen car and Tran Lee, Lilah—a brand-new junior associate with a bright future at a big law firm—marries Zack, the cop who just happened to take the first theft report—"

"Which turns out to be bogus," Bailey said. "They met when he covered her for a hit-and-run—"

"Nothing spells *love* like hiding evidence of a homicide."

"And I'd bet Zack could tell she'd been drinking," Bailey said. "He made contact with her at the bar, so he not only saw for himself what she looked like but had access to the witnesses who could tell him how much she'd had that night."

"Right. If she hadn't been drinking, she wouldn't have had anything to hide. There's no need to set up a car-theft story if it was just an accident. She's a lawyer—she knows this much. She was probably looking at a drunk-driving manslaughter. A young lawyer with a conviction like that means *bye-bye big corporate career.*"

Bailey frowned. "But if Zack saved her future when he got rid of the evidence, why would she kill him?"

"Good friggin' question." I exhaled and folded my arms across my chest. "It's not like he could ever afford to 'out' her. If he did, he'd get charged with filing a phony report, hiding evidence...the list goes on. They'd cart him away in handcuffs. So why kill him?" I sat back in my chair.

"Matter of fact, assuming she wanted to dump his ass, why not just wait for the statute of limitations to run out? What is it, six years?"

"Something like that."

"Not so long to wait. And once the statute runs, she's in the clear; they can't prosecute her."

I nodded. "And, being a lawyer, Lilah would've known that..."

"So maybe she really didn't kill Zack."

I dropped my arms and leaned back in my chair. I had the feeling we were missing something. But what? I knew we were on the right track; the Tran Lee hit-and-run figured into all of this somehow. I turned the problem over, trying to see it from different angles. It'd always seemed odd that Zack and Lilah wound up together. Though it was true they both appeared to be climbers, she was on the partner fast-track in a high-dollar corporate law firm. What could a cop—even an upwardly mobile one—do for her career? Nothing. In fact, in her crowd, it'd be a hindrance, make her look déclassé. And from what I'd seen, Lilah wasn't the romantic type who'd throw it all away for love. My thoughts looped back to the hit-and-run...Zack as the investigator...

And suddenly I knew. It was foul, depraved, and sickening, but I knew I had it. I turned to look at Bailey—she was going to like this even less than I did.

"What if Zack didn't destroy the evidence?"

Bailey sat forward and looked at me intently. "And Lilah knew it?"

We exchanged a long look.

"Zack was blackmailing her," I said. "That's how he got her to marry him."

71

It was a monstrous thing to contemplate. It was awful, but not impossible, to imagine a cop burying evidence of a homicide so he could blackmail the killer. But to use that to force someone to marry him, and keep her hostage with the threat of a murder rap hanging over her head...forever? Even though I was the one who'd raised the possibility, I found it hard to believe.

Bailey shook her head, stricken. "I don't know...it's so..."

"Pathological?"

She nodded, her expression troubled. "From every angle. Not only because it's a sick thing to do to begin with, but jeez, like we just said, once the statute ran, what's to stop her from nailing him for hiding the evidence? Doesn't that seem more than a little crazy to you?"

"No, or rather, yes. But not for the reason you think. First of all, even after the statute ran, there's no way Lilah could ever afford to turn Zack in. Remember, he didn't falsify that report alone. She's in it up to her ears. If he goes down for that, then so does she. The only thing she skates on is the manslaughter. And when it comes out that she committed the hit-and-run and then conspired to hide the evidence, even if she somehow beat the criminal charges, her big, fancy career would be toast with a capital *T*. No law firm will hire someone with a record like that. Second, I think Zack *was* more than a little crazy—not that she's a model of sanity—but he was obviously willing to take the risk that she might not be as predictable as he thought. He had to have considered the possibility that she *might* just decide being free of him was worth the downside. But I think he was willing to go down as long as she did too. It was a game of power and control, and he had it rigged so her only choice was either to live with him and endure or to 'out' him and wave good-bye to her future."

As I said those words, I envisioned Zack and Lilah locked in a macabre tango, nose-to-nose, neither of them able, or willing, to look away, hands clutching each other's throat. Had the dance finally pushed Lilah over the edge, into murdering Zack?

Bailey blew out a breath. "Damn." Then, echoing my thoughts, she said, "Then killing him would've been the only way out."

"Yeah, but is there any case that gets investigated more thoroughly than a cop killing? How could she be sure she'd get away with it? Talk about your risks. That's the mother of them all."

"True that."

We fell silent. I knew we had the hit-and-run piece of the puzzle in the right place, but Lilah's role in Zack's murder was still an open question. I looked back at Bailey, who was staring down at the floor.

She peered up at me, her expression perplexed. "It's just so hard to wrap my head around. Especially because the mom and dad...hell, even Simon, seemed so...well, normal."

"Yeah." I frowned. It *was* tough to swallow. "But there is one bright side: if there really is evidence out there, and we can find it, we'll have a good shot at nailing Lilah for not only Simon's murder but the hit-and-run too."

It was the only positive note I could find, but Bailey didn't look all that cheered.

I stared out the window. Something about what I'd just said tickled the back of my mind. Frustrated, I struggled to grab ahold of it. Simon...his murder...the evidence....It was there somewhere. I began to think out loud.

"Simon winds up on that sidewalk at the same time as Lilah. Too weird to be a coincidence."

"There had to be a reason," Bailey agreed.

"On the videotape, it looks like Simon was there to attack Lilah. And he was armed and ready. But how could he know she'd be there at exactly that time?"

She sat up and frowned. "They'd planned to meet?"

I shrugged. "Maybe." I paused. Suddenly the thought that had been circling just out of reach floated up to the surface. I stared straight ahead, mentally probing for the flaw as I pursued my new theory with a question. "And if that's true, what's the one thing Simon might've had that could make Lilah want to meet him?"

"The evidence," she said softly.

We exchanged a long look.

"If we're right that Zack hid the evidence of her hit-and-run, and Simon found out about it, that'd give Simon one hell of a great way to lure her out, wouldn't it?" I asked.

Bailey nodded. "Explains why, after disappearing once, she ended up on that sidewalk with him," she said. "But, as I recall, Simon didn't have anything on him and the surveillance footage shows the stabber didn't take anything off him."

"Simon didn't bring it. He wasn't completely crazy. But his murder proves that the evidence is still out there. Or, at least, that Lilah believes it is."

Bailey stared out the window. "And the only reason she would've had to believe that is because Zack told her so."

"Which he would have done in order to use it as blackmail. The evidence must still be out there. It's the only explanation that answers all the questions: how Zack and Lilah met, how they wound up married, maybe why she killed Zack, and why Lilah was just feet away when Simon got stabbed to death."

Bailey drove us back to the Biltmore. Though she was in no mood for fun, she had a date with Drew and didn't want to cancel at the last minute.

With a solid working theory in place, I was too keyed up to stop, so I holed up in my room and spread out the crime scene photographs of Tran Lee.

I'd looked through the autopsy report again, hoping to find some anomalous injuries—evidence of antemortem blunt force trauma that couldn't be explained by the car crash. But the body had been out in the elements for two weeks. Between decomposition and animal and insect invasion, there wasn't much left to work with. The coroner couldn't do any better than say what was already obvious:

Tran had died due to blunt force trauma. Not helpful.

I noticed that one photograph showed an officer pointing to a key in the ignition of the car. So it hadn't been hot-wired. I got excited for a moment. That could be proof the car hadn't been stolen. But then I remembered that Conrad Bagram claimed the car was stolen off his lot. He probably told the cops he kept the keys in the cars, or had a Hide-A-Key stashed in the wheel well. It might even be true, but I made a mental note to check anyway.

It was only nine thirty, but I needed a break. I gathered up the photographs and autopsy report and stacked them on my desk. Ordinarily this would be when I'd call Graden, or vice versa. We'd hash out our day, talk through our cases, and generally unwind together. I'd be lying to myself if I said I didn't miss him. But there was Daniel, in a condo just minutes away. It'd be easy to call him, maybe meet for drinks—hang out like old friends. But I knew that's not all it would be. The awareness of what we'd been to each other and the possibility that we could go there again would still be lurking on the fringes, like a melody playing in the distance, too faint to be able to distinguish the song but too loud to ignore.

I stood at the window and looked out at the night. Wispy, translucent clouds drifted across the sky. The moon glowed like a neon orb, surrounded by sharp pin dots of starlight. A soft breeze made the trees sway like wraiths, their bare branches floating like ghostly tendrils.

I saw myself reflected in the balcony window, standing alone in a hotel room. Would I always end up this way? Alone and wondering why *this* one hadn't worked out? And then the next one? My eyes fell on the street below, and I saw one of our investigators sitting in a car at the curb. The sight of my security detail hit me like a bucket of icy water.

I was standing in a lit window that faced the street—like a perfectly framed and backlit sitting duck. A really dumb sitting duck. I abruptly stepped back and drew the curtains.

Depressed, I took a long, hot shower, put on my pajamas, and slipped in a Miles Davis CD. I was in the mood for *Kind of Blue*. I curled up on a chair in my bedroom, poured myself a tall glass of Russian Standard Platinum, and pondered the accuracy of the phrase *drowning one's sorrows*. This seemed like the night to find out if that was possible. Scientist Rachel Knight conducts a groundbreaking new experiment.

I'd hoped to wait up for Bailey. But I fell asleep early with the lights on, the music playing, and an empty glass beside me.

I woke up at seven, full of energy and ideas. Really good ones, like: Find Lilah! Find Simon's killer! Find the evidence that'll nail Lilah for Tran's killing! Morning never has been my best time of day. I dressed in slacks and a sweater and went out to the living room to see if I'd managed to get up before Bailey.

"Hey, sunshine, you're up early," she said.

Clearly not. "Did you order breakfast?"

"Yep."

I poured myself a cup of coffee from my mini-coffeemaker while I waited for room service to bring the big pot. Seconds later, the waiter, Alejandro, was ushered in by DA investigators Gary and Stephen. He looked a little unnerved by his unexpected welcoming committee.

We made fast work of breakfast and headed out.

"I'd like to see Rick Meyer today, if you don't mind," I said.

She looked like she did mind, but she nodded.

"I got us lined up to talk to an expert about the watch on our stabber's wrist," she said.

Our watch expert was downtown in the Jewelry Mart area. The mart is a huge building with about a hundred different businesses devoted to all aspects of jewelry sales, design, and acquisition. Our man was in one of the little shops across the street from the main building—a bright space filled with watches in lit stands that crowded the floor, and in glass cases on the walls. Herman Rozen, a plump man with tufts of gray hair that floated around the periphery of his head like a baby bird, was dressed in suspenders and wire-rimmed glasses.

After making our introductions, Bailey handed him the blowup of the stabber's wrist. He looked at it with a large magnifying glass.

"Hmph," he said. He snorted twice, then swallowed and gave a disturbingly long, wet cough that just couldn't have been healthy. Or normal. Or tolerable.

"TAG Heuer Monaco Calibre Chronograph," Herman said. "It's worth about three thousand dollars."

"Wow," I said, referring to the watch, and his cough.

"It's no Patek Philippe, but it's nice, I suppose," Herman sniffed. Then he snorted and swallowed again. I wondered how long it would take the CDC to come and get him.

"Where's it likely to be sold?" Bailey asked.

Herman looked at her as if she'd just asked where she could find the Pacific Ocean.

"In stores that sell watches," he said. "Or on the Internet, or at an estate sale, or—"

Bailey favored him with one of her "don't fuck with me" looks. "I get the picture. Thanks."

"Sure," Herman said.

He snorted again, but this time I walked out before I had to witness the whole stomach-turning routine. Bailey followed close behind.

We stood on the sidewalk. Our investigators were a few paces away, watching in all directions.

"I'm thinking he might not be our *A* material for the witness stand," I said.

Bailey made a face. "I've got Purell in the glove box," she said as we headed for her car. "Use it."

72

We caught up with Duncan during a lull at the diner. He confirmed what we'd suspected about Tran's eyesight.

"Tran couldn't see his own hand without his glasses," Duncan said. "He couldn't have driven more than ten feet without running into...something."

Tran's glasses should have been recovered at the scene, but they weren't. If they were among the evidence Zack found near La Poubelle and then stashed, as we suspected, those glasses would likely be one of the items he'd hidden. But in order to be able to prove the hit-and-run, I'd need to link each item to Tran or to the scene itself. The glasses were a distinctive item because they were prescription lenses, so if we could link them to Tran, it would be strong evidence of a hit-and-run and subsequent cover-up.

"You know how long he was in this country?" I asked.

Duncan thought. "At least two years," he said. "That's how long I knew him."

"You met here?" I asked.

"At the diner," he replied. "Why?"

"I'm hoping to find the doctor who prescribed the

glasses for him," I said. "I don't suppose you'd know who that was?"

"No, but it had to be someplace cheap," Duncan remarked.

It was a neighborhood diner. No single tip amounted to much, and even in volume, the tips would barely pay rent on a studio apartment—split with another roommate.

"Where did Tran live?" I asked.

"Depended on how...things were going," Duncan replied carefully.

In other words, it depended on where his drug habit took him.

Duncan continued, "But he liked Venice. He liked the beach."

Venice, a beach community that was formerly a hippie enclave/run-down semislum, was now enjoying a resurgence as artistic types with money moved in and gentrified the area. But it was still a patchwork where the very poor and homeless lived just steps away from designer rebuilds on the canals. Duncan gave me a couple of addresses, and I wrote them down.

We bid him farewell and got back on the freeway, heading west to the Pacific Coast Highway.

"Can you get someone to check out the free clinics in the area?" I asked Bailey.

"How about the Hardy Boys back there," she replied, referring to our security detail. "Maybe they can spare a few minutes out of their very busy day to make a few house calls."

A testy remark, and it seemed gratuitous since the guys were pretty decent at the gig. "What's your problem? They've been staying on top of it."

Bailey shrugged. Her nasty 'tude looked to me like a classic case of what shrinks call "misdirecting." I was something of a practitioner myself, and so I knew that what was really bugging her was our upcoming meeting with Rick Meyer, and it was spilling out all over the place.

But she'd agreed to meet with Rick now, in part so we'd have a chance to get a little more ammunition before bracing up Lilah's parents. My thoughts turned to Lilah, as they seemed to do a lot lately. She'd known Graden would tell me about their encounter—her parting shots made sure of it. Where or how she'd turn up next, I had no idea. But I had no doubt that she would. I wanted to make sure I got out in front of her with a couple of my own moves.

The clouds had largely dissipated, with just a few thin streaks lingering near the horizon, and the sky stretched blue and luminous above the gently rolling ocean. But it was December, so although the sun shone overhead, its pale light provided little warmth, and the air was damp and chilly. A few die-hard surfers, who'd braved frigid waters that didn't even have the decency to provide them with rideable waves, shivered in wet suits as they packed their surfboards into their cars by the side of the highway.

The security guard let us through the gate at Rick's trailer park, and we wove around the concentric circles that led to his home. Rick was standing outside when we drove up, a can of beer in his hand. He pointed to the parking space he'd saved for us. We followed him inside, and this time he began by offering us something to drink.

"I'm good," I declined. Bailey did the same.

I purposefully took the lead and dove right into our reason for being here.

"We had a chat with Conrad Bagram," I said. "The guy who—"

"—claimed he had Lilah's car on consignment and it was stolen off his lot," Rick interjected. A defensive note crept into his voice. "Yeah, we looked into that."

"And?" I asked.

"It was a dead end," Rick said firmly. "He called it in two weeks before they even found the body. We checked the consignment paperwork, and it all looked legit."

"Did you keep a copy of it somewhere?" I asked. I'd gone back and forth over the murder book and hadn't found any trace of it.

"Nah," Rick replied, his tone dismissive. "Didn't have much on it. Just showed that Lilah's car was delivered to him, and gave the date of delivery and the terms of the deal."

"Did it say who delivered the car?" I asked. "Whether it was Lilah or someone else?"

Rick shook his head. "I would've kept it if there'd been anything to run with."

Now came the really unpleasant part.

"You check into any possible connection between Conrad and Zack?" I asked.

Rick's eyes went flat, and I heard the beer can crushing under his hand.

"I ran all things Conrad through the system, then I checked out Zack's busts. Nothing."

"You check out the auto-theft report Zack filed two weeks before they found the car with the dead body?" I asked.

Rick frowned. "Probably," he replied.

"Then you found out that the report was bogus?" I asked.

He pulled himself straighter in the chair and cleared his throat. "What are you talking about?"

I told him about the fictitious Alicia Morris and the likelihood that she was a stand-in for Lilah.

Rick took it all in, breathing heavily. "Wait, how do you know this... Alicia, whatever... didn't give Zack the false information to begin with?"

"Why would she?" I asked. "Why make a stolen report at all if you're going to misidentify the car? And you know it wasn't Lilah who gave him the wrong license and VINs. She needed to explain how her car wound up in Griffith Park with a dead body in it."

"What you're saying makes no sense," Rick said. "Zack covered up a homicide no one even knew had happened until two weeks later?" He shook his head slowly, like a buffalo that'd taken a blow to the head.

It was a lot to take in even if Rick had wanted to believe it—which he didn't. But I needed him to know where we were headed. I owed him that much. Then he'd have the chance to either step up or slink away.

"He's the only one who responded to the call, which meant he was first—and maybe the only one—at the scene," I explained. "The first thing he would've done that night was ask Lilah to show him where she'd parked. And she would've shown him. She wouldn't have thought there was anything left there to incriminate her. All he had to do was ask her to wait at the bar while he looked around. SOP," I said.

Rick's expression grew darker, but he made no effort to stop or argue with me, so I continued.

"Zack had plenty of time to search the area. Even if he wasn't sure what'd happened, there was no downside to collecting what he saw and waiting to find out," I said. "A cell phone, a shoe, a pair of glasses. Maybe they proved a hit-and-run, maybe they were just street trash. But he could afford to hold on to it and see what developed. And he could've written a legitimate report at first—in fact, I'm sure he did. He just didn't file it. He held on to it, along with any evidence he'd found, and he waited to see if anything came of it. Then, when Tran Lee turned up dead in Lilah's car, he held back the original report and filed a bogus one that would correspond to the auto-theft call he'd gotten that night."

"And if we've got it right," Bailey said, "that may be the reason Lilah killed Zack."

Assuming, of course, that she did kill Zack. But neither of us needed to add insult to injury by airing our doubts on that front. We had enough trouble on our hands as it was. "And it may also explain why Simon was killed," I added.

Rick threw the crushed beer can at the trash container and leaned forward in his chair, shoulders hunched, eyes down. "So you want me to buy that Zack hid evidence of a possible homicide...for what?" he said, his voice a low rumble. "To get a woman?"

I waited for Rick to look up, then gazed at him steadily. "Maybe."

He stared out the window for several moments before answering. "And you think the evidence is still out there somewhere?"

"It makes the most sense," I said.

Rick shook his head. "That dog won't hunt. Why

would Lilah kill Zack without knowing where the evidence was?"

"Because it didn't matter whether she knew where the evidence was. As long as Zack couldn't get to it, the odds were good that no one else could either—at least not before she did. Don't forget, that evidence also nailed Zack for some serious felonies. He wasn't about to leave it with anyone else, not even Simon. Which means Zack stashed it somewhere. And with Zack dead, Lilah figured she'd have time to look for it."

"No one wants this to be true, Rick," Bailey said. "But everything fits our theory. Including, maybe especially, Simon's murder. I've had people scouring the city and county records looking for any trace of Lilah. Nothing. But somehow Simon—who's so messed up he can barely find his way home—manages to get close enough to put his hands on her. You going to tell me that's a coincidence?"

Rick's expression hardened and his eyes narrowed, but he didn't answer.

Bailey continued, "Simon found a way to flush her out. And evidence of the hit-and-run is the only thing big enough to make her jump. He didn't have the mental capacity to bluff, or he would've done that long ago. That evidence has to exist, and somehow he got to it first."

Rick still said nothing. Simon's murder wasn't his case, and he was in no mood to shoot the breeze with us. I shifted gears back to Zack and hoped Rick would calm down enough to remember something useful.

"Do you know of anyone who was really close to Zack?" I asked. "Someone he might've confided in...at least to some degree? Because we've gotten limited snapshots but not a complete picture. I don't think anyone knew him well enough to know what he was really capable of."

Rick drew himself up and glared at me. "From everything I saw, Zack was a hell of a good cop and a decent guy. It's no snapshot, Ms. Prosecutor. My witnesses all knew him for years and I can tell you that there's no reason—*none*—to believe he was someone who'd bury evidence of a homicide just to score some tail."

I stood up. It was time to go. This had devolved into a pissing match, and I didn't see the glory in being the best pisser.

Now I understood Bailey's mood before this meeting. She'd known we were in for a brawl, and she'd been right. We got into the car and drove through the warren of trailers and out to the gates. When we emerged onto the Pacific Coast Highway, I reassessed the meeting. Sometimes it's what isn't said that makes all the difference.

"He didn't have an answer for the bogus report by Alicia Morris," I said.

"Nope," Bailey replied.

"And he had no comeback for our theory that Conrad lied about having Lilah's car."

Bailey shook her head, her expression grim.

"Rick doesn't like it, but he knows we're right," I concluded.

"Or he will." Bailey sighed. "In time."

Sometimes cold comfort is the only kind you can get.

73

Traffic was backed up on the Pacific Coast Highway, but the view of sunlight playing across the water provided a nice distraction from our obnoxiously slow progress.

"I'm on board with the theory that Simon found whatever Zack hid and used it to smoke Lilah out." Bailey paused and shook her head. "But I don't get why he didn't just turn it over to the cops."

This one was clear to me.

"His parents said he hated the cops after that trial and was more than a little paranoid. He believed the only way to be sure Lilah got punished was to do it himself." I considered what kind of evidence Zack might've found. "So we're looking for . . . what? A cell phone, a shoe, glasses . . . anything else you can think of?"

"I'd guess the original report with names of witnesses—like bartenders who'd served Lilah that night."

We pondered the question of where Zack might've stashed the evidence. At that moment, I knew what we had to do if we were ever going to bring Simon's killer to justice.

"If Simon could do it, so can we."

Bailey looked at me, then turned back and stared at the road.

"You mean, we lure her out," she said.

I nodded. "We already know I'm being followed by either the stabber or someone who works for him, right?"

"Yep. And now we've got even more reason to believe that Lilah's tied in with the stabber—"

"And last but not least, Lilah seems to know a thing or two about me," I said. My skin again crawled at the thought of her run-in with Graden. "Somebody's giving her information."

"You ask me, she seems like the one who'd be giving the orders. She's the one who's having us followed."

"Agreed," I said. "Now we make it work for us. If we're right, and she went after Simon because he had the evidence—"

"Then we go looking for the evidence, Lilah follows us—"

"And we have a shot at grabbing her," I said. "Or whoever's working for her."

"If they don't kill us first," Bailey pointed out.

There was that, of course. If Lilah had killed Tran Lee and dumped his body, then mutilated her cop husband, then had his brother killed, she wouldn't mind hastening us to shuffle off this mortal coil.

"But we're not Simon," I said. "We should be able to make it a little harder for her."

"Then we want to make sure Lilah knows we're looking for the evidence," Bailey said. "How did Simon let her know he had it?"

How could he have communicated with her?

I gazed out the window at a small inlet of water on the land side of Pacific Coast Highway. A family of ducks was gliding across the water, the mother—or whichever parent—in the lead. I pictured their little webbed feet paddling away. And then it came to me. Here was my chance to make my move, one that'd ensure we got a message to Lilah.

"Easy," I said. "Her parents."

74

It was just an average house on an average street in Beverly-wood, a neighborhood just south of Beverly Hills that, once upon a time, had been an upper-middle-class suburban enclave. But as the population grew, one neighborhood spilled into another, and the streets were no longer a place where young children played in the front yard or rode bikes to one another's houses. That's not to say it was a ghetto by any means, but it was frayed at the edges now, and the dangers of city life hovered more closely.

Guy and Pamela Rossmoyne looked like a matched pair. Of similar height, lean build, fair-skinned, and blue-eyed. Looking at Pam, I could see that at one time, she too had the mane of shining blue-black hair I'd noticed in Lilah's photographs. Now it was dulled by age and unnaturally reddened by too many efforts at chemical enhancement. Her pinched features spoke of a lifetime of disappointment and bitter regret.

Though they'd been married for decades, to watch their behavior, you'd think they were two strangers waiting for a train. They didn't touch or acknowledge each other in any way. Seated in separate matching wing chairs facing the sofa, they didn't so much as look in each other's direction.

Guy cleared his throat and leaned forward, speaking with a quiet intensity. "I only agreed to this meeting because I wanted you to know that Simon Bayer has harassed Lilah mercilessly over the past two years."

Interesting how he repeatedly said "I," not "we." And I could already see why. While Guy seemed plenty exercised about it all, the way Pam was looking down at her hands said she was more concerned with her cuticles than the fact that her daughter was being harassed. Just minutes into the interview, I'd already learned a great deal about Lilah.

I couldn't tell Guy that Simon was dead yet, so I couldn't tell him he wouldn't have to worry about the harassment anymore. But since his daughter likely had a hand in Simon's murder, this didn't weigh heavily on my conscience. "I didn't know that," I said. Though I believed and understood it.

Guy nodded. "For the first six months after the trial, he came by here every day."

"What did he do?" I asked.

"He'd just sit outside, waiting for Lilah. Sometimes he'd leave letters for her."

"And what would happen when he saw her?" I asked, making a mental note to get those letters when we finished the interview.

"He never did," Pam replied. "She was never here. The minute she got out of custody, she left."

"We told him she wasn't here," Guy said. "But he didn't believe us. We called the police a few times, but they never did anything. Just gave him a ride back to . . . wherever."

"Where'd she go?"

"I have no idea, I never asked," Pam said breezily.

I believed her because she seemed happy not to know.

"She always did whatever she pleased, whenever and wherever she pleased," Pam continued. "She didn't want any reminders of that part of her life."

It wasn't just the words but the way she'd said them. It brought to mind what Rick had mentioned about Pam being jealous on many levels. I could hear them all in the line she'd just uttered. I also noticed that Guy looked away whenever Pam spoke. They had decidedly different feelings about Lilah, and probably everything else in their lives too.

"When was the last time Simon wrote to Lilah?" I asked.

"It's been a while," Guy said. "Maybe a year?"

Pam gave him a sharp look. It was the first time she'd acknowledged her husband since we'd arrived. Message received.

"Want to try again?" I asked.

Guy looked away, then gripped the arms of his chair till his knuckles went white. After a few moments, he answered.

"A month ago?" he said, peering up at the ceiling.

I looked at Pam for confirmation.

She nodded coldly.

"I assume you kept the letters in case something happened to Lilah," I said.

I addressed the latter remark to Guy, because I got the distinct feeling that Pam couldn't have cared less whether anything happened to Lilah. As long as it didn't make Pam look bad.

"I'll get them," Guy replied. He left the room, casting a bitter look over his shoulder at his wife.

Pam turned back to inspecting her cuticles, and we sat in uncomfortable silence while we waited for him to return. Thankfully, a minute later he was back, a sheaf of envelopes in his hand.

"Here," he said, giving them to me.

There was no postage or return address.

"He put these in your mailbox?" I asked.

Guy nodded.

"Did you read them?" Bailey asked.

"They were all the same. Telling her she'd go to hell for what she'd done. That he knew she was guilty and he'd find a way to prove it." Guy stopped and shook his head. "She didn't do it. But he wouldn't accept that, had to keep haranguing her. Just couldn't let her be. It wasn't fair—a jury acquitted her, and *they* even said they thought she was innocent." His hands shook and his features were dark with anger.

His behavior seemed a bit much, but maybe he was just the overprotective type.

"Which one was the last?" Bailey asked.

"I don't have it," Guy replied.

"He gave it to Lilah," Pam added.

Guy glanced at Pam, and I saw a flash of anger cross his face. So they were still in contact with Lilah. And he hadn't wanted us to know. "Did she come here, or did you go to her?" I asked.

Guy looked at the floor. In a barely audible voice, he said, "She came here."

"Why did you give her that one in particular?" I asked, though I was fairly sure I knew the answer.

"Because it was different," he replied. "Before, he only wrote about Zack's trial and how he was going to find a way to make her pay for his murder. You'll see," he said, gesturing to the letters he'd given me. "But the last one, he said something about having evidence." Guy paused, squinting with effort. "It was a lot of gibberish, most of it made no sense at all, so it's hard to remember exactly. But he was more threatening, more immediate."

Now we knew what set the wheels in motion that put Simon at the end of the killer's knife.

"Did it say anything about a meeting place? Or how Lilah could contact him?" I asked.

Guy closed his eyes briefly, picturing the letter. "Not that I can recall," he said, shaking his head.

Not that he was *willing* to recall. It was exactly why we'd waited this long to see these two. I had nothing to hang over his head to force him to tell the truth if he wasn't so inclined. He didn't mind sharing Simon's letters, because they made Lilah out to be a victim. All except for that last one. The incriminating one. I could've had their house searched, but I knew it'd be a waste of time. Because I believed he did give Lilah the letter. What I didn't believe was that he couldn't remember what it said. But since I couldn't force that issue, I got down to the bottom line.

"How did you reach Lilah to tell her about it?" I asked.

Guy pressed his lips together, his expression stony.

"Mr. Rossmoyne, this is a police investigation," I said sternly. "If you don't turn over that number, I'll file a charge against you for obstruction of justice."

He inhaled, and I could see that he wanted to tell me to go file my charges.

But Pam pointedly cleared her throat, having reached her limit of disgust and exasperation with this whole mess. "Guy, enough."

His body momentarily went rigid. But then he slowly reached for the pad and pencil on the side table next to the telephone and wrote down the number. He handed it to me, then left the room without another word.

We thanked Pam for their time and said we were sorry to have intruded on their day. We told her to contact us immediately if they heard from their daughter. She promised they would. We were all lying.

The moment we'd driven fifty feet from the house, Bailey checked the number Guy'd given us. She got a busy signal.

"Daddy called her," I said.

Bailey nodded.

We were in play. This visit was an open declaration of war, and now Lilah would know it.

"Game on," Bailey said.

75

It was late afternoon when we headed back downtown. The time of day when I always wanted to curl up and nap. And the time of day when I was invariably stuck in the office or in court. With Bailey driving, and the monotony of the sluggish traffic, the pull of sleep dragged on my eyelids and I had to struggle to stay awake. My head had just fallen forward for the third time when Bailey spoke.

"You know, we're on the Westside," she observed. "Didn't you say you wanted someone to check out the Venice free clinics, see if Tran used one of those doctors for his glasses prescription?"

I had. I knew that if we did find a stash of evidence that included a pair of glasses, it'd be important to be able to prove that they'd belonged to Tran. I didn't expect to get lucky enough to find Tran's fingerprints on the glasses after all they'd been through. But if I could match the strength of the lenses to a prescription in his name, it would be a big help. Now I jerked myself awake and tried not to sound foggy. "You think anyone will still be around?"

"It's only four o'clock," Bailey replied. "They're usually open until five."

"I'll call and confirm," I offered.

It'd give me something to do so I wouldn't drop off and start drooling on myself. "You have a copy of his ID card on you?" I asked.

Bailey patted her jacket pocket. "Yep."

I typed in "Venice clinics" and hit *search*. "Venice Family Clinic," I said. "A few locations. But the one on Rose Avenue helps the homeless—"

"I'd be willing to bet Tran found himself in that condition a time or two," Bailey said. "Do they provide eye care?"

"Yep."

Bailey got off the freeway, but at this hour, the surface streets were even worse. It would ordinarily take us ten minutes to cover the distance, but now we crawled along for half an hour before the clinic, a small, white, low-roofed building, came into view. It didn't look like much, but the people who worked in places like this were about as close to angels as you could get.

The receptionist, a young Latina with long, shiny brown hair that was held back with a stretchy headband, said, "Do you have an appointment?"

I knew I didn't look my best, but I hadn't thought I looked homeless. I was going to have to take a little more time getting my act together in the morning.

Bailey introduced us and explained why we were there. The girl motioned to hard-looking plastic seats lining the wall and picked up her phone. Ten minutes later, a nurse beckoned us inside. We followed her to a tiny office that barely allowed room for a desk piled high with files and an aging computer.

"Vera," she said, putting out her hand.

We both took turns shaking with Nurse Vera, then, without further discussion, she sat down behind her desk and began to type. After a few seconds, she asked, "Do you have his name and date of birth?"

We did. Nurse Vera typed some more.

"Tran Lee...yes," she said. "He's been here."

I told myself we deserved to have something be this easy as I crossed my fingers and asked the critical question. "Did he ever have an appointment with the optometrist here?"

Vera tapped a few more keys, then squinted at the screen. "He did," she said. "Dr. Scarmoon. But he's not in today, I'm sorry."

"That's totally fine," I said. I didn't need to talk to him today anyway. I needed just one piece of information. "Did he give Tran a prescription for glasses?"

Vera clicked through a couple of pages. "I can't tell you exactly what the numbers mean, but I can tell you his prescription was pretty strong."

Bingo. "When does Dr. Scarmoon have hours here?" I asked.

"On Mondays and Wednesdays between one and three," Vera said. "If you like, I can ask him to call you."

"That's all right," I said. "I need to show him something, but I didn't bring it with me. No need to waste his time until then. Thank you, though. You've been so helpful."

We took our leave of Vera and the clinic.

"And that's how the big boys do it," Bailey said with a smirk as she pulled out of the parking lot.

"If the big boys had to work any harder than that, they'd pawn it off on us."

My cell phone rang. "The Crystal Ship" by the Doors, one of my favorites, which was why I'd given Toni that ringtone.

"What?" I answered.

"I'll start without you," she threatened.

"Biltmore bar in half an hour," I said. Toni hung up.

Bailey stopped for a red light, and I looked outside. A teenage boy danced around a pretty girl seated on a bus bench. She tapped his chest playfully, and he pretended to fall off the curb. She laughed, and he grinned with pleasure, a smile of almost unbearable sweetness.

"Is Drew on tonight?"

"Should be," Bailey answered. "Why?"

"Romy," I replied. "It's time to get it over with."

Bailey called Drew and told him he needed to come in a little early. When we got there, Toni was already at the bar. I motioned her over to a booth. We'd just slid into our seats when Drew sauntered in, hooked his sunglasses over the neck of his shirt, and joined us. Talk about timing.

Even though I'd already told Bailey the story, I felt my stomach tighten. I was perilously close to chickening out when Bailey forced my hand.

"Rachel's got something she wants to tell us."

I made myself take a deep breath. And so I told them about Romy and the fight that'd led to my breakup with Graden. I can't say I enjoyed it in the doing, but I can say I was glad when it was done.

Drew looked at me with pain in his eyes. "I can't even tell you how sorry I am." Then he shook his head. "Girl, the trouble you've had in your life, I'd have thought you were black," he said.

Toni smiled. "Amen, brothah-man."

We all laughed. I appreciated their efforts to lighten the moment.

Toni, who was sitting next to me, rubbed my back. "I'm glad you finally told us, Rachel."

Then her brow knitted, and she turned to face me, her expression perplexed.

"And you didn't want to tell us because...why, exactly?" she asked.

"Because when I was a kid, everyone either felt sorry for me or looked at me like I was a freak," I explained. "And I know what you're thinking. We work with 'victims' all the time. But I didn't want you to think of me that way."

"And what way is that?" Toni asked, eyebrows raised. "Everyone gets a bad break here and there. Some get worse breaks than others. Why's that anything on them?"

I opened my mouth to answer, then found I had no answer and closed it.

Toni continued, somewhat heatedly, "Rachel, there's a difference between *victim* and *volunteer.* I can't even imagine why I'd look at you any differently because some monster..." She delicately refrained from spelling it out. But then very undelicately continued, "I feel like smacking you upside your goof-assed head really hard. You know that?"

Drew kissed my hand and pulled himself out of the booth. "I've got to get to work."

After he left the table, Toni calmed down and smiled. "Your whole thing with Graden makes more sense now," she said. "It's about boundaries. If he didn't respect this one, then what happens next? Right?"

"Exactly."

"He can learn," Toni said. "You two have issues that're on a collision course, that's for sure, but it's nothing some decent communication won't fix—"

"*You're* talking?" I interjected.

"So? I can still spot the problem. When things calm down with this case, you and I are going to talk," she said, her voice sympathetic but firm.

I smiled. "It's a deal."

I didn't tell her that the way this case was going, by the time things calmed down Graden would probably be married and have grandchildren.

76

Toni and I pulled the plug about an hour later, but Bailey stayed at the bar to spend some time with Drew. It wasn't late, but it'd been a long day, so by the time I got back to the room, I was feeling warm and fuzzy but very tired. So I nearly missed seeing the note the night manager had slipped under my door, telling me to call him. Someone had left a package for me at the front desk. In light of recent events, he'd decided to have it checked out first. But the scanner had shown only a bottle with nonsuspicious liquid and a piece of paper. No dangerous materials. I told him to have it sent up.

I slipped off my shoes and sank onto the couch. It sounded like someone had sent me a bottle of hooch. Who was that thoughtful soul? Daniel? Or maybe Graden? Maybe this was Graden's makeup gesture. The thought made me smile, and I kept smiling when I took the box from the bellman.

"Thanks, Jason." Feeling magnanimous, I gave him a five-dollar tip and brought the box back to the couch and set it on the coffee table. The weight of it told me it was bigger than a wine bottle.

Using my car key, I slashed open the strapping tape and looked inside. It was a huge bottle of Russian Standard Platinum. My favorite vodka. It *had* to be from Graden. Not even Daniel knew it'd become my new favorite. My smile broadened as I lifted the bottle out of the box. Then I saw what was lying under it.

A photograph of me and Daniel, standing in front of Checkers. My hand on his chest. I stared dumbly at the image for a few seconds before recognition hit me: it'd been taken a couple of weeks ago, the night we'd had dinner together. *What the . . . ?*

It was just a photograph, but the image radiated menace. I stared down at the photo but refused to touch it. Because I knew exactly who'd sent it. *Lilah.*

I felt a hot ball of anger start to burn in the pit of my stomach. If it was meant to make me feel guilty, she'd failed. I glared at the photograph with contempt. No. Lilah's message was far more sinister than that.

This little "gift" was meant to make me feel vulnerable. It didn't. All I felt was fury. If Lilah had shown up at my door in that moment, I would've beaten the crap out of her with my bare hands. I wanted to throw the whole box out the window. But on the off chance she or one of her hounds of hell had left prints, I knew I had to preserve it for examination. I wrapped my hands in a towel and moved the box to the end table. I'd take it in to SID with Bailey tomorrow.

When the sharp edges of my anger had worn off, I decided I needed an expert opinion. I looked at my watch. It was ten o'clock, but that was the shank of the evening for Dr. Bruno Spagnotti, my favorite forensic psychologist—or, as I privately called him, "the Scumbag Whisperer." Short but with a powerful upper body, and a fuse that was both at once (short and powerful), Dr. Spagnotti had a big voice, a brusque demeanor, and a reputation for meting out visceral tongue-lashings from the witness stand to anyone who dared waste his time with "dumb" questions. But juries never seemed to doubt a word he said. On any given day, this could be a very good or a very bad thing for either side. Dr. Spagnotti had no favorites.

We'd met during a case I'd handled in the Special Trials Unit: a serial killer who raped and then set fire to five elderly women. The defense had called Dr. Spagnotti to persuade the jury that the defendant's obvious mental disturbance—while not amounting to legal insanity—was sufficient to prevent him from premeditating the murders. It took Dr. Spagnotti just five minutes to leave that defense ploy in ruins. With a patience he never showed anyone but a juror, he explained that the crimes had to have been premeditated: victims of a similar age and appearance were deliberately targeted, and the defendant made sure to attack only when they were home alone. The jury came back with five verdicts of first-degree murder in less than an hour.

Since I knew Dr. Spagnotti hated chitchat as much as he hated dumb questions, I immediately launched into the reason for the call and told him about the case, about Zack, about Lilah, and of course about the package she'd just sent me.

"First of all, your blackmail theory, unusual as it is, does seem to fit this puzzle rather well," he remarked. "And I can't say I'm surprised that union ended in carnage."

"What do you mean? Are you saying you think Lilah killed Zack?"

"That's your bailiwick, not mine. I was just reflecting on the volatility of the situation and those two personality types. Not to say someone else couldn't have killed Zack. I'd say it's likely Zack had a number of enemies—given his nature and what he did for a living."

"And what would you say his 'nature' was, psychologically speaking?"

"Psychopathic," Dr. Spagnotti replied, in a tone that broadcasted *duh*. From what you've told me, they're both fairly classic."

I remembered the conversation I'd had with Bailey. "Then normal parents can wind up with a psychopathic kid?" I asked. "Because Zack's parents don't seem to have a mean or weird bone in their bodies."

"Psychopaths can come from perfectly normal, unremarkable homes. As a general rule, a psychopath is born, not made. That's not to say environment doesn't play a part—it does, or at least it can."

"But not in this case?"

Dr. Spagnotti humphed and exhaled loudly, the sound like a blast of wind rushing through the receiver, a cue that I'd ventured dangerously close to dumb-question territory. "Not as far as I'm concerned, though his relatively normal upbringing may have prevented him from becoming homicidal. But that wasn't the question, was it? The question was whether I thought Zack was a psychopath, and the answer is yes."

I chewed on that for a moment, but then Dr. Spagnotti broke in.

"You say Lilah was acquitted. Did she give a statement to the police or testify at her trial?"

"Both, actually."

"She did well, didn't she? I'd bet particularly in front of the jury."

"On the money. Is that typical?" The last serial killer I'd had on the stand—and a psychopath if ever I saw one—was a complete idiot.

"It's Psychopath 101. They're often glib, frequently charismatic, and they're adroit liars. Lilah also has the particular advantage of being a lawyer. I'd guess she had that jury eating out of her hand. Especially the male jurors."

"You nailed it."

Dr. Spagnotti grunted. "But Lilah's encounter with Graden, sending you this package—it's obvious she's stalking you. I'd say obsessively. And she's moving in closer. She went through Graden before, but this time she went at you more directly. I'd predict her next moves are going to bring her even closer to you."

Even more than his words, Dr. Spagnotti's dark tone gave me pause.

"I agree, it's weird. And it really pissed me off at first. But when I sat back and thought about it, neither of those moves struck me as all that dangerous—"

He interrupted impatiently. "You're missing the significance of those moves. Getting close to Graden, sending that package—those were just opening salvos. I'd say it's a hundred to one she'll escalate to violence at some point. I strongly recommend you get off this case, Knight. Let someone else handle it."

"I'm okay, Doctor. I've got lots of security. And, besides, who says letting go of the case will make her stop...obsessing about me?"

"You don't want to listen to reason, then don't," he said irritably. "I'm no clairvoyant, I just play the odds. The odds are strongly in favor of you landing in the morgue sooner rather than later."

The ominous tone was meant to scare me, and it did. Just not enough to make me back down. "Can you tell me why she's obsessed with me?"

"What difference does it make? You'll be just as dead." After a moment, he sighed and relented. "Look, I can only speak in general terms, because I don't treat her. But my educated guess would be that you have something she covets."

"Do you think she's envious of my relationship with Graden? And that's why she came on to him?"

"Could be," he said. "Though that seems more likely to have been a way of letting you know she can get to you— as does this package."

"I found out that Lilah got sent away to boarding school when she was only ten years old," I said. "Might that be a sign of early criminal conduct?"

"Or that her mother wanted her out of the house, given what you've told me. Who knows? But I must say I'd be surprised if that hit-and-run killing of the Asian boy was the first criminal act she'd ever committed."

"There was no indication that she got into trouble at boarding school," I said. "In fact, she did very well. Got straight As."

"So? All that tells me is that she was smart enough not to get caught. Besides, I'm not talking about her getting away with homicides, I'm talking about small-time stuff, kid crimes." Dr. Spagnotti stopped and was silent for a moment. "I'm struck by the fact that you've got her history in boarding school. Seems to me you've gone to an awful lot of trouble for a case that hasn't even been filed yet. Do you research all your defendants' childhood histories this way?"

"Sometimes."

But after I'd hung up, I had to admit that I couldn't remember when.

77

I woke up the next morning and stretched in bed, the jabs of pain in some parts reminding me that I wasn't all the way back yet. Then I remembered our plan for the day, and my pulse sped up. Bailey and I were headed out to see Johnnie Jasper and the Bayers. Though we hadn't told the parents, the visits had two goals. One was to find out if Zack had hidden the evidence of Tran's homicide on their property. We'd figured it made sense to check places Zack had unique access to—places where Lilah couldn't go. The Bayers said Lilah never came to the house without Zack. The other goal was to give Lilah a big, bright trail to follow that'd allow us a shot at her.

We'd talked it over with the DA investigators and pointed out the risks, but they'd been on board. I had a feeling watching me was so boring, they'd do anything— even wear a bull's-eye—to spice things up. And it felt good to have a whole team primed and ready. It was one thing for Lilah to get the jump on Simon, unhinged as he was. It was another to end-run a group of trained officers.

I swung my legs out of bed, feeling a mixture of dread

and nervous impatience—the sooner we got Lilah and her henchmen in hand, the better. I went to the window and felt the warmth in the air before I even parted the drapes. The day was unusually balmy and bright. At least we didn't have to contend with weather. I slipped into jeans and a waffle shirt and pulled out my fleece hoodie, just in case we were out late enough for it to get chilly.

I found Bailey in the living room, dressed similarly. Though she was sitting back in her chair, coffee cup in hand, her hunched shoulders told me she was every bit as much on edge as I was.

"Did you order breakfast?" I asked.

Bailey shook her head.

I had no appetite either. "We can grab something on the road later."

I told her about the package I'd gotten from Lilah the night before. Though she tried to keep cool, I could see she was alarmed. "It's not that big a deal," I said. "She's obviously known where I live for a while." And I still had the bruises to prove it.

Bailey ran a hand through her hair and sighed. "I'll be glad when this case is put to bed. Let's get going. And bring that thing." She gestured to the box. "We'll drop it off at SID on the way."

It was unlikely they'd come up with anything, but we both knew better than to make the rookie mistake of assuming something when it came to evidence. The ride out was silent and tense, and the crush of morning commuter traffic didn't help.

"This is one of the weirdest cases I've ever had," Bailey remarked. In all the time we'd worked together, I'd never heard her make a statement like that. The case was getting to her. It was good to know I wasn't the only one. I told her about the conversation I'd had with Dr. Spagnotti and his diagnosis of Zack.

"So he agrees Zack was probably blackmailing Lilah into marrying him," Bailey said.

"Yeah." The words brought to mind the image of a bug pinned to a board, its legs and body pumping wildly in helpless agony.

Bailey said nothing for several moments. It had to be hard for her to deal with the notion that a fellow cop could be that twisted. We sat in silence, absorbing the horror of it all.

It was one hell of a bizarre duel. Two psychopaths locked in an unending battle of wills. Godzilla meets Mothra. Or, more precisely, Lizzie Borden meets Hannibal Lecter. I imagined Lilah looking across the table over her Cheerios every morning at the man who sadistically held the threat of ruination over her head. No matter what she did, Lilah would serve a life sentence. Her only choice was whether to serve it with Zack or in a prison cell.

"You know, I have no doubt that if Lilah ever tried to leave him, Zack would've brought out the evidence and taken the hit for his part in it, just for the pleasure of destroying her."

Bailey nodded. "He was one sick fucking bastard."

We lapsed into silence again, the hum of freeway traffic a soothing, familiar counterpoint to the dark, otherworldly revelations about Zack and Lilah. We'd decided to head out to Johnnie Jasper's colorful encampment first. Since it was Simon's last known living space, we thought he might've stashed evidence there. We got to Johnnie's by nine thirty a.m. and found him sitting in his outdoor living room, watching television and holding what looked like a large cup of Starbucks coffee.

"Hey, Johnnie," I said through the fence.

He frowned and peered at us at first. Then his eyes widened with recognition. He jumped out of his chair.

"You ladies got to go!" he shouted, agitated. "I mean it. You go on, now!"

"What's wrong?" Bailey asked.

"What's wrong?" he said. "Last time you were here, someone came by and tore my place up! I went out to do some shopping, and when I came back, everything was thrown around, broken—it was like a tornado hit it!"

Johnnie was bouncing on his toes, thrumming like a freshly tightened guitar string.

"I'm so sorry," I said. "We had no idea. Are you sure it was because of us?"

Johnnie shook his head and vibrated at a marginally slower level.

"I can't say for sure, ma'am," he said. "And if I'm wrong, I'm real sorry. But no one ever bothered my place before. Then I talk to you, and the next thing I know, my place is trashed—"

"I understand," I said, and reached into my purse. "Let me at least pay you back for your loss—"

"You can't pay me back!" he said. "The stuff they broke was one of a kind!"

"What about for your hassle? I could—"

"No," he replied emphatically. "The only thing you could do for me is get away and right now. I don't want no more trouble." He waved us away. "Just go. Please."

And with that, Johnnie went back to his chair and his television show.

We walked to the car.

"At least he said please."

Bailey looked at me, then got into the car. I joined her and put on my seat belt.

"How sure are we that Lilah's people tossed his place because we talked to him?" I asked.

"On a scale of one to ten, with ten being most sure?" Bailey said. "I'd say an eleven."

"We spread joy wherever we go," I said.

She just shook her head.

She drove south, heading for the freeway. The snow-capped San Gabriel Mountains loomed in the distance, offering a comforting sense of being encircled, protected. But, of course, it was false. The mountains protected us from nothing.

We pulled up to the curb in front of the Bayer residence and found our old friend Tracy Chernoff fiddling with a sprinkler head. I'd expected to find a FOR SALE sign out front by now. She was wearing the same men's nylon jacket. I had a feeling it was her dad's.

I decided to forgive her for not covering me better after my run-in with the homicidal mailbox rooster.

"Hey, Tracy," I called out. "How're you doing?"

She straightened up and peered at Bailey and me. After a second, she brightened and moved toward us, hand extended. "Oh, right," she said. "The cops. I'm good. And you?"

We shook, and I saw that a FOR SALE sign was lying on the ground near the side of the house.

"You put the house on the market?"

"Yesterday," she said. "But my folks got upset when they saw the sign, so I had to take it down."

"I'm sorry," I said.

Tracy sighed and looked back at the house. I'd had the feeling she was withholding something when we spoke the first time, and now I was getting it again. I gave her an opening.

"Did anyone talk to you back when Zack's case was going on?" I asked.

Tracy looked down at her feet. "Nah. I didn't live here, and I didn't really know anything."

I keyed in on the *really* part of that sentence. "What'd you think of Zack?" I asked.

Tracy sucked in her cheeks and pursed her lips. She looked off in the distance, then jammed her hands into the pockets of her jeans and hunched over slightly. It was one hell of a lot of body language.

"I can promise you that whatever you say will stay between us."

Tracy blew out a ragged breath and nodded. She turned, putting her back to the Bayers' house, and stared at her feet as she spoke.

"Zack and I...hung around together when we were kids," she said. "He was my best friend." She squinted at the ground. "And my worst enemy," she said, her voice low but hard. "We'd be having fun, playing video games, riding bikes, you name it...and then, out of nowhere, he'd turn on me—"

"Turn on you?" I asked, perplexed. "How?"

"Lots of different ways," she said. "But the first one's the one I remember best. We were playing in the abandoned house—of course we all called it the 'haunted house.'"

"Every neighborhood has one," I remarked. "How old were you?"

Tracy tilted her head, brow furrowed. "Five? Six at most. We'd just gotten inside, to the front room, when all of a sudden he was gone."

I could actually feel her fear, still palpable, after all these years.

"I was so scared, I could barely breathe," Tracy said. "I just stood there, couldn't even move, for...well, at the time, it felt like hours. It was probably more like five minutes."

I pictured her, small and terrified, standing alone in that scary house, waiting for an unknown horror to strike. I could relate to the trauma more than Tracy would ever know.

She took a moment to collect herself, then continued.

"Suddenly, he jumped down from...somewhere, screaming in this high, weird voice. Right behind me. I can still hear it." Tracy shuddered at the memory. "I screamed, and when I turned around, he was gone again. I lost it, I had to get out of there. I ran to the door, but it was closed...it wouldn't open. I didn't know what to do, so I kept yanking on the door, kicking at it, but I couldn't get it open. I didn't know whether there was a back door, but the idea of running through the house was even scarier. I cried and pounded on that door until my hand was bloody. I was so scared, I thought I was going to die. And then, suddenly, something tapped me on the shoulder." Tracy paused and looked down. "I...I completely lost it and wet my pants. It was Zack, of course, and he'd seen it all." Tracy stopped again and inhaled deeply, then resumed. "Threatened to tell everyone how I'd 'pissed' myself. He teased me about it for years."

She sighed heavily and shook her head at the memory.

"Did he ever tell anyone?" I asked.

"No." Tracy shrugged. "But he never let me forget. I kept going back to him, thinking this time would be different, he'd be nice...and he was." She paused. "Until the next time."

Tracy took another deep breath, then let it out and dropped her shoulders. "Anyway," she said, "I didn't see how that had anything to do with Zack's murder." She added with a rueful smile, "And Lilah didn't seem the type to get terrorized by anyone."

I knew the irony of Tracy's last remark had hit Bailey as hard as it'd hit me. Though it wasn't admissible evidence, what Tracy had just described confirmed everything Bailey and I had surmised about Zack.

"You're right. They couldn't have used it," I said. "But I really appreciate you telling us."

Bailey nodded. "And it goes no further."

"Thanks," Tracy said. She surveyed the front lawn with a sigh. "Got to get back to it. This grass dies, it'll be harder to sell."

We thanked her and shook hands, and she moved slowly across the yard to her next errant sprinkler.

78

We'd told the Bayers that we needed to search for evidence of any contact between Lilah and Simon, and they'd given us their approval.

At the insistence of Gary, the senior DA investigator, our full four-man security team would perform the search.

And they were doing an impressive job of it too. Gary had set up a grid both inside and outside the house, and the four investigators were moving methodically through it. They searched each area thoroughly, then put everything back in perfect order. Claire said the house hadn't looked that good in years. She asked if they'd come back next week. I wondered how long it'd been since she'd smiled like that.

Now, knowing what I did about Zack, I found myself watching Fred and Claire more carefully. After the search was under way, I'd picked up a photograph that showed Zack and Simon in swimming trunks at the beach. Zack's arm was dropped lazily around Simon's shoulder, and they both wore toothy grins.

"Zack was eleven there," Claire had said. "He was already handsome. People would come up to me on the street to tell me."

She had gazed at the photograph with tenderness. There was no hesitancy, no hitch in her voice or her manner that indicated she had any reservations about him. And though Fred was less demonstrative, I'd seen nothing to indicate an awareness that Zack was anything less than the wonderful son and great guy everyone saw.

When Bailey'd engaged him in a discussion of Zack's work on the police force, he'd spoken of his son with nothing but pride.

"It's a hard job, policing," he'd said. "But Zack said he wanted to do something important. Wanted to help people." Fred had shaken his head. "Don't think I could've done it."

How did such normal parents produce a sociopath like Zack?

We had to check the house, but Bailey and I hadn't held out much hope that there'd be anything to find. Neither Zack nor Simon had lived there at the time Tran was killed, and Zack wouldn't have wanted to risk having his parents stumble onto his evidence. So this search was just a base-covering move that'd ensure we didn't ignore what might be right under our noses.

And, of course, it was a message to Lilah. This house was beyond her reach, but if she was having us followed—as we believed—she'd easily be able to see we were here. I wanted her to be good and nervous about why and what we might find.

By the time the investigators were finishing their last grid, also known as the hall closet, Bailey and I began to focus on lining up our next targets.

"When you sold Zack and Lilah's house, who did the cleanup to get it ready for sale?" Bailey asked.

"We all did," Fred replied.

"You, Claire, and Simon?" I asked.

"Right," Fred confirmed.

"Anyone else?" I asked.

Fred shook his head. "We wanted to do it ourselves."

He swallowed and cleared his throat. I could feel the anguish behind his words. It hurt to even imagine what it must've been like to go through that house, touching Zack's toothbrush, his shoes, his ties, each item evoking a memory, a smell, a familiar feel. Whatever he'd been, his family had known only the loving son and older brother. Every second in that place, among his things—the pieces of his life—reinvoked the brutal loss of him.

"Where did Simon live before he…" I stopped short, hating the fact that I was forced to keep bringing up the most painful moments of their lives.

"He had a little apartment not far from here," Claire said. "He rented the garage downstairs as his studio."

"Do you know the landlord?" I asked.

Claire nodded. "She was a sweetheart. Mrs. Kluffman—an older lady. She lived in the main house. Simon's place was a converted apartment over the garage. But it's probably been rented out for a while now," Claire said. "I could give her a call and find out, if you want?"

I did, and she went to find the number. Bailey and I checked in with Gary, who told us the search was done. No evidence was found. I leaned in and whispered to him, "Do me a favor. Have the guys put together a couple of boxes and carry them out to your car."

"Got it," Gary said. "We'll make it look good."

"Thanks." I smiled. *Sweat, Lilah, sweat.*

A few minutes later, Claire returned.

"We're in luck," she said. "Mrs. Kluffman rented the apartment out for a few months after Simon left, but it's empty right now. I told her about what you were doing and she said she'd be happy to let you in and have a look around."

"Great," I said.

We took the address and phone number and headed to Mrs. Kluffman's place. Again, it was a long shot, but since it was a much smaller space, it'd be a lot less time-consuming than Fred and Claire's house.

As our little caravan drove the few miles to Simon's last private abode, I pulled down the visor and looked in the mirror, trying to see if we were being followed.

"That only works for Nancy Drew," Bailey said knowingly.

She was right. I closed the mirror and flipped the visor back up with an exasperated sigh.

Mrs. Kluffman, a big, round woman right out of "grandma" central casting, nodded sympathetically when we told her of our mission. She led us up a flight of outdoor stairs to a small studio apartment. The garage below, where Simon had set up his studio, was now storage space.

Gary surveyed the territory with a practiced eye and once again set up a search grid. Three hours later, the investigators had finished. As predicted, the search yielded nothing of evidentiary value—though they did find a couple of Simon's creations in the garage: a bowl and a serving tray. This time I didn't have to ask. Gary had the investigators carry three empty boxes out to the car.

We thanked Mrs. Kluffman, and I called the Bayers and told them the search hadn't turned up anything. While I was following the investigators around, something struck me, and I'd made a mental note to ask the Bayers about it. Now I questioned Claire.

"What happened to Simon's things after he left Mrs. Kluffman's house?" I asked. "Did you store all of it at your place?"

"Oh no," she said. "It was a small apartment, but Simon managed to pack a lot into it. And, of course, the potter's wheels took up a good deal of space."

"What did you do with it all?" I asked.

"We put it in storage," Claire replied. She tsked once, then continued, "Of course. Why didn't I think of that? The locker isn't far from you. I'll meet you there."

I thought that was a capital suggestion.

Until I saw the place.

79

It was dusk by the time we reached the storage facility, and darkness was quickly spreading across the sky, squeezing out the last rays of sunshine. Our destination, U-Store Lockers, a big concrete-and-beige box of a building, was at the edge of town, where real estate was cheap and ugly warehouses proliferated. Surrounded by a high fence of black steel, the place had the desolate look of a vacant house on a deserted lot. Very few people who had to rent lockers were in a good place in their lives. The building seemed to give off an air of disappointment, loss, and rootlessness.

Claire was standing at the keypad that operated the gate when our little entourage drove up. She punched in some numbers, and the gate slowly swung inward, reminding me of a door to a haunted house that opens with barely a touch—hinting at dark, unseen forces. A sudden shiver of foreboding pushed me back in my seat, an unconscious effort to resist the car's forward movement as Bailey drove through the opening.

"Any thoughts on how big this locker might be?" I

asked, just to hear myself say something—anything—to take my mind off the very bad feelings I was starting to have about this whole operation. Bailey shook her head silently. I stole a look at her out of the corner of my eye and saw that she was having a few misgivings of her own. But, of course, us being us, neither one would admit it.

We parked in the lot and followed Claire up the road that separated the rows of buildings. She stopped at an entrance on the left.

"It's on the second floor," she said. "You have to take the elevator."

You know what's worse than a storage locker? An elevator to a storage locker.

The elevator was large and empty, and Claire had to punch in her code to operate it. The security measure reassured me... sort of. We stepped out on the second floor into a freshly painted but eerily quiet and dimly lit hallway. The floors were concrete, and our shoes clacked flatly, the only sounds in the entire building. Claire stopped at the last unit on the left, inserted her key, and pulled the door open.

The locker seemed to be the size of a small room. *Seemed*, because the darkness in that room was so dense, it felt like a solid mass.

"No lights?" I asked.

"It's not a living space, so you bring your own."

Gary had a police-issue flashlight—the big, heavy kind that doubles as a weapon. He turned it on and slowly shined it around the airless unit. It was as big as a bedroom, and large pieces of furniture were piled on top of one another. A bulky object under a sheet that looked like it might be Simon's potter's wheel was standing in the far corner, and boxes were stacked in rows that reached almost to the ceiling.

"Are all these boxes from Simon's apartment?" I asked.

"All except the five up front here," Claire replied, pointing to some cardboard boxes stacked near the wall to our right. "Those are the things he left in our house."

Gary dispatched one of the investigators to fetch the rest of their flashlights, but Claire stopped him.

"You'll need this," she said, handing him a yellow Post-it note. "That's the keypad combination. It's for the elevator and the outer gate. The exit's to your left as you leave the building."

Gary handed the Post-it to one of the younger investigators, who trotted down the hall toward the elevator.

"You're not staying?" I asked her.

Claire shook her head. "No," she said. She dropped the locker key into Gary's hand. "Just let me know if there's anything else you need. You can drop off the key whenever. We don't come here, so no rush."

"Thank you for all your help, Claire," I said. "I know this hasn't been easy."

She turned to go, then stopped and looked at me, her eyes wet and bright. "I've made my peace with the fact that Lilah got away with...Zack," she said, her voice intense and strained. "I don't want to have to do it again. Whoever this monster is, he took my last baby." She blinked rapidly for a moment. "Get him."

"I will," I replied. And I meant it.

Claire left, and her footsteps echoed down the hallway. We looked around as best we could with just one flashlight while we waited for reinforcements.

"That's a lot of boxes," Bailey remarked.

Gary nodded. "But there're six of us," he said. "We'll make pretty fast work of this."

And he wasn't kidding. Box by box, including every drawer of Simon's dresser and desk, every possible space where evidence could be hidden, was explored within an inch of its life.

Bailey and I focused on the five boxes Claire had identified. In the fourth one, I found a few brochures of services and shelters for the homeless. Simon had scribbled some names and numbers on a couple of them. I figured they were probably contacts at the shelters. I showed them to Bailey.

"Take those. They'll at least give us another place to search."

And another place to find nothing. I hadn't expected to unearth a gold mine, but we were coming up completely empty on every front, and it was getting to me.

Gary came over to us. "Anything?" he asked.

Bailey and I still had the papers from our last box spread out on the floor, where we could shine the flashlight directly at them. I cleared some space and showed him the brochures.

"We might have a lot more here," he said, playing his flashlight over the other boxes that were being searched by the investigators. "But it's mostly paper with scribbles, and it's too hard to read in this light. I say we take them back to the office, where we can spend some time and see what we're doing."

I was down with anything that'd get us out of there sooner. "Good idea," I said heartily.

Gary told them to pack up all the boxes they hadn't finished searching and take them down to the cars. Each of the investigators hefted a couple of solidly packed containers and moved out into the hallway.

"I'm going to carry those out," Gary said, pointing to the last two boxes. He gave me the key to the locker. "And since you're going to see the Bayers, you may as well lock up and take it with you."

I took the key. "We'll pack up and be right behind you," I said.

I tucked the brochures into the pockets of my jacket and helped Bailey reassemble our last box. I'd just picked up the final sheaf of papers in front of me when she tapped my arm and held out a newspaper article. It involved a case that'd been prosecuted in Riverside. The defendant had been acquitted in state court of the murder of his business partner. The federal prosecutors had taken the case and won it. The article was underlined and highlighted, with names circled and notes written in pen in the margin.

"Now we know how Simon got the idea," Bailey said.

I nodded. We both scanned the article. I wanted to see why the case had gone south at the first trial and what had made the Feds pick it up. But halfway through the story I suddenly became aware that a heavy silence had settled around us. I looked up. We were alone.

"Come on," I said with some urgency. "We can read it in the car."

We threw the rest of the papers into the box, and Bailey carried it out. I yanked the door shut and nervously fumbled the key into the lock, but it stubbornly refused to turn. I had to pull it out and jam it back in twice before I finally got the damn thing locked.

Quickly we moved to the elevator, and I held the door open for Bailey. Inside, I punched the combination into the keypad. The door closed and we began to descend, but before we could reach ground level, a deafeningly loud *clang* reverberated through the walls. My stomach lurched. Bailey and I looked at each other, our eyes wide.

"What the hell was that?" I asked.

Bailey shook her head. "No idea."

She unsnapped her holster. I took the hint and pulled my gun out of my purse.

The elevator came to a stop at the first floor, and the doors slid open. Bailey picked up the box, and I motioned to her to stay there. Heart pounding, I peered out into the hallway. Nothing. I stuck my hand out to hold the elevator door open and looked around to my right. Nothing. I looked to my left. And saw where the sound had come from. I blinked, trying to clear my vision, in the hope I was wrong. I wasn't. I turned to Bailey.

"We're locked in."

80

The garage-style door to the main entrance, which was corrugated metal, had slammed down, shutting us in. Bailey dropped the box outside the elevator. The hallway to the main door was lit, but the corridor that ran perpendicular was completely dark. We'd have to cross that corridor to get to the entrance. I strained my eyes to see as far as I could, but the darkness was so total, it was like staring into a well.

I pulled out my .38 and held it in front of me, and Bailey held her .44 down by her side. Slowly, my body tensed for ambush, we moved toward the metal door. When we reached the edge of the darkened corridor, we stopped and looked from right to left. But it was impossible to see anything in the inky blackness.

Bailey mouthed, *On three.*

I nodded. She held out her fingers. *One. Two. Three.*

We ran for the entrance. I'd misgauged the distance, and my adrenaline had given me more speed than there was space. I flew across the width of the dark corridor and hurtled straight into the metal door. It would've been funny—except I was sure it would be the last joke we ever shared. I quickly searched the door for a handle. There wasn't one.

"It's probably automated," Bailey said.

I looked around. I didn't know if there was another exit. The only possibility of finding one was to venture blindly down the corridor of inky blackness. No, *gracias*.

"We need to make some noise," Bailey said.

We began to bang on the door and yell, "Hey! We're in here!"

As we were shouting and pounding, I kept anticipating the feeling of a knife in my back or the searing heat of a bullet as it ripped through my flesh. What worried me most was that with all the racket we were making, we wouldn't be able to hear if someone was coming up behind us. I motioned to Bailey to stop and looked around.

We waited in silence for a few moments. I tried to get my breathing under control, but my racing pulse made it nearly impossible. The feeling of impending danger was physically painful.

Seconds later, the door slid open.

"Sorry," Gary said, looking upset and embarrassed. "Someone leaned on the panel out here and shut the thing by accident."

I was so light-headed with relief I thought I'd faint.

"You okay?" he asked, looking at us closely.

"Fine," Bailey replied.

"All good," I said, strolling out with as much nonchalance as my wobbly knees would allow. *Whatever you do,* I told myself, *don't throw up.*

"Then what's with the firepower?" he asked, nodding toward the guns in our hands.

"Oh," I said. "Just comparing."

"She's thinking about getting a Glock," Bailey said.

We got into Bailey's car and Gary got into his, which was parked a few feet ahead. Bailey rolled down the window.

"Thanks for everything," she called out.

He waved to her and we followed him to the exit, where he punched in the code. The gate opened and we rolled out, inches behind him.

Bailey headed toward the freeway.

"Olives on the side, so there's more room for the important stuff," I said.

She nodded and punched the accelerator.

81

By the time we got back to my room, we were wrung out—and somewhat inebriated—dishrags. If Gary and the other investigators noticed our condition when we left the bar, they were cool enough not to mention it. We said a blurry good night. I showered and was about to get into bed when I found a message on the hotel phone. That was weird. No one ever called me on that phone. I punched in the number to retrieve the message and listened.

"Hi, it's Daniel. It's about…six thirty p.m. I tried you at the office, but they said you were out in the field. I was just wondering, if you don't have plans for dinner, maybe you'd like some company. Here's my number…"

I reflexively picked up a pen and wrote down the number on the notepad I kept next to my phone. I hung up and stared at what I'd written. I knew the message was about more than just an impromptu dinner invitation. What I didn't know was what to do about it.

Too tired to ponder the question after the day we'd had, I fell into bed and hoped for a dreamless sleep. So of course I dreamed all night that I was being chased by giant, faceless, machete-wielding monsters.

Over breakfast the next morning, I pulled out the brochures I'd found in one of Simon's boxes.

"He's got a pamphlet for a place in Glendale, and one in Venice." I read from the latter. "Venice Community Housing. It has low-cost housing as well as transitional housing for the homeless. Got a couple of names written on it." I squinted at the jagged writing. "Looks like…Diane?"

"Glendale's probably just a place close to home," Bailey said. "Venice's more interesting."

"And if it doesn't pan out, we can hit the Glendale shelter."

The weather was a little cooler than yesterday, and a few clouds had moved in, but it was still fairly mild for December. I wore a crewneck sweater, jeans, and a leather jacket. I figured the layering would let me adapt if it got warmer. We were on our way out the door when my cell phone played the opening bars of "The Crystal Ship." "It's Toni," I said. "Probably calling to see what we want to do tonight."

Bailey shrugged. "Let's see how the day pans out."

I nodded and let it go to voice mail. "I'll call back later."

The transitional-housing facility in Venice turned out to be a charming house with blue wood siding and brick-colored trim. Since there was no parking lot, Bailey waved the investigators toward the open spot in front of the house while we drove farther down the street to park in a red zone.

I looked pointedly at the red-painted curb. "It's not just

me this time, Keller," I said. "We've got other sworn law-enforcement officers on the scene. They might actually bust your scofflaw ass."

She strode up the sidewalk ahead of me. Gary had gotten out of his car and was watching the foot and vehicle traffic, looking up and down the street.

When we drew close, Gary leaned toward Bailey. "I was going to take that spot," he said.

She gave me a smug smile.

"This is me ignoring you," I said.

We moved up the walk, and Bailey knocked on the door. It was answered within seconds by a short, slender blond woman in her fifties, dressed in dark slacks and a long-sleeved cream-colored shirt. She had a kindly face—the sort you'd be glad to see if you'd lost your place in the world.

"Can I help you?" she asked. Bailey introduced us, and we showed our IDs.

"Come on in," she said. "I'm Teresa Solis."

Teresa ushered us into a front room with windows that faced the street. It was lined with photographs of women and children, singly and in groups.

"We're looking for a man who was homeless and who might've stayed here a few months ago," Bailey said.

She looked at us, her expression puzzled. "That's not possible."

"Because?" I asked.

"It's a shelter for homeless women and their children," Teresa replied.

Aha. Thus the photographs of women and children. But now it was my turn to be puzzled. Why did Simon have a brochure for a women's shelter?

"Does anyone named Diane work here?" I asked, remembering the handwriting I'd seen on the brochure.

Teresa's brows knitted, and she shook her head. "Not that I'm aware of, and I've been here for the past six years."

I paused and stared over her shoulder at the photographs on the wall.

"Maybe someone named Diane lived here?" I asked.

"We do have a Diane living here. I'm not sure how long she's been here, though. When were you thinking this man made contact?"

"I'm thinking sometime in the past couple of months," Bailey replied.

Teresa turned from her desk to a short metal filing cabinet under the window. She put on a pair of green-and-black-framed reading glasses and opened the top drawer. She looked through a stack of folders and pulled out a slender red file.

"Diane Nguyen," she read. "She and her daughter have been here for the past two months. Apparently she was also here four or five years ago." Teresa read some more, then looked up. "She had a young boy with her back then."

I got one of those chills you get when you just know an unexpected connection is coming.

"Is the boy's name listed?" I asked.

Teresa looked down at the file and shook her head.

Bailey began to look around. She was feeling it too.

I knew this had to pan out somehow. I went at it another way. "Does it say about how old he was?"

Teresa looked down at the file again. "Fourteen."

But boys, especially small ones, can look younger than

their years. "Are there any photographs of them?" I asked.

"Not in the file," she replied. "Sorry." She looked at me sympathetically, then put the folder back in the drawer and took off her glasses.

"Is this Diane?" Bailey said, pointing to an Asian woman in a group photograph on the wall near the window.

Teresa and I both went over to the photograph. She put her glasses back on.

"Yes," she said. "That's her."

Bailey and I looked at each other, then turned back to the photograph, where, next to Diane, the smiling face of Tran Lee beamed back at us.

82

We briefly explained who he was and what we were hoping to find.

"I'd guess Tran Lee was posing as her son so he'd have a place to stay," Teresa concluded. "And you'd like to talk to Diane about it?"

"Yes," I said.

She nodded. "I'll take you up to her, but I can't force her to talk to you. I hope you understand."

Teresa led us upstairs to the living quarters. As we walked down the hallway, I counted the doors and saw that the house had been converted to make eight separate rooms, each one presumably for a separate family. Teresa stopped in front of the fifth door and knocked sharply.

"Diane?" she said. "Are you there? I need to talk to you."

"Just a minute," said a soft voice.

We heard some rustling and a drawer shutting, then a few light footsteps moving toward the door.

It was opened by a petite Asian woman.

"Yes?" she said, looking from Teresa to Bailey to me with a slightly alarmed expression.

"There's nothing to be worried about, Diane," Teresa said gently. "Nothing is wrong. These women just have a few questions for you. Do you mind if we come in for a moment?"

Diane's face immediately relaxed. With a tentative smile, she stood aside and gestured for us to come in. The small room was neat as a pin and sparsely furnished with a bed, a dresser, a table, and chairs. But the colors were bright and cheery, which gave it a nice, homey feeling.

My heart was thudding loudly as I prayed that our theory would pan out, but I tried to act cool and calm so I wouldn't spook Diane. Bailey and I introduced ourselves and reassured her again that she was in no trouble at all, and then I dived in.

"Did you ever know someone named Simon?" I asked.

Diane looked at me blankly. Slowly, she shook her head. "I don't know anyone by this name."

This could not happen. I knew I was right. I could feel it. "Maybe you called him by a different name," I suggested. I pulled out Simon's photograph and showed it to her.

She took it from me and looked at it carefully. Then she smiled. "Oh yes," Diane said. "But his name is Zack."

I felt my scalp tighten. It made a weird, emotional kind of sense that Simon would use Zack's name. "We think he might've given you something to hold for him. Does that ring a bell?"

Diane regarded us closely but made no response.

"Diane," Bailey intervened, speaking gently. "Zack isn't coming back. Someone...killed him, and we're trying to find the person who did it."

Her face froze and she sat perfectly still for several long minutes. Then tears slowly began to slide down her cheeks. I moved to put an arm around her, but she reflexively shrank back, out of reach. I'd forgotten who I was dealing with. The world was not a gentle place for anyone, but it was particularly harsh for a homeless woman. I sat down and waited, my hands clasped in my lap to keep them still. After a few more minutes, she wiped her cheeks with her sleeve.

Then she got up and went to her dresser. She took the clothes out of the bottom drawer and set them on the bed, then turned back to the drawer and retrieved a small yellow canvas tote bag.

"This is what he left with me," she said, presenting the bag to me.

I took it, not even daring to breathe. I swallowed hard and steeled myself for disappointment. I could feel Bailey next to me, tension radiating from her body in pulsing waves.

I looked inside. And found it all. One shoe, one pair of prescription glasses, a police report—listing Lilah Rossmoyne as the victim of a car theft, a card bearing the address of this housing shelter, and a photograph of Tran Lee with Diane. Zack must have lifted the card and photograph out of the evidence locker before the reports were prepared. Who'd notice if something as minor as that went missing? After all, it was just a homeless crackhead who'd done a swan dive in a stolen car.

This was the evidence Simon had found, and it led him straight to this shelter. It took a Herculean effort to keep my reaction restrained.

"Diane, thank you so much," I said.

She nodded and gave us a tremulous smile. "He was a good man," she finally said. "I hope you will get his killer."

Elated by the breakthrough, I was in a hurry to get outside and tell Gary that he wouldn't have to endure days and nights of sifting through piles of papers. We trotted down the stairs behind Teresa and stopped just outside the reception room, where a young woman in frayed jeans and an army jacket was talking on a cell phone.

"Teresa, I so appreciate your help," I said.

"I take it this is what you were looking for?" she asked, gesturing to the canvas bag.

"It's everything we were looking for," I replied. "And more than we ever expected to find. I can't thank you enough. But it would be best if you didn't mention this to anyone for a while."

"I understand. I wish you the best of luck," she said warmly.

We stepped out onto the porch and I waved to Gary, the bag tucked under my arm. He took another look up and down the street, then moved up the sidewalk toward us. When he saw my ear-to-ear grin, he smiled.

"It's been pretty quiet, so I let Stephen take an early lunch," he said. "What'd you get? From the looks of you, it must be pretty good."

I gave him the bag, and he peered inside. I watched Gary's eyes grow big as he inhaled sharply. He looked from Bailey to me, and I nodded. We had the gold.

"You know, I was starting to doubt whether there was anything to find." He shook his head with a rueful smile. "Congratulations, you two. Why don't we meet the guys for lunch and give them the news? They're all going to Joe's."

It did feel like some kind of celebration was in order. Joe's, a no-frills-looking box that served top-notch food, had been around for twenty years, but I'd never had the chance to check it out. "Great idea," I said.

"You know how to get there?" Gary asked.

"Yep," Bailey said.

"Okay, then you lead, I'll follow."

As we turned to head for Bailey's car, Teresa walked out onto the porch with the young woman who'd been in the waiting room. Teresa waved to us, and we waved back. We got to the car just as Gary pulled up. We moved out in front, heading down the narrow street toward Abbot Kinney Boulevard.

"We might just have found the linchpin that'll nail Lilah for the hit-and-run *and* as an aider and abettor in Simon's murder," I said. I was jubilant.

"Seems so," Bailey said.

I started to tell her to unwind and enjoy our big score, but it was slow, careful going on the narrow street that was made more so by the parked cars that lined both sides, and I could see she was focused on the road. But when she stopped at an intersection and peered around me to look for oncoming traffic, I saw that she was grinning like a kid with an ice-cream cone.

As Bailey pulled forward, I chuckled. "I don't think I've seen you smile like that since—"

But my next words were cut off by the high-pitched screech of tires behind us. I turned and saw an old-model Chevy roar out of the narrow street we'd just crossed and slam into the front passenger side of Gary's car. It spun on impact, and over the sounds of shattering glass and crumpling metal came the thunderous noise of gunfire, many shots in rapid succession: *bang, bang, bang, bang!*

The blasts were still ringing in my ears when I saw the Chevy's passenger window slide down and the muzzle of a handgun turn toward our car. "Get down!" I screamed. Shots exploded through the trunk and back window. The whine of bullets whizzed right past my ear. I reached down for the gun in my purse, and I'd just wrapped my hand around the grip when Bailey suddenly threw the car into reverse and floored it. We flew backward and crashed into the side of the old Chevy, driving it into Gary's car. The force of the impact threw me forward against my seat belt and knocked the air out of me, but I had to get out, get to Gary. I managed to unbuckle and throw myself out of the car just in time to see the Chevy wrench itself out from between our cars and turn toward us. I took a steadying breath and, using our car as a shield, emptied my clip into the Chevy as it squeezed past us and then sped off.

I leaned into the car to tell Bailey. And the world shattered into a million jagged shards.

Bailey was slumped over the steering wheel, her face covered in blood.

83

My mind shut down, refusing to believe what I saw. I reached out and took her hand off the steering wheel and felt for a pulse. Nothing. My heart gave a slow, heavy thump. Afraid to move her, I looked for the source of the bleeding, praying I wouldn't find a bullet hole.

As I studied her head, her neck, her shoulders, whatever I could see, I found myself gripping her wrist, as though I could squeeze her back to life. "Bailey," I said softly. "Bailey. Come on, come on." Unshed tears closed my throat and my words came out in a strangled sob.

I couldn't breathe, couldn't think. Then, a sound. A low moan. The sweetest sound in the world. Bailey's eyelids fluttered and opened. Without moving her head, she looked at me, then down at my hand, which was still wrapped like a vise around her wrist.

A croak. I leaned in closer. "Let go," she said.

I released her wrist and she slowly sat up, groaning as she lifted her head.

"I was trying to take your pulse. I couldn't find it."

" 'Cause you don't know how, fool." Bailey shook her

head, then lowered it to the steering wheel with another groan.

I'd get even with her for that crack later. "Don't move, okay, smart-ass?"

I could hear distant sirens approaching, but just in case they weren't for us, I pulled out my cell phone and called for paramedics as I ran toward Gary's car. It was now a crumpled mess of twisted metal, steam spewing from the hood, fluids leaking out everywhere. Bullet holes had cracked the passenger window and penetrated the door. I went around to the driver's side and saw that the window was shattered and the car riddled with bullet holes. The air bags had deployed and filled the front seat.

"Gary!" I shouted. "Gary!"

No answer. I reached through the driver's window and found the door handle. Underneath the air bag, I saw Gary's face.

His eyes, wide open, stared vacantly upward. Desperate to give him air, I shoved back the air bag, but the moment I did, the blood it had been holding in streamed down the side of his neck. The source: a neat, round hole just under his jaw. I sank to the ground, too numb to scream.

I don't know how long I sat there. I only know that at some point later, I heard the whoop of sirens and the slamming doors of ambulances and squad cars behind me. Suddenly arms were pulling me away and paramedics swarmed the car. My head swimming, I grabbed a uniformed arm, pointed to Bailey's car, and tried to speak. The officer told me they were taking care of her and led me to a paramedic.

"Take a look at her," he ordered.

"I'm fine," I said, and tried to pull away. But the paramedic wasn't having any. He sat me down and insisted on taking my vitals. Suddenly, too exhausted to argue, I submitted. When he'd removed the blood-pressure cuff, I asked, "Who's taking care of Gary?" Then, without warning, I started to shake uncontrollably.

The paramedic abruptly pulled me into the ambulance and made me lie down on a gurney. "Tell me, how's Gary? You've got to tell me!" I said as a surge of fear flooded my stomach with acid, making me want to retch. The paramedic wrapped a blanket around me, and I heard the crinkling of a wrapper. I felt something cold on my arm, then a swift pinch. "Gary...," I mumbled.

The next thing I knew, I was in a bed in the emergency room and Bailey was in the bed next to me. Her head and shoulder were bandaged and she had an IV, but they'd cleaned her up and her color looked pretty good. The monitors over her bed told me her systems were in working order.

I tried to sit up, but my head began to spin. A young dark-haired doctor with a warm, sexy smile came striding in and went over to Bailey's bed. He spoke to me over his shoulder as he examined her chart and her monitor readings.

"You okay? You might be a little dizzy after that sedative."

I nodded toward Bailey. "Is she...?"

"She'll be fine. Took a grazing wound to the head and a through-and-through in the shoulder area. We'll do an MRI just to make sure, but if that comes out clean—as we expect it will—she should be good to go."

All at once, my memory came rushing back. "What about Gary? Where is he?" I tried to sit up again.

The doctor frowned. "I don't have a patient named Gary. But if you give me his last name, I can have someone check into it for you."

I gave him Gary's full name, and the doctor promised to get me some information, then left. I tried to keep myself from screaming with frustration. God knew how long it would take for someone to get back to me. I'd go find Gary myself. I was just starting to prop myself up when Eric entered with slow, tentative steps. Why was my boss here?

"Hey, Rachel." His voice was so low it was barely audible.

"No need to whisper, Eric. They've pumped her full of so much stuff, she won't wake up until next week."

"What about you?"

I quickly gave him the condensed version, then got to what was important to me. "Have you heard anything about Gary? No one here can tell me anything."

Eric put his hands in his pockets, then looked away.

"What? What?" I asked, agitated.

"Rachel, I'm sorry. He didn't make it."

I'd known, but I'd refused to accept it. I'd wanted to hear that a miracle had happened. You'd think that I, of all people, would know better. The tears came on their own, hot and silent.

84

They officially pronounced Gary at 2:41 p.m.

It was a long, hideous day and night at the hospital. Bailey and I gave our statements over and over again to a parade of officers. The other investigators, who'd gone to lunch that day, were nearly suicidal with grief and guilt. They couldn't be consoled.

Bailey's MRI showed no internal damage, and she was cleared for release. Now I was standing outside the small hospital waiting room where Bailey was giving her last statement to the reporting officers. Head down, I wrapped my arms around my waist and circled the room, suffering over the loss of Gary and the close call I'd had with Bailey. I paced in small, tight circles, glad that Bailey wasn't here to complain. As always, my grief had turned to anger, and my anger had turned to a need for action. Unfortunately action required a plan, and I didn't have one. That only added to my frustration.

I was finishing my fifty-second circle when Drew rushed in. He gave me a quick hug, then held me at arm's length and looked at me closely.

"I'm okay."

"Where is she?" he asked, looking up and down the hallway.

"In there, finishing her statement. Should be out in a second." Seeing his worried face, I added, "She's fine, Drew. Really."

His expression turned thunderous.

"When they catch that son of a bitch, I'm going to—"

At just that moment, Bailey opened the door, saving me from hearing a statement that was bound to be incriminating if we ever did catch that son of a bitch. She shook hands with the detectives and turned toward us. I'd never seen her so ragged or drained. When she saw Drew, she moved straight into his arms. He gently folded her in close, and she held on to him. Neither of them spoke for several long beats.

Drew drove us back to the Biltmore, and we immediately steered Bailey up to the room and into bed. Then I took him out to the living room and told him the whole story.

Drew leaned forward and put his head in his hands. Finally he said, "I could've lost both of you today." He shook his head as though he'd been hit with a weighted glove.

"You got anything to drink around here?" he asked.

I poured him a shot of the Russian Standard Platinum, and he tossed it back.

"Does...did...Gary have a family?" Drew asked, his expression grave.

"A wife and two daughters."

He closed his eyes. I poured us both another shot, and we downed it in one gulp.

Half an hour later, Bailey emerged from the bedroom, moving gingerly, as though her head might fall off if she made any sudden moves. She cast a longing look at the bottle of vodka.

"Don't even think about it," Drew said.

Bailey rolled her eyes, but she didn't argue. Drew settled her in on the couch. "He had to be after that bag," she said. "How'd he know we had it?"

I'd given the question a lot of thought while I was waiting for Bailey in the hospital. "The woman. Remember that young woman in the reception area? She was on the cell phone when we said good-bye to Teresa. I think she was working with the guy who was driving the car."

Bailey nodded. "So he was going to take Gary out and then come after us."

We all fell silent. The man had succeeded with half the plan.

"But, if you ask me, the move was kind of amateurish," I said.

Drew shook his head. "He may not be Blackwater, but it was good enough."

His words brought us up short, and we all fell silent. Then I heard a faint beeping sound. It seemed to be coming from my purse. It startled me at first, but then I remembered it was the signal of an unretrieved message. Toni's message. I never did listen to it. I meant to just call her—tell her what had happened—but I pressed the voice-mail button without thinking. What I heard was the quintessential last straw.

"What's wrong?" Bailey asked.

"The press got ahold of Simon's case. Lilah's photo was in today's paper—"

"Are you friggin' kidding me?" Bailey said, her voice cracking with fatigue.

Drew spotted the newspaper that'd been left on the table in the foyer that morning and read us the brief story, then we all looked at the photograph.

"They've got to be in panic mode after what happened today, and now her picture's in the paper too," I said. "Lilah's going to run."

"I don't know," Bailey replied. "The story's the bigger problem. That photo...there isn't much detail. She's in dark glasses, you can't see that much of her. I wouldn't count on her taking a powder just yet. She wants that evidence."

I hoped Bailey was right. I wanted to find her and personally choke her to death. But at the moment, my eyelids felt as heavy as concrete. I yawned and started a chain reaction that ended with Drew doing a jaw-splitting rendition that almost managed to make us laugh. Almost. Exhausted on every level, we decided to call it a night. I left Drew and Bailey to say their good-byes in privacy and took myself, and the bottle of Russian Standard Platinum, to bed.

85

In the next few days, Bailey and I had lots of reporting and updating to do with our own, and each other's, bureaucracies. How it happened, why it happened, what we were doing in that place. I must've repeated the same information about a hundred times.

But there was one thing Bailey and I had agreed to keep to ourselves: the evidence we'd gotten from Diane Nguyen.

We'd talked about it the following morning.

These people—Lilah's minions—might not be pros, but they weren't stupid. They'd know that once the evidence left our hands, there was no point in killing either of us, and they'd disappear. Now that Simon's case had gone public—and the shoot-out had ensured it got plenty of coverage—they'd expect to see some mention of the evidence we'd found at the women's shelter. If we kept it all quiet, there was a chance they'd think that it wasn't *the* evidence of Tran's hit-and-run. Or that it *was,* and we didn't realize what we had. Either way, it might encourage them to stick around, which would buy us time to come up with a plan to find Lilah and her attack dogs and put them down before they got us.

In the meantime, I was hell-bent on finding out who had leaked Simon's story to the press. It may've been irrational—maybe I just needed someone to blame for the tragedy of Gary's death—but I believed that the story coming out had set Lilah off. True, I'd been attacked previously, but it clearly wasn't meant to be lethal. The attack in Venice, on the other hand, was intended to be nothing else. I had to know who to blame. Then I'd figure out what to do to that filthy cretin.

At my insistence, Bailey worked her office while I worked mine. Eric had no idea who might've leaked and he hadn't seen Melia talking to any reporters. When I asked her directly, she denied it with a look sour enough to tell me she wished she'd had the information to give and was pissed at having been left out of the loop to begin with. Toni'd carefully asked around, but she too had come up empty. After a few days, Bailey admitted defeat.

I refused to give up.

I continued to dig around for clues, but ultimately the mystery was solved by a more direct source. I got a call from Miles Rykoff, a reporter for the *Times*. Now that the case was public, so was my involvement. He wanted an exclusive, or at least a heads-up when something big was going to break. I saw my chance.

"Tell you what," I said. "I'm not allowed to promise exclusives, but you'll be my first call on everything that happens in this case—"

Miles sighed. "What do you want?"

"The name of the person who leaked the story."

A long silence told me he knew.

"No name, no favors," I said.

"You never heard this from me—"

"Duh, Miles." The disclaimer was expected. His answer wasn't.

"Brandon Averill."

"That despicable piece of dung," Bailey said. "But it figures, doesn't it?"

I nodded, still bitter. I hadn't yet figured out how I'd exact revenge, but I would eventually. I wanted to make sure I hit him where it would hurt the most.

Bailey refilled our glasses with our latest discovery: Adastra Proximus Pinot Noir.

In part to celebrate the revelation that Brandon Averill was the leak—and in part just to take a needed break—we'd decided to hit Checkers for dinner.

"But so totally in character." I sipped the wine appreciatively.

"What're you planning?"

"Don't know yet." There was a special place in hell for bottom-feeding assholes like Brandon, but I didn't want to trust this payback to otherworldly powers. This one was mine. But I wouldn't act in haste. I'd wait and keep my eyes open for the right opportunity. I knew it'd come eventually.

"Isn't this the scene of the crime?" Bailey asked. "Where you and Daniel had your romantic dinner."

"It wasn't romantic," I protested. "It was an accident."

"Did you know that Daniel's been talking about hanging out his shingle again? Wants to get back to having his own practice. Might even buy that condo he's been renting downtown."

"Who's your source?" I asked.

"Toni, by way of J.D.," Bailey said.

The judge was about as solid a source as you could get.

"That's huge for him," I said, trying to act nonchalant.

"Maybe not just for him," Bailey remarked.

I pretended indifference, but the news rocked me. Bailey was looking at me shrewdly. My effort to appear blasé had not convinced her.

"So what're you going to do?" she asked.

I shrugged. "I don't know."

And I really didn't.

86

The next morning, I got a delivery from the mail room.

It turned out to be the return to the subpoena duces tecum we'd served on the doctor who'd done the fertility treatments for Lilah and Zack. I'd promised the head nurse we'd send out the official-records request, just to cover her butt for giving us Lilah's information on the down low. But I didn't really have any interest in the state of Lilah's ovaries, so I set the package aside and went back to my in-box.

By four o'clock, I needed a break from legalese and I remembered the subpoena return. What I read kick-started the wheels that'd begun turning in my mind some time ago. Slowly, as I put together what I was now read-ing with what I already knew, I saw what everyone had missed. It wasn't so much a legal thing. In fact, it'd never make it into court. But it explained a lot.

I called the head nurse and thanked her for the records. Then I asked her for one piece of information that wasn't in the file. She said she'd get right back to me.

I hung up and called Bailey.

"Can you set up a meeting with Lilah's parents?" I asked.

"Why?"

"I'll tell you as soon as I get the rest of the info. Just set it up as soon as you can. Tonight, if possible."

"I'll call you back," she said, and hung up.

I stared out the window at the Times Building, watching the colors of sunset paint the horizon. At four thirty, the sky was already preparing for nightfall. The phone rang, and I let Melia pick up—always a dicey proposition. But if it was the head nurse, I wanted her to have proof she'd reached the right party. I was in all kinds of luck. It *was* the head nurse *and* Melia put her call through. She gave me the last piece of information that confirmed what I'd suspected. I again thanked her and hung up. I called Bailey.

"Any progress on Lilah's parents?" I asked.

"You mean, since you last asked me ten minutes ago?"

"More like...twelve."

Bailey sighed. "They'll see us at five thirty. I'm leaving now. Pick you up downstairs."

I told Mario, the new leader of our security detail, that Bailey and I were going to pay a visit to the Rossmoynes, then packed up my briefcase, grabbed my purse out of the bottom drawer, and pulled on my coat.

While Bailey inched through rush-hour traffic, I filled her in on what I'd just learned. By the time I told her what I thought it all meant, we'd arrived.

Guy and Pamela Rossmoyne seemed more on edge than they had at our first meeting, and they hadn't been all that smooth then. All to the good, I thought. When we were seated, I deliberately set a sympathetic tone.

"I just learned that Lilah had been going in for fertility treatments for nearly two years," I said. "That's a long time to keep trying after having had two miscarriages."

Guy's expression darkened. "I told Zack to let it go. Stop torturing her." He shook his head and his face reddened. "But he wouldn't listen. Never listened. Just wanted what he wanted."

Torturing her. An interesting choice of words. Pamela, on the other hand, wore a sardonic expression. I aimed my next question at her.

"Did Lilah always have gynecological problems?"

"Not that I ever knew." She paused, as though weighing whether to say more.

I waited and hoped the *say more* part of her would win.

"But the birth control pills didn't help," Pamela added.

"Lilah was on birth control?" I asked.

Pamela gave a twist of a smile. "I saw the pills in her purse about a week before the first miscarriage," she said.

"Did Lilah ever talk to you about wanting to have children?" I asked.

Pamela gave a short bark of a laugh. "Never met anyone who wanted them less. Only kid on the block who wouldn't babysit even for top dollar."

"But we know she got the treatments. In fact, according to the doctor, Zack went with her for all of them."

Guy cut in, his voice harsh. "Of course he did. The bastard was forcing her. Just couldn't let her be." He stood abruptly and stalked out of the room.

I started to say we weren't through but decided we'd be better off without him.

"Your husband doesn't think much of Zack," I said. "Was it always that way?"

"Always," Pamela said, with a dismissive wave of her hand. "But that was nothing new. He never thought anyone was good enough for his baby girl. Hated them all. Every single one."

"But you liked Zack?" I asked.

Pamela shrugged. "I didn't know him that well. They didn't visit much." She pursed her lips. "But Lilah did complain about him once. It was about six months after they were married. Said he was abusive, said he was making her miserable. Said she wanted out. I told her, 'You made your bed, now you lie in it—just like the rest of us.'" Pamela stopped and nodded to herself. "She was just so used to wrapping her daddy around her little finger, she didn't know how to manage a man who didn't jump whenever she called." Pamela folded her arms. "*That* was her problem."

I was sure Lilah wished that was her only problem. I took an envelope out of my briefcase and handed it to Pamela.

"I know you have no contact with Lilah," I said. "But if she ever happens to drop by, I'd appreciate it if you gave her this."

Pamela raised an eyebrow and took the envelope. She made no promises, but she didn't insult me with a lie either. It was a refreshing change.

Ten minutes later, Bailey and I were back in the car and headed for the Biltmore.

"You mind if I put the DA investigators on the house?" I asked.

"May as well. But we both know it won't work. Lilah will find a way to get that letter, but no way she's going to show up here, where we can grab her."

"True," I agreed. "But what've we got to lose?"

Bailey nodded.

The letter was, in part, another ploy to coax Lilah out. And Bailey was right: it wouldn't work. It would, however, be my chance to leave a "message" for Lilah.

Bailey headed up the on-ramp to the Golden State Freeway. "I wonder if Mom would've told anyone about the birth control pills before the acquittal?"

"With her...? Anything's possible," I said.

"Do birth control pills cause miscarriage?" Bailey asked.

"They can," I said. "And if I, who isn't even thinking about getting pregnant, knows that—"

"Then so would Lilah."

We rode in silence for a few moments, considering it all.

"So now we know why Lilah couldn't afford to wait," Bailey said. "She couldn't keep forcing miscarriages forever." She turned onto Grand Avenue and parked in the loading zone.

"Yeah, but there's one more person I want to talk to."

I gave Bailey directions to Mike Howell's office, a small suite in a building just outside downtown. Like me, he always worked late, so now was the best time to catch him.

When he greeted us at the lobby door, I noticed his dirty-blond hair was already starting to recede. But he still looked trim in his slacks and shirtsleeves. He ushered us up the elevator and settled us on the couch in his office. He took the chair across the coffee table from us. "Can I get you anything to drink? No booze at the moment, but I've got water and soft drinks."

Bailey and I gratefully accepted the water.

"So you want to talk about Lilah," he said.

"I know you can't say much, but since she got acquitted, and you know I won't go to the Feds, I thought you might be able to give us a little something."

"Fire away."

"We looked into your 'skinhead did it' defense," I said. I raised an eyebrow.

Mike nodded. He looked out the window as he spoke. "Tell you the truth, when Lilah first retained me, just based on what I saw of the prosecution's case, I went back and forth: she did it, she didn't do it. It was too tough to call. But when I got into…everything else…" Mike paused, then looked at me. "I don't think she did it, Rachel."

My expression must've conveyed my skepticism, because he held up a hand.

"You know I'm not one of those true believers who think all their clients are innocent victims of a vindictive prosecution. Ninety-nine percent of the time, my clients are guilty as sin." He shook his head. "Not this time."

"You know about Zack forcing her to get pregnant? And that she took birth control pills to miscarry?" Bailey asked.

"Yeah."

"And you're sticking with the skinhead story?" I asked.

"No." Mike looked down at his hands and frowned. "I didn't like it myself. But Lilah insisted. She wouldn't let me go after the real killer."

"And that was?" I asked.

"Her father."

* * *

Bailey and I drove back to the hotel in silence. When we got up to the room, I finally spoke. "Lilah's either a world-class manipulator, or—"

"It really is the truth."

There was nothing unusual about a defendant lying to his lawyer about being innocent. Defendants think—with some degree of accuracy—that a lawyer who believes in his client's innocence will fight a lot harder than one who knows his client is guilty. But I'd never heard of a defendant offering up a straw man and then refusing to let the lawyer use that information at trial. It was a heck of a curveball, and I wasn't sure what to make of it. Was it an incredibly clever ploy to work her lawyer? Or did her father really do it? "What do you think? You believe Daddy might've done it?"

She shook her head, looking perplexed. "Before today, I probably would've said no. But now? I don't know."

I remembered Lilah's father's fury when he spoke of Zack and his efforts to get Lilah pregnant. It made him a somewhat plausible suspect. And yet...

I headed for my bedroom. "It's hard to believe Lilah'd take the fall for her father. I would've expected her to throw anyone she could under that bus."

"Who says Mike is right? Smart as he is, he could just be another Lilah Moonie who can't believe the pretty girl's an ax murderer. And like you said, she might be a world-class manipulator. Matter of fact, I'd be willing to bet she is."

I nodded. "And even if she thought she stood a better chance than her dad of getting the jury to acquit, there's no telling what a jury will do. Any lawyer knows that."

Bailey sighed, and we both went to bed. Though I was skeptical of the theory that Lilah's father had killed Zack, I knew I wouldn't be able to resolve the question tonight. But I was too keyed up to sleep right away. I wondered what Lilah would make of the letter I'd written to her. I'd deliberately lied—hopefully not enough to be obvious but just enough to get her to pop off and do something stupid. It was the long shot of the century, but it cost me nothing. And I enjoyed the possibility that at the very least, I'd make her worry. A satisfying thought. And a good one to fall asleep on.

87

Lilah waited until she'd gotten back to her condo and locked her bedroom door. Then she took the envelope out of her purse and examined it for signs of tampering. It looked intact. Her mouth twisted in a bitter half smile. She knew it wasn't respect for her privacy. Her parents just didn't want to know. She used the nail of her index finger to slice open the envelope and unfolded the letter.

Lilah,

I know why you killed Zack.

You never did find the evidence he hid on the Tran Lee hit-and-run, did you?

And I know he was trying to force you to get pregnant.

The thought of carrying the child of the animal who held you hostage was too much, wasn't it? And if you had children together, you'd never be free of him. It was a game that would go on forever. So Zack had to die, and you deserved to get away with it. By the way, the ax was a nice touch.

Of course, you wouldn't have had to deal with any of that if you hadn't gotten drunk and run over that boy, Tran Lee. So when it comes right down to it, you only have yourself to blame.

Still, I'm willing to offer you a deal.

Plead guilty to aiding and abetting in Simon's murder, and to Tran Lee's hit-and-run. You do that, and I'll let you plead to second-degree murder for Simon's killing and I'll agree to a concurrent sentence for Tran's killing. That'll give you fifteen years to life for two homicides.

It's more than fair.

Call me, and I'll arrange for you to surrender discreetly.

But if I find you first, the deal is off.

Rachel Knight

Lilah barely managed to choke back the scream of rage. Her fault? *None* of it was her fault! That stupid kid— it was all his fault! She'd done *nothing* wrong! Lilah's breath came in ragged spurts as she tore the letter again and again, until the pieces were too small to hold. Then she put them in the sink and burned them.

88

Morning came a little too early, but then, for me, it always did. I wanted to go back to sleep, but the clock said it was already seven thirty a.m.

I dressed for work in slacks and a blazer, put on heels just for a change of pace, and packed my sneakers in a bag. I went out to the living room and found that Bailey'd ordered a devastatingly evil breakfast of French toast, scrambled eggs, and bacon and sausage. I lifted the silver cover on my dish. Instead of my usual egg-white extravaganza, there was a plateful of the best-looking pancakes I'd seen in quite a while. And a side of bacon. I tried to act pissed off, but a big smile spread across my face, which undermined the effort considerably.

"Just enjoy it for once," Bailey said.

"How can I ignore such sage advice?"

I sat down, snapped open my napkin, and spread it across my lap. Then I got busy with my pancakes. They tasted even better than they looked.

I noticed Bailey had a copy of the *Daily Journal* open in front of her. "What're you reading that thing for?" I asked.

"Toni told me the story Hemet gave to the press about you being a useless goldbricking Special Trials cherry picker—"

"You are allowed to abbreviate now and then," I said, stone-faced.

"—was supposed to come out today," Bailey finished. "Why didn't she tell me?"

"She didn't want you to stress over it," Bailey said. "And now I'm really glad she didn't."

"Because?" I prompted.

"Because it's not here."

I stared at Bailey, perplexed. Good news might evaporate, but bad news rarely did. "Why?"

She shrugged.

Bailey dropped me off at the courthouse and headed for the cop shop. Though I'd been working through the stacks of motions, reports, and messages that'd accumulated during my stint in the field, I still had a daunting array to get through, so I decided that today would be the day I got caught up all the way. I kept my head down, not even breaking for lunch, until eight thirty that night.

When I'd finished, I leaned back in my giant chair and took in the scene with satisfaction: it was only a temporary condition, but my in-box was empty and several clean square inches of desk had emerged. I stretched and looked outside, surveying the view of downtown L.A. at night. The glowing windows in dark buildings, the faint hum of traffic, the stars hanging like silver dust in the night sky. I never tired of the view.

But it was time to pack up and get out. It was Wednesday night and I had a date. I put my files in order, tossed my heels into the bag, pulled on my coat, and picked up my purse. I made it down to the lobby in mere seconds and trotted out to Chinatown, my destination the Oolong Café. I ordered double helpings of orange chicken, fried rice, beef chow mein, and steamed vegetables, and added an order of chow fun. They packed it up neatly in a grocery bag with handles, and I headed back down Broadway. Though Chinatown still had some action, the streets got emptier as I moved south. By the time I passed Temple, I was the only one on the sidewalk.

The stretch between First and Second Street was the darkest, and I started to feel shaky as I drew closer to the corner. I considered going back to the courthouse, but that didn't feel any safer. I started to fish out my cell phone, but using a cell would only distract me and keep me from hearing an approach. And I couldn't hold the food and my gun in the other hand. I had no choice but to keep moving. I stood at the intersection of Broadway and First and peered into the darkness but saw no one.

The light turned, and I stepped off the curb. I moved as quickly as I could on the uneven sidewalk, paying attention to every step, every second, and every inch of the space around me. I crossed the street and forced myself to move forward, into the darkness ahead. My throat felt tight, my mouth dry; it was an effort to swallow. I'd call it a panic attack, but there was nothing irrational about the fear I was feeling.

Slowly but deliberately, I moved down the street, seeking out the one particular spot that was my destination. When I got to the middle of the block, I saw it. There, in the doorway on the corner, was the pile of blankets with the Lakers hat on top—my friend Cletus's rig. I owed him big-time for his help on Simon's case, and this was his

Wednesday-night spot, where I usually brought him Chinese.

I started to head for the blankets when suddenly there was a *whoosh* of air behind me, the precursor to a lethal swing. I ducked down and turned to see a slender man in dark clothing and a watch cap. Without thought, I doubled up and threw my body into his solar plexus. A black sap flew through the air where my head had been and landed with a heavy thud on the pavement. The flight of the sap drew my eye, and I reflexively looked up. A lucky move, because it pushed me back just as I felt his fingers reaching for my neck. I spun away and dug into my pocket for my gun.

But he saw my move and knew what it meant. Before I could get it out, he lunged forward. I lifted my knee and swung out my foot, putting all of my body weight into a vicious kick, not caring where I connected. My foot hit his body with force, and I heard him grunt, but when I tried to pull it back, he grabbed and yanked. I landed flat on my back on the concrete, the wind knocked out of me. Momentarily stunned, I saw the glint of a knife in his hand and tried to pull my gun, but it was caught in the lining somehow.

My hand trapped, I had to improvise. I put my finger on the trigger, did my best to aim, and fired from inside my pocket. And missed. The shot startled him, causing him to drop his knife. But he only paused for a second before reaching into his own pocket. I heard sirens in the distance. I hoped they were headed our way...and that they'd get here in time.

Before he could withdraw his hand, two shots exploded from under Cletus's blankets farther down the street. The man turned and fell back a step, momentarily stunned. Bailey burst out from under the blankets and raced toward us as she fired another round, hitting him in the thigh. That stopped him cold. I scrambled to my feet and had just regained my balance when he reached out and grabbed my arm. He pulled me toward him and went for his pocket again. Acting on pure instinct, I wrapped my hand around the barrel of my gun, turned into him, and smashed the butt of it into the side of his head—once, twice... by the third time, he let go and fell back.

Bailey slammed him to the pavement and rolled him onto his stomach. Pinning him with a knee on his back, she ground his face into the concrete as she pulled out her zip ties. Just to be on the safe side, I held my gun to his head while she cuffed him. When he was thoroughly trussed, I patted his jacket pockets and found a .38 revolver. I slid it on the ground, out of his reach. Police cars arrived in a screaming phalanx, responding to the sounds of gunfire. Bailey and I held up our shields. The police moved in fast and took over. As Bailey quickly explained the situation, I had a chance to get a clear look at our attacker, who'd lost his watch cap in the scuffle. He had the sinewy appearance of someone who was strong but flexible, and the watch cap had fallen off to reveal a shock of curly dark hair. There was something feral about his features—what I could see of them through the blood coursing down his face.

Bailey pointed out the knife and the sap that'd fallen to the ground during the fight and made sure they got bagged and tagged. It looked like the kind of combat knife that'd been used to kill Simon. I doubted there'd be anything left on it to allow for DNA testing, but it was pretty distinctive. If all the other evidence panned out, it'd be a nice addition. After the police had loaded the suspect into a car, Mario, one of the investigators, showed up, looking like a balloon that was about to burst.

"You two okay?" he asked, concerned.

Bailey nodded.

"Yep," I replied. Though it hadn't gone exactly as planned. We'd thought the attacker wouldn't make his move until I had stopped at Cletus's rig. Bailey would've been able to take him down before he knew what hit him. It was a flawless plan. Except, of course, it wasn't. All he'd had to do to derail it was what he did: jump me a little sooner—just a half-block away from the blankets. Only now did it begin to hit me how crazy this whole idea had been. I decided I didn't need to tell Mario every little detail.

"Good," he said flatly. With our welfare out of the way, he was free to let go of one giant hunk of pissitivity. His nostrils flared, and he put his hands on his hips and fixed me with an angry glare. "You were supposed to call me before you left the office." He turned to include Bailey. "And you two idiots obviously planned this—"

"Hey!" Bailey interjected.

But Mario was on a roll. "What the *hell* did you think you were doing, setting this up without telling anyone? And *you*"—he turned to Bailey—"I know *you* know better than this. So what the hell...?"

Bailey ground her lower jaw. Her voice was harsh and raw. "I tried to talk her out of it, okay? But she wasn't listening. She would've done it alone. How'm I going to let her do that?"

I opened my mouth to protest, then clamped it shut.

Bailey was right. I'd always had a tendency to push the envelope, riskwise—I called it *tenacious*. Carla the Crone diagnosed it as survivor's guilt. But even for me, this plan was a bridge too far. This time it wasn't just me; I'd endangered Bailey's life as well. How could I have done this? Why on earth had I taken it so far? Gary's death, this case—something about Lilah—it all had me more unhinged than I'd realized.

Mario turned on me, eyes blazing, then stormed off, venting, "This is why no one wants to guard you—no one!"

When he was in a more receptive mood, I'd explain that we didn't think we could tell him about the plan because we suspected that Lilah had a source somewhere in the police department or the DA's office—maybe both. By then maybe he'd be able to hear me, and even agree. But maybe not.

The bags of Chinese food I'd been carrying were splayed all over the sidewalk. Crows had already found the banquet and were cawing their victory over the orange chicken.

"Bailey," I said, "where'd you put our buddy—?"

She motioned to me to follow her. "Be right back," she called after Mario.

One of the police officers yelled out to us, "You'll have to give statements, so don't go far."

We moved quickly down the street and turned the corner. Bailey led me to her car. There, stretched out in the backseat with a feast of Chinese food, was Cletus. Bailey knocked softly to warn him we were there, and he sat up and gave us a semitoothless grin. She opened the door.

"How you doing, Cletus?" I asked.

"Just fine, missy. Cletus's just fine," he replied in the gravelly voice that seemed to come from the middle of the earth. "Not as good as yours, though," he said, pointing to the boxes of food.

"I had to make do," Bailey apologized.

"Cletus, you might want to get inside tonight," I said. "There're going to be cops all over your space."

He frowned. "What'd you two get up to?" he said suspiciously.

"Don't ask," Bailey said.

He shook his head. "Got to bother an old man like this. Ain't right, ain't right." He sighed. "I got a ride," he said, looking around the interior of Bailey's car. "May as well use it. Take me to Johnnie's."

I looked at Bailey. We weren't exactly Johnnie Jasper's favorite people at the moment.

"You mind if we let someone else give you a lift there?" I asked. "We've got to hang around for a bit."

"Sure, sure," Cletus said, digging into his fried rice.

We headed back to the crime scene to find someone to give Cletus a ride. And to spend another million hours giving statements.

89

Bailey and I got up the next morning at the crack of dawn. One of us was happy about this.

"You know," I said when she shook me awake at six fifteen a.m., "you can probably go back to your own pad now." I sat up, rubbing my eyes. "Besides, what's the rush? I'm not filing on that guy without ballistics and DNA results—"

Bailey held up her cell phone and waggled it under my face. "You got 'em. The blood on Simon's shirt came back to him, and the gun he was carrying matches the one used to shoot Gary. Good enough for you?" she asked.

That had to be the fastest I'd ever seen DNA come back. This case had a lot of people fired up. "It'll do," I replied.

Bailey drove us to the courthouse for what I figured would be the last time. With Simon's killer in custody, I'd be walking to work again. Though we hadn't lucked out and caught Lilah going to or from her parents' house, I was confident our newly arrested killer could be persuaded to tell us where she was. Besides, now that she knew we had the evidence on Tran's case, Lilah had nothing to gain by killing us. She seemed to be a fairly pragmatic murderer.

We were so early, we beat the morning courthouse crowds and got an elevator within seconds. Two minutes later, we'd settled in my office. I woke up my computer.

"So do we have a name for our perp?" I asked.

"Chase…" Bailey fished out her notebook. "Erling. Was a bouncer at Les Deux a few years back. But his full-time gig—that is, before he went to work for Lilah—was in computer hardware and electronics. Used to work for a gadget company named Omni—"

"Electronics and computers?" I frowned. "What the hell?"

"Must have something to do with Lilah's business."

"When he's up and running, do you think he'll be willing to cough up some information on Lilah in return for a choice of prison placement?"

Bailey shook her head. "I'd say negatory—"

"Though you really shouldn't, 'cause it sounds silly," I observed. "But why not?"

"Because we found this inside the lining of his jacket," she said, holding up her cell phone.

It showed a photograph of a watch. TAG Heuer, to be exact.

I frowned at Bailey. "Okay," I said. "He's got the watch we saw on the video. So why does that mean he won't talk?"

"Check out the next picture," she instructed.

I hit the arrow. A photo showed the underside of the watch. It was inscribed. *Fondly, L.*

"Lilah," I said. Then I put the rest of it together. "After he saw our photo, he knew he couldn't be seen wearing the watch anymore. But he didn't want to dump it because it was a keepsake from his...girlfriend?"

Bailey shrugged. "I wouldn't necessarily go that far, but there was obviously some kind of relationship, and it meant something to him."

I turned back to my computer. "Two counts of murder...use of a deadly weapon on Simon...use of a firearm on Gary. Even if the judge stays sentence on the deadly weapon, this guy's getting seventy-five to life."

We shared a satisfied smile.

"I'll be done with this in fifteen minutes," I said. "If I walk it down, we'll be ready to arraign him within the hour. Think you can get anyone to move him in for the afternoon session?"

"Let me find out," Bailey said. She went into the hallway to make the calls.

Fifteen minutes later, she was back. "Our boy will be on the afternoon bus."

"Excellent." With a DA investigator as one of the victims, the press would likely get interested in the case. It'd be nice to at least have the arraignment done without the hoopla. I hit print and took the pages as they spit out.

I looked at the clock on the Times Building. It was only ten thirty. I stood up and put the papers into a plain file folder to shield them from view. "I'll be back," I said. I turned on my heel and left.

The clerk got the case filed as fast as I've ever seen. Within half an hour, I was on the elevator and headed back to my office. I dumped some sandwiches on the desk in front of Bailey.

"Turkey and Swiss for me, ham and cheddar for you," I said.

"Looks great," Bailey said. "I do miss that silver tray, though." Her cell phone rang. She looked at the number on the screen.

Bailey answered the phone. "Keller here."

That was pretty formal for her.

Suddenly she dropped her feet to the floor and grabbed the desk. Her face looked pale. "When?"

She listened, and I stood up. *What?* I mouthed. But Bailey wasn't looking at me.

"How?" she asked.

I was ready to pull out my hair. What the hell was going on?

When Bailey ended the call, her expression was thunderous. "Chase Erling," she said. "Someone attacked him on the transpo bus."

90

"**Someone shanked** him when they were loading up the bus for court," Bailey said.

"I thought they had him as 'special handling.'"

"Yeah, so did I," Bailey said, hands on her hips. She stared out the window.

"We got the guy who did it?" I asked.

"Oh yeah," she said. "He's looking at about a hundred years to life himself—"

"Figures." He had little to lose.

"And he's a skinhead," she continued. "Nazi Low Riders."

We stared at each other as the significance of what she'd just said settled in the air.

"Lilah," Bailey said simply.

Though I'd come to the same conclusion, I didn't want to believe it.

"How could she possibly manage to get to someone in the jail that fast?" I demanded.

Bailey shook her head. "They just told me the skinhead claims he heard the guy was a chomo."

Chomo. The slang for child molester. It was a skinhead credo that they had an obligation to kill any known child molester on sight, and it was a badge of honor to carry it out.

There was nothing whatsoever in Chase Erling's file that indicated he was a child molester.

"Bullshit," I said.

"Definitely," Bailey agreed. "But it's great cover for the skinhead, and who's going to bother proving that Erling *wasn't* a perv?"

No one. The Low Rider would enter a fast guilty plea and get carried into prison like he was Cleopatra.

"She used them as the fall guys for Zack's murder—," Bailey said.

"And now she's done it again," I said with cold fury. "What would it take to bribe a cretin who's already doing one hundred years to life?"

"Nothing."

We sat in silence for several minutes. The skinhead would never admit he'd been put up to it. And, for all I knew, he really believed Erling was a chomo. It wouldn't have taken much to convince him—just a few well-chosen words. I couldn't say I minded Erling's death. What I did mind was the giant fuck-you it came with.

"Chase Erling was our only way of getting to Lilah," I said.

Bailey nodded, her expression stony. "And now there's no way we'll find her. She's in the wind."

91

Lilah took one last glance around the empty office. She'd made sure every inch was scoured. There'd be no trace left of her. She'd always known this day would come, one way or another. What she hadn't been prepared for was Chase. Hotheaded, yes. Impulsive at times, yes. But going after that prosecutor? Suicidal. Now, in hindsight, Lilah realized the screwup in Venice had affected him more deeply than he'd let on. And she couldn't afford to leave him behind. He was too big a liability. Loyal as he was, she knew better than to believe he'd never crack. She sighed heavily as she closed the door for the last time. Somehow, everyone always failed her in the end. She should be used to it by now. No one was as strong, or as smart, as she was.

The car was waiting for her at the curb. She looked around and saw the street was deserted, then gestured to the driver. "In there," she said, pointing to the luggage just inside the entranceway. The driver nodded, opened the back passenger door for her, waited while she got seated, and closed it behind her before trotting up the walkway.

Lilah pulled out her phone and called Maxwell Chevorin. "I'm on the way out. Is it ready?"

"All set. Only the pilot knows the destination, and he works for me."

"I'll be in touch as soon as we land," she said.

Chevorin seemed satisfied with that. She ended the conversation and closed the phone, her expression grim. Now she was beholden to him—not something that sat well with her. It gave him too much power. She tapped the back of her cell phone, thinking about how to even the score. A little smile lifted the corners of her mouth as a possibility came to mind. Half an hour later, the driver pulled onto the tarmac.

Lilah boarded and buckled up. Within minutes, they'd ascended over Van Nuys Airport and climbed into the clouds. She couldn't stay gone forever. But she couldn't come back until she'd eliminated the threat. Lilah pulled out her throwaway phone.

92

"They'll probably pronounce him in the next half hour or so," Bailey said.

I clamped my jaws shut to keep from screaming in frustration. Chase Erling had been rushed into surgery, but it was a doomed effort—the kind they make out of duty, no real hope involved. The skinhead had managed to stab him five times in the head and torso.

My office phone rang. I snatched it up angrily. "Yeah."

It was the mail room. A package—another response to my subpoena for records—had come in. Arturo, the mail room clerk, offered to drop it off on his way out. "Great, thanks," I said with no interest whatsoever. Lilah's medical records were of little import now.

When Arturo dropped off the slim package, I barely glanced at it. But after a moment I absently tore open the manila envelope and read the document.

"What?" Bailey asked, seeing my expression.

"Lilah was almost five months pregnant when Zack was killed," I said.

Dr. Aigler had been the last to see Lilah and Zack at

the clinic. It'd been his pleasure to give them the happy news that she was four months pregnant. But two weeks later, Lilah had canceled her prenatal checkup. When the office had called to reschedule, she'd said she was changing doctors—she'd send them the address of his office so they could forward the records. So the office had packaged her file and set it aside, ready for mailing. Which was why, when my subpoena was served, it'd taken a little longer to find it. They'd never heard from Lilah again.

"Didn't she get arrested right after the murder?" I asked.

Bailey shook her head. "Not for a while. I can check, but it was at least three or four months." She frowned. "And she definitely wasn't pregnant when she went into custody."

"According to Audrey's records, Lilah never went back to work after the arrest." I stared out the window. "She might've been able to find a doctor who'd abort it—"

"Wouldn't be easy, though."

"No."

"So what happened to that baby?"

I leaned back in my chair, and we fell silent. But in the next moment, Bailey and I simultaneously stopped and stared at each other. Like a blast of cold wind that blows away the fog, the revelation left a view that was crystal clear. Finally, the last piece of the puzzle clicked into place.

"If she'd had that baby with Zack still around—," Bailey began.

"She'd never be free of him," I finished.

Bailey nodded.

"She did it. Lilah killed Zack."

* * *

My cell phone buzzed in my hand. It was a text message.

> Did anyone ever tell you that one month after Romy disappeared, a parking citation was issued to a red pickup truck just twenty miles away from your home? And that a black dog was in the cab?
>
> Or that six months after that, a man in a red pickup truck was given a speeding ticket up in Eureka? And that his "daughter" was asleep in the backseat?
>
> You didn't know any of that, did you? And there's more, so much more that I could tell you...

I stared at the message with such intensity, it got blurry. I could barely breathe.

"Rachel? What's wrong?" Bailey asked.

But my heart was pounding so hard, I couldn't speak. I handed her the phone.

If the kidnapper hadn't killed Romy within the first forty-eight hours, there was a chance he hadn't killed her at all. I had hope—real hope—for the first time in decades that my sister might be alive.

The sudden adrenaline rush left me trembling. I wanted to jump on this possible lead with all fours. But I couldn't afford to dwell on it right now. I looked down at my shaking hands and willed them to stop. Because I had a message for Lilah.

I set my phone to camera mode, held it up to the hospital bed in front of me, and clicked. And sent Lilah the photograph of Chase Erling. Who had miraculously survived.

Then I typed: Don't you wonder what else I know?

EPILOGUE

I felt fairly certain that when Chase woke up and learned that Lilah had put out a hit on him—and I'd make sure he did—we'd have an important source of information on her. Not only where to find her but also her involvement as the mastermind of the murders of Simon and Gary. I'd find her eventually. And when I did, I'd make sure she was locked up for life.

For now, Bailey and I found some consolation in the fact that we'd caught the actual killer responsible for Gary's and Simon's murder, and thanks to the efforts of the fine doctors at Harbor General, Chase Erling would get to live for quite some time. Long enough to serve at least one of his multiple life sentences.

I'd asked the Bayers if they'd mind donating the bowl and serving tray Simon left behind in his studio to Johnnie Jasper. They'd been happy to do it, and they'd enclosed a beautiful, loving note to Johnnie, thanking him for the kindness he'd shown to Simon. We braved Johnnie's wrath and delivered the items, including his vase, personally. I called out to him, and when he emerged, I placed everything just outside the fence. He waited until I got back in the car, but I saw him open the gate before we pulled away.

Toni told us we owed her dinner—why, she didn't say. But we'd been meaning to check out Rivera, a Nueva Mexicana restaurant downtown that was supposed to be the bomb, so I got us reservations. Whatever Toni thought we owed her, I figured that would settle the score.

She was resplendent in a leopard-print dress, and Bailey looked hot as usual, in her Calvin Klein sweater and slacks. We ordered our Ketel One martinis and toasted to "Girls' night."

"So give it up, Tone," I said. "Why do we owe you?"

Toni gave us a sly smile. "Remember I told you if we wanted to shut Hemet down, we needed to get dirt on him?"

"Yeah."

"I got to thinking," she said. "Who has the eyes and ears closest to management?"

"The secretaries," I said.

"And Hemet's secretary, Rosa, has been a friend of mine since I was a baby DA," Toni said. "She's about fifteen months pregnant, and she's not real interested in coming back after her maternity leave—"

"So she was willing to talk," Bailey surmised.

"You *are* good, Detective," Toni said. "We were looking over a Ross-Simons catalog when Hemet called in and told her to sign him out at five p.m."

"So?" I asked, puzzled.

"It was one thirty p.m.," Toni said. "And he was not in the office."

"He has her fake his time cards?" I said with disbelief.

She nodded emphatically. "Like crazy. When I see this go down, I ask her, does he do it all the time? She says, this was nothing. Last month, he went to Maui and called in to tell her to sign him in and out every day for *a whole friggin' week!*"

The man who was dogging me about playing hooky on company time was falsifying his own time cards.

"But how would you ever prove it?" I asked.

"Well, we have Rosa's word for it," Toni said. "But girlfriend did a smart thing. She told him she was thinking of going to Maui and asked him to send her pictures. Hemet, the dumb shit, never dreamed his little secretary would dump him out, so he sent 'em to her—"

"On her cell phone, which shows time and date," I said.

Toni nodded and chuckled.

"Is he in any of them?" Bailey asked.

"Huh, try *all* of them!" she replied. "The man should not wear shorts!"

We covered our mouths and tried to laugh without snorting.

Toni continued, "I told her what Hemet was doing to you and that I wanted to confront him with the dirt myself, but Rosa wouldn't let me. Said she'd been waiting for years to get the chance to mess him up. So when she heard about you, she wanted to do it for you too. And, like I said, she doesn't care about keeping the job anymore—"

"So she went out with a bang," I said. "And I assume that's what made Hemet pull out of the news story?"

"Unless he wanted to be the featured player," Toni said. "He's got connects, so he won't get fired. But I'd guess he'll be put out to pasture in a land far, far away, where the only career he can ruin is his own."

"It's better this way," I reflected. "If he's fired, he has to find a new life. This way, he stays, but he's invisible—"

"And powerless," Toni added. "But here's the kicker: with Hemet gone, Averill's days downtown are numbered. He can kiss his dreams of the big time good-bye. Ten bucks says he's out in Newhall by Easter."

"No bet, Tone," I said. "But I'll drink to that." I started to lift my glass, but it was empty.

"Mine too," she said.

Bailey nodded. I raised my hand to get our waiter's attention.

He spotted it from across the room and made a circling gesture, asking if we wanted another round. I gave him a thumbs-up. When he returned with a tray of drinks, he pointed to a table at the other end of the dining room. "The gentleman over there is buying this round."

Detective Stoner lifted his glass and smiled. We joined him and mouthed, *Thank you.*

It was a great night. And as I got into bed, I remembered a saying I'd heard: If you wait long enough, all your enemies will be vanquished. Hemet's—and Averill's impending—demise might just be proof that it's true.

Sometimes, I can be very patient.

The next day, Bailey moved back to her apartment.

She looked around the hotel room one last time and sighed. "I guess all good things have to come to an end eventually."

"I'll miss you too," I said.

"I was talking about room service."

"Get out."

Having the room to myself again gave me a lot of time to think. Along with the new hope of finding Romy—a hope I could barely let myself touch—was the sadness of Gary's loss and a profound loneliness. I was glad to get back to work Monday morning. I buried myself in the double homicide that was set to go in two weeks, and before I knew it, the office lights in the surrounding buildings were glowing warmly against an ebony sky.

Time to pack it in. I slipped into my coat, grabbed my purse and briefcase, and headed out through the now-quiet hallways. I crossed the lobby and stepped outside into the chill night air.

"Rachel."

I stopped. My heart gave a slow, heavy thud. I knew that voice. I turned to see Graden standing behind me. He walked over, looked down at me, and brushed my hair from my face.

"We should probably talk," I said.

"Later." He folded me into his arms. And I exhaled in a way I hadn't done in a very long time.

ACKNOWLEDGMENTS

Once again, I am forever indebted to Catherine LePard—whose brilliance, talent, and support are the inspiration and mainstay of my life. Cathy, I might never have attempted to live the dream of writing novels if it weren't for you.

Dan Conaway, how on earth did I get lucky enough to have you for an agent? You're not just phenomenal at the job, you're a gem of a person. It's a delight to know you and to work with you. And fantastic assistant Stephen Barr, you are such a pleasure. What a team! I couldn't love you more.

I again owe boundless thanks to wonderful editor in chief Judy Clain and publisher Michael Pietsch. Terrific people who are also terrifically talented—a rare combination. I'm incredibly fortunate and honored to be working with you. To marvelous assistant Nathan Rostron, thank you once again for all your hard work behind the scenes.

And to senior copyeditor Karen Landry—another great job. Thank you.

My profound thanks to all of the wonderful folks at Mulholland Books, and especially the publicity all-star team: Nicole Dewey, Sabrina Callahan, Miriam Parker—aka my buds. Your smarts, energy, creativity, and sheer resourcefulness are phenomenal…and you couldn't be more fun! A million thanks to you for all your hard work.

To Marillyn Holmes, I can't begin to tell you how grateful I am for your help. Your keen eye and knowledge were indispensable. My love and endless thanks to you.

To Lynn Reed Baragona and Hynndie Wali, who helped keep me sane through the writing of this book. You set the gold standard for girlfriends, and somehow always know how to talk me down off the ledge and how to make me laugh through my *mishigas*. I love you guys!

PROLOGUE

Rocky mountain peaks glowed lonely and austere under the nearly full moon. But the trail that led to God's Seat, a throne-shaped outcropping high atop Backbone Trail, wound darkly under thick canopies of branches and overhanging boulders. One false step on that narrow path meant a thousand-foot drop and certain death, but the two lone figures walking single file up the trail moved at a heedless pace.

The night was still except for the crunch of their footsteps on sun-baked earth: one confident and driving, the other stumbling gracelessly forward, blinded by terror, steps punctuated by weeping, a nearly inaudible murmuring—*This can't be happening... Can't... No, no, no, no. Please, let me wake up. Please, please. This is just a dream.* At the top of the ridge, beside a waist-high boulder, the larger figure stopped and threw a shovel to the ground, the clang of metal hitting rock.

"Dig."

The smaller figure stared at the shovel, then abruptly doubled over, stomach heaving convulsively as the vomit rose up too fast to control. The larger figure watched for a moment, then, with cold disdain, flashed a vicious-looking blade. "You hear me? Pick up the fucking shovel and—"

"Okay, okay," came the reply, as clammy, trembling hands took the shovel and thrust it into the earth. *Okay, okay... okay, okay...* repeating it over and over, mantra-like—wheezing with the effort to breathe through a fear-constricted throat.

"Faster."

Slowly, the hole grew deeper and longer. *Okay, okay... This will be okay. Someone will come. Someone will come. Okay, okay...*

And then, miraculously, someone *did* come. A soft rustling, the sound of slow, tentative steps approaching. And, as if in a dream, a moonlit face emerged from the darkness.

Three Nights Earlier

Hayley and Mackenzie spilled out of the chauffeur-driven Escalade and into the throng of twenty-somethings in front of Teddy's, the "it" club in the Hollywood Roosevelt Hotel. Long sparkling earrings and sequined minidresses on spray-tanned body beautifuls, well-toned pretty boys in carefully torn jeans and three-hundred-dollar T-shirts—the air heavy with the tension of feigned indifference, as though each and every one of them wasn't desperate to gain entrée into the exclusive club. Hayley led the way through the crowd, her blonde head thrown back, stiletto heels hitting the ground with confidence.

Mackenzie trailed behind, nervously pulling down her tube skirt as she instinctively reached for Hayley's hand. Her eyes focused on the ground to avoid the angry glares of the waiting crowd. The jackhammering of her heart made her breath come in short, shallow gulps.

When they reached the door, the bouncer, slender and sinewy, a spider tattoo wrapped around his neck, raised a skeptical eyebrow from beneath the worn brim of a black hat. Mackenzie wiped a nervous palm on her thigh before relinquishing her license. But Hayley, with a sexy-lazy smile, smoothly dipped into the cleavage of her leopard-print halter top and flipped her license out between two fingers. As always, Mackenzie watched with awe and envy, knowing she'd never master that kind of breezy nonchalance.

The bouncer briefly scanned their IDs, then handed them back with a dismissive head shake. "Not even close."

Mackenzie's heart stopped. *Busted.* But then Hayley stepped in and shoved a card under his nose. She looked him straight in the eye. "You sure?"

The bouncer frowned and peered at the card, then took back Hayley's license and gave it a second look. Suddenly, his face broke into a lopsided grin. "Your dad know you're here?"

Mackenzie felt giddy with relief—and foolish. After all this time she should surely know better. Clubs, private parties, restaurants—hell, even the *Vanity Fair* after-party on Oscar night—all happily opened their doors to the daughter of megastar director Russell Antonovich.

"My dad *sent* me," Hayley joked, with an intimate look that brought him in on it.

Chuckling, the bouncer lifted the rope, then reached back and opened the door, unleashing a blast of music. "Have a nice night, ladies," he said.

Hayley grabbed Mackenzie's hand and led the way through a wall of dancers whose bodies glowed under pulsing multicolored lights, their only guide through the near-impenetrable velvet darkness. A hand shot up and waved to them from a crowded horseshoe booth next to the DJ—the sweetest spot in the house. They inched their way over and squeezed in, Mackenzie practically sitting in Hayley's lap. The walls seemed to vibrate with the thunderous bass, making conversation impossible. But it didn't matter. They weren't there to talk and they wouldn't need to place orders: hors d'oeuvres were served continuously, and they always had bottle service. Tonight's offering was Patrón Silver, and she and Hayley had doubles in their hands by the time they sat down. A cute curly-haired guy—was his name Adrian?—moved forward with a sexy smile and pulled Mackenzie out onto the dance floor. She didn't sit down again till unknown hours later when she and Hayley collapsed into the back of the Escalade.

Now

Could that really have been just three nights ago? From her perch high on a hill in Laurel Canyon, Mackenzie barely noticed the spread of twinkling lights, the crawl of traffic across Sunset Boulevard and up La Cienega. She glanced to the west, where, just a few miles away in the Hollywood Hills above Sunset Plaza, Hayley's dad had his "party house." It was a favorite hang of theirs when her dad wasn't around. They loved to skinny-dip in the infinity pool that stretched from the edge of the hilltop and flowed under a heavy plate-glass wall, right into the living room.

Laughing, partying, playing, sharing. The past year had been the best of Mackenzie's life, and she owed it all to Hayley. Tears sprang to her eyes, turning the red and white lights on the streets below into long, blurry streaks. She pulled the photo, normally enshrined on the mirror in her bedroom, out of the back pocket of her jeans. It was a picture of her and Hayley at Colony, loose, boozy smiles, arms looped around each other's shoulders. Her first night out with Hayley. And her first step out of the purgatory of "new girl" and, even worse, "poor girl" at the Clarington Academy prep school, aka high school for rich kids. Mackenzie got in on an academic scholarship, but she was a charity case and everyone seemed to know it. For the first few months she'd slunk through the hallways, a lonely, miserable misfit. Until one day, in gym class, she and Hayley had discovered a mutual hatred of field hockey. That's all it took. Her life, her whole world changed overnight. How could that have been just a little over a year ago?

Mackenzie clutched the sides of her head and tried to breathe. Hayley had said not to worry. That it would be okay. That she'd call and she'd explain everything. But for now, don't tell anyone. Don't tell.

But that was three days ago. Three days, with no word from Hayley. Was she supposed to wait this long? What if something had gone wrong? Should she call someone? But maybe nothing was wrong and her call would just screw everything up. It'd be all her fault and Hayley might never forgive her. What was she supposed to do? Mackenzie dropped her head, hugged her knees, and squeezed her eyes shut against the tears. It would be okay. Hayley would be okay. Hayley was always okay. She *had* to be.

1

"I'm guessing by your expression that dinner went pretty well after all," Bailey said. *Her* expression had an obnoxious "told-you-so" tinge to it that made me want to lie. But I knew there was no point. Bailey was not only a top-notch detective in the elite Robbery-Homicide Division of LAPD, she was also one of my very best friends. She would see right through it. Still, I didn't have to give it up all at once.

I gave a noncommittal shrug, hung my purse on the hook under the bar, and slid onto the cushy leather stool. "It went okay."

It was ten o'clock on a Monday night, so the after-work crowd had largely cleared out of the Biltmore Hotel bar. The only exception was a well-dressed middle-aged couple on one of the velvety couches against the wall. They were enjoying Manhattans with a leisurely attitude that told me they didn't have to worry about a morning commute. Though I didn't recognize them, I guessed they were staying in the hotel. Being a permanent resident of the hotel myself, I could usually tell who was a guest and who had just dropped by for a drink.

Drew, the gorgeous bartender, who'd been my buddy ever since I'd moved into the Biltmore a few years ago, gave me a knowing smirk. "Just okay? I don't think so." He tilted his shining black head toward the mirror behind him. "Take a look at yourself, girl."

Even in the dim light I could see the sappy expression on my face. Damn. Drew and Bailey exchanged an amused smile. They'd been together for about two years now—the longest stretch either of them had ever managed with a single partner. Most of the time, it was a beautiful thing. But there were stomach-turning moments like this, when their "oneness" made me want to bang their heads together. Hard.

Bailey turned back just in time to catch my nauseated look—and ignore it. "And in case you were worried, you're not alone out there. Graden was actually whistling." Bailey made a face. "All day."

Since Lieutenant Graden Hales was Bailey's boss, she knew he never whistled. But I refused to give her the satisfaction of seeing how good it made me feel. I looked at her, deadpan. "Funny how annoying little things like that can be."

"Isn't it?" Bailey deadpanned right back at me.

Graden and I met a couple of years ago when he worked the case of Jake Pahlmeyer, a dear friend and fellow Special Trials Unit prosecutor, who was found dead in a sleazy downtown motel room, not far from the Biltmore. We'd begun dating, and I was just starting to believe Graden and I would go the distance when we had a major blowout over a violation of privacy; specifically, his violation of my privacy. He'd done some digging, otherwise known as "Googling" me, and found out that my sister Romy had been kidnapped when she was eleven years old. And was still missing.

He hadn't known that Romy's abduction was my closely guarded secret, one I'd kept from even my besties, Bailey Keller and Toni LaCollier, also a Special Trials prosecutor. But my breakup with Graden had forced me to tell them about it. Bailey and Toni had been sympathetic to my upset—well, actually, fury—at what I called the trampling of my boundaries, but they'd made no secret of the fact that they thought I'd overreacted...wildly. "He surfed the Web, Knight," Bailey'd said. "Hardly an act of high-level espionage," Toni'd added. I knew they were right, but knowing something intellectually and dealing with it emotionally are two very different matters. It'd taken me a while to come around.

But I did get there. At least enough to recognize that my reaction was over the top, and that I wanted to give Graden another chance. So we'd been taking baby steps, getting together for coffee breaks and lunches over the past few months. Tonight had been our first real date since the breakup—or, as Toni and Bailey called it, breakdown. I'd been a little apprehensive. Would he try for a sentimental play and take us to the site of our first date, the Pacific Dining Car? Or to the romantic hilltop restaurant that had become a mutual favorite, Yamashiro? I'd hoped not. I wasn't ready for any trips down memory lane.

"So where'd you go?" Drew asked.

"We went to Craig's—"

Drew nodded sagely. "My man, Graden. Excellent choice."

It really was. The leather and white tablecloth steakhouse in West Hollywood had that same Sinatra–Dean Martin feel as the Pacific Dining Car—great food and a comfortable ambience for real dining and conversation— with none of the emotional undertow of having been "our" place. It wasn't cheap, but money was no concern for Graden, who'd made a fortune on Code Three, the video game he'd designed with his brother.

Bailey studied me for a moment. "You look ridiculously sober. You stuck with water, didn't you?"

I nodded.

"Didn't trust yourself?" she asked.

"Of course I trusted myself." I cadged a cube of cheese off Bailey's plate. "I just want to keep a clear head."

"Time to put a stop to that," Drew said. "What'll you have?"

I ordered a glass of pinot noir, and Drew moved off.

"So...you didn't trust yourself," Bailey said.

"Nope, not for one second."

We laughed, and when Drew set down my glass of wine, we toasted.

"To knowing your limits." Bailey raiséd her glass, and I clinked it with mine.

"To that."

We took a sip.

"And he really didn't see anyone else?" I asked.

"Not unless she worked the cleaning crew at the station. From what I saw, he was in the office night and day. I'd guess he was keeping himself distracted."

"Know what I'd guess?"

But I never got a chance to say, because Bailey's work cell phone rang. If Bailey was next up on the roster, she wouldn't have been drinking, so it couldn't be work. I listened, hoping to get some information, but all I heard was "Yep" and "Got it" and "Let me write that down." Finally, Bailey ended the call and drained her water glass in one long gulp. Then she took my glass of wine—still practically full—out of my hand and set it down.

"Hey!"

"O'Hare's sick, so I'm up. Got a kidnapping call. Russell Antonovich."

Russell Antonovich. A name attached to so many blockbusters even I, who knew nothing about Hollywood hotshots, recognized it.

"Someone kidnapped him?"

"No." Bailey made sure no one was near us, then lowered her voice. "His teenage daughter, Hayley. Antonovich delivered the ransom and was supposed to get her back within the hour. That was two hours ago."

Bailey motioned to Drew that she'd call, and we headed for the road.

2

Bailey got off the 405 freeway and headed east on Sunset Boulevard. I was about to ask where we were going when she turned onto Bellagio Road—which led to the heart of Bel Air. If I were a billionaire director I'd live there too.

Bel Air is in the foothills of the Santa Monica Mountains, and it's the highest of the three legs known as the Platinum Triangle—the other two being Beverly Hills and Holmby Hills. The most expensive homes in the world occupy real estate in that wedge of land, and the majority of those homes are in Bel Air. The biggest and most lavish are usually closest to Sunset Boulevard, but you'd never know that, because massive trees and dense shrubbery hide all but the gated entries, and even those gates are tough to find, hidden as some are by deliberately overgrown leafy climbers.

Which explains why Bailey was frowning and muttering to herself as she scanned the road for house numbers. But when we reached Bel Air Country Club, she made a U-turn and pulled over. "Do me a favor and look for this number. The navigation says we're there, but I don't see a damn thing." She handed me a scrap of paper with an address and headed back down the road. One minute later I told her to stop and peered closely at a set of massive black iron gates that were almost completely obscured by towering elm and cypress trees. The tops of the gates met in an arc, and there in the apex, woven into the iron scroll-work, was the number.

"This is it." If I hadn't been parked in front of it and looking hard, I'd never have seen it.

I pointed out a discreet black metal box mounted on an arm in the brick wall, and Bailey pushed the button. A voice that sounded like a British butler's said, "Yes?" Bailey identified us, and he told us to hold out our badges. I couldn't see any cameras, but I didn't imagine he'd have asked us to do that just for giggles, so I held them outside the window, not sure where to aim them. After a couple of seconds the gates swung open, and Bailey steered up the brick lined road.

Los Angeles has some of the most outrageously opulent manses in the country and Bailey and I had seen our share over the years, but nothing compared to this. The road opened to a bricked-in area that was the size of half a football field, in the middle of which was a massive Italian Renaissance–style fountain, complete with cherubs' and lions' heads that spewed water. Towering over the grounds was a palatial two-story Tudor-style house all in that same matching brick. It was tastefully covered in ivy that obediently climbed where it best accented the archways and latticed windows and formed a large *L* around the perimeter of the front area. Judging just by what I could see from the outside, that "house" was at least thirty-five thousand square feet if it was an inch.

Bailey parked and we both stepped out of the car and took in the view.

"Damn," said Bailey under her breath.

"A quaint little 'starter.'"

By the time we'd made it up to the arched brick entry, the door was open and a slender man in his fifties, with thinning hair combed neatly back and dressed in a cardigan and dark slacks, beckoned us in.

"Right this way, please."

We were eventually ushered into a room that was sectioned off by furniture groupings of leather couches, ottomans, and cherrywood tables. Large wall-mounted flat screens hung on opposite walls. The room was big enough that both could be watched at the same time without anyone suffering noise interference. I supposed it was what the Realtors called a "great" room. Cozy.

Several people had gathered and the room buzzed with tension, though no one was moving. It was an odd sensation, as if everyone were vibrating in place. A tall wire whip of a man approached me with a smooth, athletic stride. Something about him looked familiar. I studied the brows that arched expressively over green eyes, the full lips, the faint spray of freckles across the bridge of his nose, and the dampish, freshly showered–looking dark red hair that curled down the sides of his neck. When recognition hit, shock made the name spring from my mouth. "Mattie!"

A brief look of annoyance was quickly replaced by a self-deprecating smile; it got me at first, but there was a too-polished feeling about the expression that said he'd probably been working it from his earliest child-star days. "Right." He held out his hand. "Though I actually go by Ian Powers."

We shook, and I collected myself. "Sorry," I said. "I just wasn't expecting—"

Ian Powers held up a hand. "Hey, don't apologize. At my age, I'm only glad that people can still recognize me."

It was somewhat remarkable. Though he definitely didn't look it, Ian Powers had to be in his forties. I knew it'd been more than thirty years since he'd starred as the eight-year-old boy in the sitcom *Just the Two of Us,* about Mattie, a charming, wise-beyond-his-years boy and his single father. I remembered watching the show when I was a kid, though by then, the show had long since been in reruns. It was weird to see the vestiges of that sweet little-boy face in this fully grown, casually elegant man.

"I take it you two are the detectives?"

"Actually no. I'm Rachel Knight, deputy district attorney."

"Detective Keller." Bailey put out her hand. "And your connection . . . ?"

"I'm Russell's manager."

Ian led us to the left side of the room, where a short man, no more than an inch taller than me, dressed in a baseball cap, faded jeans, and a forest green Henley, sat on the arm of a plush burgundy couch. "Russell, this is Detective Bailey Keller and, ah—"

"Deputy District Attorney Rachel Knight," I filled in. Clearly, I was already making quite the impression.

Russell stood and rocked on his toes—I'd bet so he could look down on me. But he'd have needed a step stool to look down on Bailey, all five feet nine inches of her. He took her in with a sidelong glance that avoided his having to look up at her, and didn't offer his hand to either one of us. He took a deep breath, expelled it through his nose, then started to dive in. "Got the first message about—"

Bailey held up a hand and looked around the room. "Mr. Antonovich, before you get into it, can you tell me who all these people are and why they need to be here?"

With a pained expression he said, "Russell, okay? Call me Russell." His tone was peremptory, almost impatient, and his voice was high enough that if I hadn't been looking at him I'd have thought he was a woman. "They all pretty much live here." He pointed to a willowy blonde who looked to be in her mid-twenties and easily twenty years his junior. "My wife, Dani. That's her assistant, Angela," he said, nodding at a trim young girl with a mop of curly brown hair who was pouring bottled water into a glass for the missus. He pointed to a sturdy-looking girl in overalls and a matching baseball cap. "My assistant, Uma." I noticed she was the only one in the room who was shorter than Russell. I was sure that was no accident. An older woman came in carrying a trayful of plates bearing finger food. Russell followed my gaze. "That's Vera, the cook." No last name—unless you counted "the cook." In fact, none of these people had a last name. Not as far as Russell was concerned anyway.

"And that...?" I asked, pointing to a young man wearing jeans that sagged below sea level who was sitting on an ottoman at the other end of the room.

"Jeff, my runner. Assistant too, sometimes."

And then there was the butler who'd answered the door, and all the others it would take to keep this place going. If we kept taking attendance, we wouldn't get to the case until sometime next week. Bailey had apparently reached the same conclusion.

"I'll need a list of everyone who's been in the house today and who's in the house now," Bailey said.

"Right, got it, got it."

"When did you first realize your daughter had been kidnapped?" Bailey asked.

Russell pulled off his baseball cap, which now showed me it was his substitute for hair. The hem of tight straw-colored curls just above his ears was all that remained. He rubbed his head and then his face. With the cap off, I could see the worry and fear etched in his features. Suddenly the celebrity director was just the frantic, distraught father of a child in danger. And in that moment, the picture of my father's face filled my memory: the panic and confusion in his eyes, turning to frozen shock when, sobbing and hysterical, I told him of the stranger who'd taken Romy while we were playing in the woods near the house. I brought myself back to the present with a stiff jerk. That was Romy and my father. Not Hayley or Russell. This daughter still had a chance of a safe return.